Kathleen Mitchell
867 Ruby St.
N. Fort Myers, FL 33903

Booth

Booth

A NOVEL

David Robertson

LARGE PRINT BOOK CLUB EDITION

Anchor Books
DOUBLEDAY
New York London Toronto Sydney Auckland

This Large Print Edition, prepared especially for Doubleday Direct, Inc., contains the complete unabridged text of the original Publisher's Edition.

AN ANCHOR BOOK
PUBLISHED BY DOUBLEDAY
a division of Bantam Doubleday Dell Publishing Group, Inc.
1540 Broadway, New York, New York 10036

ANCHOR BOOKS, DOUBLEDAY, and the portrayal of an anchor are trademarks of Doubleday, a division of Bantam Doubleday Dell Publishing Group, Inc.

Photograph of Mary Surratt, courtesy of Surratt House and Museum. All other photographs courtesy of the Library of Congress.

ISBN 1-56865-599-1
Copyright © 1998 by David M. Robertson

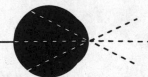

This Large Print Book carries the Seal of Approval of N.A.V.H.

This book is for Catherine

List of Illustrations

"When the shadow of any figure is thrown upon the prepared surface, the part concealed by it remains white, and the other parts speedily become dark."

—THOMAS WEDGEWOOD AND SIR HUMPHRY DAVY,
An Account of a Method of Copying Paintings Upon Glass, and of Making Profiles, by the Agency of Light Upon Nitrate of Silver, 1802

"I often feel that people come to me to be photographed as they would go to a doctor or a fortune teller—to find out how they are."

—RICHARD AVEDON,
Minneapolis Institute of Art Catalog, 1970

Part One

From the wire services, April 22, 1916

JOHN H. SURRATT DEAD
Last of the Alleged Conspirators In Lincoln Assassination

BALTIMORE, Md., April 21.—John Harrison Surratt, last survivor of the corps of alleged conspirators tried for implication in the plot to assassinate Abraham Lincoln, died at his home here tonight in his seventy-third year. He retired as general freight agent of the Baltimore Steam Packet Company recently and had lived in Baltimore for many years.

Mr. Surratt was living in Washington at the boardinghouse maintained by his mother when he learned of President Lincoln's death from the newspapers. Booth's conspirators seriously injured Secretary of State Seward, and also attempted to kill Vice President Johnson. Friends advised Mr. Surratt to flee, and nothing further was heard of him for some time, although all the United States Consular agents and secret service men were combing the world for him.

3

During Mr. Surratt's absence, his mother, Mary Surratt, was arrested and tried with several others for alleged complicity in the Lincoln assassination. Testimony at her trial established that she had met frequently with John Wilkes Booth, the presidential assassin, at her Washington boarding house. Mrs. Surratt and three others were executed by the government on July 7, 1865.

Two years later, Mr. Surratt was recognized abroad and arrested. He was returned to this country to stand trial before Judge George P. Fisher of the Criminal Court of Washington, D.C., on June 10, 1867. Intense interest was shown all over the country in the trial of the last of the Lincoln conspirators. It ended when the jury reported, on Aug. 10, that it had disagreed on Mr. Surratt's guilt, after being out for more than seventy hours. The Judge then discharged the jury and Mr. Surratt received his liberty.

Mr. Surratt subsequently shunned the public spot light for many decades, refusing to speak from his modest Baltimore home to the news reporters and other writers who attempted to question him on the events of the Lincoln assassination. In recent years, he was said to be considering a lecture tour to speak of his friendship with John Wilkes Booth and of his mother's innocence, but these plans apparently had not been acted upon by the time of his death.

Details of the funeral are incomplete.

*From the diary of John H. Surratt, April 17,
Monday, 1916*

1.

"I'm Billy Bitzer," the man said.

We stood outside the National Theatre at the corner of E Street and Pennsylvania Avenue. Behind us a jitney cab backfired at the curb, and a party of officers and ladies getting out of the automobile laughed in nervous excitement. There seemed to be officers in military dress uniforms everywhere in the crowd in front of the theatre. The ladies wore fashionable richly caped dresses and plumed hats. Tomorrow a military parade for what President Wilson had called Preparedness Day was scheduled; tonight was the army's night on the town.

"I'm John Surratt," I said to the short, somewhat disheveled man before me, and we shook hands. His hand was very small, the fingers almost delicate.

He pushed a bowler hat back on his head and wiped the perspiration from his face. He reminded me of an overgrown boy sweating inside a suit of adult clothes as he scanned the crowd behind us with a quick, calculating glance.

"Jesus, we might have a sold house," he said.

I turned, and followed the direction of Bitzer's gaze. The crowd of people illuminated by the theatre's electric light marquee spread along a full city block, past the restaurants and oyster saloons on either side of the National. I was struck by the remarkable youthfulness of the audience that turned out for these photoplays, or movies, as everyone seemed to call them. I wondered for a moment how Bitzer had been able to recognize me among the hundreds of figures milling about on the sidewalk. Then I realized I was the oldest person there, and one of the few who yet dressed in formal black to go to the theatre.

Bitzer plucked at my coat sleeve. "Let's get a move on, Mr. Surratt. We need to be inside before the curtain goes up."

I followed him awkwardly as he made his way through the crowds. A thin, worried-looking manager behind a glass door inside the theatre recognized Bitzer and beckoned to us to come quickly, allowing Bitzer and me to enter by the side door.

"*Surely you will not ask* me *for a ticket?*" For a moment, I visualized John Wilkes Booth's handsome, jeering face beside me. This mock question had been Booth's favorite jest during the war to the theatre managers of Washington City.

Not since 1864 have I been inside a Washington theatre on opening night. Grover's National had once been Booth's favorite theatre, seating over two thousand for his performances. Tonight the crowd inside the lobby was pressed together even more closely. There was some confusion ahead of me as several couples blocked the way into the lobby's interior, thrusting men's hats and overcoats at a harried-looking girl behind a small counter.

"*I'm playing in* Romeo and Juliet *this week,*" Booth had told me in 1864. "*It's poor stuff, but the best I can do in a wartime theatre.*"

"Excuse me, pops." A young soldier, holding the arm of an equally young woman, squeezed past on their way into the lobby. The young woman's breasts were pressed briefly against my shoulder, and, for a moment, I caught a lingering scent of lavender from her hair.

Bitzer had remained behind, talking with the man by the door. I worked my way around the crowds and made my way to the lobby wall.

No doubt Booth would have been saddened at the changes in his favorite theatre. Since the advent of the movies, someone had redecorated the interior of the National Theatre as a fantasy from the Arabian Nights. The wall behind me was painted with gilt ziggurats, and a trash container on the floor was disguised as a Grecian burial urn. At the open anteroom to the men's lounge at my right, the officers of the republic stood beneath a ceiling mural of a small boy on a flying carpet.

From the lobby ceiling overhead, a row of what appeared to be Oriental oil lamps hung suspended only a few feet above the trimmed feathered hats of the ladies before me. *Please don't let me fall,* my mother had cried from the gallows. *Oh, please, don't let me fall.* I hesitantly walked closer and saw that what appeared to be burning oil lamps were only colored electric lightbulbs inside *papier-mâché* cones.

10

Bitzer suddenly appeared beside me, handing me a program. "You want something?" he asked. "You look a little pale. Candies, chocolates, a cola drink?" He jerked a thumb toward a near corner of the lobby, where at a concessionaire stand three black men costumed as Moors were shoveling popcorn and chocolate nonpareils into white paper bags for a crowd of eager customers. This was a modern innovation I could appreciate. During the Civil War, theatre-goers had to rush out of the theatre during intermission to drink hastily at the saloon next door.

"No." I smiled. "Just thinking about the last time I was here."

"Well, we better go upstairs. We've got good seats—we're sitting across from Woodrow Wilson, if he shows. The papers say maybe he will."

Bitzer's face kept a deadpan expression. I was stunned and sickened. No one in extending me the invitation had told me the president might appear tonight. I have experienced three presidential assassinations in my lifetime. I did not want to witness another one in a theatre.

The rows of electric lights in the lobby

dimmed three times in rapid succession. I forced myself to smile. "I'm ready," I said.

Bitzer and I joined into the press of theatre-goers up the stairs to the balcony. The good seats for the National in the age of the movies were, I now understood, in the uppermost balcony rather than the dress circle or the rows on the main floor below. At the top of the stairs, Bitzer showed a pass and waved aside the uniformed usher, and I followed him into the interior. It took several moments for my eyes to adjust to the darkness.

The inside of the theatre was as I remembered it so long ago. Bitzer and I stood in a wide aisle that curved like a giant horseshoe around thirty or forty rows of dark velvet seats in the balcony in front of us. They were now almost fully occupied. The general admission seats below us were just visible. There were easily two thousand people in the theatre tonight. On either far side of the balcony I saw two private boxes projecting over the main audience and overlooking the stage. Bitzer had been correct; from where we would be sitting at the front row of the balcony, we could look directly into the state box.

Before we took our seats, Bitzer paused before a small, closet-sized wooden room built against the rear wall. Although I had been inside movie theatres before, I had never noticed such a structure. As Bitzer opened the door, brilliant light fell across the first rows of darkened balcony seats.

Inside I saw two men in cloth hats, stripped to their undershirts, kneeling beside a piece of large machinery which I recognized as a film projector, whispering in Italian. They fell silent as they looked at Bitzer. From within the small enclosure I could recognize the familiar smells of the nineteenth-century darkroom: nitrocellulose, guncotton, and human sweat.

"Remember, you bastards, three speeds," Bitzer hissed in a kind of stage whisper. "Three." He shook three fingers into the illuminated interior. The two Italians remained crouched in front of him mute and immobile, as if they were figures in a religious tableau. Bitzer slammed the door shut with satisfaction.

"I directed each scene," Bitzer said to me after we had taken our seats. "A different scene means a different exposure time and frame speed. Three different speeds for each reel." I understood little of what he said. In my day, photographic exposure was determined by sunlight, and I was puzzled by his reference to himself as the director.

The orchestra below began playing an overture. Directly in front of the stage, below the screen and the proscenium arch, a Wurlitzer organ played a song I recognized from Wagner. The stage-right box across from us in the balcony was still empty. The audience, impatient for the show to begin, started to clap along to the music.

Suddenly the orchestra struck up "Hail to the Chief." All the theatre lights went out, except for a single spotlight that now illuminated the still-empty stage-right box. In the general confusion, we all stood up and some in the audience applauded. Bitzer particularly was quick to his feet, clapping his small hands together with enthusiasm. For a moment the box seat above the stage remained empty.

Then he appeared. There was a momentary confusion, a scattered whispering of his name among the audience, and then the applause came again, even more thunderously. From his photogravures in the theatre sections of newspapers, I recognized the man in the box as D. W. Griffith. I felt a rush of relief that I would not be present at a theatre when the president attended, and joined in the applause. Next to me, Bitzer clapped his hands more vigorously.

Griffith seemed genuinely humbled by the applause. He turned away for a moment from the audience and placed his arm around the shoulder of a young woman who entered the box after him, in a gesture both protective and public; Griffith seemed both to present and to shield her from the crowd. Next to his tall figure, she appeared to be almost childlike. He leaned down and said something to her with an amused expression on his face, and they both broke into laughter.

As the clapping receded, I thought for a moment he might speak. But Griffith simply bowed deeply before the filled rows of theatre-goers, then quickly drew himself upright and swept his arm with an elegant, silent gesture in the direction of the screen. He seemed to be crediting our response to the motion picture we were about to see, rather than personally to him.

The applause died, and the spotlight was extinguished. From the balcony rows behind us I heard the reshuffling of clothing and adjustment of bodies, as if the audience were some great collective animal, settling itself into the darkness. The orchestra below resumed playing, and from the small room at the rear of the balcony came a muffled, clacking noise, like a distantly heard machine gun from the European war. Then the first of the giant images appeared on the screen in front of us.

I had not expected to see color. I had been to the movies years before, of course, usually in the company of young men from our firm at Baltimore, but the disconnected movements, the low physical clowning, or the simple melodrama that so pleased the young people disinterested me. The black-and-white images of the movies never seemed real to me, accustomed as I was to the more subtle tones of the albumin prints of the nineteenth century. But scarcely had the curtains opened in front of the audience tonight, and the title appeared in white letters on the screen, than the entire theatre was suffused with a rose-colored light. Some in the dress circle below us gasped. The light gradually shifted to a peach shade on the screen as the actors first appeared in the opening scenes; then, to my surprise, the film became a familiar sepia tone as the story proper began. It reminded me of the photographs and magic lantern shows of my youth.

I had read the novel by the Reverend Thomas Dixon on which the photoplay was based and considered it poor stuff. It was the same tired story, as tired as I who had once lived through it, of two families in the North and the South, the Stonemans and the Camerons, and their suffering throughout the Civil War. But the novel had sold well, and D. W. Griffith had high hopes for the success of tonight's showing. One generation's tragedy becomes another's melodrama, I reflected to myself, to be enjoyed fifty years later in a movie theatre balcony while eating popcorn and chocolates.

The opening scenes took place at the Cameron family's South Carolina plantation. I had to admit that the clothing and buildings appeared authentic, although I knew they had been photographed in California. Miss Lillian Gish, who played the sweetheart of one of the Cameron boys, was very beautiful. The youngest Cameron sister, who silently giggled throughout her scenes

17

like a natural stage *ingénue,* was a young woman whom I did not recognize. According to the program in my hands, her name was Mae Marsh.

"Her name is Sarah Ravenel," Booth once said to me as we spoke in the darkness before the terrible cataclysm of events fifty years earlier. *"I immediately saw that she had an immense talent for the theatre."*

The scenes quickly shifted to the Civil War battlefields. Once again, I was impressed by how real they appeared. Nor had I forgotten what the battlefields looked like; I recognized the trenches at Petersburg and the dark shape of Malvern Hill before the title cards appeared identifying them. Some of the battle scenes were composed identically to the famous photographs of Brady, and I knew the resemblance could not have been accidental. Someone must have studied the original photographs closely. I was impressed, too, by the large number of "extra people" in each of these battle scenes. I realized this must have been a very expensive production to photograph.

Yet there was something puzzling to me about the movements of all these actors in uniforms. There were no unsynchronized and uncoordinated gestures on film, such as I knew actual battle scenes must have presented.

As the Civil War scenes ended, there were several interesting chance encounters between Miss Gish and John Wilkes Booth in Ford's Theatre. Of course, the actor for Booth was all wrong. He was handsome enough, but the way he skulked in the dark balcony aisle behind the president's box was very overplayed.

The assassination scene was realistic, and very disturbing. As the pistol shot rang out—a sudden bang on the orchestra's drum below us—I felt my heart catch in a beat of *No, no,* as the heads of the entire audience turned involuntarily to look into the box above the right side of the movie screen. But the box above the stage was darkened, and it was impossible to see whether D. W. Griffith or anyone else was seated there.

Earlier, we had watched the assassination from a distance, so that the dress box above the stage right at Ford's Theatre and Booth's leap from it (he had moved with surprising speed) filled the middle foreground. But while the dress box remained in focus, we seemed to be moving closer to it on the screen. The camera moved, not toward the president's body, which had slumped out of sight below a corner of the screen, but toward the face of the president's wife, Mary Todd Lincoln. We watched as her face registered at first surprise, discomfort, and then horror. It occurred to me that Bitzer somehow had managed to mount a motion picture camera at the end of a construction crane, and then extended that crane and camera smoothly over the heads of the extra people below in Ford's Theatre, all the while keeping Mrs. Lincoln's face in clear focus. I heard several people in the audience cry out in pity; a few applauded, apparently in praise of the photography.

No legitimate theatre company could have achieved anything near that performance without a complete change of scenery, or of actors shifting clumsily behind a darkened set. I turned to look at Bitzer, who was smiling happily.

I was spared, at least in this Washington showing of the film, any further scenes of Booth's death or of the subsequent hanging of his four conspirators. *Oh, please, don't let me fall.* I was glad the darkness partially hid the expression of pain and loss on my face.

The rest of the movie interested me very little. The Cameron and the Stoneman families were reconciled by the marriages of their children after the Civil War. The remainder of the story flashed by with title cards like pages from the photogravure section of a newspaper, recounting the rise of the Ku Klux Klan, the reunion of the nation, the beginning of our modern era.

As the movie neared its conclusion, I found my mind replaying the earlier scenes of the war. Bitzer, of course, had manipulated the images on the screen like a puppet master with his two Italian mechanics in the projection room. But I could not dismiss from my mind how these scenes had slowly taken on a life of their own. Sitting in the balcony, I realized suddenly the truth of the common man's name for this drama: we watched still pictures that *moved.* They moved, not to our time in the audience or even to Billy Bitzer's time behind the camera, but within their own time. I thought of all the thousands who had been photographed during the Civil War; all the thousands who yet moved their lives within the frames of their own time, finite and endless. I myself had helped to photograph hundreds of them. "There were so many," I found myself saying aloud. My voice trembled with something almost like grief.

"Bums," Bitzer whispered back to me. He apparently thought I was referring to the large number of extra people he had filmed in the battle scenes. "Migrant laborers, mostly, from outside San Bernardino. We hired them for a song from the bean and wheat fields."

Below us the organ was playing an exit march. But I scarcely heard it. Everywhere around us in the balcony people were standing up and applauding, telling one another what a marvelous piece of work this new movie, *The Birth of a Nation,* was.

2.

Bitzer and I remained sitting in the balcony even after the theatre seats below us were empty. The houselights long since had been turned up, and in the orchestra pit the musicians had packed their instruments and left.

In the darkened balcony interior, I was reminded of the few times I had attempted to pray at church after the death of my mother: there was that same large emptiness pervading the air around me.

Finally, Bitzer said, "Come on. He's had time to rest. We need to talk." It was time to meet the famous man in the state box.

I followed Bitzer's bulky form up the balcony steps. The electric lights had been turned out at the rear of the balcony, and only a few gas lamps remained lit. I noticed with some satisfaction that the darkened balcony steps had been left littered with uneaten popcorn kernels, ticket stubs, a discarded handkerchief. No longer were we in the world of animated and illuminated photographs from the nineteenth century created magically for us on the screen; instead Billy Bitzer and I were back where we belonged in the twentieth century, inside a theatre in downtown Washington with fake decorations, empty seats, and uncollected trash.

Bitzer stopped for a moment beside the open door to the projection booth. The two men inside were now busily stacking round metal canisters. Bitzer silently counted the canisters and gave the two men and the projection booth itself a proprietary glance, before he wordlessly walked on.

At first I thought we were headed toward the entrance to the president's box at the far right side of the balcony. But he turned suddenly without warning into an unmarked alcove built into the balcony wall. The alcove concealed an open door that led down a short, unlit hallway.

I had forgotten that theatre buildings are full of these odd, out-of-the-way passages the public never sees. I remembered the basement tunnel at Ford's Theatre that enabled us to pass from the back stage to the front of the building while a play was in progress; or the trapdoor built into the stage floor so that stagehands could prepare one scene while hidden from the audience by the drop curtain in front of them. Or the short passage leading from the back stage to the alley behind the theatre, where Booth had fled the night of the assassination.

At the end of the hallway, Bitzer stopped before an unmarked door. He opened it without knocking.

Inside I saw a tall man lying full length on a sofa underneath an old-fashioned gas lamp, his right hand resting across his eyes. A young woman sat in a chair, reading a magazine.

The furnishing of the small room startled me. It seemed to have been unchanged since the 1860s. The man lay on what we once had called a swooning sofa in the nineteenth century, a piece of furniture I had not seen in homes since the Civil War. The young woman was sitting in a chair of similar Victorian design. Grover's National continued to present occasional live performances as well as movies, and it occurred to me that this room must have been furnished with cast-off pieces from past stage performances.

"Billy!" The man swung his legs off the sofa with surprising speed. The young woman looked up from her periodical and smiled.

"I see you've brought our honored guest to our little hideaway." He looked up at me and smiled. "You will forgive my appearance on your first entering, sir. I find anticipating the audience's reactions to our filmed performances almost as exhausting as the photographing of them."

He stood and offered a firm handshake. "David Wark Griffith," he said.

"John H. Surratt," I said.

Griffith was one of the most impressive-looking men I had ever seen, dressed in a two-piece suit of dark tweed and a white shirt with one of the new, folded-down collars, giving him a studied, informal look. I found myself staring. It was the type of attire I would have expected an English squire to wear on his estate for shooting. In person, he looked precisely like the hundreds of photographs I had seen on the theatre pages of newspapers—there was the same aquiline nose, far too large for his face yet somehow handsome; his shock of coarse, black hair; and his eyes, inquiring and intelligent, friendly and predatory.

"But I forget my manners, Mr. Surratt." He turned to the young woman. "May I introduce you to Miss Mae Marsh, whom of course you know from our photoplay as Little Flora Campbell?"

"How do you do," she said in a perfectly adult tone of voice, despite her childish frame. I took her hand. She had the bluest eyes I had ever seen.

Miss Marsh remained seated throughout

the introductions; I noticed that she was so short that her feet barely touched the floor. I wondered if Griffith deliberately surrounded himself with diminutive people to emphasize his own tallness, or if for some technical reason the motion picture camera required smaller people.

"I enjoyed your role very much," I said with sincerity. There was an awkward pause before Griffith regained the reins of the conversation.

"Well, sit down, sit down, Mr. Surratt," Griffith said. He waved his hand toward a heavy mahogany table and chairs at the center of the room. "I trust our Billy talked your ears off before the show?" Griffith laughed mischievously, giving an affectionate look toward Bitzer. "You know, I fear Billy talks only to that Pathé camera of his. Even then, when he's hidden his head underneath the black hood behind the lens, Miss Marsh and I hear only the bad language he so often employs."

I joined Bitzer, who had already seated himself at the table. He seemed to pay no attention to Griffith's remarks. Apparently his taciturnity was a long-standing joke among them. He pulled a cigar out of one of his pockets and lit it. I was somewhat shocked that he did not ask Miss Marsh's permission.

"You know, the magazines say the camera loves me." I turned to look at Miss Marsh. "It's true," she told me. "But I sometimes think the only one who loves the camera back is Billy. That's all he loves, the camera and the movies."

Bitzer stared dispassionately at Miss Marsh. "Sure, I love the movies," he said. "It's the nuts." He flicked a cigar ash onto the floor and then looked sharply at Griffith. "What the hell got into the orchestra tonight? Where was Woodrow Wilson?"

Griffith gave out a prolonged low chuckle that could have been heard at the back row of a theatre. "That *was* a trifle embarrassing, wasn't it?" He cast a sly glance sidelong at Miss Marsh, who smiled back at him radiantly. "We had been told to expect President Wilson in the state box with us tonight. I sent word to the orchestra to play 'Hail to the Chief' just before the box was lit. At the last moment the White House telephoned and canceled his appearance. I gather the word didn't get to the orchestra pit in time. So when Mae and I stepped into the spot, there they were, playing 'Hail to the Chief.' I imagine that Mr. Poli, our poor theatre manager, is furious."

Griffith paced the room as he talked. The forced good humor suddenly was gone, replaced with a kind of barely restrained aggression. He reminded me of an oversized animal pacing inside a small cage. "Apparently some of Mr. Wilson's advisors thought it would be unseemly for the president to appear at a public theatre the night before the military parade. Mr. Wilson's friends also had heard some reports, probably exaggerated, of a minor disturbance in the street outside the theatre tonight. Oh well. We've arranged a private showing at the White House for tomorrow night."

Griffith paused momentarily, and his face took on an abstracted look. "But in a larger sense, the playing of that song was wholly appropriate, don't you think, Mr. Surratt?" His remarkably intense gaze fastened on me.

"After all, are not we, the captains of this new motion picture industry, the unacknowledged leaders of this nation and the world?" He raised his hands in front of him, the fingers spread wide. "For one thing, the

29

telling of history, the education of old and young, may be entirely revolutionized by its strange new process."

Griffith turned toward the table, facing us. Miss Marsh remained smiling steadily; Bitzer was expressionless, studying his cigar ash. "Pictures are the universal language, Mr. Surratt," Griffith said, fixing me with the intensity of his performance. For I could see that it *was* a performance, though a convincing one. "Pictures are the only medium that can carry big stories. Epochal poetry!"

I expected him to continue, but Griffith shook his head good-naturedly, as if suddenly amused at his own enthusiasms. I reminded myself of having read in the newspapers that Griffith had been a professional actor before he became a movie impresario.

Griffith smiled. "But perhaps I get ahead of myself," he said. "We should ask *you,* Mr. Surratt, what you think of our motion picture."

I sensed negotiations for my photographs and diaries had begun. I chose my words carefully. "Your work is very accurate, Mr. Griffith. Very historical."

"Precisely." Griffith sighed, as if in relief

that I understood, and then moved to join Bitzer and me at the table.

"I'm sure you noticed the thousands of yards of cotton sheets required for the Klan scenes, and the hundreds of horses we required in the battle scenes," Griffith said. "Both very difficult to purchase in California during the European war, I can assure you." He shook his head sadly. "We had hoped to open the first showing tonight at Ford's Theatre, but that idea flivvered. Apparently, even after all these years the theatre is still permanently closed to the public.

"And surely you noticed the pains we took with each set, Mr. Surratt, how Billy here so carefully followed the details in each of his camera shots, to correspond exactly to the historical authenticity of Brady's photographs of the Civil War?" He nodded toward Bitzer. "We studied them for months before shooting."

Griffith leaned closer to me. "And that's when we discovered *you,* Mr. Surratt." His eyes were remarkably intense. "Imagine our surprise when we learned that you had photographed many of the very scenes for Mr. Brady that we were then including in our movie production. And then, as a corker, we

31

learn that you also had personally known John Wilkes Booth.''

Griffith looked down at his reflection on the mahogany table as if he were momentarily troubled by his thoughts. ''And, of course, there is your own family's tragic history after the Lincoln assassination.''

Fifty years of publicly hiding the past, of living obscurely and insisting that I was just a clerk at a Baltimore shipping company, also had made me something of a professional actor, although it was a skill in myself I did not cherish. I kept my face carefully neutral. ''Of course,'' I said.

Griffith's features brightened. ''That's when we decided I must meet with you.''

What he said was true. Griffith had written to my home at Baltimore the previous year, inquiring whether I was the John H. Surratt listed as a photographer in a Washington City directory of 1864, and the same John Surratt tried as a conspirator with John Wilkes Booth. Throughout my life, I have received numerous such letters, written either by Civil War historians, admirers of Booth, or, on occasion, zealots threatening my life.

In earlier years, I had thrown all these letters away unanswered. But I had replied to

Griffith's Majestic Motion Picture Company. For over half a century, I had kept my word to a secret bargain, remaining silent, so that my wife and I could live obscurely and un-molested by powerful authorities. But upon receiving Griffith's letter, I reconsidered. After all, the participants in that drama, excepting myself, were now dead: my mother, Alexander Gardner, Allan Pinkerton, and, of course, Booth and Lincoln. And so I had written back to Griffith, informing him that I was indeed that John Surratt, and that I was in possession of significant Civil War photographs and also historically important, previously unpublished diaries. Perhaps, I had decided, it was time to tell the full truth about the Lincoln assassination.

For several months there had been nothing more forthcoming from California. In the meanwhile, I read in newspapers of the openings of *The Birth of a Nation* in theatres in Los Angeles and New York City. The most recent telegram from Griffith had arrived at my home only yesterday, inviting me to be his guest at the movie's premiere in Washington, and asking that I bring my photographs and documents to the city.

Now meeting him backstage and telling

him my story, I wanted to be at least super-
ficially honest with Griffith. "Actually, I never
photographed for Brady," I said. "During
the war years he claimed many other photographers' work as his own. I worked during the Civil War in the studio of one of
Brady's competitors, Mr. Alexander Gardner."

D. W. Griffith waved my words aside.
"But you *saw,* Mr. Surratt, you saw, and
that is the real thing." He looked at me earnestly. "People only believe what they already know. And they know only what they
can see. That's why I asked for you to be
with us here in the city tonight. Surely you
observed the audience's reaction after our
production." He spread his arms from his
chair to include the theatre room in which
we were sitting. "I tell you, the public's appetite for real history, particularly the authentic history of our Civil War—which can
be presented only upon film—is insatiable."

Bitzer and Miss Marsh remained silent.
Apparently, this was Griffith's scene to play.
"That reminds me," he said. "How are the
rooms we engaged for you at the Willard? I
trust that everything is satisfactory?"

It was time to offer him a little bait. "They

are very fine. During the war, I met Booth at Willard's Hotel several times."

Griffith looked at me with renewed intensity. "Your photographs? They are here in the city?"

I felt a moment of panic as I visualized the packet of photographs and the two diaries unprotected atop the desk in the hotel room. I had considered placing them in the hotel safe, but had realized, having taken this trip to the city and unlocked the past, I would want to look at them tonight. "They are in a safe place," I said.

"One hears the strangest stories," Miss Marsh said. I turned in my chair to look at her. Under the light of the gas lamp I noticed for the first time that she rouged her cheeks and cosmetically colored her lips, although she had not appeared on stage tonight.

"So many people believe Booth never died," she said. "And only last month I read an article in the *Saturday Evening Post* about a man claiming to be John Wilkes Booth's illegitimate son, exhibiting himself at carnivals throughout Texas." She brought the fingertips of her right hand to her mouth, and I saw the same silent giggle I had witnessed on the screen.

"No, you're mistaken, Miss Marsh," I said, more harshly than I intended. "Wilkes Booth was shot dead in Virginia, and his remains buried at Baltimore. I myself have seen the grave."

"Wilkes Booth?" Griffith gave me a sharp look.

I experienced the familiar feeling of being interrogated, as I had been during my three months' imprisonment after Lincoln's murder. It was a memory that I recalled with dread. "That's right. Booth went by his middle name, out of respect for his father, who had christened him. When Booth and I were together, I was the one always called John."

"He was so young and photogenic," Miss Marsh said.

"We were all young then," I said, nodding my head slightly toward Miss Marsh. I hoped by this small galantry to bring the conversation back under my control. "Booth was only twenty-seven when he murdered Lincoln. I was twenty-two."

I saw Miss Marsh's eyes widen slightly, as if suddenly realizing she was speaking to someone who had actually rubbed shoulders with John Wilkes Booth. I thought back to what I had written one night in my diary in

36

1864, when I had been twenty-one: *Mother is right. Booth is a good man, so much better a man than I.*

Fool, I thought now. I involuntarily shuddered in my chair, a consequence, perhaps, of the growing fever I had felt since leaving Baltimore.

"After Booth's capture and death, three of his friends were arrested and hanged," I told them.

"And the fourth person to hang, Mr. Surratt?" Griffith paused. "Mary Surratt, your mother, I believe?" Griffith shook his head as if in great indignation. "The first woman to be hanged by our government in U.S. history. And whose only crime was to have been the innocent owner of the boardinghouse where Booth and these three others happened to meet."

Oh, please, don't let me fall. Although I had anticipated Griffith's question, after fifty years of locking away those painful memories and my own profound shame, the emotions that swept through me made my tongue thick, and words failed me.

"I read of her boardinghouse in the newspapers," Miss Marsh said. "It's still standing on H Street, isn't it?" She covered her

37

mouth with her hands, and once again I saw that inaudible giggle. "It's become a chop-suey palace!"

I felt my face redden. "There have been many changes in Washington since I was young," I answered carefully. "Before to-night, I had not been back in the capital district since my trial. After the assassination, I fled to Europe. If at any moment during my flight I had known that the government had seized and intended to murder my mother, if I had thought that my testimony in any way could have—"

I stopped. "When I was seized and brought back here to trial in 1867, the temper of the times had changed. I was able to get a fair hearing and was acquitted." I had already revealed more about myself than I had planned, and I was angered that these two actors, less than half my age and presumably amateurs at concealment, had succeeded in drawing more out of me than I intended. It occurred to me to wonder whether their conversation and questions had been planned, and, for all I knew, re-hearsed, before I had entered the room. I looked at Bitzer, who regarded me with what I thought was a sardonic expression.

"Mr. Surratt, I shall be candid with you." Griffith spread his hands upon the table. "You have seen the audience's reaction to our film. In the next few weeks, I intend to take it to the national markets, touring the cities of the South and New England. *Birth of a Nation,* assuming its popular success, is only one of many epics on our nation's history I intend to complete. For a number of years now, I have been determined to bring to the public a motion picture of the true history of the last year of our martyred Lincoln. I can think of no one better qualified than you to assist in its production and historical authenticity."

Griffith kept his gaze fixed directly on me as he spoke. "I intend this future picture to portray the tragic events of that week in April when Lincoln was taken from us, and when you personally moved among so many principals of that drama." He smiled. "I'm thinking of calling it *Lincoln: A Tragedy and Photoplay.*"

As he fell silent, my mind raced. Could I, I wondered, tell the truth about Booth, about my mother, about myself, and be believed? "It's a difficult story to tell," I said slowly.

"The Lincoln assassination happened a long time ago."

"I discovered time when I invented the movies," Griffith said, with the conviction of a true believer. "And novelists were my inspiration. I borrowed the 'cutback' from Charles Dickens. Novelists, Mr. Surratt, think nothing of leaving one set of characters in the midst of affairs and going back to deal with earlier events in which another set of characters is involved. I tell you, all great story-men of past ages, whether novelists or historians, were directors of motion pictures."

Griffith leaned closer. "And you, Mr. Surratt, with your photographs and firsthand knowledge of the Lincoln assassination, you can make these pictures move for me." His eyes darted slightly to the empty chair at my left. "Wilkes Booth," he said, as if to test to himself the sound. "Not John Wilkes Booth, but Wilkes Booth. I never dreamed such a familiarity."

He quickly turned to the business at hand. "Here is my proposition. I propose that you join us on our present Southern and Northern tour. Your presence onstage at the end of the show, particularly in the

Southern states, will guarantee the commercial success of *Birth of a Nation.* And throughout the tour you will be available to me in order to share your photographic reminiscences, your vivid personal retellings, so that I can block out each shot of the Lincoln story here." He tapped his forehead. "I never shoot from a written script. Each scene is visualized in my head before the first strip of film is unrolled."

Griffith looked at me earnestly, a look, I gathered, calculated to convince me of the seriousness of his intentions. "Your time will not be wasted, Mr. Surratt. You will receive generous remuneration. I intend to pour every cent of profit from *Birth of a Nation* into my new Lincoln photoplay. I have learned that in the motion picture industry, one must be always moving ahead, not looking backward."

Griffith touched my coat lapel lightly. "And you won't be appearing on the stage alone. The eldest surviving son of Abraham Lincoln, Robert Todd Lincoln, is himself a permanent resident of Washington. Like you, he is a mature gentleman, but of good health. Can you imagine the audience's reaction if the two of you were to appear onstage together after each showing of *Birth of a Nation* to offer your thoughts?"

Griffith jumped from his chair, extending his opened hands to the light in the ceiling. "Imagine! The son of the murdered Abraham Lincoln shaking hands in peace with the friend of John Wilkes Booth and the son of Mary Surratt, the woman judicially sacrificed for Lincoln's assassination! A true birth of a new nation!"

He turned to look at me, and for the first time, I wondered whether I might have been talking with a madman. Robert Todd Lincoln was wealthy—what need had he of appearing onstage hawking his memories? "Let them make of that grand gesture what they will with their petty demonstrations in the street. It will guarantee the success of *Birth* and whet the public's appetite for my new Lincoln epic," Griffith had gone on. "I have not yet received a definite reply from Mr. Lincoln or his family, but it can happen, Mr. Surratt, it can happen. It *will* happen!"

I was speechless. The very idea of my shaking hands with Robert Lincoln on a theatre stage was obscene. For years I had withheld my name, my photographs and diaries from publication, refusing all blandishments to exploit that period of my life for commercial purposes. With all the other participants dead, I had thought that perhaps it was time to tell my story, and, in a measure, to clear my mother's name, if not my own. To confess to my sins, if you will, in a public act of contrition. Instead I was being asked to become a vaudeville entertainer, performing from theatre to theatre like a second-rate failed character actor.

There was a sudden knock at the door. "Come in!" Griffith said. For a wild moment, I feared Robert Todd Lincoln himself would walk into the room. Instead, I saw the tall, worried man who had been at the theatre entrance at the doorway. He carried a tin cashbox and an account ledger.

"Ah, Mr. Poli, our theatre manager and general factotum of the cinema arts." Griffith advanced to him and put an arm around his shoulder, his attention utterly diverted. "So how did we do?" Griffith and Poli spoke in hushed tones for a few moments, before Griffith smiled, accepted a slip of paper from the theatre manager, and ushered him to the door.

"Not bad, Billy, not bad," Griffith said, as he handed the slip of paper to Bitzer. "Who said the two-dollar feature ticket would never fly for *Birth of a Nation*? A full house, plus a percentage of the concessionaire's receipts." He smiled roguishly at Miss Marsh. "Now if only the gentlemen of the fourth estate will speak kindly of our players in tomorrow's newspapers, all will have gone well for our Washington opening night."

Griffith looked over at me with a startled expression on his face, as if suddenly remembering who I was. "Mr. Surratt, you're welcome to join us in having a late supper at our hotel. We can discuss the further details of our arrangement."

But I had had enough of these people. I stood up, with my overcoat and hat in hand. "It's been a long night," I said, with as much civility as I could muster. "Perhaps we can talk again later."

It didn't occur to Griffith not to take my answer at face value. "Well, tomorrow night we're at the White House. Could you not stay in town through this following week and call on us after Tuesday? We'd be happy to accommodate your bill at the Willard. You could be on the train and back home at Baltimore by Good Friday."

"Perhaps." I bowed slightly to Miss Marsh and shook Bitzer's hand.

Griffith acted the solicitous host, helping me into my coat. "May I have Poli telephone a taxicab for you?"

I shook my head. "My hotel's only a few blocks away. I'll enjoy the walk." Griffith's hand hesitated on my shoulder. His eyes seemed to be trying to read my reaction in my face.

"This week for sure, then? I'll walk you to the theatre door."

As Griffith and I walked around the balcony aisle in the semidarkness, the movie screen in front of the empty seats was a pale and surprisingly small rectangle below us. "The colors in your motion picture tonight were very beautiful," I said. I was anxious to avoid any further talk with him of Lincoln's assassination.

"As well they should be," Griffith replied, as he walked before me. "Nearly every frame was hand-tinted by a warehouse full of young girls working night and day in Los Angeles. Billy practically tore out his hair over the costs. At some point I predict the

45

motion pictures will have true Kinemacolor film. But we're a ways from that yet."

"They are all so young," I commented. "The actors, the actresses, even the audience."

Griffith stopped and turned to me. "Youth is what the movies are about," he told me. His words hit me like a blast of cold air: I am old, I realized. If the story of my youth is to be told, these new motion pictures may be the only means to do it.

"We gather and sit in the twilight in the company of youth, and look upon young faces enlarged on a screen," Griffith continued, his face lit by one of the gas jets set into the balcony wall. I was strangely reminded of a conversation with Booth half a century earlier on a dark, lamplit Washington street.

"In the privacy of the audience we see thoughts that are personal to our own past," Griffith explained, looking directly at me. "With the silence of film, Mr. Surratt, we have the privilege of supplying our own words and messages." Griffith's eyes in the low flame of the gas jet appeared hard and yet translucent, like two pieces of quartz set into a mask. "We go to the movies to relive our youth."

I thought of the ghost of Booth that pervaded my viewing of the movie, and nodded silently to Griffith.

"That's what I hope to accomplish with my current motion picture and my new Lincoln tragedy and photoplay," Griffith said, as we resumed walking toward the balcony exit. "I want America to see its youth before we embark on the mature challenges of this new century."

The theatre lobby below us had remained brightly lit with electric lights. Griffith and I walked down the stairs and made our way eerily across the ornate, empty space. A young black man, still in Moorish costume, was desultorily pushing a carpet sweeper across the floor. Griffith appeared to be completely at ease. I had the feeling I was being led to the door of his personal mansion after a successful dinner party.

"I look forward to seeing you again later this week and viewing your photographs," Griffith said. He leaned toward me conspiratorially. "These aren't just ghost operas, Mr. Surratt," he said. "The motion pictures are a new way of seeing. They are a new way of knowing."

I nodded my head noncommittally and shook his hand. "Good night, Mr. Griffith."

3.

Pennsylvania Avenue was clean and well swept for the parade tomorrow. Barricades had been put across the side streets to keep out the automobile traffic, and at the intersection of 12th Street toward the Capitol a banner had been stretched over the pavement: PEACE THROUGH PREPAREDNESS. A turn to my right on Pennsylvania Avenue, toward 14th Street, would bring me in a few blocks back to Willard's Hotel and to my room; to my left, at the far end of the avenue, was the Capitol Building and the H Street house. My thoughts were interrupted by a brief, painful spate of coughing, and for a few moments I had to fight for my breath. Leaning against the theatre facade as I recovered, holding my sides, I considered that at my age this might well be my last visit to Washington.

After a moment of hesitation, I turned left

and walked toward the city of my nine-teenth-century youth.

The sidewalks were much improved since the Civil War. I looked across Pennsylvania Avenue at the new post office building. Behind the post office building, and obscured by its architecture, were the streets and alleys of the Washington neighborhood we had known as Hooker's Division during the Civil War. I still remembered the names of some of the houses which had been there—Wolf's Den, Bake Oven, and Headquarters, U.S.A. The bodies of newborn infants were occasionally discovered in the privies behind the houses.

My footsteps echoed against the storefront windows as I walked on. A single trolley car rolled past on its tracks in the middle of the street, its illuminated interior almost empty, making its last run to Georgetown. At the corner of 10th and Pennsylvania, I cast a look up the street to the darkened hulk of the building that was once Ford's Theatre. The facade had collapsed near the turn of the last century, killing a number of government clerks who worked in offices there. The government had seized the property after the assassination, and the three-story building had not been used as a theatre since the night of Lincoln's murder.

As I continued to look down the darkened corridor of 10th Street, I could see the intersection with H Street, and my mother's old boardinghouse. Although I wasn't ready to look at the house itself yet, I felt a certain sense of relief for my having talked to others tonight, even if it was Griffith and his Los Angeles colleagues, about my mother's death and my ill-fated friendship with John Wilkes Booth. For years after my trial, I had denied the reality of these places, refusing to speak in public, or even to look at the photographs and diaries I possessed. Was it not my fault that my mother was disgraced? Was it not my fault that she was hanged, and my own life had been ruined?

As I walked on, I reached the corner of 7th and Pennsylvania, the Market Square. Behind me the post office clock struck twelve. The sidewalks on either side of the avenue were lined with rows of wooden booths of the fruit and vegetable vendors, padlocked for the night. Across the avenue was the city market building itself. When my father was alive, my sister, Anna, and I would ride in his wagon here when he went to Washington City to sell the produce from our farm in Maryland.

I could still remember the chemical smell of this place. After the start of the Civil War, the city market had grown enormously. By the third year of the war, the expanded market had reached the undertaking establishments that had sprung up in the city blocks behind it to serve the army. Newspapers wrote angry editorials. I often shopped in the market after our move to Washington, and the stench from behind the building was at times unbearable.

For the first time in decades, I wondered what had ever become of the two Light sisters. The girls had been the terrors of respectable Civil War Washington. With their mother they ran one of the most notorious brothel houses in Hooker's Division. One insufferably hot summer day in 1864, while Grant's army was being butchered in Virginia, they danced naked in Market Square. The hammering of coffins behind the market had been an incessant din to shoppers for weeks, and the formaldehyde smell from the undertakers' shops had hung over this section of the city like a cloud of pestilence. That afternoon, when the casualty lists from

Cold Harbor and Spotsylvania were posted ever higher on the brick walls of the market building, the Light girls hired an organ grinder and monkey to play for them in the center of Market Square. As the organ grinder cranked out patriotic tunes, the Light girls began to cavort and dance and finally strip off their clothes, first a stocking or two, and then their petticoats. A crowd of men gathered in front of the market building and urged them on. I think the two sisters acted less out of natural depravity, or their usual drunkenness, than as a taunt to all that death that surrounded us. Finally, they had danced themselves stark naked, one of the sisters running in circles about the monkey, waving over her head a pair of pantaloons. When a provost marshal's wagon with barred windows arrived and carried them off, they huddled together in a blanket at the back of the wagon, still laughing.

When I arrived back at the Willard, I immediately went to the books and photographs I had placed on the writing desk earlier that evening. The first, much thicker than the others, had my name printed on the cover: *The Trial of John H. Surratt in the Assassina-*

tion of President Lincoln. The other two books were private diaries, one covered in a cheap red buckram, and the other, more expensive, sewn in a dark leather with interior compartments to hold maps and letters. A small parcel wrapped in brown paper contained photographs of the Civil War era; they were tied with a finely worked gold chain.

As I sat down at the desk and stared at the small package, there was a tremor to my fingers. The shame, anger, and guilt of so many years flooded my thoughts. It would be the first time these documents had been examined since I had first put them away, fifty years before. After several moments of hesitation, I finally unslipped the gold chain off the paper wrapping. On one side I saw again the engraved inscription, "St. Anthony Pray For Us," along with an image of the saint. On the other side was an inscription scratched with the point of a knife: "Te amo. JWB."

The first photograph I encountered as I unwrapped the paper covering was that of Lewis Powell, the youngest of the Lincoln conspirators to be hanged. The photograph was taken just hours after Lewis was arrested at my mother's house. In his torn jersey sweater, he could almost be a modern-day football player photographed on campus at Georgetown or Johns Hopkins. One scarcely notices the heavy iron manacles on his hands. *He is dead,* I think, *and he is going to die.*

An hour later, I have spread all the photographs, images both of horror and of art, across the desk. I hear the post office clock on Pennsylvania Avenue strike three outside my hotel window. I am very tired, but I know that sleep will be an impossibility, the consequence, perhaps, of my having lived too long. I pick up the diary bound in the cheaper red buckram and open it to my own handwriting: "The Personal Diary of John H. Surratt, 1864–1865" is carefully inked on the first page in a formal style. For a moment, I pause on the threshold, afraid to take the plunge. Then I begin, rereading my first diary entry, dated November 28, 1864.

Part Two

Part Two

From the diary of John H. Surratt,
November 28, Monday, 1864

1.

Today I began my career as a diarist and a photographer.

Earlier this morning I had stood on the sidewalk at the corner of 7th Street and Pennsylvania Avenue, impatiently watching the columns of blue-uniformed Union soldiers marching down the pavement in front of me, as I looked for a break in their ranks, hoping I could quickly dart across the street in time for my appointment at Gardner's. Stamping my feet on the curbstones for warmth in the wintry sunlight, I sensed rather than heard the presence of someone stepping up behind me.

"There are so many," a familiar, deep voice boomed. From the angle of my vision I saw that he was a well-dressed man, wearing a fully cut riding cape, and carrying expensive gloves in his right hand, as if he had just stepped out of one of the fashionable shops fronting Pennsylvania Avenue.

"Dear God, there are so many," the man said again. His voice had a distinctively musical quality, as if he were accustomed to hearing his thoughts spoken aloud in public places. The familiar face smiled at me as I turned to face him, and I found myself almost against my will extending my right hand.

"How are you, Wilkes?" I asked.

I stop, and read what I have just written in my diary. For the moment, this boarding-house room where I write is mine alone, as Louis Weichman, my mother's favorite boarder, has not yet returned to the sleeping quarters we share. Two iron-framed beds run the narrow length of the room. At the far end there is a washstand and a pitcher. Next to it is my clothing trunk and the small writing desk where I now sit, which I silently claimed as my own the day Weichman arrived. I look again at the date of my first diary entry. Already our nineteenth century is more than half finished, and I feel a moment of doubt. Will we be remembered, I suddenly wonder, only as an age that kept diaries and took photographs: the private records of men and women, sitting alone in furnished rooms, set down in tones of light and black?

I dismiss my doubts, dip my pen purposefully into the inkwell, and begin to write. My purchase of this diary today was my first act of confidence after securing employment at Gardner's. Despite my earlier failures as a playwright, despite my decision to avoid taking up arms in the War Between the States, I may have yet something useful to say and to do, after all. Through the eyes of the photographer and the chronicler, I may yet participate in the events of the war, if only as an observer. Before today, I had had no role to play at all in the events of the day, even as provider to the family finances. Walking home from Gardner's studio, with this book's blank pages concealed under my coat, I felt as if I were in possession of a great secret that lifted me above the anonymous crowds in their black coats, and above the shabby meanness of this sparsely furnished room in our family's boardinghouse. Yet my chance meeting with Booth on the street earlier this morning still troubles me.

I had awakened early this morning at seven o'clock to the sounds of Weichman's morning ablutions and half-muttered prayers. Feigning sleep, I listened to his splashing water from the basin, interrupting his exertions occasionally to mutter an almost inaudible "Ah, sweet Jesus!" and "Dear Mary, heavenly Mother!" He withdrew the chamber pot from its cabinet under the washbasin and noisily used it. It seemed to take forever for him to put on his coat and clump down the stairs in search of breakfast.

As the City Hall clock outside struck half past seven, I threw back the covers and rushed to the washbasin to attend to my own washing and attire. Everything depended upon my appearance today. Despite my family's financial circumstances, I was determined to put up a good front at the job interview.

I knew little of Alexander Gardner, the photographer, except that he had resided briefly at one of the socialist communes out West during the fifties. It seemed probable to me that Gardner would see humanity through the eyes of both the commercial photographer and the artist, and that he expects the same perception in an employee. As a result, I chose the more aesthetically pleasing gray-striped trousers and waistcoat to go with my black coat, the same style black coat practically all men wear today on the streets of Washington City. Everywhere, civilian men and most women are dressed in black, as if, in the third year of the war, we are all deeply in mourning. I touched the slip of paper inside my right coat pocket, signed by the provost marshal. I needed only Gardner's signature today to remove me from all this senseless violence.

I combed out my beard and hair, grown long in the latest military style that is commonly in vogue, and tied my cravat under the stiff, sharply pointed white collars of my shirt. The German immigrants at Baltimore call this style of linen shirt the *Vatermörder,* or father-killer: according to German legend, a university student wearing such a stiff-collared shirt, embracing his father on returning home, had inadvertently cut the old man's throat.

Downstairs, I hurried through breakfast, taking only a cup of boiled coffee from the tin pot Mother had thoughtfully left warming on the stove. Mother, Anna, and our other female boarder already had left for their morning visit to Father Wiget at St. Aloysius Church. Although I love my mother and sister dearly, I am occasionally vexed by the almost exclusively female nature of the boardinghouse my mother operates. Nor, I realize, am I recognized as the male head of the household and business, despite the fact that my father is deceased and that my brother, Isaac, joined the Confederate army.

For a moment I felt a stab of jealousy, recalling Wilkes Booth's visit to my family last month. What a flurry of excitement there was when I announced I would be bringing home the most famous actor in the nation. If my presence as the male in the house had been ignored, Booth's was immediately acknowledged. Even my mother's face had flushed unexpectedly. The neighbors, too, had noticed Booth's arrival, and I overheard them weeks afterward talking about his visit. He seemed to have made it a point to linger at his departure, laughing and shaking hands with me at the curbside.

Yet, for all his kindnesses to me, there is something disturbing in Booth's company. We seem almost *too* intimate for a friendship based upon only a few months' acquaintance.

I had first met Booth by chance in the lobby of Ford's Theatre, shortly after our move to Washington City a month before. I had stopped by the theatre with the manuscripts of my plays, thinking, out of naïveté, that the owners might be interested in producing them and that I could make a name for myself. Booth was standing in the lobby, having come to call for his mail. While I recognized him, I did not presume to speak to the great actor.

"I don't have time for this romantic nonsense," Harry Ford, the theatre's treasurer, said to me, dismissively thrusting the loose manuscripts back into my hands. Booth, overhearing the remark, approached me and introduced himself. When I told him my name, he drew me aside, and said, "I believe we have mutual friends in Maryland." I understood immediately that Booth was referring to my small efforts to send letters and newspapers to the South, in support of my brother's cause.

"Come, let me show you around," Booth said, sweeping his arm before him to indicate Ford's Theatre. After a brief tour,

Booth, to my amazement, offered to take my plays and read them himself. I couldn't help wondering, however, whether he was helping me because of his affection for the theatre or because of my Southern sympathies.

In the following weeks, as I had searched for work—any type of work—I encountered Booth so frequently on the streets our meetings almost seemed to happen by design. And, to my surprise, he had, indeed, read my plays.

"They are really quite good, John," he told me. "A few changes in the basic motivations, a different resolution here and there, and I think you will do something very memorable." On these occasions, Booth frequently bought me an expensive meal at Taltavul's Restaurant or the Willard Hotel and encouraged me to talk of my artistic ambitions. At first, it had seemed too wonderful, and Booth was the friend of one's dreams: sympathetic, wealthy, experienced with women, a famous actor who was himself the son of a more famous father. But I could not but wonder at times what he found so interesting in such an obscure person as myself. Was it just my ambition for theatre that had brought him to me?

Then last week I had received written notice from the provost marshal that I was liable for the Union draft. I may have been singled out because of Isaac's loyalties, or because my family came from the South, from Maryland. Booth had seemed genuinely alarmed when I had told him, claiming that my mother would find it unendurable to give up two sons to the war. I feared he was right. Moreover, while my Southern sympathies were not strong enough to compel me to fight for the South, I couldn't, I knew, find it in my heart to take up arms against them. Booth promised to make inquiries on my behalf with the provost marshal's office. He later assured me that he had made certain arrangements and that, if all went well at Gardner's studio today, my employment problems would be solved.

I finished my cup of coffee. Perhaps it was only churlish of me to think that because Booth is a celebrated figure, he is incapable of human kindness to people such as my mother and me. I rose, straightened my coat. I knew that by the end of this day I would either be a photographer's assistant or be gone for a soldier. I exited the front door determined to see the world through a photographer's eyes.

Outside I found the same familiar, dreary H Street in Washington City as ever in the late war years, completely devoid of photographic interest. An early morning rain had passed, and there was a weak sunlight, but the unpaved city street in front of our house remained more a brown liquid of mud and horse manure in the sunlight rather than dry dirt. Already carriage wheels have left deep ruts on both sides of the street. Today was coal delivery day in our neighborhood, and, at houses up and down the block, heavy wooden doors built level with the sidewalk have been lifted up and left gaping open, exposing the coal cellars underneath. At irregular intervals down the sidewalk, planks had been leaned against the curbing by the more careful householders, so that they can step from the sidewalks into hired hacks on the street without soiling their shoes or boots.

I turned the corner at the sidewalk onto 7th Street and immediately collided with a fat gentleman in a black coat, who stepped backward, awkwardly trying to keep from dropping a basket of vegetables and wrapped packages from the market. I was too startled to apologize or to assist him. "Damn you, sir, for your insolence!" he shouted, regaining control of his packages. Surprisingly, his face showed not anger, but a great fear. He rushed around me onto H Street. For a moment, I had the strange idea that he was fleeing a battlefield just around the street corner.

As I turned fully down 7th Street, the image of a battlefield suddenly seemed to become fact. Down the corridor of narrow city blocks toward the street's intersection with Pennsylvania Avenue, I saw a confused welter of cattle, wheeled vehicles, and, between them, flashes of blue-legged trousers. An officer stood in the middle of 7th Street, amidst the twisting horns of beef cattle, wildly hitting on the backs of the beeves with the flat of his sword. A group of drovers stood nearby on the curb, cursing the officer and raising their bullwhips menacingly. Another officer rode his horse down the sidewalk, shouting at civilians to go back into their houses and shops. Ahead, I could see an immense backup of traffic on upper 7th Street, with all manner of the horse-drawn vehicles jammed too closely together in the street for any one of them to turn around: private landaus and barouches in shaking hoops of black fabric; crowded public hackneys; light, two-seated chaises; and two-horse dray wagons loaded with barrels and furniture.

As I walked nearer I saw the reason for the impasse. A herd of beef cattle had been led down 7th Street, the drovers no doubt, as was their custom, planning to turn the animals onto Pennsylvania Avenue in front of the city market. From here their usual route would take them down the avenue past the Executive Mansion to the grounds around the half-completed Washington Monument, where the army kept its holding pens and slaughtering houses to feed its troops. The area was known humorously in the city as the Beef Depot Monument.

But the cattle and their drovers had been blocked at the intersection of Pennsylvania Avenue by troops marching from the direction of the Capitol Building and the railway station, turning left by the market building and continuing down 7th Street to the Potomac wharves, where they would be shipped to Virginia to replenish Grant's army. Cattle and men had collided in a typical Washington City confusion.

I cursed and looked at my pocket watch. I could not afford to be late for my appointment with Gardner. His studio and gallery was only a few blocks farther down 7th Street, but I stood on the wrong side of the street. Between me and the opposite curb was a mass of cattle. The herd now had begun to bawl nervously, their cries echoing off the brick walls on either side of the street, as if this Washington neighborhood had become an unfamiliar and frightening holding pen. One look at these animals, thrashing their necks and rolling their eyes under the whips of the drovers, convinced me that I could not force a passage to the sidewalk opposite. There was nothing for me to do except continue down the sidewalk on my side of 7th Street to the corner at Pennsylvania Avenue. There, when the last of the soldiers had passed and before the cattle were driven onto the avenue, I could race across the street and up to Gardner's.

Civilians in black coats stood under clusters of stovepipe hats at the curbs of Pennsylvania Avenue, discussing business or politics, seemingly not paying the slightest attention to the traffic behind them or to the conscripts from this year's draft call marching down the avenue in front of them. The soldiers themselves seemed equally indifferent to the civilians on the sidewalk.

Looking at the patriotic banners and the anonymous men marching beneath them, I couldn't help but think what a waste of life the war represented. Everyone knows the South will be defeated, and only the desperate or the conscripted continue to fight on. I am glad my brother, Isaac, is out of it. Standing at the curb, I remembered reading, when the war was still young, of the hundred or so Union soldiers, all volunteers, killed at the battle of Ball's Bluff outside Washington City. Heavy autumn rains that year had washed their bodies out of the shallow battlefield graves and into the Potomac. Days later, I had read in the *Washington Star,* residents of the capital were shocked to see these same swollen bodies floating into the canals at Georgetown and against the edges of the city's wharves. Today, as the conscripts marched down the city's main avenue toward battlefields where the casualties are numbered in the tens of thousands, no one bothers even to look.

I shuddered, although not from the cold wind. If my interview with Gardner was not successful, I was resolved, despite the risk of death, to take my place without protest in the Union ranks as a conscript. It is obviously the winning side, and a soldier's pay will contribute at least a little money to Mother's and Anna's upkeep. As a man now twenty-one years of age, I feel I must *do* something.

The new conscripts in front of me continued to march down Pennsylvania Avenue in silent and unbroken companies, as if these men in uniforms were being slowly unspun from a giant spool of blue thread hidden behind the Capitol Building up the avenue. I saw one young Dutch-looking boy with curly blond hair, about sixteen or seventeen, eating an orange. Orange pips spilled down the front blouse of his uniform. Fruit and candy vendors from the city market had been running along the curbs beside the soldiers, and many of the conscripts, without breaking ranks, had been able hastily to hand over paper currency for bags of roasted chestnuts, oranges, or cheap chocolates. Like the others in his rank, the young boy carried a full field pack on his back; the blue sleeves of his uniform seemed one or two inches too long for his arms, giving him a raw, untutored look. It was as I watched him marching down Pennsylvania Avenue that, turning my head, I encountered John Wilkes Booth standing nearby at the curb. Several pedestrians walking behind him, ignoring the military parade in the street, silently nudged their companions in the ribs, pointing out Booth to one another.

I turned. "How are you, Wilkes?" I asked.

I would have preferred that Booth had not noticed me. Perhaps it was only my embarrassment at knowing Booth had obtained my interview with Gardner; or perhaps it was the unease I felt in his presence, as if he wanted something of me I didn't know if I could give.

He smiled and inclined his head toward the soldiers passing in the street. "At least, John, you're well out of all *this*."

I nodded. "Yes. That is, if I can only get across the street after the whole damn Army of the Potomac has finished marching through Washington City." For a moment we said nothing further, the cold air around us filled with the rhythmic drumming of the soldiers' boots on the pavement. "It will all be over soon in Virginia," I said at length. "Reinforcements like these have been moving through the city for months. Lee's army will fold before spring."

"Oh, no, not at all, John." Booth looked at me with an intensity I found disturbing. "Lee is preparing a fine defensive line between Richmond and Petersburg. His troops are well dug in, and supplied with enough wire, artillery, and ordnance to hold those lines indefinitely. I myself was in Richmond last week and have seen these preparations with my own eyes."

I put my hand on the right shoulder of his coat and cast a quick glance at the cluster of civilians standing near us on the sidewalk. Several had recognized Booth. His Southern sympathies were well known. "For God's sake, Wilkes," I whispered. "Keep your voice down."

I led him away from the curb toward a storefront window facing Pennsylvania Avenue. My fear of bystanders was real. Secretary of War Stanton often boasted of the number of informants he employed through the provost marshal's office to listen for just such disloyal talk on the streets of Washington City. Stanton bragged in the newspapers of the little bell he kept in his office, where he interrogated suspected disloyalists. One little ring of his bell, he said, was sufficient to summon his guards and carry away any suspected man or woman to incarceration at one of the many prisons in the city. Or, perhaps, to a worse fate.

Booth seemed amused by my caution. In front of a milliner's window, we stood a moment without speaking. Behind the glass, I could see a row of ladies' heads, each carved out of wood in coquettish expressions and topped by creations in velvet and ribbons. A card beside the mannequins' heads behind the shop window read:

LADIES! THE UNION MAY BE IN PERIL, BUT YOU
ARE NEVER IN PERIL OF APPEARING
UNFASHIONABLE IN OUR LATEST TRIMMED SPOON
AND CURTAINLESS BONNETS!
PRICES REASONABLE.

Looking at our reflection in the plate glass, Booth in his black riding cape and I in my black frock coat, we made an incongruous pair.

"I am an enemy to neither the North nor the South," I said. "I only want all this senseless killing to stop."

"Really, John?" Booth's patient eyes seemed to search mine in mild disbelief. "Then I envy you, and your calmness of mind." Booth turned from me to light a cigar, and spoke in a low voice as he slowly shook his right hand in the wind to extinguish the match. "Of course, I would have expected an *artist* such as yourself to feel much more passionately about the events of our times." Behind an aurora of cigar smoke, Booth seemed to regard me with laughing eyes.

"Oh, stop it, Wilkes," I said, irritated that Booth had spoken so sarcastically to me.

We were interrupted by a small boy running up to us carrying a rag and a wooden box. "Give your boots a Union shine, sirs?" he said in a small, piping voice. "Cost you only a dime." He was perhaps eight or nine years old, wild and hungry-looking, with a dirty face and a torn cloth cap. Irritated at my delay in reaching Gardner's, I started to sharply tell him to be on his way. The street urchins had become a great nuisance in the city in the last year; many of them were children abandoned by women working in Hooker's Division, and it had become impossible to cross the city's main streets without being accosted by one or another with their cleaning rags.

Booth threw his cigar into the street and reached inside his cape to take out his coin purse. "Here, son," he said. "Now leave us." I saw that Booth had handed him a gold dollar piece, in an act calculated, I sensed, to put me in my place.

He now turned his full attention back to me. "But I forget my manners, John. I remember how well I enjoyed my visit with your family last month. Is there any news of your wounded brother? And how is your sister, and your dear mother?"

"All are fine, Wilkes," I said, somewhat abashed. "We've learned Isaac's wound was not fatal; he's invalided out to Texas. And Anna thinks life in wartime Washington is very romantic."

"Good, that's good," Booth said, as if to himself, unconsciously turning to look at his own reflection in the shop's window glass. Booth was commonly known as the most handsome actor in America. The newspapers frequently described him as beautiful;

John Wilkes Booth seemed to have inherited the best of the features of his late father, the famous tragedian Junius Brutus Booth: dark, mysterious eyes, curly hair, and an athletic, almost acrobatic build.

Booth leaned against the wooden frame of the shop window. His left hand—remarkably white despite his habit of not wearing gloves—was crudely marked with the letters *JWB* in India ink.

"Wilkes, you were a fool to disfigure such a fine hand with your initials," I said.

Booth smiled at me, aware that I had been studying him. "A childish prank. I honestly think at the time I was just trying to vex the priests at school. Anyway, I am relieved that Isaac is well, and that he is safely out of the war."

"At the moment, it is my mother's other son that I am most concerned with. I'll not do my cause any good by being late to see Gardner." I turned toward the curb. I could at last see an end in the distance to the columns of soldiers moving down Pennsylvania Avenue. Far behind the Capitol Building, the blue thread of soldiers was finally playing itself out. I impatiently fingered the slip of paper inside my coat pocket. *God-damn* this war.

"I'm sure you'll get on with Gardner," Booth said. "I've spoken to him several times on your behalf. Gardner tells me that my *cartes de visite* at his shop outsell those of any other actress or actor, including Laura Keene's and Edwin Forrest's." Booth laughed. "Even Mr. Lincoln's."

"I must find *something*," I said, half to myself, looking out over Pennsylvania Avenue.

"We both know you were made for greater things, John, than the front lines." Booth stood very close to me, his voice almost in a whisper. Once again, he seemed to have read my thoughts. "I've read your plays, and I understand the dramas within your mind. You already think and visualize scenes as a cameraman, John, whether you realize it or not."

I nodded. Booth did understand me. And I have long had an interest to learn something of photography and the visual arts.

"You're remarkably observant," Booth went on. "Surely a steady eye must count for something in a photographer's studio. And a future in photography can bring you financial rewards long after this wartime popularity in pictures of battle scenes is over. I've often thought that when peacetime comes, portrait photography and the theatre must inevitably combine. Of course, that will mean the end of classical drama."

Booth turned to face me, reaching inside his cape. "That reminds me," he said. He withdrew a small piece of cardboard with his photographic print affixed to it. It was a *carte de visite,* one of the most popular of the recent photographic innovations. Everyone since the war began seemed to be purchasing these cards and sending them to friends. Their popularity was by no means limited to celebrated subjects such as Booth; photographers followed the common soldiers into their camps, where the young men had their photographs taken on payday and mailed their *cartes de visite* to their families from Grant's front lines.

Booth took out a small gold pencil from inside his cape and began to write on the back of the card. "I'm staying at a hotel near the National, where I'm playing in *Romeo and Juliet* this week. It's poor stuff, but the best I can do in a wartime theatre."

Booth finished writing on the card and

handed it to me. "I know that Gardner keeps half-day hours at his studio on Saturdays," he said. "I've written the address of a restaurant near my hotel. I'd like you to join me there next Saturday. There will be some people present that I would like you to meet."

As I started to shake my head, Booth smiled at me and closed my fingers over the card. "John, I know your desire to make something of yourself, to be the head of your family. With your father's death and your mother's troubles, it's understandable and I respect that desire. I am not asking anything of you. These are people who can help *you,* John." After a moment's hesitation, I nodded and slipped Booth's *carte de visite* inside the pocket of my black coat.

A moment later, an unnatural stillness fell over Pennsylvania Avenue. As I turned we saw the last company of blue-uniformed men turn the corner by the city market building toward the wharves. Almost immediately I heard the cattle bawling up the blocks on 7th Street and the crack of drovers' whips echoing off the brick buildings. "I must go," I said.

"I won't hold you," Booth said. He

grasped my right hand. "Saturday afternoon for sure?"

I nodded, reluctantly, and pulled my hand
away from him. Stepping into the traffic, I
crossed 7th Street just ahead of the drovers
and began to hurry up the opposite sidewalk.

"John!" Booth called out. He stood in the
middle of Pennsylvania Avenue, his hand
cupped to his mouth. The cattle already had
been turned into the avenue, toward the Executive Mansion, but he paid no attention to
them; their broad backs and curved horns
calmly parted around him, as if they, too,
realized his extraordinary presence. At this
moment, a ray of brilliant sunshine fell
where Booth stood in the mired pavement.
The sight was strangely impressive; Booth
appeared both youthful and also very old,
and weary. He shouted to be heard above
the noise of the animals and the rapidly
moving carriages.

"Remember me to your mother."

I ran the last two blocks to Gardner's studio and was at the entrance to the building with a few minutes to spare. The studio and gallery was in the top floor above Shepard and Riley's Stationery and Bookstore at 511 7th Street. Two huge wooden signs covered most of the building's brick facade over the second and third stories, and were visible from several blocks away: PHOTOGRAPHS and VIEWS OF THE WAR. I stood in the sidewalk for a few moments more, catching my breath, before opening the door into the bookstore.

The clerks were busy with customers. I rapidly walked by the merchandise displays; a hand sign painted on a small board directed me up a flight of rear stairs to Gardner's studio and gallery.

At the top of the stairs, I found myself on a small landing, a frayed carpet covering the floor and a single gas jet burning fitfully in the corner. The walls on either side were covered with dozens of framed photographic prints. A large, ruffian-looking man occupied the only chair, chewing tobacco and eyeing me with an unmistakably sardonic expression. His pug hat was pushed back rakishly on his head, and he made no attempt to withdraw his legs, stretched out across the narrow width of the landing and blocking me from the studio's closed door. His cowhide boots were liberally covered with manure from the streets; he looked remarkably like one of the cattle drovers I had passed on the avenue.

I assumed he must be a customer who had an appointment with Gardner preceding mine. Even the laboring class of people in Washington City now found portrait photography to be within their means. He was plainly of great physical strength, and in good health. I wondered why he was not in Grant's army.

"Mr. Gardner's in a *conference*," the ruffian said. Without taking his eyes off me, or changing his expression, he leaned over and projected a brown stream of tobacco juice into a brass cuspidor next to his chair. "I'll tell him you're waiting."

I stared at him with barely concealed astonishment. This man was obviously an acquaintance of Gardner, not a patron. Was it possible that this pug-ugly at the top of the stairs was an employee at Gardner's studio? Speechless, I handed my calling card to him, and watched him open the studio door just wide enough for him to step in sideways, his broad shoulders preventing me from seeing into the interior. He quickly shut the door behind him.

Alone on the landing, I turned my attention to the photographic gallery on the walls. The photographs seemed to stare back at me in a ghostly and pale crowd in the dim light of the single gas jet. The portraits were hung in innumerable sizes, from the *cartes de visite* a few inches across to the standard-sized prints about the size of a book page, with a few life-sized imperial portraits, which I estimated were a good seventeen inches wide. Booth had been right; his portrait was easily the most frequently represented on the walls, alongside those of Laura Keene and his brother and fellow actor, Edwin Booth. President Lincoln and his secretary of state, William Seward, also were prominently displayed.

I found myself staring at a group of landscapes hung separately on the wall a little distance from the others. They were prints of Brady's famous photographs taken after the battle following Lee's invasion of Maryland near the little town of Sharpsburg, as the battle became known in the South, although the North, forever divided, referred to it by the name of the river nearby, Antietam. They had caused a public stir when first exhibited in 1862 at Brady's gallery at New York City.

The imperial print directly in front of my eyes was composed of a long row of Confederate bodies, the dead roughly aligned in the shape of a giant fishhook at the base of a slight hill. They apparently either had been shot there leading an advance, or had been laid in a row by a Union burial party soon after the battle. Their bodies did not appear to be swollen in the sunlight. A caption underneath the photograph read: "Eighty rebels are buried in this hole." In the cold darkness of the landing, I touched the slip of paper inside my coat pocket, and thought, *It will either be photography or the army.*

I turned away from the prints, and found myself reading a curiously worded notice tacked to the wall directly underneath the gas jet:

TO MY PATRONS

PHOTOGRAPHY

Is not a branch of mechanics, whereby a quantity of material is thrown into a hopper, and with the grinding of grim, greasy machinery, beautiful portraits may be turned out. To produce such beautiful pictures requires skill, culture, much study and practice, to say nothing of an expensive commercial outfit and a properly arranged studio. With all these, the photographer must also know how to manage a most obstreperous class of chemicals. Therefore he needs all the assistance from you that you are able to give him. He is entitled to the same respect and consideration from you as your minister, your physician, or your lawyer, and it is just as essential that he should have rules for the best government of his establishment as it is for anyone else whom you patronize.

WHEN TO COME

A bright day is not necessary. In fact, the light is best when the heavens are clouded and the sun shines through the clouds. Never come in the early morning, and never come in a hurry or flurry. Although times for exposure can be as little as five to ten seconds, ladies who have shopping and an engagement with the photographer on the same day will please be careful to attend to the latter first. Remember, red takes black, and red faces hurried out of their natural countenance will photograph as black.

THE CHILDREN

We are always glad to take a reasonable amount of pains with the little ones. We can always get something out of them. Never threaten a child if it won't sit, and never coax it with sweetmeats. Please permit the photographer to manage it from the beginning.

HOW TO "SIT"

The headrest must be used, not to give the position but that you may keep it. The natural pulsations of the body cause it to move (in spite of the strongest will) sufficient to make your negative useless. To avoid the fault so generally and justly complained of, the light within the sitting area has been constructed so as to obliviate all heavy and unnatural shadows under the eyebrows and chin.

PRICES

Our prices are kept at reasonable rates.

There may be work done for less, *but we ask that* quality *be given your preference.*

Suddenly I heard the studio door open behind me, and turned to see the ruffian in muddied boots walk out, followed by a man in the uniform of a Union colonel. The colonel was speaking to someone else behind him. "Well, it's settled, then, Captain. We can expect the cartographic work no later than the end of next week."

A barrel-chested, middle-aged man in civilian clothes followed them partly out into the landing. "They'll be ready as I promised," the man said. "There will be no doubt about the results." The colonel nodded, and he and the ruffian walked past me down the stairs.

"You're punctual," the barrel-chested man said to me. "A virtue which is its own reward, but a virtue nevertheless." I stood unable to think of a reply, certain that the man before me was the person I had hoped to work for. In a moment all the felicitous phrases I had rehearsed beforehand fled from my brain. "I'm glad we'll have ample time to talk before my afternoon sittings."

He stuck out his right hand. "Alexander Gardner."

Embarrassed, I returned his greeting. Short, stocky, and indistinguishable in his outward appearance from the dozens of merchants and bankers I had seen today on the sidewalks of Pennsylvania Avenue, Gardner was far from the man I had anticipated. I realized I had made a mistake in dressing to make an "artistic" impression upon him. An expanse of ginger-colored whiskers neatly combed down his shirtfront emphasized his businesslike demeanor. He spoke with a noticeable Scottish burr to his voice, and reminded me of a type which I instantly recognized, and dreaded: the Scots merchant, frequently seen at the docks of Baltimore or Richmond, interested only in trade, whether he was engaged in the business of selling slaves, tobacco, or, in this case, photographs. They are seldom interested in the ambitions of artistic young men.

"The waiting was instructive to me, Mr. Gardner," I said. "I passed the time agreeably by looking at your gallery of photographs. I particularly was interested in Mr. Brady's prints of the battle of Sharpsburg."

Gardner looked at me with disdain. "They are popularly known as Brady's prints because he was the first to sell them," he told me. "But I hold the copyright, and I was the photographer on the scene in 1862 at Antietam."

Before I could apologize for my mistake, Gardner seized my shoulder and began to lead me toward the studio door. "We can talk in there," he said. "It's warmer."

Following him inside, my first impression was of walking into a furnace where the walls had become superheated to a blue intensity. An enormous potbellied stove with a blazing fire occupied the center of the long, rectangular studio. I saw now that the entire room was painted a light blue. Mounted on one wall was the largest and most detailed map of northern Virginia and Maryland I had ever seen. It was easily six feet across. I could even make out the spot marked Surrattsville, the hamlet in Maryland where I had been born, and where my father had been postmaster.

Gardner walked briskly across the studio and covered the map with a large black tarpaulin. "You'll not need to be studying that," he said. He then walked to the stove, inspected its grate critically, and turned his backside to it, spreading the tails of his frock coat in front of him for further warmth. "I find the heat accelerates the action of the photographic chemicals," he said by way of explanation, rubbing his hands against the tails of his coat. "And having been reared in Glasgow winters, I've no great fondness for the cold."

Except for a doorway which seemed to lead to a small room above us on the third story, there was no entrance or exit other than the way we had come. It occurred to me that Gardner's studio would be a great firetrap in winter. Pushed to the sides of the studio was a jumble of tables, chairs, and divans, some on top of one another, like an odd lot purchased from an auctioneer. I recognized some of these pieces of furniture as "props" in the photographs outside. Other than the stove, the only object in the center of the room was a rosewood box supported by a tripod about four or five feet in height. Four metal tubes projected from one end of this box, each covered with a brass cap.

Gardner was grinning at me from behind his ginger whiskers. "My four-barreled solar camera, capable of four exposures on one plate. I immediately saw, as some, like Brady, did *not,* that this patented device multiplied the effects of one operator while greatly reducing the material losses on our side of the business."

Gardner's exuberant arrogance, which I would find off-putting in most people, was strangely appealing, as well. "Rather like the new Gatling machine rifles suggested to the army this year, which, had the military taken my advice and employed in the spring offensive, which it did *not,* would have ended the war by now." He dropped his frock-coat tails but continued to rub his hands together energetically. "Don't you agree, Mr. Surratt?"

I did not have the slightest idea what he was talking about.

Gardner suddenly began to pace around the room energetically, as if there were a steam engine inside his stocky body that at last had received sufficient heat for locomotion. "But we've come to meet this morning to discuss your possible employment, Mr. Surratt, not the future of the war or the future of photography."

His hands were now busy pulling a sheaf of papers out of the inside pocket of his frock coat. I saw my calling card among them, as well as a number of other papers I did not recognize. "I cannot deny that you've come highly recommended by some of my best patrons," Gardner said. He peered at me over the sheaf of papers. "You say, Mr. Surratt, that you come originally from southern Maryland?"

I had said nothing to him of the sort. "Yes, sir. A small town named for my father, a former Union postmaster."

"And after the unfortunate death of your father, your widowed mother relocated herself to our capital, some two months ago? And you have a brother in the Confederate army, do you not?"

Gardner had not asked me to sit down, or more accurately, to untangle a chair from the stacks against the walls. I remained standing uncomfortably in front of his four-barreled camera while answering his questions. I must admit I found it disconcerting that he knew so much beforehand about my family history. Someone other than Booth had told him extensively about my past. I chose my words carefully.

"Yes, we moved here in October. Like so many others in this tragic war, my family was divided in loyalties. I'm happy to say that my brother is no longer in active service for the Confederate army. My mother is currently settled with the rest of our family here in Washington City, where both she and I run a boardinghouse for a respectable citizenry. One of our boarders is a most loyal and trusted clerk in the U.S. War Department."

"Ah, yes, your mother, a Catholic lady," Gardner said, not taking his eyes off the papers in his hands, "and I see you were educated by priests at St. Charles College. I'll say this for the Roman Church, it instructs its members well, if not wisely." Gardner quickly folded the papers and returned them to his inside coat pocket. He seemed to regard me with a fresh interest. "I understand you write in a good hand, and you're adept at copying out details, whether from ledgers or sketchbooks? You can even reproduce the handwriting of others?"

How had Gardner come to know so much about me? I wondered again. I could see my face reflected in the polished brass circles of the lens caps of the four barrels of his camera in front of me. I replied that what he had heard was true.

Gardner stroked his beard reflectively. "Well, I'll not deny that I'll be needing another hand about the studio. With the victory at the polls this month of Mr. Lincoln's party, I expect to continue to be favored with the patronage of his administration. I am proud to say, *very* proud, Mr. Surratt, that I have been privileged to have taken more photographic portraits of Mr. Lincoln and members of his cabinet than the owner of any other photographic establishment in Washington City. Mr. Lincoln himself has sat for his portrait several times in this very room. And with the advent of next spring's offensive at Petersburg, I'm certain to find an assistant useful on trips to the field, should you prove able."

I replied that I had always had a great interest in recording a photographic history of the Civil War.

Gardner brought his right hand down possessively at the opposite end of the rosewood box that stood between us. *"I take the photographs here, Mr. Surratt."* For a moment he seemed to stare at me with a fierce but amused expression on his face. "You've not the slightest idea of what I'll be needing you for, do you?"

Before I could answer, Gardner stepped around the tripod and planted himself in front of me. To my alarm, he screwed his face into a contortion, and in a high-pitched, wheedling voice asked of someone invisible over my shoulder, "Ah, Mr. Gardner, could you not do something about that terrible 'squint' your camera has given my eyes? It quite puts me out of countenance."

"Oh, my dear Mr. Gardner, I fear your shadows have added at least twenty-five years to my age."

It occurred to me that he was caricaturing a procession of his more plaintive elderly customers. Gardner threw back his head and laughed, and then continued in his own voice, "Well, how young would you care to be, madam? I can have my youthful assistant Mr. Surratt here make you twenty-five again, but I fear my reputation would not bear that. Forty-five is as low as I'll go!"

Gardner laughed again, before taking on a serious expression. "There's a skill, John Surratt, an art in presenting objects or people not simply as they appear, nor as they wish to appear, but as they *should* appear. That's as true for my military work as it is for my civilian portraits. A steady hand in spreading the chemical agents on glass, a pen sharpened into the fine point of a scribe, the judicious application of a piece of holystone upon the emulsion, all are as necessary to my art as a camera and lens."

Gardner seemed to be regarding me already as a retained employee, and my hopes rose. "Do you know, Johnny, what you will be most struggling against here in this studio, and what will be your greatest enemy?"

I shook my head.

"Bombazine!" Gardner thrust his ginger whiskers to within a few inches of my face shouting with such force I thought he was naming another unknown weapon of the Union army.

"I beg your pardon?"

"Why, bombazine, man, the cotton and silk fabric, *always* black, which the ladies insist upon draping around themselves by the yard. The damned stuff is the bane of the photographer's art, and it absorbs light as your blotter paper absorbs ink. It was bad enough when the gentlemen chose always to wear black. But now, with the fashion in ladies' dress, a pretty maiden of twenty who comes to my studio in her best bombazine outfit becomes, without a skillful application of the emulsion or an apt re-touching of the negative, a fleshy blob of a face swimming in an inky darkness."

My own face must have shown incomprehension, for Gardner grabbed my arm impatiently. "Ah, I'll not waste words. Come along upstairs, for I will show you better than tell you."

Without further explanation, Gardner directed me by the elbow across the studio and opened the small interior door. He paused to throw to one side a heavy piece of black fabric that hung suspended from a row of rings at the top of the door frame, and pushed me through the doorway. As he closed the door the black curtain fell behind us. I found myself at the bottom of a rickety staircase; in the darkness I could barely make out the flickering of an orange-colored light in the attic room above us. It took several moments before I could discern the whiteness of my hand in front of my eyes. "Why, go on, man, go on," Gardner shouted from behind, pushing me up the stairs.

At the top of the attic stairs, we came to a small half-room. A single gas jet, hung from a ceiling joist and masked by a cone of reddish-orange paper, provided the only light. A shallow vat about half the length of a man's body, filled with a brownish liquid, occupied most of the room. On wooden shelves about me were numerous smaller metal troughs, water pipes, and long rows of vials of chemicals. There was an acrid, penetrating odor that reminded me unpleasantly of the undertakers' sheds behind the city market.

"Here's where you'll be working if you prove satisfactory," Gardner said. He had turned his back to me and appeared to be searching for some items among the chemical vials in a small cabinet jammed against a corner. "Cyanide, formic acid, nitrate, these, among others, will be the tools of your trade," he said. When Gardner turned around, he was holding a vial of liquid and a rectangular piece of clear glass.

"The negative is made on glass, Johnny, which must be *absolutely* clean of any dust particles, ashes, or any of your pocket trash, or my whole art is spoiled, and at great expense to me." Gardner gave me a questioning look, and in the reddish-orange light his beard and features appeared surprisingly malevolent. "You'll not be a user of tobacco, are you, John?"

I assured him I was chaste in all my habits.

"Ah, that's good, that's good." My answer seemed to satisfy Gardner, who continued to smile while he poured a syrupy liquid from the vial over one side of the glass. A sharp smell of ether and alcohol filled the attic room as he had uncorked the vial.

"Here we have a photographic *plate,* John Surratt," Gardner said. "Covered on one side with an emulsion of sulphuric ether, iodide of potassium, and guncotton." He held the piece of glass at a distance from him with a pair of gutta-percha tongs while he spoke, letting the excess liquid drop into a metal trough. "A fine chemical combination for an explosive, actually, much more satisfactory in its results than gunpowder. But in this case, almost ready to preserve the beauty of our young ladies in their bombazine dresses."

Holding the glass by a pair of tongs, Gardner carefully placed it into the brownish liquid of the vat. "The excitement bath," Gardner said. "The ether and alcohol evaporate very quickly, mind you, leaving chiefly iodide of ammonium upon the organic material of the emulsion." Gardner stood over the vat while he spoke, gently moving the plate through the solution with obvious pride in his skill. "We plunge the plate into the excitement bath knowing a chemical reaction will take place, causing our plate to become charged with iodide of silver, and eminently sensitive to light."

I nodded as if to show I understood this chemistry.

Gardner looked up at me critically from his work at the vat. "I see you're wearing fine linen, Johnny. That won't do here. You'll find that iodide of silver will blacken all that comes into contact with it. You've no objection, I suppose, to getting your hands dirty?"

I thought of Booth's hand marked with India ink. He had stained his hand out of vanity; like a lesser actor in a play, my hands apparently were to be marked by hard work. I shook my head to show I had no objection.

"Done!" Gardner cried. He lifted the plate of glass out of the vat. The side of the glass which Gardner had covered with the emulsion liquid was now the color and opacity of an egg white.

"It's ready for the camera now, Johnny," Gardner said. He stood with his body partially blocking the plate from the reddish-orange gaslight at the attic ceiling. "But the plate *must* be used while it's yet wet, and until my exposure in the camera it must be zealously shielded from any direct sunlight." Gardner placed the damp glass onto a rack inside a metal box japanned to a flat black on the inside.

"Well, Johnny, do you think you can do it?" Gardner closed the box with a snap, pressed it under his left arm, and stood facing me, rocking back on his heels. "I can't be running up and down these stairs every few minutes for my wet plates while I'm having the afternoon procession of sittings. That will be *your* job, provided you find twenty dollars a month satisfactory."

I was pleasantly surprised at his offer. This salary was substantially more than the sixteen dollars a month paid to Union privates, and I would be trained to record life, not destroy it.

Distracted by the red-masked light of the gas jet inside the attic room reflecting off

Gardner's black coat, giving him a somewhat demonic appearance, I paused for a
moment. My future employer seemed to
take my silence for hesitation. "Later on,
Johnny, after I've shown you how to print
the positive images on paper, how to handle
the shellac on a paper print and retouch our
prints so that the matron of fifty years becomes a mere forty, we can possibly talk of
more money for you."

I smiled. "Mr. Gardner, I am certain that I
am your man."

Gardner extended his right arm toward
me, as if to confirm our conversation with a
handshake. "There's just one other, small
matter," I said.

"There certainly is. You must have your
own photograph taken!" Gardner, instead
of taking my right hand, suddenly grabbed
my right elbow, and, keeping the boxed
plate tucked slightly against his left side,
began pulling me violently down the dark
stairs.

"Mr. Gardner!" I cried as I half fell and
half followed him down the attic stairs. As I
had turned my back on the single gas jet,
the stairwell below seemed plunged into total darkness. I heard, rather than saw, my

boots tripping over the wooden stairs. "But I'm not prepared, sir, and I fear my appearance—" I felt Gardner's grip on my elbow tighten in the darkness.

"Ah, I'll not take no for an answer, Johnny," I heard from the steps below me. "I'll not waste a plate once it's wet from the excitement bath, and I make it a policy to take photographs of *everyone* who enters my studio."

I felt the curtain at the bottom of the stairs brush across me as it was pulled aside, and the door was opened to the studio light. The heat from the blue room struck me like a blast from a furnace, and I involuntarily shut my eyes.

"You'll do fine if you just act naturally," Gardner said. He led me like a blind man to the center of the studio, and positioned me five or six feet in front of the camera. A large skylight of frosted glass was angled into the ceiling over where I stood. "But the light, Mr. Gardner, surely the sunlight—"

"The light will be perfect," Gardner said. "I deliberately kept us talking until I knew the sun would be at a proper height." He had placed the box containing the wet plate on top of the camera and was now rummaging through the stacked furniture against the studio walls. "Besides, the blue walls of my studio are scientifically prepared to diffuse the light as much as possible." Gardner came toward me with my hat in one hand and a folded metal contraption that appeared to be an instrument of torture in his other. He thrust the hat into my hands. "Put your hat on, man, put your hat on! How shall we recognize you otherwise?"

It was an odd request, for we were indoors. But I did as Gardner demanded.

"Now, if you'll just be so kind as to lock your head into this iron brace," Gardner said. He stood behind me, adjusting what I had assumed to be the instrument of torture. It was a metal rack, now unfolded to about the height of a man, with projecting metal hoops and adjustable screws. Gardner fitted my head into the hoop at the top of the rack and began turning the screws to an uncomfortably tight pressure at the small bones at the base of my ears. He bent to make a lower adjustment at my back, and I suddenly was jabbed in my kidneys by the prongs of another metal hoop, forcing me to stand upright.

Gardner tightened two smaller metal

bands around each of my kneecaps. I was now rigidly locked into place and prevented from looking anywhere except directly at the camera in front of me. "Must I keep my eyes open entirely during the camera's operation?" I asked. The iron prongs of the headrest made speaking difficult.

"Blink as often as you please," I heard Gardner say from behind me, "but don't roll your eyes, or try to avert your gaze from the camera." Gardner stepped in front of me, surveyed me critically, then adjusted my hat and spread the tails of my frock coat to conceal the immobilizing iron instrument behind me.

I struggled to form words against the restraint of the headrest. "But, Mr. Gardner, what do you advise for an appropriate facial expression? What shall I think about while my portrait is being taken?"

My question seemed to infuriate Gardner, who was now crouched at the back of the camera, his head and arms entirely covered with a black cloth that resembled a large hood. "Damn it, man, think of what you please! Whistle 'Yankee-Doodle' in your head if it damn well pleases you!" His voice was quite loud, despite the black cloth covering his head. Without withdrawing his head from the hood, Gardner removed the four lens caps facing me and pulled the box containing the wet plate underneath the black cloth. He recovered the lens caps, and moments later I heard the back of the rosewood camera slide open.

"If you will merely think that it is your job not to move a whit, I will be very gratified," Gardner said, with a heavy sarcasm, underneath his black hood. I heard the sounds of the glass plate being mounted inside the camera.

"Prepare yourself," Gardner said. Without moving his head from underneath the hood, he raised his right arm behind the camera. My eyes fixed upon his open fingers. His other hand was busy outside the black cloth, skillfully uncovering the lens caps once more. "You must remain absolutely still for fifteen seconds, Johnny. I'll lower my right hand when the time's elapsed. Until then, don't move, and try to breathe shallowly, if you must breathe at all."

I stood encircled in the iron hoops of Gardner's headrest and back stand, trying to obey his injunction not to breathe. I began to feel that this art of photography was not so directly removed from the pain and suffering of the war, after all. The two prongs of the headrest behind my ears were now compressing the back of my skull in a manner much more painful than a few moments before. I felt a bead of perspiration warmly congeal just under my collar band, hesitate there a moment, and then roll, uninterrupted, down the entire length of my spine; it *was* insufferably hot inside this studio. The round lenses of the rosewood box in front of me continued to look upon me like four impassive eyes. I thought of how within a few moments the negative of my image would be floating within the brownish liquid of one of Gardner's vats upstairs; removed from the vat and thoroughly dried, printed as a positive upon paper and shellacked to an impenetrable hardness. The image of my face would then join the company of innumerable others in the dim light of Gardner's gallery at the top of the landing, my features preserved eternally there, as if in the darkness of the tomb.

Surely fifteen seconds had gone by; but Gardner remained hidden beneath his black hood, his right arm rigidly stuck into the air.

The pain at the back of my skull was now becoming unbearable, and I had lost all sensation of feeling in my legs from below where Gardner had fastened the metal hoops around my knees. I began to fear that I would become unconscious, toppling myself and the iron apparatus behind me in a crash to the studio floor, and I thought I felt my body begin to sway. The camera was all I could see; the iron prongs behind my head seemed to be squeezing into blackness all else on either side of me, and I was certain that I was dangerously swaying forward from where my knees stood locked into place. Just before the camera box itself disappeared into the darkness and my consciousness began to fade, I thought of the caption on one of the photographs outside: "Eighty rebels are buried in this hole."

Gardner cried out, "Finished!" and dropped his right arm. My arms flew to the back of my head, and I began unscrewing the hoop from behind my neck. Gardner emerged at last from underneath the black hood and stood upright with the glass plate inside its box. "Well, that's all the time I have for you today, Johnny," he said. "I'll expect you here at eight o'clock sharp tomorrow morning so I can begin to show you how to mix the guncotton and potassium in a safe manner. I'll deduct the costs of today's plate and any paper prints from your pay."

Gardner left me to free myself from the rest of the metal back stand as best I could. I finished quickly, and stepped forward, like a prisoner at last paroled. I felt it was time to make my confession about the military draft. "Mr. Gardner, I must speak further with you," I said.

Gardner was already at the door to the attic stairs. He looked at me irritably, the box containing the exposed plate tucked underneath his left arm. "Not now, Johnny. I must put your image into pyrogallic solution and hydrofluoric acid."

I persevered. "Mr. Gardner, did not the Union officer here earlier today call you captain?"

Gardner stopped, and smoothing his ginger whiskers with his free hand, a motion which provided him, I suspected, a moment to consider his answer before he spoke. "I have the honor of holding that brevet rank for the duration of the war," he said.

"You also mentioned possible photographic trips into the Virginia theatre of war, and I've read that your photographic work there is officially sanctioned by the War Department."

Gardner was looking at me closely. "I do provide officially commissioned photographic portraits of selected general staffs there, it is true. I am on occasion also officially requested by our military to do certain other work in the Virginia theatre from time to time." His voice was gravely serious when he spoke, a concerned look on his face.

I took a deep breath. The next moments would determine my fate either as a soldier or as a photographer. "My own relation to the military is of some concern to me, Mr. Gardner. As you know, Mr. Lincoln called this year for one hundred thousand additions to our Union army. Already large numbers of conscripts are being called upon, as the supply of volunteers proved inadequate. The provost marshal's office here in the city has notified me that my own name has lately been added to the list of possible conscripts."

Gardner's face lost its serious expression, and he seemed to regard me with a look of amusement. "You must know that my own family is not a wealthy one," I went on. "Under our circumstances, neither my mother nor I can afford the three hundred dollars commutation fee in order for me to buy a substitute for my military service, as the law allows. I'm quite willing to go, even if it means passing by this splendid opportunity. However, if I can document my employment with you, with a firm that provides services otherwise deemed necessary and useful to our Union military—"

Gardner suddenly threw back his head and laughed. When he at last had exhausted himself, he began shaking his ginger-colored whiskers, looking at me. "Oh, dear heavens," he said. His features suddenly took on a look of mock alarm, and, despite the heat of the studio, he began pulling the lapels of his frock coat closer over his chest. "Does our Johnny feel a *draft?*" Gardner began to laugh again.

I felt my face redden. But, despite my embarrassment, I reached into my coat pocket and handed him the slip of paper Booth had obtained for me. "In fact, a friend provided me with this chit, signed by the provost marshal himself," I said. "It needs only your signature to validate my employment and, in doing so, secure my services to you." I passed the slip of paper to him.

Gardner read the words on the small slip of paper:

November 1864
Office of the Provost Marshal
Washington City
The below named individual has permission for taking "views on the march" in lieu of service to the Army of the Potomac:
John Harrison Surratt, Jr., to be associated with the photographic firm of Alexander Gardner of this city.
(Signed)

Alexander Gardner
Major General C. C. Auger,
Military Department of Washington City

Gardner seemed to find these proceedings highly amusing. At last, continuing to shake his head, he placed the slip of paper atop the plate box in his left hand and, with a grease pencil, scrawled "A. Gardner" in a large script.

"There you are," Gardner said. "I suppose I'm lucky to find an assistant who hasn't an arm or leg shot off." I quickly accepted the signed paper back. "No war for you, eh, Johnny?" he asked, smiling. For a man his age, Gardner displayed an impressive number of white teeth behind his ginger whiskers.

I did not want to be thought a coward, or unheroic. "Mr. Gardner, I assure you, I'm ready to assist Mr. Lincoln and his cause whatever my services—"

Gardner shook his head dismissively. "I don't have time for such talk," he said. I was reminded of how my awkward beginner's dramas were rejected at Ford's Theatre, and I felt my face redden again.

Gardner suddenly thrust a stubby finger against the breast of my frock coat. "Consider yourself drafted into *my* service, John Surratt." He held me in his steady gaze. "And if we should travel to the Virginia theatre together, I promise you that you'll see your share of the war."

Abruptly, Gardner broke his gaze away from mine and walked to the attic door. "Now I *must* get your image into the developing and fixing baths," he said. "Remember, Johnny, eight o'clock sharp tomorrow." He quickly opened and shut the attic door.

I fairly burst with relief as I left Gardner's studio, grinning disrespectfully at the gallery of faces looking down on me from the walls. I considered how, with my newly obtained prosperity, I could likely obtain a diary on credit from Shepard's bookstore below. I had acquitted myself honorably, both from the military conscription and from my dependence upon my mother. I was now to be a photographer. And diarist, if I had my way. I had found my fate in the war.

3.

December 3, Saturday, 1864

Mother was greatly pleased by my new *carte de visite.* I have been working at Gardner's studio a full week now, and even Mr. Gardner has been satisfied at how quickly I have "caught on" to the photographer's art. I spend my late mornings and early afternoons in the darkroom at the top of the attic stairs, preparing the glass plates and running them downstairs for Gardner. I have become justifiably proud of my skills at retouching the negatives and at toning the paper positives with a gold solution or with a colored crayon. Mr. Gardner, however, insisted himself on printing the negative of my own portrait, and he allowed no retouching or alteration of my resulting *carte de visite.*

I have received no further messages from Booth, though we are due to meet at the restaurant later today.

"John, I think it's a very good likeness," my mother said, as we sat at the informal pine dining table in the basement kitchen of our house. She had begun to clear away the dinner plates of the family and the four boarders under our roof. How I have come to dread these weekly Saturday dinners with the boarders! It seems an obscene parody of the time when Father was alive, and he, Mother, my brother, sister, and I would gather as a true family around our own table at our house in Maryland. Since our move to Washington City, however, Mother insists upon our taking meals together with the boarders at least once a week. She refers to them as our "Washington family." Last week I endured a Thanksgiving supper with them at our upstairs dining table. Mother, good soul that she is, even obeyed Mr. Lincoln's suggestion, as well, that Washington City residents purchase baked turkeys and send them, anonymously, to the Union troops in the lines at Petersburg. "Perhaps someone unknown to us is doing the same for Isaac," she answered me when I made a disapproving face.

"Oh, John, let me see." My sister, Anna, sat at the opposite end of the table with Louis Weichman, the boarder who rooms with me. Our two other boarders, young Miss Fitzpatrick and Mr. Holahan, had already left the table, Mr. Holahan to retire to his room, and Miss Fitzpatrick to wander among the new shops opening at the Willard Hotel. Weichman, predictably, had stayed on for dessert—an economical rice pudding. I myself had shopped for the ingredients at the city market after my first payday at Gardner's.

My mother handed the paper print to my sister. Anna and I share the fine but dark and abundant hair we inherited from our mother, and which once made my sister and me look almost identical as children. We were very close then, sharing each other's confidences, as well as the same thin, prominent cheekbones and jet-blue

117

eyes from our father. We seemed to form a natural conspiracy in childhood against our older, larger brother. But since Isaac's departure for the army and our father's death, I have sensed a subtle change between Anna and me. Growing up, she had deferred to me, but since living in Washington City, I feel that I have lost importance in her estimation. Anna seems to be almost impatient to begin her own life as a woman outside our household, and she is much more free and informal with strangers than I would wish. I find these changes in her at times disturbing, especially with my own situation, until recently, so uncertain.

Anna laughed and whispered something to Weichman as she held my *carte de visite* between them. Embarrassed, I examined the contents at the bottom of my coffee cup. Could that really be me in the photographic print? The young man on the *carte de visite* is resting his hands in a relaxed, almost confident manner despite the excruciating pain of Mr. Gardner's headrest; and my hair and my beard, although styled in the correct military fashion, appear far too long and unkempt. Because of the length of the exposure, my eyes in the print appear almost to be black. Worst of all in photographic etiquette, I appear to be smiling in my portrait, although I can recall nothing from the period in front of the camera that in any way justified a smile.

Could there really be such a difference between how we perceive ourselves and how our identity is taken by others? Anna looked up at me, her eyes bright and merry. "It *is* a good likeness, John," she said.

Weichman folded his napkin and dabbed officiously at the corners of his mouth. "He looks like the cat who ate the canary," he said.

Mother took back the *carte de visite* and carefully put it inside a cream-colored paper envelope at her side. She has expressed hopes, since I have begun work at Gardner's studio, of having photographic portraits made of all her children, to be placed alongside the glass daguerreotype of her as a young woman in the frame upstairs on the parlor mantel.

"John, it was kind of Mr. Booth to help you get a place at Mr. Gardner's studio," Mother said to me.

I am sensitive to the issue of Wilkes Booth within my family. At his advice, I had not

119

mentioned to Mother my problems with the draft or how he had helped resolve them, as Booth has intimated such talk would only trouble my mother. And although he is my distinguished friend—more mine than my family's—Booth has done nothing more than enable me "to take your place with us on the public stage," as he likes to phrase it. I regretted that I even had mentioned to Mother that Booth intended to speak to Gardner on my behalf. "It's my own skills that secured me my place with Mr. Gardner, and that will keep me there," I told her, with what I hoped was finality.

"John, could you not ask Wilkes to come visit sometime before Christmas?" asked Anna. I looked with some surprise at her across the table. Her face had the same pleased but slightly embarrassed expression she had as a child when she would shyly plead with me to join her in some girlish game, and I was, next to Father, the most important man in her life. "It was so wonderful when he visited us when we first came to the city, and we've scarcely seen him since."

The *Star*, of course, had reported Wilkes's return to Washington City. His triumphant theatrical appearance in New York City with his brother Edwin in *Julius Caesar,* to raise money for a statue of Shakespeare in the city's Central Park, and the attempt that same week by unknown Confederate agents to set afire Barnum's Museum and the hotels of New York City, had filled the pages of the *Star* for days. Still, I was taken aback by my sister's request, and by the familiarity of her reference to Booth. Booth prefers to be called by his middle name only by his most intimate friends. To all others, he is John Wilkes Booth.

"I'm sure Mr. Booth is far too busy during the holidays to visit his poor friends here at a boardinghouse," I said.

My answer sounded more sharp-tongued than I intended. Anna gave me a quick, hurt look. I saw her cheeks blush, as she looked down at the pine table. I felt rather than heard my mother's disapproval as she stood up beside me and silently began to remove the used dessert bowls from our places around the table.

I felt my own face redden. I had spoken thoughtlessly to Anna out of jealousy of Booth, and, perhaps, jealousy at sharing my intimacy with my famous friend. I realized with shame that it had been at Booth's insistence, not mine, that he had been introduced to my family last month.

"John, I fear your last remark has made our Miss Anna resemble a fashionable carriage," Weichman said, wiping once more at the corners of his mouth with his handkerchief. Never have I seen a man more obsessed with cleaning himself after each meal. "Your sister has become a little *sulky*."

"Oh, fie, Mr. Weichman, fie! This must cease!" Mother laughed. She put the dirty dishes on the table and began waving her hands in a good-humored gesture toward Weichman, as if to shoo him out of the kitchen. I am constantly surprised by my mother's reactions to Weichman's attempts at wit. Even my sister managed a thin smile, though she continued to stare down at the table.

A sweet, familiar odor had begun filling the kitchen as Weichman waved about his handkerchief and returned it to his shirt pocket: night-blooming cereus. Daily he soaks his handkerchief in this *eau de Cologne* until the attic room we share practically stinks of it.

"John, I believe you should get out of the house more often and visit others, particularly on leisurely Sunday mornings." Weichman continued to regard me with a patronizing look. Like most men in both the North and the South since the start of our Civil War, Weichman has grown a beard—in his case, a pale blond half-beard under the chin—but the result has been only to make himself appear even more immature, although we are both twenty-one years of age. He turned toward my mother and Anna, who gave him their complete attention. "Ever since he has begun work at Mr. Gardner's studio, John spends all his free hours at night writing in that diary of his. Scratch, scratch, scratch. Between the sound of his pen across paper and the oil lamp burning late at night, I can scarcely get my sleep."

Weichman turned toward me again, deliberately tucking his chin down into his recently grown whiskers in striving for a serious expression. "John, if you would only go with us to confession, and talk more frequently with Father Wiget, I do not believe you would find it necessary to confide so much in your diary."

I sat speechless. Never before had I hated Weichman so much as at that moment. I had not mentioned my diary to either Mother or Anna, and I was outraged that Weichman had made such a casual reference to it. I had assumed that he had been asleep while I made my nightly entries sitting at my desk in our upstairs bedroom. It suddenly occurred to me that my diary was left unlocked in my desk and that Weichman, arriving back at the H Street house from his work earlier than I in the late afternoons, might be reading my *journal intime* in my absence.

Weichman folded his hands and sat smiling at me across the table. He apparently was enjoying my discomfort with a quietly vindictive air. His comment about my attending more to church had clearly won the approval of Mother and Anna, who remained determinedly silent. I was stung by the half-truth of his malice; my diary, as well as being an artistic attempt, has somehow taken the place which the Church has never filled for me. I feel that only on its private pages can I reveal my soul openly, and I was as outraged as if I had seen Weichman eavesdropping outside my confessional stall.

Weichman had been our first paying boarder, having arrived at Washington City from what he said was a good Catholic family and from what I believe was just a few steps ahead of the Union draft. He claimed he planned to establish a business college in the city, and Mother had decided that he and I should share a room together as two young men with similar scholarly ambitions. After a few months, however, as General Grant's calls for more conscription fodder in Virginia increased, and as did the likelihood of Weichman's being called to military service, he began to exhibit a concern for his soul which I had not previously detected. His wild exclamations in his sleep, and his half-muttered prayers as he twisted in his narrow bed beside me, had begun to keep *me* awake at nights.

Weichman also had begun in these months suddenly to talk of attending seminary and becoming a priest after the war. Along with my mother and Anna—how he loves being in the ladies' company!— Weichman began to attend Mass three or four times weekly at Father Wiget's St. Aloysius Church. Father Wiget, a strong Union man, had noticed the young man's piety and had taken a personal interest in Weichman's case; and the priest eventually had succeeded in obtaining a safe sinecure for Weichman out of the war, an undemanding civilian clerkship in the War Department.

I felt my anger continue to rise in the face of Weichman's chiding. I had not chosen to take advantage of my family's Catholic faith, nor had I a powerful patron in the Church to help me avoid the military draft, although I do admit the assistance of Booth's good works. And, unlike Weichman, I contribute something of my weekly salary to my parent's financial maintenance.

"If I chose the nightly relaxation of writing a diary, it is because *I* work very hard at my daily employment," I said. "I do not have the time to seek the consolations of the Church." I stood up from the table to leave the room. "I'm going out. I don't know when I'll be back." I was in no mood for company of any sort, and I silently cursed my reluctant agreement to meet with Booth again. I then became even angrier; I would have to put on my frock coat before entering the street, and I suddenly remembered I had left it hanging in the upstairs hallway. I wanted very much simply to walk out of the service exit to the alley outside.

Weichman had assumed his favorite, patiently suffering expression, raising both his uplifted palms to the two women in the kitchen, as if to say, "What can you do with such a son?" Anna simply appeared uncomfortable. My mother seemed genuinely shocked. She remained standing and speechless, an empty dessert bowl held in her hands. I shut the kitchen door.

I stood at the bottom of the stairwell and considered what to do. The gas jet at the top of the staircase was turned low, and just beyond it I could see the central hallway on the first floor. I could continue up the main stairs to the attic bedroom and make certain that my diary was locked away from Weichman's eyes before I left the house. I considered, though, that Weichman might not have actually read my writings. He did not seem so directly malicious. His remarks in front of my family about my keeping a personal history secret from them and my lack of attendance at confession may have been made solely for the effect it would have upon me; I determined not to give him the satisfaction of my immediately running upstairs to lock my diary away. I would hide it later today when he was absent from the room. I had gone several steps to fetch my coat for my appointment with Booth when I heard my name called.

"John." My mother stood at the bottom of the darkened staircase, below me. She closed the door to the kitchen behind her.

I expected her rebuke for my sharp words toward Weichman. I knew we needed the money he gives us. Weichman is our only regularly paying boarder; even the man in Maryland to whom Mother has leased our farm has been laggard in his rent payments.

"John, I do wish you would consider Anna's request to invite Mr. Booth to visit us," she said. I was so surprised at my mother's statement that I could think of nothing to say. She looked up at me with renewed warmth in her face. Since my father's death, my mother had ceased arranging a once-elaborate coif of dark curls at the nape of her neck that fascinated me as a child; she now severely parts her hair in the middle and pins it back. But this new hairstyle only sets off the high, fine beauty of her forehead and makes me think of how she must have appeared many years earlier. The low gas jet at the top of the darkened stairs highlighted the top of my mother's hair and concealed the lines that I know have been written by the past few years into her face. Since I began work at Gardner's studio I have begun to think almost exclusively in terms of light and shadow; as my mother stood in front of me I could not help but recall Mr. Gardner's many tricks of shadows and exposures to make an older woman appear much younger.

My mother looked away from me, as if embarrassed. She was wearing a white cotton kitchen frock over a plain black dress. The golden chain of what I knew was a St. Christopher's medallion was just visible in the light around her neck a few inches above the trim of the frock.

"It's been hard for Anna since we moved to Washington City," she said. "Anna is a young woman, and with our concern over Isaac's welfare and the domestic work here, she's had very little time to meet any eligible young men for a beau."

Mother traced her finger across the wooden slats of the stairwell wall, and, without thinking of it, began to rub a spot of soot

129

on the wall, darker than the dark wood about us, which had doubtless been deposited from the coat of one of our boarders. "I'm afraid that other than me and Mr. Weichman, all Anna has had for company are Mr. Holahan and Miss Fitzpatrick."

I nodded sympathetically. Mr. Holahan, a middle-aged man, is a mystery to all of us, even Weichman; he is an occasional boarder and says nothing during his meals, only to retire immediately afterward to his room. At least he usually pays punctually, if not as punctually as Weichman. Miss Honora Fitzpatrick is a young woman Anna's age, genteelly vapid, even by Anna's judgment. Miss Fitzpatrick was literally left at our doorstep by her father, an energetic widower with commercial textile interests from Boston, a few weeks after we had opened our boardinghouse. She seems to know no one in the city other than us, and spends her days either looking at merchandise in shop windows or accompanying my mother and sister to church. Her father pays her room and board irregularly, not so much out of miserliness, I believe, but from a frenzy for war-profiteering, when he occasionally forgets he has a daughter. Miss Fitzpatrick has mentioned that her father has a contract to supply goods, probably shoddy, to the Union army.

"So, you see, John, it would mean a great deal to Anna if you would ask Mr. Booth to visit us. She would enjoy the company."

As reluctant as I was to reintroduce Booth to our lives, it seemed at the moment a small thing to please her. "Perhaps I will see Wilkes in a day or two."

Mother's voice took on a tone that seemed to me to be almost imploring. "Mr. Booth always has been a good friend to us, John. And I believe he is also a good man."

I started to reply that Booth was, more accurately, *my* good friend rather than our family's, but I kept my words in check. Standing in front of Mother, I was ashamed at how I had hurt Anna's feelings by my earlier comments.

"Mr. Booth and I went several times together to Mass when we first moved to Washington City," Mother said. I did not at first comprehend her remark. For some reason, my eyes and attention had become fixed upon the gold pencil my mother kept attached to a pocket at the front of her kitchen frock with a light chain, and which she used to keep our household accounts. I saw her hand twisting the chain in agitation. "After your brother was wounded, Mr. Booth went with me to St. Aloysius to light a candle for Isaac."

"You have taken communion with Booth?" My surprise and, at last, understanding of Mother's remark now registered in my voice. I was aware, of course, of Booth's habit of keeping many acquaintances and never mentioning one to the other; it simply had not occurred to me that Booth would extend his silence about his friendship with my mother to me.

Mother seemed to take my question as surprise at Booth's religious observance, rather than that she had met with him without my knowledge. "Oh, yes. I believe Mr. Booth is quite devout in his way. He had recently gone to confession while visiting Dr. Mudd in Maryland at the church near Surrattsville."

As Mother continued to speak, I think I really *saw* her for the first time as she is: a plain woman in late middle age, standing before me dressed in a mended and simple kitchen frock. The straitened circumstances of her life almost brought tears to my eyes.

The beautiful woman she must have been, her life full of promise, was no more. The only passion left for her is in the Church.

"Well, I don't know whether or not I'll see Wilkes," I lied. "But if I do, I'll ask him. If I can do it for Anna, I will."

"Thank you, John." My mother gave me a relieved smile and turned to go down the stairs toward the kitchen door. Although I stood on the staircase only a few steps above her, suddenly she seemed to be very far away from me.

Mother stopped at the bottom of the stairs, turned to look up at me, and smiled again. "And by the way, John, despite Mr. Weichman's teasing, it *is* a handsome photographic portrait."

I went up the back stairs to the front hallway and began to put on my black frock coat. I was still somewhat shocked by my mother's sudden revelation to me of her friendship with Booth, and at the fact she hadn't mentioned her attending Mass with him. This knowledge, however, made me feel less bad about deceiving her as to my destination this afternoon. If Mother could have her secrets about Booth, so could I.

A stiff piece of paper inside the pocket of

my coat caught my hand as I put my arm through the sleeve. It was Booth's *carte de visite,* which he had given me earlier this week.

For a moment, I considered destroying it, and looked toward the coal grate in the front parlor. I had not mentioned receiving the card to either Mother or Anna. On reflection, however, I decided not to throw the *carte de visite* into the parlor fire. If Booth did visit, the card might be called for, and I would be at a loss to explain its absence. I also was determined not to provide Weichman any satisfaction, or suspicions, by going up the main stairs and hiding the *carte de visite* somewhere in the attic room. But my coat eventually would have to be turned over to my mother for her brushing and cleaning, and the card would have to be disposed of.

I walked into the front parlor, where Mother's daguerreotype was in its place on the mantel. The parlor is not half the size it was when we purchased the house; the back half of the room is divided by some haphazard dressing screens, behind which, I am embarrassed to acknowledge, my mother keeps her bedroom. There she sleeps, balances her accounts, and reads

her devotionals, separated only by a thin screen from the room where we entertain strangers, in order to free more upstairs space for our paying boarders.

I took down Mother's daguerreotype from its place on the mantel in the front parlor and quickly unhasped its case. The manufacturer's name was embossed on the brass front of the case: E. T. Anthony and Company, the same photographic firm in Philadelphia that supplies many of the chemicals I use in Mr. Gardner's studio. The daguerreotypic process of the forties and fifties, I reflected, was much more beautiful and three-dimensional than the paper prints we now use, but the daguerreotype had the disadvantages of producing only a single negative image on glass and cannot be mass-produced in multiple printings, as we now do with modern photographs. A piece of black paper or dark velvet is placed in the daguerreotype case behind the glass negative to restore the subject to its usual tones.

I carefully slid the glass negative of my mother from its place inside the case—how quick and adept my fingers have become since beginning work at Gardner's studio! I then placed Booth's *carte de visite* behind the velvet that backs my mother's daguerre-otype. I can easily retrieve the card from its hiding place a few days in advance should Booth's visit make its presence necessary. I placed the daguerreotype back into its case, and returned the case to its position on the mantel, before going out the door of our H Street house to my appointment with Booth.

4.

From the transcript of the trial of John H. Surratt, Jr., in the murder of Abraham Lincoln, Criminal Court of Washington, D.C., 1867

Q. [For the prosecution] Please state your name, occupation, and residence.
A. I am Benjamin W. Vanderpoel, Jr. Before and after the war, I have been an advisor in the financial brokerage firm of Chauncey Schaffer, 243 Broadway. I am a lifelong resident of the city of New York.
Q. Did you leave your civilian employment at any time after 1861?

A. At the commencement of the war, I enlisted in the 69th New York Volunteers.

Q. What position did you hold in the Union army, and where were you stationed?

A. I was first lieutenant of Company G of that regiment, and for the first three years of the war I was assigned to aid in guarding the security of the port of Manhattan against any possible enemy action. In the latter part of November 1864, I was transferred to administrative duties in Washington City.

Q. While you were stationed in New York, did you know John Wilkes Booth?

A. Only slightly, just well enough to exchange casual greetings with him. He used to visit a club that I belonged to in the city of New York, next to Laura Keene's theatre.

Q. And during the war, did you ever see Booth here in Washington City, or speak to him?

A. Once, yes. On a late afternoon in the first week of December, we recognized each other among the crowd of people inside a restaurant, or a sort of concert hall, located on the left side of Pennsylvania Avenue as you go toward the White

House. I wish to emphasize he spoke to me, and not I to him. That is, Booth smiled at me as he went toward his table and called me major. Such was the humorous title by which he had addressed me ever since he had learned in New York of my enlistment.

Q. Tell the jury the further circumstances of your seeing him that day.

A. I had been up to the paymaster's department that afternoon on some business relating to my accounts. In coming out, I came down the avenue on the opposite side from the place I have described, and, hearing music, I went across Pennsylvania Avenue to see what was going on at this place. It was called the Washington Hall, or National Hall, or some name like that. As I went down the stairs, I think there was a woman dancing a sort of ballet dance. There was a stage or something of the kind in the back part of the room.

Q. Describe what Booth did after he greeted you.

A. He went on to his table, where he was shortly joined there by three rough-dressed and ruffian-looking fellows. It was a round table, and after they had been there a while, there were a great many empty glasses upon it. That is all I can recollect of the three ruffians.

Q. Now tell the jury of the arrival at this restaurant, or concert hall, of Booth's fourth companion at his table.

A. It was about twenty minutes before another person joined them. This person was neat in appearance—very neatly dressed—and he immediately entered into conversation with Booth and the three others at the table. I remember the face of this best-dressed individual very distinctly. It was that face that I afterwards saw in my dreams.

Q. Can you identify that man now?

A. I can.

[The defendant is made to rise.]

A. He stands there [pointing to the prisoner].

Q. Are you certain that is the man?

A. I am. I have seen that same pale and excited countenance many times in the dreams I have had since the assassination. He does not now have the beard which he then did, but I have daguerreotyped his features within my mind. I am certain he is the same man.

Q. Thank you. No further questions.

While sitting at my writing desk in the Willard Hotel, I look up from reading the court transcript of my trial. I consider how the incidents of real life dangle in a most hopeless manner.

An officer from New York State receives his paycheck one day in late 1864 in Washington, D.C., and decides to have a drink. He knows that for him the war is largely over, unlike those already trapped in the lines at Petersburg for the expected spring offensive against Lee, or those in the distant western theatre. He goes into a restaurant, or "a sort of concert hall," and sees me sitting at a table with John Wilkes Booth. So he testifies three years later, a damning bit of testimony for which I might have been hanged for conspiracy to the murder.

Q. [For the defense] Please state your name, occupation, and residence.
A. My name is Oliver Jellicoe. I am the owner and sole proprietor of the National Hall establishment between 11th and 12th Streets on Pennsylvania Avenue, just above Willard's on the sidewalk. I have been the owner since before 1861, and I

am a long-term resident of Washington City.

Q. Now, Mr. Jellicoe, at any time since your ownership of the National Hall, have you ever employed a woman there to perform any sort of ballet dance, or have you employed entertainers of any sort there?

A. Oh, no, sir. We are exclusively a fine dining and drinking establishment.

Q. And at any time from 1861 to 1864, did you ever recognize John Wilkes Booth among the patrons there?

A. No, sir. Although we did on occasion receive the lunchtime patronage of theatrical troupes from Grover's up the street, Mr. Booth to my memory was never among them.

Q. And at any time from 1861 to 1864, did you ever recognize the defendant, Mr. Surratt, among the patrons there?

A. No, sir, to my memory, I do not.

Q. Thank you, Mr. Jellicoe. No further questions.

Q. [For the prosecution] No questions.

I close the printed volume of transcript, with its permanently recorded voices of truths and half-truths. The trial now seems like so long ago. But the events with Booth leading up to the assassination seem like yesterday. I open my diary again and continue reading.

December 3, Saturday, 1864

"No ranks" was posted on a sign above the two swinging half-doors at the entrance of the National Hall, in the basement of a building off Pennsylvania Avenue. I heard music from within the room. Through the doors, I had a glimpse of a crowd of men, mostly Union officers, at a long bar. The sign above the doors was in observance of a citywide ordinance to prevent public drunkenness among the common soldiers; it is surprisingly well enforced, except in Hooker's Division.

As I entered I heard a loud burst of laughter among the Union officers at the bar to my left. Booth was sitting well beyond the bar at a table facing the entrance, about forty feet from where I stood. His face appeared pale in the darkness of the place, but he was smiling, and easily recognizable among the crowd. Booth nodded at me across the room and motioned for me to join him. Three other men were sitting with him at the table.

I slowly worked my way around the crowd of Union officers at the bar. Judging by the insignia on their blue sleeves and by the conversations I overheard, they were mainly from New York State. The ceiling of this basement room was very low, with few gas jets on the walls. There was no cross-ventilation; cigar smoke hung like a battlefield haze in the air above the polished mahogany of the bar where the officers stood. As I brushed against the heavy woolens of their uniforms, there was an overwhelming aroma of whiskey and human sweat. There was a noticeable stench from the men's sinks, located somewhere beyond the room. Strangely, I did not find these sensations repellent. At this moment, I felt a certain regret at not having joined the Union army, perhaps obtaining a commission and taking my place with these officers at the bar. I then considered all the young men on both sides who had died in the war already.

There was an elevated, empty stage at the center of the room. A small Negro boy was kneeling at the front of the stage, lighting oil lanterns in front of brass reflectors placed along the stage edge. These preparations were doubtless for some sort of flesh show, perhaps a *camera obscura* of a woman undressing behind the curtain and projected in shadow upon a screen placed on the stage. I have heard that these entertainments had become very popular in places like this since the start of the war. Booth's table was close to the stage.

"John!" Booth rose quickly from his chair and grasped my hand. His grip was surprisingly firm. "I knew you wouldn't disappoint us."

"I was delayed somewhat by my mother," I said. I took the place Booth indicated at the table directly opposite him.

None of Booth's three other companions seated at the table offered any greeting, and only one of them acknowledged my presence—a remarkably large, muscular young man who sat at Booth's right. He held his broad shoulders noticeably erect in his chair with what seemed to me the tensile alertness of a soldier, or an ex-soldier. As I took my place at the table, this man turned to gaze at me, his face both inquiring and yet strangely remote. He did not speak. His silent countenance reminded me of a large, silent dog who watches faithfully over his master.

145

"John, may I introduce you to an old friend of mine from before the war?" Booth said. "Mr. Lewis Powell." The young man raised two fingers to a lock of black hair that had fallen across his forehead. At first, I thought he meant to brush his hair back from his eyes, but then I realized that this gesture was an informal, and perhaps furtive, salute. "Captain," the young man said.

"And this is Mr. David Herold, of the city," Booth said. He indicated a callow-looking young man at the table, who seemed embarrassed at the attention. "Davy is a student at Georgetown, and the pride of his mother and sisters," Booth continued. Booth was evidently enjoying these introductions, but I could not determine whether or not he was being humorous in a manner only he and I were expected to detect.

"And this gentleman is from your neck of the woods in southern Maryland. Mr. George Atzerodt." Booth opened his hand in the direction of a small, middle-aged man in a slouched hat. An almost empty glass of beer rested on the table in front of him. At the sound of his name Atzerodt looked up at me from a pair of pale, watery-blue eyes, drawing his elbows closer to the beer glass in front of him as if he feared I intended to take it away. None of Booth's companions offered to shake my hand.

"Drink with us, John." Booth now moved his open palm in an expansive gesture over the table. There were a great many empty glasses on it.

As Booth knows, I am not much of a drinker. "I'll take a light ale," I said.

Booth smiled at me. "Ale for friendship." He picked up an empty glass and held it in front of him, as if examining it critically. "And brandy is for heroism."

I realized then that Booth was quite intoxicated. I well knew the signs of his indulgence. When drunk, Booth did not become violent or crass, as did many other men; instead, his intoxication expressed itself in elaborate courtesy toward others and an ironic distance toward commonplace objects, as if he had put on a mask that momentarily separated him from all others around him.

Booth reached into his pocket and withdrew some silver coins.

"Lewis, please go to the bar and buy a glass of ale for Mr. Surratt and another brandy for me. Mr. Herold and Mr. Atzerodt can go with you; buy them another beer each, as well."

Powell nodded. "Lewis, there is also a sideboard at the bar with pickled eggs, oysters, and beefsteaks for sandwiches," Booth said. "You must get yourself something to eat. It's all right. The man at the bar won't care what you take, so long as you buy the liquor." Booth's voice when he spoke to Powell was very kind, as if he were addressing a favorite child, and he suddenly seemed my clearheaded and sober friend again.

Powell nodded once more, and I watched as this giant of a man took Booth's coins, stood up from the table, and began to move toward the farther gloom at the bar, followed by Herold and Atzerodt. There was a long pause at the table before I spoke.

"Dear God, Wilkes, who are these people? And what do they have to do with me?"

Booth looked at me steadily, and there was none of the affected humor he had exhibited a few moments ago. "Lewis Powell *is* an old friend of mine. I met him years ago in Florida, before the war. I was playing in the northern part of the state, *Julius Caesar* I believe. Lewis was a country boy, and had paid his quarter to see this, the first play of his life, on a whim. Afterwards, he came up to me in the little lobby of the place to shake my hand, and to tell me how much he had enjoyed the show, as he called it." Booth looked at me earnestly. "I really found his sincerity and his plainness of manner to be quite affecting."

Booth glanced at the other tables around us before he went on. "Last year he recognized me on the street in Baltimore and called out to me. Lewis had been drafted into the Confederate army, captured at Gettysburg, and paroled as a prisoner of war at Baltimore. He was penniless, and starving to death. Of course, I recognized him. He simply wanted to shake my hand again, and to tell me how he had remembered my 'Will'um Shakespeare,' as he put it. I must have been the only familiar face he had seen in years."

Booth now seemed completely sober. "I bought him some new clothes and tried to buy him a meal. Lewis has suffered greatly in the war. Because of his impressive size and strength, he was always put in the front rank when the Confederate army charged a breastwork. He had survived the war physically unharmed until his capture, but I fear Lewis's mind has been affected. He now thinks like a child, and despite his great strength, he eats very little. He cannot abide the sight of rare roast beef."

"And the others," I asked. "Herold and Atzerodt?"

Booth laughed and seemed to relax. "David Herold is a young man who lives in a house of women, with his widowed mother and seven sisters. He is desperate for a father. I think he would do anything I ask."

For the second time today I found it disconcerting to consider that Booth was so easily able to win and manipulate the affections of others—and under so little compunction about doing so. Was I like Davy Herold in his estimation, an insignificant figure whom he found totally malleable to his will?

Hidden to us from behind the curtain on the stage, a flute and drum began to play, rather loudly, and I had to shout to make my next question heard.

"And George Atzerodt?"

Booth gave me a confidential wink. "He is a piece of work, isn't he? Before the war,

George was engaged in smuggling untaxed tobacco, slaves, and God knows what else across the Potomac River from southern Maryland into Virginia. I believe he now gets his living doing odd jobs here in Washington City. But he still knows the swamps and rivers of southern Maryland like the back of his hand."

From the darkness of the restaurant, I saw Lewis Powell and the two other men approaching our table from the bar. I began to fear that if Booth continued to drink with them, he would lose his clearheadedness and not be in a condition to appear at the National Theatre later tonight. "Wilkes, shouldn't you be getting ready for your performance?"

I saw that Booth already had put on his handsome, drunken mask. Never have I witnessed a man alternate so wildly between sobriety and intoxication. Booth smiled pleasantly at me. "Everything's fine. I've arranged for my understudy to take my place tonight."

The three seated themselves at our table, but before there was any further talk among us, the noise of the flute and drum increased in a loud crescendo. The gas jets were extinguished suddenly, leaving the room lit only by the flickering row of lanterns on the stage. A short, very fat man in a cook's apron jumped with surprising agility onto the stage.

"Gentlemen, officers of the Republic, and distinguished guests." His words brayed distinctly over the music and the noise from the bar. "We now present for your entertainment a living picture, a representation in actual flesh of allegories of virtue and vice." The short man strutted along the footlights as he spoke, and I noticed how the lights from the brass reflectors shone in highlights on the baldness of his head. He had absurdly combed three long strands of wet hair across his pate. "Our first presentation for your pleasure is entitled 'The Temptation of Eve.'"

There was a great deal of applauding and banging of glasses from the officers at the bar. I now understood what type of flesh show was to be performed. It was a *tableau vivante.* Young women, usually in stages of undress, arranged themselves in public to represent the figures in some scandalous French oil painting, or posed themselves in one of the more licentious scenes taken from the Bible. It was supposed to be morally uplifting.

The flute and drum behind the curtain segued into a vaguely Oriental tune. Two pairs of hands appeared outside the fabric and partially pulled back the curtain. It opened to reveal a crudely painted backdrop, representing the Edenic garden. I was shocked when a man, naked except for a ridiculously shaped piece of cloth covering him in front, stepped into the small stage from behind the curtain.

In his mid-forties, he was far too old to be playing an Adam. His chest had a caved-in look, probably from decades of manual labor, and his left thigh seemed misshapened. He had a squared, rural-looking beard.

The crowd of officers at the bar was disappointed; catcalls and whistles sounded from the darkness. The old Adam mechanically struck a series of poses in front of the painted backdrop, admiring the beauty of his surroundings to the accompaniment of the flute and drum.

The naked player had the same distant look on his face I had noticed on Lewis Powell's. In the flickering light, I saw an odd

grouping of rounded scars on his left but-
tock, like pox marks, only much larger and
spread over a greater area of his skin. Then I
realized: artillery shell fragments.

The catcalls in the darkness grew more
shrill. There was a loud thumping of beer
glasses on the bar, and angry voices in the
dark. "Sold! We've been sold! Humbug!"

Then the woman stepped from behind the
curtain.

I thought at first that she was nude. But
as she stepped to the front of the stage, I
saw that she was wearing flesh-colored
tights from her waist downward. A small
fabric fig leaf covered her sex. She was perhaps twenty-one or twenty-two, with hair
that appeared auburn-colored in the stage
lights. She circled the man with half-danc-
ing steps, and as she did so cradled in her
arms the coils of a long, absurdly artificial
stage snake that almost concealed her
breasts.

The applause from the men at the end of
the room was instantaneous, and another,
more enthusiastic banging of beer glasses
upon the bar followed. Shouts of encour-
agement arose out of the darkness.

"I propose an immediate advance upon her flanks!"

"The 69th New York was never bashful in seizing breastworks!"

The woman moved to the beat of the drum in a delicate type of ballet dance around the man on the stage, who stood stiffly, shifting his weight slightly to favor his right leg. Neither she nor the man paid any attention to the remarks from the audience. Still cradling the coils of the stage serpent in her left arm, the woman began to extend the head of the snake with her right arm, weaving it about the man's shoulders and chest in an enticing manner. This serpent was the most ridiculous stage property I have ever seen. The head was painted a bright green, with a pair of childishly evil eyes and a forked fabric tongue. The rest of the creature's body, three or four feet in length, was a tube of red flannel stuffed with rags, and appeared once to have been the leg of a man's pair of winter long johns.

I turned in my chair to look back at my four companions sitting at the table, to see how they regarded this performance, and perhaps to take a cue from Booth's expression as to how a man of his experience deported himself. Herold was staring greedily at the woman on the stage as if he had never before seen a revealed female form. Atzerodt looked at the stage as if calculating how to steal something from it. Powell's expression was as blank as the older Adam beside the dancer. But Booth took in the performance of the woman before him with mixed expressions of pity, anger, boredom, and perhaps physical interest. I told myself that such was the proper expression for a man of the world in this situation, and turned back in my chair to the stage determined to mirror Booth's expressions as much as possible.

The woman onstage was now standing with her back to us, her face turned in profile looking at some point on the wall behind our table. Her features were surprisingly beautiful. She began to sway her body in rhythm to the flute. Her tights were laced very low down upon her hips, and as she moved I plainly saw her two sacral dimples, the two indentations in the flesh above a woman's pelvis which are like two finger touches pressed into clay, and which the French photographers consider the perfection of feminine beauty. As she swayed, I could not help but consider her symmetry and beauty, especially in comparison to the jagged and irregular holes in the flesh of her partner.

Gazing at her, I suddenly became aware of my own heightened arousal, which made impossible my sustaining the bored countenance of an experienced man of the world. I quickly glanced down to my lap. I was noticeably in the male state. At that moment I was thankful for the darkness.

Embarrassed, I turned my chair away from the stage and made as if to finish the last of my glass of ale at the table. I then saw what the woman was looking at behind us. A large mirror was mounted on the far wall. The woman had turned fully to face our table and the mirror behind it. As she danced, I saw that she was looking not at our table or any of the other tables surrounding her, but at her own eyes in the mirror. *She is dancing for herself and not for others,* I thought.

Emboldened by my state of arousal, I became determined to obtain some acknowledgment from this woman that I was not like the others, and I, too, stared into the mirror, directly and unwaveringly at her eyes and ignoring the rest of her exposed body. For a moment, I believe she saw my reflection, and our eyes met. I then saw the reflection of another face. Booth, too, had turned in his chair and was facing the mirror.

The music was reaching a crescendo. The full height of the woman's body was reflected in the mirror in front of me. She put down the snake, and stood as if a statue in front of my eyes, her hands turned slightly outward. Her breasts were now fully exposed.

The applause came like a shock from the tables around me, and the gas jets suddenly lit the room. I blinked my eyes at the unaccustomed brightness, and discovered I was no longer in a state of sexual excitement. But when I looked back at the mirror, it reflected only an empty stage.

I turned in my chair, but all I saw was the bare arm of the woman partially glimpsed from behind the curtain, as she offered her hand to help the old Adam exit the stage. The crowd at the tables around us continued applauding with cheers and an enthusiastic thumping of beer glasses. I overheard some disgruntled remarks from the Union officers at the far end of the room, who had not been as near as we to the stage.

Booth turned away from the mirror and now sat facing me across the table. His expression was very serious. "We should go outside and talk, John," he said. He threw a paper dollar down onto the table with a significant glance at Lewis Powell, plainly intending that Powell and his companions stay here.

As Booth and I rose from our chairs, the short, fat man ran up to our table. "Mr. Booth, Mr. Booth, you will not be leaving us so soon, I hope." He twisted his greasy cook's apron with his hands as he spoke, and there was an imploring note in his voice. "You'll miss our second performance, taken from the opera *Mazeppa.* We enact the scene where the heroine is stripped quite naked, sir, and tied upon a wild horse to ride across the German landscape until she dies of exposure. We've devised a wooden bucking horse that you'll find amazingly like the real thing."

Booth looked at this man with the same pity in his expression as he had looked upon the woman onstage. "I'm sure it's a wonder,

159

Oliver. But my friend and I need to step outside and discuss some business."

The man brought his hands from the apron and brushed them over his almost bald pate, plastering down the same three strands of hair. "It was an unexpected pleasure to have you as our guest today, Mr. Booth. It brought back to my memory the good years, prior to the war, when I was privileged to act in the same Shakesperean troupe as your father at the Winter Garden in New York. He played in *Richard III,* you'll remember, and I was Puck in *A Midsummer Night's Dream."* The fat man continued to worry the three strands of hair atop his head as he spoke. "Those were the glory years of American theatre, Mr. Booth, when your father was alive. The glory years."

I feared that Booth would become angry. Despite his income and fame from acting, he is remarkably sensitive to comments that imply he is not the great man onstage that his father was. Indeed, it was one of the causes of his break with his brother Edwin. Booth looked at this man, however, with continued kindness. "I'm sure you're right, Oliver. The theatre is not what it once was. And there never was a Puck such as you."

The cook continued to twist his apron. "You'll not regret it if you stay, Mr. Booth," he said. He leaned forward confidentially. "There is also private entertainment available for the gentlemen in the back rooms."

"That's enough, Oliver." Booth turned brusquely away to face our three companions at the table. "Lewis, please make sure that Davy gets safely home tonight to his sisters. And be certain that after this dollar is spent, George does not try to ask for credit at the bar."

Booth placed his hand upon Powell's right shoulder as he spoke. "And you must get yourself something to eat." Among the loud voices of the soldiers and the smoke of the restaurant, Powell sat in his chair quietly looking up at my friend, as if Booth were a calming vision he once had seen moving among the carnage and horror of Antietam or Gettysburg.

I suddenly felt an urgent need. I went to the men's sinks, and then rejoined Booth outside on the street.

Booth was waiting with his back to me on the sidewalk above the basement steps. "It's good to be out of that place," he said

161

as I approached. He turned and took my arm. "We both need some fresh air. Come. Let's walk toward the Capitol Building."

Booth seemed to become more comfortable after we put some distance between us and the National Hall. He resumed his old habit of addressing me as he would a trusted confidant. "They are not like us at all, are they, John?" he asked.

I thought of the three men we had met, and of the crowds that now moved on the pavement around us, and realized Booth was right. The short winter afternoon was ending, and there was an early December chill in the air. Along the sidewalk, gas lamps had been lit, illuminating the great rows of trees that lined both sides of Pennsylvania Avenue. Crowds hurried to the curbsides to get into or out of hackneys and carriages as Booth and I passed by shops open for the last hour of business. Some of the shop windows, even though it is early yet in the season, displayed Christmas merchandise.

"No one has seemed at all like me since the start of the Civil War," I said.

"I feel the same way," Booth said, stopping to fasten his riding cape about his shoulders. "That is why I had asked you to meet with me today with such men. I wanted you to see the coarsening effects of this continuing war. Not simply upon other people, John, but upon you and me. Ourselves, in comparison to who and what we were before the war. That is what I truly hoped you would see here tonight."

Booth kept his eyes intently focused upon me as he fastened the last of the horn buttons of his cape, as if he were trying to find entrance to my innermost thoughts. "Everyone has been coarsened, John. That woman who danced for us there, for instance. I knew her once in Richmond before the war. She was once a woman of immaculate virtue."

"Really, Wilkes?" I found his statement unbelievable.

Booth looked at me with complete sincerity. "Her name is Sarah Ravenel. She was a schoolmistress to the small children within the household of a prosperous Richmond merchant. But he paid her such a niggardly salary she was barely surviving. One night, her only free night a month, she took all the money she had and went to see me onstage. We met in the lobby after the perfor-mance, and we talked there."

This I could accept. Much of Booth's popularity as an actor was due, I believed, not so much to his theatrical ability, but to his remarkable habit after his performances of mixing with the audience outside the the-atre. He seemed happiest there, discussing the performance and dissolving the barriers between himself and the audience.

We resumed walking. "I saw immediately that she had an immense talent for the the-atre," Booth said. His face was half hidden within the upturned collar of his cape. "I ar-ranged for her to move to Washington City at the time, and receive at least a living wage while she trained at theatres here. Now, four years later, I find that the only way this woman can make a theatrical living in a wartime city is by exposing her body to drunken louts."

I thought of my own feelings at the bar, and said nothing. How could I admit that I was half smitten with her myself? Was this a sign of my own coarsening?

We reached the intersection of 10th Street and Pennsylvania Avenue. Booth looked down the street to the row of carriages at Ford's Theatre. "It seems that Harry Ford is making some money tonight," he said distractedly.

"How is your work coming with Gardner?" he asked suddenly.

I felt it best to be evasive, not because Booth had been so mercurial earlier—I was accustomed to this trait of Booth's personality—but because I realized I knew so little about Booth, a man who visited so many others, including apparently my own mother, about whom he told *me* nothing.

I replied offhandedly that my success at photography exceeded expectations.

"That's good, that's good," Booth repeated, as if talking to himself.

As we reached Market Square, my companion turned and faced me. "John, I have a confession to make." Booth hesitated before he spoke again. We had left the crowds behind us. A horse trolley rolled by almost silently, on its way to the other end of Pennsylvania Avenue toward the fashionable shops, theatres, and the Executive Mansion.

"I often go to such places as we were at today, and sometimes to places even more vile in Hooker's Division," Booth said.

"Usually, I go alone. At times I go in stage disguises. I try to ignore the panderers and whoremongers there. And I never degrade the women."

Booth stood apart from me, directly under the lighted circle of a gas lamp. "I do it as a spiritual exercise, John. I wish to see if I can keep my own purity, my own sense of myself, in the midst of all this carnality and death."

Booth's face was as pious as if he were confessing to a priest. Yet it made me uneasy, for it just didn't fit comfortably with the man I knew—much less the man the reporters and gossipmongers whispered about—a ladies' man of enviable reputation to those so inclined. Then he smiled. "And I have another secret, John. Since this terrible war has continued, I have returned to the true Church. I now frequently take holy communion. *That,* if nothing else, is a great gift to me from all these years of national suffering and degradation."

With a surprisingly quick, elegant gesture Booth reached under his cape and shirtfront and withdrew a medallion attached to a short chain around his neck. There was a glint of gold as he held it in his hand.

"Surely you recall Dr. Mudd in Maryland?" he asked. "He was a good friend to me in my Southern enterprises, and he has remained a good friend to me since. We went together to confession at the church near your mother's. I have worn this medal ever since."

I stepped closer. The medallion Booth carried around his neck was the image of a saint. At the bottom were inscribed the words "St. Anthony Pray For Us."

I was too surprised to speak at this revelation. I couldn't help but believe Booth—his sincerity was utterly convincing. In an instant I felt mean and diminished, a mere callow youth before my more sophisticated friend. Booth's return to the Church was a further instance of how, despite his moodiness and his secretiveness, he could be so much better a man than I. Mother was right; Booth *is* a good man. Once again, I reflected upon how lucky I was to be able to call a man like John Wilkes Booth my friend.

A sudden wind had sprung up between the wooden sheds on the square, causing me to shudder. I had become quite cold since we had stopped walking.

"I've acted thoughtlessly," Booth said.

"You're without an outer coat. Would you care to wear my cape?" he asked solicitously.

I dismissed his offer with a gesture. "I'm fine. We'll both feel better after we clear our heads. Wilkes, I greatly admire your decision."

We continued along Pennsylvania Avenue up to Capitol Hill. I felt my confidence in Booth flood back stronger than ever. Though he might be rich and famous, at heart, I was convinced, Booth and I were kindred souls. "By the way, Wilkes," I said. "Mother asked today if you could visit with us before the holidays. I know it's a bother, but she said Anna would greatly enjoy seeing you again." I paused. "I would, too."

Booth turned suddenly to face me. "Really, your mother asked?" He seemed genuinely surprised. His face, for an unguarded moment, became animated by interest that I hadn't seen before. His face was so different in its appearance that he almost seemed for a moment a stranger.

"Well, of course, if that is what you wish," he said. "Should it make Anna and your mother happy, I shall be pleased to visit with your family before Christmas."

We had reached the stand of large elm trees at the base of Capitol Hill. Above us on the hill was the uncompleted dome of the Capitol Building, its gaping iron girders and wooden scaffolding exposed and empty to the winter sky. The district government had hoped to have construction on the new Capitol dome finished in time for Lincoln's second inaugural, but it seems unlikely. Just beyond the trees, Booth paused to light a cigar. In the flare of the match, I again saw illuminated on his hand the ink tattoo of JWB.

"Do you know what our Havana friends say about lighting a cigar?" Booth asked. He seemed in a particularly jovial mood on the heels of his confession. He drew on his cigar for a few moments, then threw the match into the darkness. "It is inviting the gods to the party."

We walked onto the Capitol grounds. Around us stood the wooden shanties used by the Irish workmen during the day, and beyond the workmen's huts the abandoned piles of huge, squared granite stone with which they were building the dome and the new wings to the Capitol Building. Close by was the railyard of the Baltimore and Ohio

Railroad, which had brought the Union soldiers I had seen marching earlier this week.

We walked up the hill in silence for a while. The frozen mud underneath our bootheels cracked in the night with a sound like broken iron. When Booth spoke, it was in a quiet, close voice. "John, I shall be leaving you soon," Booth said. I looked toward him in astonishment, but all I saw in the darkness was a red glow from the lighted end of his cigar. "I feel my work here on the stage is almost done. I shall be going to England, or perhaps to France or Italy."

I could not believe what I had heard. "Wilkes, don't act foolishly," I exclaimed. "Your career on the stage has already brought you fame, and you're still a young man."

Booth stepped closer, and in the darkness I saw his pale face shake slowly from side to side. "We both know what all people say, that I will never be the great man in the theatre that my father was," he replied. "And I have had problems with my health that will hinder me onstage. My leg has been bothering me very much lately."

"Oh, Wilkes, don't talk such nonsense." I tried to dismiss Booth's statements humorously, but there was an undertone of pleading in my voice, for myself as well as for him. "It's just too many cigars, too many brandies, and too many women."

Booth looked at me with complete sincerity. "No, it's not that simple. I know it sounds unusual to say, John, but I feel as if the process of my aging has become strangely accelerated."

I considered that there might be some truth in what Booth said. Before his spiritual reconversion, I had often witnessed Booth's physical dissipation, and he still drank excessively. There were rumors that he had once supported a woman in Hooker's Division. There were also other, uglier rumors of his past repeated by his theatrical rivals which I refused to credit, of illegitimate children or of some inherited "bad blood" from his father, Junius Brutus Booth.

"But, Wilkes, what do you propose to do if you go abroad? If your health does not permit you to go onstage, how shall you occupy your time?"

Booth had begun to walk up the hill. He

turned to look at me over his shoulder. He smiled. "Why, teach acting, of course."

"Teach people how to act?"

"Why not?"

We had reached the Capitol Building steps. Booth and I stood there among the piles of wood shavings, jumbles of stone, and construction cranes where within three months Lincoln would stand to take his second inaugural oath. Below, the lights of Washington City appeared in miniature. At my left side, beyond a wide spread of darker night which I knew was the eastern branch of the Potomac River, I could see the lights of myriad campfires among the Union army stationed around the city.

"John, as a photographic assistant," Booth asked almost casually, "did you receive a pass signed by the provost marshal to cross the Potomac and go among the Union lines?" Booth asked.

"Certainly," I said. "It is because of Gardner's service to the Union army that I, as his assistant, am made exempt from the draft." I did not mention that Booth's efforts in obtaining that safe passage had put me under a certain obligation to Booth.

"Once among the Union lines passing as a photographer, it would be a relatively easy thing to slip away and find your way to Richmond?"

"What is it that you want me to do, Wilkes?"

Booth placed his hand upon my shoulder. "To go before me, and to prepare a place for me, John."

My face must have shown my incomprehension. "When I leave," Booth said slowly, "I will first be traveling southward, with these men you met today. I want you to alert the keepers of safe houses I've used in the past. I want you to tell them to expect me, and to help me."

Booth kept his gaze fastened upon me. "With your pass, you can cross and recross the Navy Bridge across the Potomac at will. The military guard will never suspect a photographer. You can say you're on Mr. Gardner's business. What Gardner doesn't know will not hurt him."

I was startled at Booth's request—and as I thought about it, more than a little put out. True, it was, I had to admit to myself, Booth who helped get me my position with Gardner, but I had no idea there might be strings attached. And in light of what Booth had just asked of me, I couldn't help but wonder whether that was the reason he had been so persistent and persuasive in helping me to get the job. Suddenly, my renewed trust and confidence in Booth were rattled, and I felt at a loss.

Moreover, my reaction, I knew, was deepened by my keen sense of loss and abandonment at Booth's leaving. My glamorous friend was already planning to remove himself from my life. I felt bereft, even though I knew Booth's departure was still some months off.

"Do you have to go, Wilkes? And must you go this way?"

"I fear that if I attempt to openly leave, I will be arrested on the spot. My sympathies for the South are well known. The fact is, I have no future here. It is better that I leave now, under my own terms. And that is why I need your help in planning my route to Richmond."

Booth paused. "When you go in advance of me, I want you to take with you the woman you saw tonight, Miss Ravenel. I decided as we've walked together tonight that one of my last acts will be to save her from this war, just as surely as I saved you, John," he said, underscoring my obligation to him. "Get her safely back to Richmond, and a chance at a respectable life there. I have friends in high places in the South. They will not care what she had to do to survive in a Northern city."

It seemed impossible to me that only a few days earlier I thought I had escaped my obligations to people, including Booth, and could begin to make a fresh start.

"Think of your own family, Wilkes. Think of how they would suffer because of your action."

Booth released his grip upon my shoulder. "My family? My brothers Edwin and Junius, and I are so divided over this war we cannot bear to speak to one another. My dear sister, Asia, has married a man of such coarse political sympathies he has forbid me to visit their house. The others I rarely even speak with." Booth looked away from me and down the marble steps. "And don't forget my father, 'the Prince of American Players,' " he said bitterly. "He died a raving lunatic in New Orleans."

Booth looked up at me. "And your father, John, died a drunken failure in Maryland, and your mother now makes her living by taking strangers into her house."

I was shocked by both the suddenness of the plan and the subterranean passages of Booth's mind. At Gardner's studio I had learned of what is called a latent image, the picture hidden upon an undeveloped photographic plate until, under the right conditions, the image can be seen. I felt as if I were seeing signs of such a latent image in Booth.

Booth touched my shoulder again in the darkness. "John, I helped to get you a job when you most needed one. I asked you for nothing in return. Now all I ask is that you try to save a woman."

I did not immediately reply to Booth. I had never before considered myself as a man who rescues a woman. I looked down the Capitol steps at the jumbled granite blocks on the lawn. In the starlight they appeared primitive and disturbing, not as the beginnings of a new construction but as the ruins of an abandoned and dead city. Above us, in the night sky over the ringed iron of the uncompleted Capitol dome, the constellation Orion hung among the wooden scaffolding.

Booth stood at my side waiting for an answer.

"Yes," I said. "Yes. I'll do it for you."

Part Three

1.

From the diary of John H. Surratt, April 18, Tuesday, 1916

I was seated in my chair at the Willard dining room when Billy Bitzer appeared at my table. I had intended on taking my morning meal alone, and my attention had been fixed on my opened diary in front of me. Lately, I have been making new entries on its pages, as if I were writing the resolution of a story to which after more than fifty years I do not yet know the ending. My photographs were rewrapped and safely placed near the center of the table. Unless Griffith asks for them, I had determined not to look at these photographs again, and to place them securely in the hotel safe after my meal. Then, looking up, I saw the cameraman.

Bitzer was wearing a light pinch-back suit and a round straw hat. He held an unlit cigar between his teeth. "Let's have breakfast," he said, and pulled back a chair. I quickly shut my diary and put it aside while Bitzer settled himself at the table. He took a clean handkerchief from his coat, carefully wrapped his unlit cigar into a neat package, and put it back inside his coat pocket. *Saving it for later,* I thought. Bitzer then propped a newspaper and menu on the table.

Moments later, our waitress came over, wearing one of those attractive white blouses styled after the men's Arrow shirts, with black elastic bands above her elbows. "Yeah, honey. I'll have the scrapple and kippers with a side order of home fries and tomato catsup. The coffee black." Bitzer was obviously very experienced at ordering meals in such establishments.

After we ordered, he nodded toward the newspaper. "Will you look at this?" Bitzer said. He made no motion to show me the page he was looking at. "The colored in the city are griping about our picture. I don't know why everybody's got their nose so out of joint over *Birth of a Nation.*" He suddenly seemed very animated, and I realized I had just heard the longest conversation Bitzer had ever spoken with me. "We opened in Los Angeles and we did okay," Bitzer said. "Not terrific, but okay. Same story in New York. Not terrific, but okay. Christ, I only hope Woodrow Wilson tonight doesn't give it the goddamn kabosh.''

Our food arrived more quickly than I would have thought possible. ''That's why I'm talking to you this morning,'' he said in a low voice, his attention fixed on his plate. ''D.W. wants me to look at your photographs. He wants to know you've got the real inside dope.''

I stared at the food in front of me. I had not thought I would have to face the pictures again so soon after last night. But I decided to show Bitzer something of the horror they contained. I pushed my plate aside and began to unwrap the package. I took out the photographic print on top. ''This is a photograph of a dead Confederate soldier I took early in the spring of 1865,'' I said.

Bitzer raised his eyes from his breakfast and looked at the photograph on the table in front of him. His face had a look of concentration, although he continued to chew his food in a way that seemed absent-minded, as if he had seen death before and found it commonplace.

I took out several more prints and glass negatives and spread them across the ta-

ble. "These are photographs of the execution of my mother, Mary Surratt, and the three other Booth conspirators," I said, careful to keep all emotion out of my voice. "The tall young man with his arms tied behind him standing next to my mother is Lewis Powell." I looked down at the photographs. One of the executioners on the wooden scaffold held open an umbrella above my mother's head in order to provide her a few moments' shade. It was well over one hundred degrees that day inside the brick courtyard of the Old Arsenal Prison. "The young man on the scaffold second from your right is David Herold. They haven't put a noose around his neck yet; he's staring down at his shoes. The one at the far right, the short man turning his head as if he's trying to say something, is the German carriage painter, George Atzerodt."

I glanced up at Bitzer. He had stopped chewing his food and was looking at the photographs with an absorbed expression on his face. I pointed to another brown albumin print on the table between us, determined to speak of these pictures in purely professional tones. "In this photograph, the four conspirators are on the gallows. The sentence of execution has been read. A noose and hood have been placed around each one's head."

I rested my finger at the bottom of the print. "Do you see the two Union soldiers standing underneath the gallows?" I said. "Their job is to knock away the two wooden posts you see that are supporting the gallows trap above them. The soldiers are included in this composition to give a sense in the picture of the proportions of the gallows. It's at least a ten-foot drop from where the four sentenced to die are standing above them."

I tapped my finger on the image of one of the Union soldiers. "This soldier is holding onto his post and leaning forward," I said. "He's becoming sick, either from the heat of that morning or more likely from his anxiety over his realization that he soon would receive the command to push away the wooden post."

I moved my hand to another image on the table. "This photograph was taken a few seconds after the trap was dropped," I said. "The body of Lewis Powell is the only image of the four that isn't blurred. I suspect that Lewis didn't try to fight the fall, and that his neck was cleanly broken and he did not suffer."

I pointed to the images of the three other hanging bodies in the photographs. "Blurred images mean motion," I said. "The three others are still alive, at least for a few moments more. Notice that David Herold must be swinging three or four feet back and forth, fighting against the binds that hold his hands behind his back and the noose around his neck." I kept my gaze carefully on the image before me, willing the tears not to come.

Bitzer's mouth had fallen. "Jesus H. Christ," he said. "Jesus Harry Christ." He reached forward to pick up one of the glass negatives on the table between us.

"Don't touch the negative," I said, alarmed. My hand intercepted him in midair quicker than I thought possible. Bitzer withdrew his hand and placed it in front of him. There was a long pause before he spoke.

"Do you know who took these?" he asked. I thought he was beginning to understand.

I nodded my head silently.

Outside the dining room, the Preparedness Day military parade was beginning along Pennsylvania Avenue. The window-panes of the room rattled slightly in their frames from the beat of the drums and the sound of horns. Several of the patrons stood up from their tables to look through the windows at the parade of men in khaki uniforms on the pavement. There was a long pause before Bitzer spoke again.

"Are you willing to talk more about these?" he asked.

I shook my head. "Not now," I said.

"Oh, hell, not here." Bitzer waved his delicate hands in the air as if he were wiping away a small understanding. "I meant on the Gramophone. D.W. telephoned from the train station. He's got the idea you can record a talk, and then at the end of *Birth of a Nation* we can splice in the film of your talking, see?"

Bitzer looked at my photographs spread across the table. "Maybe we can use two screens at the end of the show. You can be on one screen, with the Gramophone speaking offstage, and I'll run your photos onto the second screen. I'll use rear projection."

I looked across at him. "I'd never thought of being in the movies," I said evasively.

The waitress put the check for our meal on the table. I reached for my wallet, but Bitzer shook his head and waved me off. "Well, you should think about it. D.W. wants to see you this afternoon. You two can talk about it then."

We walked through the lobby toward the front entrance of the Willard. My photographs were rewrapped and held under my arm. Bitzer had put on his straw hat and lit his cigar. I started to wish him success tonight in showing *The Birth of a Nation* at the White House, but Bitzer made a dismissive motion with his free hand as if he had something else on his mind.

"Maybe I shouldn't be telling you this, Mr. Surratt," he said. "But I like you. Generally, I can take or leave people. But you've seen a lot. You're all right."

We had reached the revolving door at the front of the hotel. Bitzer stood aside letting a crowd of men and women pass through. Despite his smart tailoring, he seemed to me gnomish and somewhat frumpy in appearance among the other men and women in the lobby, his suit and straw hat somehow too large for his body.

"Watch yourself when you talk to D.W.,"

Bitzer said. "Watch yourself around Mae, too."

"They seem all right," I said. I was anxious to put my photographs inside the hotel safe.

Bitzer turned to go out the revolving door. He took the cigar out of his mouth, and for a moment a look of distaste came across his small features. "They're all such *actors,*" he said.

2.

December 18, Monday, 1864

I finished developing the last of the afternoon's negatives at Mr. Gardner's studio attic. Without Gardner's knowledge, I have completed several scouting expeditions southward for Booth, presenting my pass "to take views on the march" to the military sentinels at the Navy Bridge over the Potomac. Booth was correct; after one look at my pass and a glance at the boxes labeled as photographic plates and chemicals which I intentionally carried on my saddle, a bored Union sergeant waved me over the bridge. And I have paid attention to what

Booth calls the details of stagecraft: I have always rented my horse at the same livery stable in the city, making a point to tell the owner that a late afternoon ride is a necessary exercise after the confines of a day in a photographic studio.

Approaching the war from the Maryland side of the Potomac is curiously like entering a theatre from the rear entrance of the building. A few miles south and west of Surrattsville, beyond the swamps that mark the border with Virginia, is the great drama of the war. I visualize the two armies drawn up in their separate lines between Richmond and Petersburg, like audiences gathered for a mutually lethal performance. But while I ride in Maryland, the scene is much more informal, with Union soldiers in casually equipped uniforms moving among civilians like partially costumed actors mingling among stagehands backstage.

Booth's tasks are easy to accomplish. I quickly sketch the cattle paths or country lanes that will enable him to travel through the swamps into Virginia unobserved by the Union patrols, or deliver to his ''safe houses'' the messages or packages of morphine plainly intended for the relief of

191

wounded soldiers. Occasionally, the occupants of these houses, who never identify themselves, ask that I return a message to Booth, usually a coded, enigmatic phrase such as "Comes the spring, there will come retribution."

I am acutely aware that what I now write in this diary could be used as evidence for my imprisonment should the wrong eyes read it. The Union authorities would not care or believe that I carry these medicines behind the lines to help both Northerners and Southerners. Why, then, am I compelled to write? Perhaps I cannot separate myself from this diary because, as Booth phrased it, we are engaged in a secret heroism of which the two of us dare never speak. In any case, I have taken pains to secrete this diary in a place in the attic at my mother's boardinghouse where Weichman's prying eyes will not see it. In reading over these diary's pages, I have noticed that I have always referred to my friend here as "Booth," although in conversation he has always been "Wilkes" since we first met. It occurs to me that this use of two names, and my keeping a secret diary, may be an unconscious effort to keep Booth at a distance, at least on these diary's pages. It is a means of establishing *control,* I believe, over Booth's presence in my life.

I heard the clump of Gardner's boots coming up the attic steps. I was surprised, for the sunlight was too low in this late afternoon for him to request another wet plate for a sitting.

Gardner appeared in the reddish-orange light at the top of the stairs and advanced toward the vat where I was washing the glass negatives. "Well, Johnny, you may think your work for the afternoon is almost over, but I have something else for you," he said. In one hand he carried a folded newspaper and in the other a positive photographic print. He thrust the paper print at me. "What do you make of this?"

I looked at the photograph. It showed a middle-aged gentleman in a black coat, slumped dejectedly in a chair, holding his head in his hands in the classic posture of despair. There were the usual studio props around the man in the chair—familiar to me now from developing literally hundreds of negatives—the intentionally broken pillar of plaster of Paris, a vase of probably artificial flowers, and a faded and somewhat greasy-looking carpet on the floor. To the gentleman's right was an underexposed image of a young girl, perhaps thirteen or fourteen, who appeared for some reason to be wearing a large sheet of light muslin over her head. She was affectionately touching the hand of the seated gentleman, who did not notice her presence. The pattern of the carpet on the floor was clearly visible through the image of the girl's bare feet.

"It is a double exposure," I said. "The photographer either forgot that he had previously exposed the plate, or knowing that the plate had been exposed used it again, hoping that the first exposure would not appear and thereby save himself the expense of preparing a second plate." I thought this was some kind of test.

"Why, Johnny, I'm disappointed in you," Gardner said. He pushed his ginger-bearded face toward me, and in the reddish light of the darkroom his features so close to my face were leering and goatlike. "You hold in your hands a wonderful instance of spiritualistic photography. It is an *ec-to-plas-mic* materialization." Gardner pro-

194

nounced each syllable distinctly, with an evident sarcasm.

"Look at this," he said, and held his newspaper up to the masked gas jet in the darkroom ceiling. I stepped closer to the light and took the newspaper from Gardner's hand. The pages had been folded so that a display was visible in the lower left-hand corner.

It was an advertisement for a spiritualistic medium, a certain Monsieur Daoud. I was not surprised. Mediums, like prostitutes, had flooded into Washington City at the start of the war, and these commercial representations now had become a daily part of the city's newspaper pages, along with advertisements for patented wooden limbs and reasonably priced mourning clothes. In the midst of so much death, shipped from the battlefields by the Union army in the tens of thousands each year to the sheds behind Market Square, and the daily arrival in the city of so many distraught family members and spouses desperate for contact with a loved one, these people made a very good living. Even Mrs. Lincoln is said to have once employed a medium to contact the spirit of her deceased eleven-year-old boy, an act which I find of questionable taste.

M. Daoud promised more than most. In addition to offering his patrons readings in palmistry and "the genuine Egyptian secret for causing the married to be happy," his advertisement assured his readers "the almost-certainty of communication with the spirits of the recently deceased." For those skeptics not otherwise convinced of his powers, M. Daoud offered to provide at his Connecticut Avenue quarters irrefutable photographic evidence that the spirits of the dead move among the living.

I handed back the photograph and the advertisement. "I don't believe in such humbug," I said.

Gardner smiled at me under the red light. "Neither do I, Johnny. But some people do. And *some* people take advantage of the credulity of others, peddling these fraudulent photographs and all other sorts of rubbish. Their influence has extended even into the private living quarters of the Executive Mansion, where Mrs. Lincoln still grieves over the loss of her poor Willie."

Gardner held the spiritualist photograph at arm's length. "This is the sort of thing that could put all honest cameramen in a bad odor with the public, and could threaten the continued science and art of photography. And it could be very embarrassing politically to the war administration if this M. Daoud continues to boast to his clientele of his influence over a certain member of our foremost family." Gardner gave me a conspiratorial wink. "So *some* highly placed members of the administration have asked me and other friends to see if we could not persuade M. Daoud from making such a public nuisance of himself. I'm afraid your work will not be over when you've finished these negatives, Johnny. You're scheduled to join me and other friends for a séance tonight at M. Daoud's. We intend to have a wee bit of prayer with him."

Gardner turned and clumped down the stairs. At the bottom step he shouted back up to me that I was to meet him after closing time at a carriage parked in the alley behind the studio. I was not taken aback by his request. After a few weeks of working in his studio, there was nothing Gardner could say or do that would now astonish me, and I knew better than to try to argue with him.

Just as the bookstore downstairs closed,

I ran out into the street to see if I could find a bootblack boy to carry to H Street a note to Mother that I would be late for supper. Of course, this time there were none on 7th Street; but to my surprise I recognized George Atzerodt slouching against one corner of a building. I then remembered that the oyster saloons and drinking establishments along Pennsylvania Avenue lowered their prices for a few hours in the late afternoons, and Atzerodt doubtless was waiting for the drop to favor his personal fortunes. I gave him the note and a twenty-five-cent piece, and hoped he would deliver the message before he became too hopelessly drunk.

Gardner was waiting beside a carriage in the alley, talking to two other men. One was the ruffian in checkered trousers I had not seen since my first day at the studio. The other, shorter man had his back turned to me, and as he stood talking with Gardner I overheard that he, too, had a slight Scottish burr to his voice.

"Ah, John, you're here at last," Gardner cried out over his companion's shoulder. "May I introduce you to a good friend of mine, Mr. E. J. Allen?" The shorter man turned around.

Never before have I seen a man who was so simian-like in appearance. Like most residents of this city, I have heard the bad jokes about President Lincoln's long arms and legs and his resemblance to a gorilla, and from the few times I have seen Lincoln, I considered these remarks both unkind and untrue. But this Mr. Allen in front of me absolutely appeared to be a chimpanzee dressed in men's clothing. He held both his arms, far too long for his body, clasped tightly behind his back and simply thrust his face toward mine. A round black hat, much too small, was pushed down his head onto an enormous pair of ears, and it did not quite conceal a forehead that was alarmingly sloped. His eyes, underneath a bushy pair of eyebrows, were both intelligent and malevolent.

I bowed my head slightly. "John Surratt," I said. Neither Allen nor the ruffian offered to shake my hand.

Gardner opened the carriage door. "Well, let's be off," he shouted. "Though they have all eternity, we mustn't keep the spirits waiting." Gardner seemed in an extraordinary good humor. He told the address in a loud voice to the driver at the front of the carriage.

Gardner and the ruffian sat across from Allen and me. At closer quarters, I saw that the pug-ugly I had met that first day at the studio had the facial scars and swollen knuckles of the professional pugilist. He glared at me, saying nothing.

The carriage rocked through the traffic on upper 7th Street. Allen spoke first. "Mr. Surratt," Allen said, "your employer, Mr. Gardner, tells me you have a brother wounded in the Confederate army and invalided out in Texas." He and Gardner nodded to each other across the cramped space of our carriage compartment like a pair of Scottish churchwardens. "At least, that is what you'll tell Daoud," Allen went on. "Tell him you've received no word from your brother since he was wounded, and you want to know if he's alive or dead. Just keep him talking, that's your job." Gardner could not repress a chuckle from the seats across from us, and Allen scratched a chimpanzee ear. "We'll handle the rest," he said, and smiled toward the pugilist, who cracked his knuckles and gave me a significant look.

The carriage had almost reached Connecticut Avenue. At a sudden stop in the traffic, I was jostled in my seat toward Allen. A long metallic-like object jabbed me in the ribs. I realized that Allen was carrying a pistol underneath his coat.

The carriage stopped at the Connecticut Avenue address of M. Daoud. It was a very respectable-looking one-story brick house with no sign in the front advertising Daoud's profession. I saw a pot of geraniums set inside upon a windowsill.

"Don't tie up at the hitching post and don't set the wheel brakes," Gardner said to the driver as we got out of the carriage. "We may have to leave in a hurry."

I led the way up the stone steps to the front door. Just as my hand reached for the brass knocker, however, the door opened of its own accord. I found myself looking down at a small boy about eleven or twelve years of age standing inside the hallway. His features were Arabic, or at least Levantine, but the most remarkable fact about this boy was that he was dressed precisely like a miniature man, down to his small black frock coat and formal shirt linen. "He awaits you," he said.

We all tramped into the narrow front hall-way. Everyone took off their hats. From a shuttered door to a room at our right, I heard someone playing an improvisational tune upon a piano, vaguely reminiscent of Chopin. I noticed a large mirror in the hallway, angled so as to reflect a small curtainless window set in the wall beside the door. This doubtless would explain the boy's trick of opening the front door before I had knocked. The only other furnishings in the hallway were a marble pedestal and, set atop it, a small statue of a dancing god that was really quite beautiful.

The playing of the piano in another room abruptly stopped. I heard the wooden shutters to the room open. "Ah, Mr. Surratt, my six o'clock appointment." Monsieur Daoud stepped into the hallway.

Never, even backstage at the theatre, have I seen a man who so painted his face as did M. Daoud. His eyelids were carefully tinted a lavender shade, and there was a noticeably heavy application of rouge to his cheekbones and lips. Otherwise, he presented an appearance that was almost respectable. Very slight and short, Daoud was no more than five feet or so in height, with a neatly trimmed mustache and heavily Macassared black hair that appeared to be his own. He was roughly thirty years of age, perhaps a bit older. He wore a conservative black coat, with wide lapels nearly concealing his white shirtfront and flowered cravat, with matching black trousers. For some reason, he wore carpet slippers, rather than shoes. Judging by his name and accent, Daoud was French, or pretended to be.

"The playing of music before a session relaxes me, do you see, Mr. Surratt, and it makes me more receptive as an instrument myself to the spirits and the messages they may bring me." Daoud smiled, and stretched his fingers in front of him. They were marvelously long and tapered, and appeared to be double-jointed. Each finger was bejeweled with rings, both large and small.

"And I see you have brought others with you?" Daoud turned his lavender and, I sensed, larcenous eyes toward my three companions. "Friends or family, perhaps? Well, so much the better." He softly clapped his hands. "Aman. Please show these gentlemen to our parlor."

Their parlor was not, as is usual in most

houses, a room located on one side or another of the central hallway. The door from which Daoud had entered the hallway remained shuttered, as did the door to the room at our left. I suspected that this door concealed, as did our own parlor door on H Street, a makeshift and shoddy bedroom. Instead, we silently followed the formal little boy down the hallway to a windowless room at the interior of the house. Daoud came behind us in the hallway. I thought I overheard him humming, or giggling, to himself.

We entered an ill-lit room with a large, round table at the center. Allen and the pug-ugly cast looks into the shadows at corners of the room, as if they suspected other thugs might be lurking there. Gardner critically inspected an unlit gas fixture in the ceiling above the table. On the table itself were placed a small drum, a tambourine, and a banjo. The only other furnishings in this room were a large wooden cabinet pushed away from the table in a corner, an Empire clock audibly ticking alone on a mantelpiece, and a jumble of chairs pushed against the walls. The sole light was a single gas jet in the wall, turned very low and partially covered by a damask cloth. The furnishings and arrangement of this room reminded me very much of a photographic studio.

"One, two, three, four." Daoud had stepped up closely behind me, moving very lightly in his slippers. He apparently had been counting heads. "It is my custom, Mr. Surratt, to charge one Union dollar for each patron at a sitting, and as I see you have brought three others—"

I heard Allen sigh, and he brought his money purse out of his coat. He counted out four paper dollars and began to hand them to Daoud.

"Oh, no, no!" Daoud held up his hands flat in front of him, and beneath his painted face, I think I saw a look of genuine alarm. "It is a gift which I possess. If I accepted money for it, the gift would no longer be mine." Daoud continued to hold up his hands, but he then crooked one long and ringed finger in the direction of the little boy. "Still, one must live, and if you will be so kind as to give to Aman—"

Allen handed over the dollars to the boy. He accepted them very seriously, never taking his brown Arabic eyes away from Allen's face.

"Sit, sit!" Daoud now exclaimed, and he began pushing chairs toward the table as soon as Aman had accepted the money. "We shall all sit together at the table, and in a few moments join our hands for our communication with the spirits. Mr. Surratt, I shall sit at your left. You shall sit here, here, and here." Daoud pointed to each of my companions and indicated a chair.

We took our places at the table. There was an empty chair at my left for Daoud; Gardner sat next to him on the other side. Allen and the pug-ugly sat across the table from me. I could not help but think how several weeks ago I had sat at a table in a similarly darkened room with Booth and his three ruffian companions.

Daoud stood behind his chair, putting on a pair of black velvet gloves. He self-dramatically rolled up his coat sleeves and his shirt linen, then rolled them down his thin arms again.

"I promise nothing, you understand?" Daoud lightly touched my shoulder, and there was a look of complete earnestness on his face. "The spirits sometimes visit, sometimes they do not. Anyone who claims otherwise is a fool, or worse."

Daoud brought his painted face closer to mine. I was acutely embarrassed. "There are so many who do not have the gift, or very little of the gift, but, you understand, like the good life. That beautiful boy from New England, that D. D. Home, who *levitates* for gentlemen in hotel rooms. And that terrible Mrs. Guppy from England. All they are really interested in is this." Daoud brought his thumb and forefinger together and rubbed them, as if touching money.

He giggled. "And the spirits can be droll. *Very* droll. Just last week I had a rich widow visit me. A very rich widow. She is concerned, you see, about her husband's moral deportment in the afterlife. I suspect he had many special friends among the ladies during his time on this side. She is worried that he will find such a special friend on the other side. Perhaps a sweetheart of his youth who passed away before he married his wife. Or perhaps an attractive young girl of twenty or so, dead of typhoid, who does not wish to spend all of her eternity alone and unattended, you understand? So my widowed client asks for a sign, a little lover's gift, a token of affection to show that her husband is thinking of her on the other side."

Daoud giggled again. "And would you believe? She is *showered,* right where you sit underneath the gaslight, with a gift of sugarplums, sweet currants, and some very delicious figs from Turkey. We were all so happy."

I started to say that these items could be had from any Washington City confectionery shop, without spiritual intercession from the other side, now that the Christmas season was upon us. But I decided to hold my tongue.

Daoud seemed to think of me as his special confidant. "If I have a success in contacting the spirits, do not become alarmed if I speak in another's voice or sound as if I speak from another part of the room," he said. He placed his gloved hand into mine. "I am but a medium. Think of me as a clear pane of glass through which another sees and speaks, and do not under any circumstance let go of my hand, and you shall be safe." He offered his other hand to Gardner, and Allen and the pug-ugly joined hands and then linked theirs to ours around the table. The pugilist gave me a nasty smile and painfully squeezed my fingers.

"So. We are ready," Daoud said. "Aman,

extinguish the light and then leave us." The Arabic boy reached up to the gas jet and closed the gas cock. In the total darkness I heard the door to the parlor open and shut.

Daoud giggled unseen beside me. "Usually, I begin a séance by asking my patrons to sing some holy song or poem. But as none of you gentlemen appear musical, I shall do so myself."

Daoud then began a type of wordless singing, or humming, remarkably toneless for one who had supposedly been playing Chopin improvisations a few moments before. This humming went on for a long while. *Whistle "Yankee-Doodle" in your head if it damn well pleases you,* I remembered Gardner telling me on the day I was first photographed. In the darkness, I tightened my grip on Daoud's hand.

Suddenly I became aware of a new sound. Unseen to us on the table I heard the drum begin to beat, slowly at first and then energetically and very regularly. I heard the tambourine shaken. I then barely discerned a pale white oval hanging several feet above the table. There were the sounds of the banjo strings being plucked in the air above our heads.

Daoud ceased singing, and he was now breathing in and out apparently with great difficulty. I felt his hand twist in my grasp, but I tightened my hold. The pugilist across the table squeezed my other hand far too tightly.

The invisible music at the table abruptly stopped. The banjo remained floating in air. Daoud's breathing sounded less forced, and his fingers relaxed slightly in my hand. "With whom do you wish to speak?" he asked, his voice sounding harsher, seeming to come from slightly behind me.

"With my brother Isaac," I said. "He has been wounded in the war, and I wish to know if he's alive or dead."

"Have you heard from your brother since learning of his wound?" Daoud asked.

"No," I lied.

"I see him," Daoud spoke next to me in the darkness. His voice had regained his usual tones, and was not so harsh now. "He is in a desert land. He is alive, but his flesh is very badly torn. He is on one side of a very great river which he cannot cross. Perhaps it is your Mississippi, where the Union soldiers are."

My breath caught in my throat—Isaac

was on the other side of the Mississippi, in Texas. How could Daoud have known?

Daoud suddenly began his stentorian breathing again. I felt him twitch in his chair next to me, and his hand twisted as if to free himself from my grasp. I tightened my grip on his hand with so much pressure that I felt his rings under his glove cut into the flesh of my palm.

"You also are there," he said. "On the other side of the river with another man. He, too, is your brother, yet he is not your brother. Perhaps another family member to whom you have grown more familiar since the start of the war? No. I see now. You are not brothers, but two parts of the same man. You are together the young and the old parts of the same man."

I felt Daoud begin twitching violently again in his chair in the darkness, and I felt my own flesh begin to burn. When he spoke once more, his voice was harsh.

"I also see a woman there," he said. "She also is both young and old. Or she is no longer young and she feels old. Who is she? Your sister, your ancestor?" Daoud's stentorian breathing beside me continued, and I became worried that this little man might work himself up into some kind of apoplectic fit.

"Now this great river changes colors in its waters," Daoud said. "It is like a channel of blood that runs by the woman who stands there. The river flows for many years. Is it the Red River in Texas where the Union soldiers still fight? No. It is now like a theatre where the ropes hang behind the stage. It is like the ropes that hang behind the red curtain at a theatre with large bags of sand tied to the ends of them. No, it is not like that at all. Oh, my God, this is most terrible—"

Daoud began a violent spasm in his chair, and for a moment his hand slipped away from me. Quicker than I thought possible in the darkness, I regained his hand and held it even harder. The pugilist across the table never loosened his iron grip for a moment upon my crushed and numb right hand.

I no longer heard Daoud's labored breathing, and when he spoke, his voice was normal, although his words again seemed to come from behind me. "I shall now materialize for you the one who always stands beside you," he said.

With a sudden click in the darkness, the doors of the wooden cabinet in the corner flew open. A luminous veil was visible hung inside the cabinet. I presumed we had all startled upward in our chairs, as I had done. Even the pugilist removed his hand from mine. But I reminded myself that what I witnessed was probably only a trick of clock-driven springs in the cabinet doors, and my hand never left Daoud's for an instant.

A black image reminiscent of an inkblot began to appear on the luminous screen. As I sat in the darkness, it slowly began to take on an appearance more familiar, gradually shaping itself into the form of a man's face. *It is Booth,* I was certain. I felt a moment of absolute fear. Was this all a trap for me? Had the Union spies already learned of my trip across the Potomac, had Gardner and the others enticed me here only to confront me in this grotesque manner with the evidence of my treason? Would I hang?

I felt myself violently pushed backward in my chair, still holding onto Daoud's hand. There was a crash at my feet, as the table overturned in the darkness. From one corner of the room, I heard a muffled curse, then the smack of a fist upon flesh, and the sound of a body falling to the floor. The whitened circle of the banjo swung crazily in the air before my eyes. From another corner of the darkness I heard Gardner's loud voice: "Hold him, hold the catamite! I've got a match!"

Light returned to the parlor room. Gardner stood across the room, his hand on the gas jet. Allen stood beside me where I still sat in my chair, his hands on his hips. He had kicked over the table. The Arabic boy was crouched where the table had been, clutching musical instruments identical to those we had heard played. The banjo, still spinning in midair, hung suspended from the ceiling by a very visible wire. M. Daoud was sprawled on the floor, barefoot, in a corner of the room, holding his palm over his right eye. The pug-ugly stood over him a few feet away, his fists raised and the red mark of fingernail scratches on his face.

"*Merde!*" Daoud cried. He brought his hand away from his eye and squinted at the blood and facial paint smeared on his palm. "You have ruined me! Ruined me!"

But how could Daoud be slumped in a far corner of this room when I sat the length of the floor away from him holding onto his hand? I looked at what I held in my left hand. It was a wooden limb, such as are

214

commonly issued to Union soldiers who have lost an arm in the war. It was even complete at one end with rings and a glove filled with warm putty or paraffin. I then remembered Daoud's last sudden spasm, and how easily I had recovered his hand in the dark. I dropped the thing in horror.

There were a few moments to take in other details. The overturned bottom of the table included a pair of wooden levers, which Daoud doubtless had been able to manipulate with his bare feet once he removed his carpet slippers, to raise or lower the wire attached to the banjo. A very long hearing horn, of the kind frequently used by the deaf, was tossed on the floor. Gardner walked purposely over to the wooden cabinet in the corner. He tore the veil and looked inside.

"It's a *camera obscura*," he said. "He's got a bull's-eye lantern in here, and silhouettes and all other sorts of trash to project upon the screen. Though I'll be damned if I know how he managed to light the lantern without striking a match."

Daoud was attempting to rise. "Unworthies!" he shouted. His right eye was swollen shut, and the cheekbone beneath it was bleeding copiously. "I have the true gift, and I use such theatre tricks only because you will not otherwise believe. I give, and I give, but you will not believe! You have betrayed yourselves!" He turned his head to look at all of us from his ruined eye of lavender paint and blood, but I felt that his gaze was particularly directed at me. And I knew at that moment that Daoud was right, he did have a gift. For I had not imagined the portrait of Booth upon the screen. What had Daoud seen as he'd collapsed in a fit? What, dear God, did the hanging ropes and the river of blood signify? I felt a cold shiver in my bowels, as if the shadow of death had sent a chill wind through them.

Allen quickly took command. He walked from around the overturned table, his long simian arms loose and free at his sides. "Stay as you are, Daoud," he said. "Maguirre, if he gets to his feet, knock him to the floor again. And this time make sure that he stays on the floor."

Daoud had risen to his hands and knees. He was a pathetic figure with his smeared facial paint and naked feet. His blood had spilled down his white shirtfront and as he hung his head down between his shoulders, a thick thread of saliva fell from his lips. Still, he continued to try to stand.

Daoud lifted his head from his shoulders. "I am superior to you all," he said. The pugilist a few feet away began a shuffling dance, moving both his fists in a circular motion in front of him.

None of us anticipated the boy. With a high, inarticulate cry, he suddenly sprang forward between the pugilist and Daoud, spitting and glaring his teeth like a feral animal.

E. J. Allen, with a sure, unhurried movement, walked across the room to stand just beyond the boy's reach. Then he withdrew the pistol from inside his coat.

Allen cocked the pistol and leveled it at the boy's head. The weapon was enormous, a Colt Navy .44 revolver with a barrel at least five or six inches long. I could not help but think that one pull on its trigger would splatter the boy's brains across the length of the room.

Allen scornfully looked down at the kneeling figure of Daoud. When he spoke, his voice was thick with anger. "Call off your cur, Daoud. Or I swear before God I shall bust a cap on this boy."

There was a long silence in the parlor room, the only sound the ticking of the Empire clock on the mantelpiece. When Daoud at last spoke, his voice was calm. "Aman," he said, "come to me, please. Move very slowly away from this gentleman."

The boy obeyed reluctantly. Daoud put his right arm protectively around him, and they huddled together in the corner with a greater dignity, I thought, than anyone else in the room at this moment.

"That's much better," Allen said. The pugilist slightly relaxed his stance, and Allen kept his pistol leveled at the pair.

"Now you listen to me, Daoud," he said. "I've already seen enough tonight to have you taken up on a dozen charges of being a confidence man. But you *may* keep your liberty, and you *may* keep your four dollars. But there will be no more séances at the Executive Mansion, do you understand, and no more peddling of photographs and bragging of your clientele. If you do not do as I say, I shall personally take you and this boy to the Arsenal Prison, and I shall see that both of you hang there on charges of sedition. I am in a position to do what I promise. Now *do you understand?*"

Daoud looked at him with his one good and one bruised eye, his arm closely around the boy. "Yes," he hissed. I have never before heard such hatred in a human voice. "Now get out of my house."

There was a moment when no one spoke. Then Gardner cocked his head toward the parlor door. The four of us walked silently out of the room and gathered in the hallway to put on our hats. It was as if nothing had happened. Allen slipped his pistol into the leather holster underneath his coat. Glancing at the dancing statue on the pedestal in the hallway, he brought his hand across the top of the pedestal, knocking the statue to the floor and breaking it.

We left the house and got into the carriage, and the driver carried us away. For a while, no one spoke. I thought I might become physically sick in the carriage, both from the momentary fear I'd felt at my possible arrest and from my deep shame at what I had been an accomplice to in that house tonight. The pugilist seated across from me touched the fingernail scratches from Daoud on his face with a dirty handkerchief.

Gardner finally broke the silence, laughing

with a loud, harsh, braying sound. "You played your part well tonight, Johnny," he said. He reached across the carriage compartment and tapped me on the kneecap. "You're one of us, after all."

What did my employer mean by this statement? Had Gardner begun to suspect my secret trips for Booth, but now perceived me as loyal because I had helped these two Union bullies? Was he telling me that I was almost as skilled a deceiver as was he himself? Or simply that I was no better than Gardner and his companions, because I joined with them in beating a frail man? No one said anything further, and I sat silently, an actor among actors, as our carriage jolted forward into the night.

3.

December 23, Friday, 1864

Last night my sister and I went to the theatre with Booth. True to his word, earlier in the week he had sent an envelope embossed with his initials to our H Street house, addressed to our mother. She opened it with, to my eyes, a surprising urgency to her fingers; it was an invitation to join Booth as his guests at the theatre this Friday. Mother handed each of us a ticket from inside the envelope and then placed the envelope and the enclosed note into the pocket of her house frock.

The tickets were to the opening night revival of that old theatrical chestnut *Our American Cousin,* playing at Ford's Theatre. Booth apparently was taking another night off from tragic drama at the National Theatre and letting his understudy fill in for him. *Our American Cousin* was just the sort of light-hearted comedy that pleases the occasional theatre-goer, and I knew that Booth had chosen it for Anna's enjoyment. Mother then told us that Booth, in a gesture of thoughtfulness that can be so characteristic of him, had also enclosed a ticket for our young female boarder, Miss Fitzpatrick. But why would Booth invite Miss Fitzpatrick, whom he barely knows, and not my mother? And if a ticket *had* been intended for my mother, and she did not wish to go, why would she not say so? Why the need or desire for secrecy?

In the evening before our theatre date, I heard shrieks and laughter from Anna and

Miss Fitzpatrick as they completed their appearances in the bedroom upstairs. Miss Fitzpatrick had generously offered to let Anna borrow from her wardrobe, crammed with the most fashionable and expensive of crinoline dresses, most of them never worn. I myself brought out of my trunk my best black suit, which I had not worn since my father's funeral. Brushed and pressed, it hung nicely on me, I reflected, as I stood in the hallway and awaited Booth's arrival.

Moments later, I heard the harness jingle of a hansom cab as it stopped at the curb outside our house. There was a confident knocking on our door, and when I opened it, there stood Booth, elegantly dressed in black, with a gray cape over his suit.

"Wilkes," I said, and warmly shook his hand as he crossed the threshold. "It's good to see you." And, then, in a lower voice, I added, "I have much to tell you," referring to my efforts to assist Miss Ravenel.

"Good evening, John," Booth said loudly. "I want to know everything," he went on more softly. He smiled. "We can talk after the performance."

To my surprise, I saw the figure of Lewis

Powell standing behind Booth. "John, I'd like for you to meet an old friend of mine from down South," Booth said as they entered the hallway together. "He'll be accompanying us to the theatre tonight. Mr. Lewis *Paine.*"

I understood that Booth meant to conceal Powell's real name, though why I couldn't imagine. I shook hands with Powell and repeated aloud his newly assumed name as if we were meeting for the first time. Powell played his part well, as well, in exchanging greetings, although the poor man may have in fact already forgotten that we had previously been introduced. He was dressed in a decent suit of gray which I was certain Booth had bought for him.

A frantic patter of footsteps above our heads told me that Anna and Miss Fitzpatrick had heard Booth's arrival and that the ladies were making last-minute preparations for their appearance downstairs. Booth looked around the hallway good-naturedly. "Where is your mother?" he asked.

"I am here, Mr. Booth."

My mother stood in the hallway, just outside the parlor door; apparently she had been rearranging her hair in the parlor bedroom. I saw that it was styled down the nape of her neck in the beautifully elaborate and dark coif I remembered from my childhood and which I see daily in the daguerreotype of her as a young woman. But my mother was dressed in a way that seemed almost deliberately to contradict the youthfulness of her hairstyle. She wore a severely plain dress, with no ornamentation, of blackest bombazine, the fabric of which Gardner despairs when he is taking photographs and which he claims is suitable only for the eldest of matrons.

Booth's face showed genuine surprise. "Why, Mrs. Surratt, you're not dressed for the theatre."

My mother gave him a strangely ambiguous smile. "I have decided to forgo such pleasures, Mr. Booth. I am a widowed mother with a commercial boardinghouse to maintain. I think it best tonight that you divert yourself with my children and other younger people." My mother's voice was grave as she spoke these words, but she involuntarily raised her left hand to adjust the coif of hair at the back of her neck.

My suspicion that Booth had enclosed a

theatre ticket for my mother, as well, in the envelope had been correct.

Booth turned in confusion, raising his right arm to indicate the unintroduced Lewis Powell in the hallway. "But the company, Mrs. Surratt, will be unbalanced. I had planned upon three gentlemen in order to accompany three ladies. And otherwise a ticket will go to waste."

"I am sure you will manage, Mr. Booth," my mother said with finality, looking at Booth with an odd intensity.

Booth held her gaze for a moment, then shrugged as if accepting an unavoidable and unaccountable whim of my mother's. He then proceeded to introduce her to Powell, or Paine as he called him, taking care to emphasize to my mother that Powell came from "a devoutly religious family" in Florida. Booth's remark seemed a very tactful criticism of my mother's decision, that although she considered Booth to be appropriate company at Mass, she refused to accompany us to the theatre.

My mother put aside her graveness of manner when she greeted Powell. She displayed the same unqualified kindness she had when she greeted strangers at our house at Surrattsville. "Mr. Paine, please be assured that any friend of Mr. Booth's is considered a good friend of my family's."

Powell managed to mumble a few monosyllables. Mine was probably the first family into which Powell had been welcomed since he had become a Confederate soldier.

I heard the sound of excited female voices behind us, and as I glanced up I saw my sister and Miss Fitzpatrick appear on the staircase at the back of the hallway.

Never have I seen my sister more beautiful. Both she and Miss Fitzpatrick wore full hooped skirts of crinoline covered with silks; as the two women made their way down the stairs, carefully holding onto the banister, the hooped contraptions at their waists swayed from side to side like two gracefully swinging bells. My sister's skirt was a silk of dramatic blue that wonderfully complemented her dark hair. Miss Fitzpatrick wore a more extravagant, and to my eyes less tasteful, magenta skirt with emerald-green stripes. At such times I regret, since the recent invention of chemical dyes and the adoption of colors not found in nature, that photography in our nineteenth century cannot capture the subtle or dramatic hues of the dresses young women like my sister wear for an evening at the theatre. Succeeding generations will think that they always dressed only in tones of black, like the respectable gentlemen, or that they all appeared as my mother chose to do so tonight, as matrons in darkest bombazine.

My sister's *décolleté* was cut very low in front, and she had arranged her hair like our mother's in a chignon at the back of her neck. Usually my sister's boldness discomforts me, but at that moment seeing her stand there, looking so beautiful, I was filled with pride.

"Wilkes," she said, and extended her hand.

"Anna," Booth replied, smiling. He took her hand between his. "You are very beautiful tonight. You don't know how many times over the past few months the images in my mind of you and your brother have cheered me on my theatrical travels."

Booth released my sister's hand and turned her toward her companion. "And you must be Miss Honora Fitzpatrick," he said in his best theatrical voice. "Anna and John have told me so much about you." Miss Fitzpatrick simpered, and actually curtsied, and for a moment I thought this witless girl simply would collapse in a magenta silk heap of delight at Booth's feet.

Booth nodded imperceptibly toward my mother. "My only disappointment in this evening's experience is that your mother has unaccountably decided not to join us." The look of surprise on my sister's face told me that neither had Anna known of the extra ticket.

"No experience is ever wasted, Mr. Booth," my mother said. "And the ticket shall not go unused. Our other boarder, Mr. Weichman, has, like you, Mr. Booth, been a good friend to my family, and he also deserves an evening out. I have taken the liberty of passing on your gift to Mr. Weichman."

At that moment we all heard a loud clumping of boots at the top of the hallway stairs, and an even louder voice shouting, "Hold, hold! Don't leave without me!" And then Louis Weichman barreled down the hallway stairs, costumed as I have never before seen him.

Weichman was dressed, from top to toe, in an absurd, lavender-colored suit. The fabric was still creased and stiff from the

tailor's shelf, where Weichman apparently had purchased it earlier this afternoon to wear specially for this occasion. The choice of lavender was bad enough; but Weichman had added, to complete his ensemble, a brightly colored paisley waistcoat and matching paisley cravat that positively hurt one's eyes.

Mother and Anna appeared to be as astonished as I was at this unexpected transformation in Weichman. For months we had grown accustomed to seeing him dressed only in the rusty black coat of an insignificant government clerk. Weichman almost never spent his money on extravagances, laying out his salary after his board and religious tracts, parsimoniously. But tonight he clearly had decided to indulge himself and dress the part of a sophisticated play-goer, or at least Weichman's vision of such a sophisticate.

"John Wilkes Booth! The Prince of American Players, like your father before you!" Weichman cried, as he advanced on Booth, seizing my friend's free hand without an introduction. Weichman's eyes showed an enthusiasm, and, I must add, a spontaneity which I had never before seen in him. "I never dreamed, sir, that I would have the honor of knowing you socially." He continued to pump Booth's hand energetically, and the heavy scent of night-blooming cereus filled the hallway air.

Booth chose to play this scene ironically. He gently disengaged his left hand. "Well, you certainly have a flare for the theatre, yourself, Mr. Weichman. And you're most welcome to join us tonight."

Booth turned his attention back to Anna. Entwined among the chignon at the nape of her neck was a pretty arrangement of paper roses and pink honeysuckle. These paper artifices were quite expensive, but my mother somehow had managed to scrape together the money from her weekly accounts to buy them for Anna for tonight's engagement. I was certain that Booth knew, without my telling him, the effort to which my mother had gone. It was almost as if she were complementing Anna's beauty while obscuring her own.

"Anna, your flowers are most refreshing," Booth said, "particularly in the wintertime of this war year. They remind me that there will always be another springtime. Please permit me." With a quick, graceful gesture,

Booth slipped his right hand from Anna's and removed a rose from her hair.

Booth advanced toward Mother, holding out the paper rose in his open hand. When he spoke, his voice had the musical quality for which he was so noted on the stage. "And this is for the flower that stays at home," Booth said. "The flower whence all this beauty has come."

My mother's face reddened, but she accepted the rose. She understood, as I think we all did, that because she had chosen tonight not to go to the theatre, Booth was bringing a theatre to her, offering a private performance in our hallway by one of the nation's most acclaimed actors.

It was Weichman who broke the magical spell. "Well, come on! Come on!" He clapped his hands. "It'll be Christmas Day at this rate before we get to Ford's Theatre." He evidently was eager to show off his new suit.

There was a general bustle in the hallway. As the ladies put on their shawls, my mother seemed relieved. Everyone checked to make certain that they had their tickets, and Powell, as Paine, was again introduced to the newcomers. I saw my mother kiss Anna good night. Booth nodded a silent farewell to my mother without a touch of his hands, and as I was then putting on my gloves, I did the same.

Just as we were going out the door, I realized that in the initial confusion over the extra ticket, Booth had forgotten to ask my mother what she had thought of his *carte de visite*. Nor was he alone in forgetting, for I had not yet disposed of it. As the door swung to a close, I visualized Booth's image in the brass case behind my mother's negative, where in the excitement of the past weeks I had failed to remove it.

The driver, a dignified middle-aged Negro man, helped the ladies inside the enclosed seats of the small hansom carriage. Of course, as soon as Anna and Miss Fitzpatrick had taken their places and leaned back, the stiff, hooped skirts of their crinolines raised upward and threatened to engulf the small seating area. Amid a great deal of giggling, glimpses of white stockings, and attempts to press down unruly flounces of tulle and silks, we men tried to squeeze ourselves into the cab. It was just as well my mother had decided not to go with us tonight, as I questioned whether there would have been room for her. Lewis Powell finally volunteered to ride at the back of the cab with the driver. Booth, Weichman, and I managed to find places among the voluminous folds of the ladies' skirts inside the cab; and, somewhat humorously for a party on its way to the evening theatre, the cab jolted forward, its male occupants softly crushed by crinoline and silks. Booth joined in the good-natured joking at our expense. I was tempted to tell him and the others a comically altered story of my visit to the medium, but I thought better of it. It was, after all, a far from comic enterprise.

The driver avoided the heavy traffic along Pennsylvania Avenue by taking the carriage on F Street. The windows of many of the shops were illuminated for the Christmas season. Miss Fitzpatrick sat beside Booth. She gazed about her as if she could not believe her good fortune in traveling with such company. "Mr. Booth, this is all so wonderful," she said.

Booth smiled at her. "Please call me John," he said.

"Now, this could be deuced confusing!" remarked Weichman, who sat jammed into a corner of the carriage with Booth and Miss Fitzpatrick, across from my sister and me. He was so engulfed in colors of magenta, blue, and lavender that we scarcely could discern his face and his blond half-beard.

"Perhaps I should rechristen myself tonight as John, too, as the general catchall for this male company," Weichman giggled. He seemed in extraordinarily high spirits. Weichman managed to raise an arm from the crinoline folds around him, and pointed to himself and to Booth and me. "One John, two Johns, three Johns," he giggled again.

No one knew for a moment how to respond to Weichman's ridiculous and pointless witticism. It was my sister who acted first. Turning to smile pleasantly at Weichman, she said drily, "Mr. Weichman, you are a caution," with an understated but delicious irony that was the equal of Booth onstage.

In the close confines of our carriage, I squeezed her hand. Booth smiled conspiratorially at us.

Our cab pulled up at the entrance to Ford's Theatre on 10th Street and took its place along the curbside in the line of carriages discharging passengers. The giant gas lamp in front of the theatre brilliantly lit the crowds of people outside, many of them Union officers arm in arm with the ladies they escorted. Wooden benches had been placed outside the theatre by the treasurer, Harry Ford, so that the Union noncommissioned soldiers and the plainer laboring class of civilians in the city, not able to attend the theatre, could sit and watch the arrivals of the well-dressed theatre-goers.

Miss Fitzpatrick's eyes grew wide in amazement. "Do you ever perform here, John?" she asked.

"Sometimes," Booth replied.

A theatre employee dressed in livery—the leftover costume, I suspect, of some previous historical drama at Ford's—helped the ladies from the cab. Booth told the driver to wait for us after the play, and we clustered around the small entrance to the building beneath a sign marked DELIVERY OF TICKETS.

A harried-looking man stood at the theatre door taking tickets. Booth positioned himself in front of this man and asked in his best theatrical voice, "Surely you will not ask *me* for a ticket?"

The man looked up, and I recognized him as Harry Ford, treasurer of the theatre his brother John owned. His features quickly brightened. "John! John Booth! It's so good to see you." Booth's rhetorical question was an old joke between them; Booth had often in my presence greeted the theatre's proprietor with this humorously mocking question, even on nights when Booth himself performed here. When I had first moved to Washington City, Booth had introduced me to Ford in hopes of obtaining a position for me at the theatre. Ford, however, did not appear to remember me now. His attention was fixed exclusively on Booth as the two shook hands.

"Is everything prepared for my guests tonight?" Booth asked.

"Of course, John." Ford seemed eager to please Booth, to the point of ignoring the line of ticket holders behind us. "State boxes seven and eight, in the dress circle, furnished just as you requested. I took down the partition between the two boxes. I'm sure the ladies will be pleased. Peanut will unlock the outer door for you."

Ford went back to his task of collecting and ripping tickets. But as we passed by him on our way into the foyer of the theatre, he called back over his shoulder, "We're all

237

very happy to have you back with us, John. Even if tonight you're on the wrong side of the stage. Talk to me after your engagement ends at the National."

We found ourselves jammed with fifty or so other arrivals inside the small lobby of Ford's Theatre. Most of the lobby's area was occupied by the two incongruously grand and sweeping staircases at our right and left which led up to the dress circle seats.

"Hello, Peanut," Booth said affectionately to the slow-witted boy who now stood in the lobby beside him, and passed him a fifty-cent coin. Johnny Peanut was a parentless child of very limited mental abilities, nicknamed for the refreshment he sold between the acts to the patrons in the theatre's cheapest gallery seats. He was employed by Ford out of charity. Booth also was in the habit of making small gifts of money to this unfortunate child whenever he visited Ford's Theatre. It was a kindness of which my friend never spoke, yet which many in the theatre world were aware of. While such kindnesses were, I had no doubt, utterly sincere, I couldn't help but notice that he was keenly aware that he was being observed when he carried them out.

Booth laid his hand deftly upon the boy's shoulder; he appeared very relaxed and jovial, as he frequently did in a theatre lobby before or after a performance. Several of the other theatre patrons around us recognized him, and pointed and spoke to their companions in excited, inaudible voices. Weichman preened in his new suit and in his proximity to Booth. Miss Fitzpatrick, who stood closest to Booth, seemed bedazzled by her surroundings. Booth leaned confidentially toward her and whispered that Peanut was rumored to be an illegitimate child of European nobility, spoken in a voice just loud enough for Anna and me to overhear. It was all part of his elaborate offstage performance. Even to one who knew him as well as I, one couldn't always tell where the performance ended, and where Booth the man began.

My sister and I followed Booth, Miss Fitzpatrick, and Peanut up the carpeted staircase to our right. Weichman and Powell, an incongruous pair, brought up the rear. Someone had spilled sugared almonds on one of the stairs, and I held Anna's bluesilked waist so that she would not lose her footing in her dress slippers. She smiled at me, and for a brief moment it was as if we were as close as we were as children. I had found us moving further and further apart, much as it pained me. My sister seemed to have developed more self-possession, and was less drawn to the infatuations and enthusiasms to which I was still subject. While I was firmly bound to my family's support and goodwill, my sister had become more independent and self-assured, in a conventional sort of way. She didn't seem to harbor the same fears and doubts that haunted me. As a result, perhaps, we no longer shared our deepest fears, or greatest joys, as we once had.

Peanut opened the entrance to the back of the dress circle, and the full theatre sprang to life in a pandemonium of noise and color. Below the balcony were seated nine hundred or more on the main floor. Directly in front of us were dozens of curving rows of dress circle chairs, all occupied by spectators engaged in private conversations—the officers in their light blue uniforms and the ladies beside them in crinoline dresses of great splashes of color under the gaslights of purple *moiré antique,* violet-slashed magenta, and reddish solferino. But none of them, I noticed, appeared to me as beautiful as Anna.

Our party moved around the last row of seated spectators, some turning to look at us or to allow us room to pass. I felt, as I always do on entering a theatre, a sense of physical intimacy with the strangers before me. Hundreds of individual perfumes, *eaux de Cologne,* and the closer scents of women commingled as I moved and brushed against these spectacularly dressed people. Other than opening nights at crowded theatres, I have experienced this strange sensation of mass physical union only at one other time. When I was a very small boy, I was in the habit, unknown to Anna or to anyone else in my family, of stealing into my mother's bedroom and re-moving the paper currency she kept in her purse. I did not take the money; instead, in my childish way I raised it to my face and secretly enjoyed the scent of it. The banknotes were vaguely perfumed from my mother's purse and also smelled dramatically of so many other people's bodies. It was an experience both intimate and yet

241

private, a rather secretive way of drawing close to her without interference from anyone else, that even now filled me with nostalgia.

"Just like the president, Mr. Booth," Peanut said enthusiastically, as he unlocked the outer door to the state boxes. He seemed very proud of himself. In a way, Peanut was correct; the two connected state boxes at the right of the dress circle usually were reserved for high-ranking government or military officials in their visits to Ford's Theatre, as were the boxes' two counterparts on the balcony left. Booth warmly thanked the boy and led the way into the short passageway to the interior door. It was my first glimpse into the most exclusive seats at Ford's Theatre, and it was something of a disappointment: this short passageway was unlit, narrow, and probably not very clean. But then Booth opened the interior door for us, and we entered another world.

Our theatre boxes were beautifully furnished, with a velvet-backed settee for the ladies and three comfortable chairs for gentlemen. On a sideboard near the ladies' seats, Booth had ordered placed an assortment of dainty tea cakes, sweet breads, and sugared fruits in jewel-like assortment. Between the ladies' and men's chairs a silver-chased container was filled with crushed ice and a large bottle of sparkling wine, cunningly entwined with what appeared to be real ivy. In a corner of our double state box stood a dramatic arrangement of blooming roses, though how Booth had obtained these beautiful flowers in the dead of December, and at what cost, I could not guess.

Anna slipped out of my grasp and turned in full circle, taking in the splendor before us. "Wilkes, you have outdone yourself," she said. I was flushed with gratitude for Booth's efforts, and would have told him the same, had she not spoken first.

"Not at all, Anna," Booth replied. "I am the most of what I am capable when I make the members of the Surratt family happy. And I do not forget the ones with us tonight whom Mrs. Surratt so kindly considers her Washington City family," Booth said generously, as he indicated the others standing behind us with a gesture of his arm.

We then took our seats, except for Powell, who indicated that he wished to stand behind Booth. Weichman, of course, seated himself beside the sideboard and immediately began stuffing himself with the sweet breads and cakes. Booth removed from his coat a small leather case containing theatre glasses, engraved on the brass tubes with his initials, JWB. He gazed intently down at the crowd and the stage below us. Our double box was very close to the stage, practically overhanging it, with no more than a ten- or twelve-foot drop to the stage floor.

There was a sudden excited bustling and turning of heads among the crowd seated in the chairs below us. At the elevated state box opposite the theatre from our own, a burly man entered, who began energetically shaking the hands and slapping the backs of all those men who stood near him.

"That's Vice President Johnson," Booth said, looking through the glasses. "Or he will be vice president, when Lincoln is inaugurated next March."

"Oh, John, do please let me see," Miss Fitzpatrick said, with what now seemed a newfound confidence. Miss Fitzpatrick accepted Booth's offer of the glasses and then peered through them at the occupants of the opposite box, as if she were calculating the purchase of even more new crinolines and bonnets. "My father says he *pins* a large number of hopes on the new vice president," Miss Fitzpatrick tittered, and put down the glasses. "You see, Mr. Johnson was a tailor before he decided to enter politics, and my father sells contracts for textile goods to our national government." Miss Fitzpatrick tittered again.

Booth in response bowed elegantly and wordlessly from his chair, as if Miss Fitzpatrick's expression of her father's wit were so overwhelming that no further comment were possible. I think that only Anna and I saw the wicked light in his eyes. Weichman laughed uproariously.

As soon as the vice president-elect had been seated, the orchestra in the pit below us began to play a medley of silly songs, which I recognized as the introduction to *Our American Cousin.* The enormous red curtain, scarcely more than ten feet from our box, began to be pulled upward with a straining of ropes in their pulleys that was audible to me above the music in the pit. At last, those around me settled down in our chairs to enjoy the comedy.

(Lawyer Coyle) —*I see one means, at*

least, of keeping the estate in the family, by marrying your daughter.

(Sir Trenchard) —*You insolent scoundrel, how dare you insult me in my own house, sir!*

Written by the Englishman Tom Taylor, *Our American Cousin* has been as popular for the last ten years as any modern novel, and its plot was full of mysteriously missing documents, clandestine meetings, and surreptitious romances. I had seen it performed several times, though never in the company of Booth. It concerned a lovably eccentric but impoverished nobleman who is threatened with foreclosure on his estate unless he agrees to marry his young daughter to an unscrupulous financial broker. The family's fortunes are set aright, however, by the arrival of their American cousin, reputed to be fabulously wealthy, who eventually reunites the daughter with her true love and defeats the nefarious mortgage holder. The play was of interest to me only because of the presence tonight of Laura Keene. Miss Keene played the role of Florence, the high-spirited *ingénue* daughter. Booth had said to me several months ago that in his opinion Laura Keene was now getting a little long in the tooth for such roles, as she was approaching a certain age, which I took to be of about forty. But she appeared very convincing to me tonight in front of the footlights.

At last the American cousin made his first entrance below us on the stage.

(Florence Trenchard) —*Ah, it is our American cousin.*

(Asa Trenchard) —*Wal, yes, I'm Asa Trenchard, born in Vermont, suckled on the banks of Muddy Creek, about the tallest gunner, the slickest dancer, and generally the loudest critter in the state. I ain't got no objections to kiss you, as one cousin ought to kiss another.*

In the dark intimacy of our box, I saw Booth lift two crystal hock glasses from the sideboard, and, with an inquiring look at Anna, indicate whether the ladies chose to take some wine. Miss Fitzpatrick shook her head, but my sister boldly accepted half a glass. As Booth had begun to place the bottle back into the ice, Weichman seized a hock glass from the sideboard and like a greedy child, thrust it toward Booth. Booth silently shook his head and withdrew a silver flask from his cape. Discreetly hiding his ac-

247

tions from the ladies at his left, he filled Weichman's glass with brandy. He then filled another glass and handed it to me. Lewis Powell ate or drank nothing.

As the play progressed, I found myself increasingly amused, and, at last, caught up in this revival on the stage. The character of Lord Dundreary, a pretentious nobleman, was quite comical. With his absurdly foppish clothes and his outlandish side-whiskers, he reminded me of Weichman, and I laughed several times aloud.

As we approached the end of Act II, when the American cousin physically overpowers the villain and recovers the mortgage, Powell stepped forward to the railing, absorbed in this scuffle on the stage. In the dim illumination of the footlights below us, I saw that Powell possessed a type of unaffected good looks that might have made possible his becoming a supporting actor, had he been better educated and had the war not so ravaged his young mind. Was this part of the reason Booth was so kind to him?

At last, the theatre gaslights went up for the intermission between the second and third acts. With the exception of Powell, I and all of Booth's guests looked about us in the light to assure ourselves that this wonderful dream of a private box with roses, wine, ivy, and, most importantly, Booth all were still there. "I believe the gentlemen would like to go outside for a cigar," Booth told the ladies, as he stood up. This was a euphemism for us to go to the Star Saloon next door and drink more brandy, and perhaps use the sinks.

"Of course! Of course! The gentlemen will go outside and smoke cigars!" Weichman happily shouted. He followed eagerly behind us down the stairs after we excused ourselves from the ladies. The brandy apparently had gone to his head.

The inside of the Star Saloon was even smaller than the lobby of the theatre next door, and the crowd at the bar was three or four men deep, all dressed in the uniforms of Union officers. Booth told Powell to wait outside. Weichman, who actually had accepted Booth's offer of a cigar and was puffing contentedly away, went off to the sinks. Despite the crowd in front of us, the bartender recognized Booth and raised his hand to indicate he would take our order. "Hello, Patrick," Booth called. He raised three fingers over the crowd in front of him.

"Three very large brandies, please, for three very thirsty theatre-goers."

We took our drinks to a corner of the noisy room. "Wilkes, Anna was right," I said. "You've really outdone yourself tonight. I don't know why you've gone to such lengths."

"I didn't," Booth replied. He winked at me, then quickly tossed back most of his brandy. But clearly Booth had. I couldn't help wondering what Booth wanted.

"No price is too high to see you and your sister happy," Booth said. "I meant what I said tonight about often thinking of you and Anna on my theatrical travels. The roses in the box, incidentally, were intended for your mother. Please tell her that."

Booth studied the last of the golden-colored brandy in his glass and then finished it off. "John, when I see you and Anna so happy, as you are tonight, you seem more than just brother and sister to me. You are like twins, and I feel somehow like your sibling. My only regret is that before I begin my travels abroad, the two of you cannot meet my sister, Asia. I really think the four of us would have gotten on wonderfully together. We could have been as close, and as similar, as a family. I have always wanted to be more like Anna and you.''

I was surprised. I had to speak loudly to be heard above the noise of the crowd. "Wilkes, you've got it all wrong. It's *you* that everyone wants to be. Harry Ford, Johnny Peanut, the Irish paddy behind this bar. Everyone wants to be you. Even poor Weichman.''

Booth's face showed that he took my reply seriously. "If what you say is true, John, remember that what fate, or the gods, give me with their right hand they take away with their left. Being John Wilkes Booth can be as much a burden as a blessing.'' He regarded me carefully for a moment. "I need to talk to you alone for a few moments after the play is over.''

I nodded my head in agreement.

Weichman approached us from the sinks, unsteady upon his feet. His ridiculous, knock-me-down cigar and his lavender suit brought some hard looks from the Union officers behind his back, but he seemed oblivious. Weichman's fleshy face was now very pale and sweaty, but he eagerly accepted the glass of brandy Booth offered, and consumed it in one noisy gulp.

"Mr. Booth, John, this is all so wonderful," he said, wiping his face. "I've often hoped of going to the theatre in just such a company as this." He looked about him, as if trying to put into words his description of this overcrowded and vulgar barroom. "It's all, it's all so *miraculous.*" He swayed slightly in front of us and seemed to be searching his vocabulary for a more grandiose phrase.

Booth put a steadying hand upon his shoulder. "That's very well put, Mr. Weichman." Booth looked earnestly into Weichman's eyes, speaking loudly to be heard over the drunken noise at the bar. "The early Christians knew of what you speak with their performance of mystery plays, and the ancient Greeks knew it before them. Whenever one goes to a theatre, for whatever reason, there is always the possibility of rebirth."

The gaslights in the ceiling dimmed three times in succession, signaling that the third act was about to begin next door. We joined in the press of men going out the barroom to the theatre.

"Shall I spoil the performance of *Our American Cousin* for you?" Booth asked, leaning teasingly close to Anna and Miss Fitzpatrick after we had rejoined the ladies in our darkened box. "The American cousin gives away his fortune to the pretty English dairy maid, so that the two of them may marry for love. He finds suitable employment for the very young sweetheart of Miss Keene. And he avoids the clutches of the fortune-hunting Lady Mountchessington."

Anna playfully tapped Booth on his knuckles with her program and smiled. "Really, Wilkes, we are not so naïve as all that. We did anticipate how this play will end. And I do believe, despite what you imply, that Miss Keene is presenting a very credible performance." Anna slightly fanned herself with her program, although I found our box to be underheated. She glanced at the stage beneath her, where the performance of the third act was under way, and asked in a low voice, "Do you know Miss Keene well, Wilkes?"

"Laura and I were good friends once," Booth said softly, so that it did not interfere with the voices from the stage. He glanced at the figures below him. "A little less so now."

I realized that Booth probably was referring indirectly to one of his many amatory conquests. I was somewhat shocked, for Miss Keene was more than a decade older than Booth. I wondered if my sister had guessed the same.

"Laura is a very independent woman owning her own business, like your mother," Booth said. "The actors work for her production company; Harry Ford has merely rented the theatre to her tonight. He gets very little of the profits."

All of us, even Weichman, had leaned forward in our chairs to hear Booth, finding his background on the players more compelling than the action on the stage. "The most talented player in her company tonight is, in my opinion, Joseph Jefferson," Booth said to us. "He is only a comedian, like my brother-in-law, but I'll have to admit he has given a wonderfully comic turn to the character of Lord Dundreary, as I believe, Anna, your brother has noticed."

To my amazement, Booth seemed to notice everything. He managed to refill two hock glasses while he spoke, and Weichman and I accepted the glasses of brandy Booth discreetly passed to us.

"The most interesting point about *Our*

American Cousin is neither its plot nor its acting," Booth continued. "It is in the pacing. Mr. Taylor has written it so that one comic scene follows another, each in greater intensity. It's just the same with tragedy, of course, except that pain follows pleasure. But by the end of our comedy tonight, the audience will be laughing out of all due proportion to the humor of the lines. Personally, I find it a little grotesque, but it is wonderful how happily people can be swept along by anticipation of a scene, making it seem greater than it actually is."

Booth raised a finger on his right hand. "Look toward the stage," he pointed. "The last line of this scene always is anticipated in delight." As if with one head, we turned to look as he told us.

Onstage, the American cousin was telling Lady Mountchessington and her daughter that he no longer possessed a fortune.

—*No heir to the fortune, Mr. Trenchard?*

—*No. Not a penny, madam.*

—*Ma! The nasty beast!*

—*I am aware, Mr. Trenchard, that you are not used to the manners of good society, and that, alone, will excuse the impertinence of which you have been guilty.*

255

The two actresses left the stage, leaving the American cousin alone and facing the audience.

—*Don't know the manners of good society, eh? Wal, I guess I know enough to turn you inside out, you sockdologizing old mantrap!*

At the sound of the word *trap,* Booth brought down his finger. The reaction from the audience below us was instantaneous, as the theatre exploded into laughter. For a moment we could not have heard one another shout within the close confines of our box. Booth had been correct. Onstage, the actor playing the American cousin nodded happily toward the audience, an unforgivable stepping out of character in my opinion. The red curtain was run down quickly for the next scene.

The two ladies in our box gazed at Booth in wonderment. "John, you really should direct drama," Miss Fitzpatrick said. The poor girl had confused comedy with drama.

"Thank you," Booth said. "Perhaps I shall."

The orchestra in the pit below us now began playing a merry tune from Mendelssohn. By the play's conclusion, all the principals in the comedy, except for the villain, were happily married, and even Lord Dundreary found a mate. As the curtain was lowered for the final time, all of us in the theatre stood up and applauded, and the players reappeared and joined hands in a circle at the footlights. Weichman particularly was enthusiastic in his applause, and for one terrible moment as he stood next to me in his lavender suit I actually feared that he would shout *Bravo!* Miss Keene, dressed somewhat inappropriately in her juvenile costume, caught Booth's attention in our box above her, and smiled at him in a way that won her another round of applause from the audience below us. Booth, however, had already put on his cape and gloves and was preparing to open the door to our box, apparently eager for us to leave before the crush of the crowd.

As we stood waiting for our cab, none of our party seemed to want to leave the romance of the theatre, and the company of Booth, behind. A late-night December wind had cleared the coal smoke from over Washington City. Looking upward to the sky from between the narrow width of buildings on 10th Street, it was just possible to see the winter constellations. The paste jewels on the ladies in the crowd around us glinted in surprising ways, and as the Union officers put on their greatcoats, I noticed that many of these men had pinned sprigs of holly to their military lapels, in anticipation both of Christmas and of the coming of peace. The slaughter in Virginia seemed very far away.

As our cab arrived, Anna hesitated in front of Booth. "Wilkes, do please join us for tea at home. I'm sure Mother awaits our arrival. You can tell her all about this wonderful night at the theatre."

Booth placed her hand between his. "Anna, there is nothing in this world that I would desire more. But I'm afraid your brother and I need to meet privately tonight to discuss a mutual enterprise. Mr. Weichman will see you home."

"What, say?" Weichman stumbled clumsily up to us at the curb. "But I thought that we men could say good night to the ladies here and adjourn to some other place, like at that establishment next door. You and I could talk further, Mr. Booth."

"I'm afraid not this evening, Mr. Weichman. I would be grateful if you would see the ladies home," Booth said firmly.

Anna and Miss Fitzpatrick regretfully bade their farewells and turned to the hansom cab.

Weichman seemed confused. "But could not your boy, that colored boy there, see the ladies home, and you and I could talk some more? You see . . ."

"The driver's name is Johnson," Booth said curtly. "He is twenty years older than you, has a family, and is a freed black. And that is not his job." Booth then added, somewhat more kindly, "We all have our parts to play, Mr. Weichman."

"But we could talk to one another some more, don't you understand, Mr. Booth?" Weichman reached forward to touch Booth on the shoulder.

My anger at Weichman's behavior tonight and toward me over the past months suddenly boiled over. "Damn you, Weichman, go back with the ladies! That's where you belong." It was as if another person shouted these words as I grabbed Louis Weichman by his lavender suit, turned him roughly around, and thrust him in the line toward our carriage.

Weichman tripped and almost fell face-forward on the paving stones. A Union officer standing nearby fortunately grabbed his right shoulder and set him aright. Anna and Miss Fitzpatrick were at this moment being helped inside our hansom cab by the driver, Johnson, and I do not think they witnessed the scene.

A small circular area among the crowd opened around Weichman and me, everyone discreetly watching without interference. The theatre-goers apparently thought they were witnessing some minor, drunken quarrel on the street. I had the strange sensation that I was acting a part on the stage. I sensed Booth's presence behind me.

Weichman tottered unsteadily on the pavement in front of me. His right hand remained extended where it had helped to break his fall. With a look of shock, then outrage, he looked down at the scraped skin on his hand and then at me. I had an image of Weichman onstage extending his hand in friendship and me dramatically drawing a knife and cutting his open palm across the life line.

As Weichman looked down at his hand again, we both seemed to realize that we stood outside the theatre on a public street. Without a word, the pathetic little man turned his back on us, walking away toward the carriages and returning to the ladies, with as much dignity as I suppose he was capable.

Booth and I walked together down Pennsylvania Avenue without speaking. Lewis Powell followed behind us. Booth lit another cigar, his second in the past hour, a sign, I thought, of his nervousness. "John, that was very indiscreet," he said finally. "Weichman is in a position to learn a great deal about our affairs."

I was still angry about Weichman imposing his company upon us tonight, and, to write honestly, at Booth's casual announcement to me three weeks ago of his plans to go abroad. "Well, you don't have to live with him," I said. "Sleep in the same room with him, and breathe the same air."

"That's true," he said after a brief pause. We continued for several minutes along a dark section of the avenue. I was aware of Booth only by the presence of the glowing embers of his cigar.

He looked behind us to make certain that only Powell followed nearby. Booth then turned to me with a look of gravity about his face that sent shivers down my spine.

"Now, tell me about your travels in Virginia, John, on my behalf. This may be the last adventure we share together, as you can see now why I must escape to Europe immediately after our escapade. I want you to tell me everything."

I felt perversely pleased that Booth had resumed talking to me, confiding in me on our familiar terms. "Dr. Mudd is willing to help you in any way he can," I said. "The others along my old courier route are a little less willing. They say they want to know more of your enterprise."

"They shall know more," Booth said. "All in due time." We had reached the commercial section of Pennsylvania Avenue. Despite the late hour, the hotels and saloons around us were brilliantly lit. "And how are the roads leading toward Richmond?" Booth asked in a low voice. "Could you safely escort Miss Ravenel there, and can you provide a way so that I and my party could escape there?"

I think that I then realized for the first time that Booth was literally putting his life and Miss Ravenel's into my hands. "The back roads from Surrattsville to Richmond are very lightly patrolled," I said. "I am certain I can get Miss Ravenel across the Rappahannock and safely to your friends at Richmond. And after a few more rides I can tell you in exact detail the route you and your party should take."

"John, I haven't been as forthcoming about my plans as I feel I need to be with you. Up to this time, I've restrained from involving you too deeply in the historic role I intend to play on the world's stage. But I can keep you in the shadows no longer." He glanced at me apprisingly, as if monitoring my every reaction. "You see, I am not planning on escaping to the South alone. In addition to several comrades, I plan to take one other person southward with me."

"Who is that?" I asked, half hoping and half dreading that Booth would speak my own name.

"President Lincoln."

I looked at him in shock, speechless, hoping against hope that he would break into laughter at any moment and admit the cruel joke he was playing on me. But his face remained utterly serious.

"What I've just admitted, if relayed to others, would result in my execution," he went on. "But I assure you I am deadly serious. I know you must think me insane at the moment, John, but think about it for a moment. The terrible losses the North is inflicting on us in the South are abominable; young boys are being slaughtered daily, with no end in sight. I've stood by uselessly this entire war. I cannot, I will not, continue to stand by and not do the one thing I believe I can do to bring the fighting, and the bloodshed of our people, to an end. I am *determined* to stop it one way or another." He paused, spittle flying from his lips, his eyes filled with a fierce, almost merciless intensity. "What I intend to do, John, is to capture Lincoln at some social event and whisk him away to the South. You've seen Lewis Powell," Booth said in a lower tone of voice. "He has the strength of three men. And the other two will do anything I ask. And I must tell you that I have additional friends here in the city, people high up in government, who share my feelings about Mr. Lincoln and about ending the war, who are willing to lend us a hand. After all, there is nothing different about capturing the chief federal executive officer than taking a private individual as a prisoner of war, just as poor Lewis was taken. And think, John—it would mean a negotiated end to this war and the saving of so many lives."

Booth put his hand on my shoulders in the darkness. "John, I need your help. I do not want to involve you in the plot itself—it is too dangerous. But I do need your help in escorting Sarah Ravenel to Richmond, as you had agreed. And I need the maps only you can prepare for our journey south. For as you can see, neither I nor those with me will be able to travel on the main roads. We must have alternative routes through the Virginia swamps if we are to make our way successfully to Richmond. You're from the South, John. Surely you can't want the bloodshed of our people to go on. All I'm asking for, for friendship's sake, for the sake of the as-yet-unspilled blood of the South, is your secrecy, and your continued help in mapping out the routes we might take in Virginia. Will you do it?"

I looked at Booth with a kind of terrible fascination, feeling the almost animal attraction of his persuasiveness and charm, the terrible weight of my friendship with him, and of society's adoration of him. Against my will and better judgment, I felt myself giving way. How could I turn him down? How could anyone?

"All right, Wilkes, I'll help you. Though God forgive me if anything goes wrong."

"Good, John, good. And thank you. You won't regret it. What we're doing will be far more important than anything else we could do."

Booth looked at me in admiration. "You have begun well, John. I know that you have a good hand for drawing. As soon as possible you must prepare maps that I can carry with me when I go. You must leave them in sealed envelopes at my hotel. After my engagement ends in the next few weeks at Grover's, I will be in and out of the city a great deal, but I will call for my mail. And only I will read what you leave me. But now I must let you get some sleep. Powell and I will get a hansom and take you home. You've got a full day tomorrow with Mr. Gardner, and it wouldn't do to upset him at this stage by arriving late for work."

And so an evening that had begun with such merriment, and in such glamorous surroundings, ended on such a somber note, on the dark and deserted streets of Washington City. And I can't say that when I left Booth, I didn't feel a tremor of fear.

4.

January 6, Friday, 1865

I made several more trips to Virginia scouting out alternative routes through the swamps on my days off before Booth asked to see me again, to discuss his plans. It was with some trepidation that I met him late at night in the commercial section of Pennsylvania Avenue again, near the Executive Mansion, following Booth's evening performance. He greeted me with some warmth, as if a new bond existed between us, drawing us inextricably closer together. After asking after my mother and sister, he suggested that we take a walk together and enjoy the unseasonably warm night air.

As we reached the entrance to the curving, block-long facade of the Willard Hotel, I saw miniature U.S. flags snapping in the night air from their mountings at the second-story balcony of the hotel. A few figures stood there outside their rooms watching the evening drama of traffic on Pennsylvania Avenue. From where we had stopped at the curb, I could not help but glance from the hotel entrance across the street to the most feared address in the city, 217 Pennsylvania Avenue, the two-story brick offices of the U.S. War Department's Secret Service. It was from there that Stanton sent out his secret agents and the dreaded provost marshals to ferret out suspected disloyalists, often imprisoning civilians without hearings or trials. Even at this late hour, close to midnight, the office windows were lit, and there was a long line of hooded and empty barouche carriages parked outside the building.

Booth partially opened his cape and showed me a brass hotel key. "John, I've taken some rooms at the Willard for a friend. I mentioned that there are others in the city and elsewhere who are willing to help in my attempt to find peace for the South. I want them to see you with me here tonight. It's not necessary that they learn your name, but I want them to know your face as one they can trust."

I was surprised, and more than a little nervous. Booth already had rooms at the National Hotel, and the proprietors of the Willard were well-known Unionists. Why had Booth dared it?

We entered the hotel by the side door, near the lobby barroom, and Powell and I followed Booth up the back stairway to the second landing. Booth motioned for us to stop in the corridor in front of a room door, and, rather than using his door key, knocked twice. He paused, and knocked once more. The door opened, and Davy Herold stood in front of us.

We stepped inside a sitting room that was apparently connected to a bedroom next door. The gas jet was turned very low, and the room was crowded with six or seven other men, all of whom grew silent when we entered. I thought I recognized one or two of them as prominent legislators. At my right, I could just make out a sideboard on which a large number of near-empty bottles and a half-eaten oyster loaf rested. I could see George Atzerodt and Dr. Mudd standing back among the shadows, but Dr. Mudd affected not to recognize me. My attention was fixed, however, upon another man in the room, the only one sitting down, or reclining rather, upon a full-length sofa with a curving back.

"Well, so the great John Wilkes Booth finally makes his entrance," this man said. His face was remarkably similar to Booth's. He remained lying full length upon the sofa, and he had let his left hand fall slightly away from his features, where it had been resting over his eyes. "Where the hell have you been, Booth?" He pointed at me with his left hand. "And who the hell is that?"

I stared at him in surprise. I had never before heard anyone talk so insolently to Booth in public. At first I thought he was Booth's brother Edwin, but then I remembered Booth's telling me that they no longer met or spoke because of the war. Was he a cast-off actor, one of the many who were less talented or permanently "between engagements," whom Booth always had been willing to partially support from his greater earnings onstage? This man even dressed like Booth, in an expensive black suit and imported riding boots, the heels of which rested on the fabric of the sofa.

"Hello, Samuel," Booth said, with an embarrassed smile. "Your tongue is as sharp as it was in our school days together. I see you've made yourself comfortable." Booth stood with his gray cape folded over his left arm while he spoke, and Powell remained close beside him. "You know Lewis," Booth said. He raised his right arm to indicate me. "And this other man is a good friend to us all, perhaps the best friend I shall ever have."

"Well, you asked all of us here to talk, so, goddamn it, let's talk." The man's face, smaller and equally handsome to Booth's, jeered upward at him from the sofa.

Booth seemed remarkably deferential toward him. "Of course, Samuel. Please pardon us a moment."

Booth took me outside to a chair on the balcony and spoke to me in a lower voice. "John, I really think it best that you do not know all the details of our enterprise," he said. He handed me his flask from inside his coat. "Why don't you make yourself comfortable while I talk to these men for a few moments?"

I sat down with a great tiredness. I hadn't seen any clean glasses or tumblers inside, so I drank directly from Booth's flask.

I must have nodded asleep, for I awoke to the sound of an angry voice from within the room. "No, goddamn you, Booth, that won't do! We'll be taken up by Stanton's men, I tell you, and hanged before we reach Virginia." The man on the sofa was shouting at Booth, who stood patiently over him. Despite the insolent man's anger, he made no move to raise himself, and it occurred to me that he might be permanently crippled.

"Capture is one thing, Booth, but this is another," the man said. He gave me a nasty look from the sofa. *"They* have their spies, too, you know. I'm out of it. I'm out of it as of this moment."

"We're all on this together, Samuel," Booth replied softly. "None of us can leave it now."

"By God, are you threatening me, Booth?" The insolent man's face twisted into what seemed an ugly reflection of Booth's, and his right hand began to move underneath his black coat. "Because if you are, *two* can play at your game, John Wilkes Booth."

I stood to my feet in alarm and slipped back into the sitting room. Powell moved quick as a panther between Booth and the man on the sofa. I was certain that Powell would either take into his body any bullet

272

aimed for Booth or tear this insolent man on the sofa into pieces before a shot could be fired.

I think Booth deliberately prolonged this tense scene before giving Powell a quick glance that stopped the young giant. Booth's left hand was still hidden within his gray folded cape. I almost had the impression that Booth was mentally completing a stage count. When he finally spoke, his voice had the musical quality he often employed on the stage.

"Of course I'm not threatening you, Samuel," Booth said. "We are so good a pair of friends, and have known one another so long, we could never harm one another. I would sooner harm myself. I was only suggesting that we have a fresh drink, before we leave this matter."

His answer seemed to satisfy the man on the sofa. Booth brought up the back of his right hand and wiped his mustache in what I believed was a deliberately coarse manner. He grinned at the pale faces of Mudd, Atzerodt, and Herold, and the others in the room. "Hell, boys, I think we could *all* use a fresh drink," he said.

Everyone in the room relaxed, and Davy

Herold laughed aloud. "Hell, yes, another drink." How often I have envied this ability of Booth's to act the common touch just when it was most needed. It was disconcerting to remember, however, that inside the theatre or outside, he always pulled it off without the slightest overacting, and he always seemed to know just what people wanted to hear. Even I, I knew, could not tell the difference. Booth looked across the room at me. "Friend, could you do me a small favor?" he asked, walking to where I stood. "Thank you for being ready to come to my aid," he said in a very low voice. "Sam Arnold is a ruined man in this world, but I need him."

Booth made a great show of handing me the brass hotel key and also a smaller key. "In the next room is my portmanteau with a full bottle of whiskey inside it," he said in a louder voice, clearly intending that the others in the room hear. "Would you unlock my suitcase and bring us the bottle, please?"

"Of course."

I walked past the others, unlocked the connecting door, and shut it behind me. The hotel bedroom in which I stood was small, with an unmade bed and a mahogany washstand in front of me. Booth's portmanteau and a standing mirror were at my right. Some indirect light from the streetlamps outside filtered into the room through the open balcony doors.

Booth's leather-hinged portmanteau, when unlocked, spread open to both sides, like a very large, opened book. Inside the left compartments were his stage costumes, including the false beards and the wooden daggers he used in performances of *Julius Caesar.* In the right-side compartments I saw military passes and bills of lading for the port of New York. I was somewhat shocked to find, as well, a length of chain, handcuffs, and a revolver. Were these the instruments to be used in Booth's suicidal plot to capture the president? Cushioned among newspaper clippings of his theatrical appearance in the North, I located a full bottle of whiskey. I had just hefted the bottle in my right hand when I heard a motion at the balcony doors behind me.

"Mr. Surratt."

I stood frozen in fear. I expected in that moment the hand of the provost marshal on my shoulder. I thought simultaneously of rushing toward the balcony and jumping to safety, and reaching for Booth's revolver in front of my hand.

"I did not intend to startle you, Mr. Surratt," I heard a distinctly feminine voice add. I turned, and saw Miss Ravenel walking toward me from the balcony doors. She drew the folds of her blue wrapper closer to her nightgown. Her rich auburn hair hung loose to her shoulders in a way that further took my breath away. "John had asked me if he could use my sitting room tonight to meet with some friends. I was awakened by voices in the other room. You men are certainly keeping late hours."

My fear turned to relief, but almost immediately my mind was full of questions. How unlike it was of Booth not to have warned me that I was entering a lady's bedroom unannounced. Had Booth arranged this meeting as a "gift" for my having done so well on the rides into Virginia? But I quickly dismissed this possibility from my mind— Booth was no more a panderer than I was, I convinced myself. Certainly his oversight was due to the brandy he had consumed this evening.

"I apologize for this intrusion," I said. I attempted to say more, but I could not find the words. I suddenly felt very foolish standing in front of her with the bottle of whiskey in my hand.

"There is no need for us to apologize to one another," Miss Ravenel said calmly, and advanced toward me. Although her voice was devoid of a Southern accent, it was a voice I felt I had heard at some unremembered time in my past, as much a part of myself as a part of her. She did not seem surprised by my presence. "John has told me of your bravely volunteering to escort me through the Union lines. I would gladly meet with you under any circumstances, Mr. Surratt. Nor should I apologize to you. There have been many changes for the better in my life since we last have seen one another."

Miss Ravenel raised her head in front of me as she made this statement, but she could not quite conceal the tilt of her face toward the standing mirror next to us, as if to assure herself that she was presenting at least a modest appearance in her dishabille. Her features were very delicate in profile, and with her auburn hair and her long, pale neck she reminded me of the ethereal female models favored by the painters in England. Her eyes were bluer than any I had ever seen before.

At this moment, I realized that I was again looking at her reflection in the mirror, as I had in the bar when I first set eyes upon her. Embarrassed by the memory and the circumstances of our first meeting, I turned aside. "John Wilkes Booth is a good friend," I said, speaking somewhat clumsily, as if to convince both her and myself.

"He is mine also," Miss Ravenel said fervently. She gazed into my eyes with almost unseemly intensity. "John, and you, Mr. Surratt, are the ones responsible for the changes in my situation in life. After I first saw you at that horrid concert hall, John came back and insisted that I leave there immediately. He has arranged for me to stay at these rooms alone and under my true name until you, Mr. Surratt, can take me southward to his friends."

I considered that Miss Ravenel referred to Booth by only his first name. Despite his charity to her, it reassured me to know she was simply one of many he had helped in life. The sound of the men's voices, arguing again, became audible through the door behind me. I found that the darkened walls of the small room seemed to sway on either side of me, like the interior of a hansom cab on a rough ride. For no reason, I thought of Weichman's ridiculous joke of two weeks ago inside the carriage on the way to the theatre: *One John, two Johns, three Johns.* Was I just another John?

"I will be glad to help you any way I can," I said, with more feeling than I could express. I put down the bottle behind me and steadied myself against the closed portmanteau. "A gentleman never inquires into a lady's past." I made this last statement as the type of worldly remark that I imagined Booth might say in this situation. But it had the reverse effect to the one I had intended.

Miss Ravenel abruptly turned her face from mine, bringing her hands to her face. I sensed I had made a mistake. "I will admit that there is much in my past, Mr. Surratt, that is not admirable. And a *gentleman* such as yourself is under no obligation to interest himself in the fate of a woman such as I. But perhaps any other woman whom you might know, Mr. Surratt, and who found herself in my situation, may not have acted as well as I."

She looked at me again with tearstained

eyes. "At the beginning of the war, I found myself stranded in Washington City, unable to return South and bereft of all family and friends. John was my only acquaintance among all these strangers, and he often was away on his theatrical travels. Because of my prior residence at Richmond, I came under the suspicion of the provost marshal's office; and legitimate theatre owners, out of fear of association with me, began to refuse me all employment.

"I am certain that rumors of my disloyalty were deliberately spread by rivals of mine on the stage, who wished to eliminate me from the theatre. Of course, I could have written John asking for financial help, but he already had been so kind to me. I believe that he, too, has suffered professionally from malicious rumors spread by these people."

Miss Ravenel spoke to me more frankly than any other woman of my experience. I was acutely aware that we were standing in a darkened hotel bedroom. "So I took an assumed name and did what was necessary to survive," she said. "But even in my fallen state, I still dreaded that some enemy of mine would recognize me and I would suddenly be arrested by the provost marshal's men, or the Secret Service agents. I used to have dreams of my being cast into chains and locked inside some dark room from which I could not escape."

She raised her arm and turned it to indicate the unmade bed behind her. "I was having such a dream tonight when I was awakened by the men's voices in the other room. I stepped out onto the balcony to look at that evil building across the street, and to reassure myself that those cruel men there were not coming for me."

"Stanton's goddamned little bell," I said. I myself have had such dreams since my association with Booth. I thought of her standing on the balcony, her body exposed and vulnerable, as I had entered the room.

"Miss Ravenel, I shall help you travel to Richmond and to find a new life there," I said. I felt as if I stood on a stage, and remembered Booth's comment about the theatre. "There is always the possibility of rebirth," I heard myself say.

From the closed door behind me, I heard more loud arguing and recognized the voice of the man on the sofa querulously asking why I was taking so long with the whiskey. Booth's voice was not among them.

"Do you believe what you say, Mr. Surratt, do you truly believe that?" Miss Ravenel stepped closer to me and took both my hands into hers. As her hands touched mine, the blood rushed to my head, and all doubts and fears fled like shadows before a bright light. "For if you truly believe what you say, then I am certain that you are a good man, John Surratt. You are as good, or a better man, than is John Wilkes Booth."

And I did believe it, in a way.

I had never before kissed a woman in passion. As her face drew closer to mine, I cupped her cheek in my hand. As our lips touched, there was a delicate scent which I could not recognize among the fallen locks of her hair, one that I would never forget. I buried my face deep into the auburn luxuriance of her hair, until she finally turned her head from mine and rested it against my chest.

The voices from the door behind me grew louder. I released her with a start, and turned to pick up the bottle I'd been sent to retrieve. As I began to apologize for leaving her so abruptly, Miss Ravenel only brought one finger to her lips in an admonition to remain silent, smiled, and stepped back into the shadows of the room.

I opened the door and rejoined the men. Booth glanced at me briefly as I made my way to the sideboard.

5.

April 18, Tuesday, 1916

"My name is John H. Surratt. I am the last surviving member of the alleged conspiracy to murder Abraham Lincoln."

I repeat to myself these words in time to the turning wheels of the trolley car beneath me, carrying me and the other passengers down Pennsylvania Avenue. I had decided to forgo walking the few blocks from the Willard to my appointment at Griffith's hotel, as my fever and coughing had increased. As I looked out the glass window beside my seat at the passing Washington traffic, the images moved as rapidly across the flat surface in front of me as in one of D. W. Griffith's motion pictures. Was life always this way, I thought, passing before me in a blur?

The events leading up to Lincoln's assassination had unfolded in my mind's eye with the almost painful slowness of a train wreck, unforeseen yet inevitable.

The lobby of Griffith's hotel was an expanse of potted ferns and expensive leather chairs that made even the comfortable appointments of the Willard look spartan by comparison. I asked at the front desk for Griffith's suite and was irritated that the porter assigned a bellboy to accompany me upstairs. I wasn't feeling that bad and I didn't need help. The boy knocked several times at what I assumed was the suite door on the fifth floor. I heard Bitzer's voice answer. "Keep your shirt on," he said. "It's unlocked."

I dismissed the boy without a tip and stepped inside. My first impression was a sitting room filled with innumerable telephones and thick with telephone wires on the carpeted floor. A large, detailed map of the western front was mounted on a collapsible wooden stand in one corner, and at the center of the room was a massive card table supporting what appeared to be a model in miniature of an ancient Babylonian city.

Bitzer was seated above all this confusion, very precariously to my eyes, on an open windowsill at the far end of the room. Coatless in a blue-striped silk shirt with a straw hat pushed far back on his head, he was, of course, smoking. He looked like a well-dressed gargoyle contemplating throwing his cigar down at the heads of the passersby below. "D.W. is changing *clothes,*" he said, and twisted his head significantly toward a bedroom door to my right. Bitzer seemed to be in a particularly bad humor.

"Mr. Surratt!" The bedroom door swung open and D. W. Griffith advanced toward me, smiling and spreading his arms generously out from his sides. Griffith was extraordinary in appearance even for him. He had cut his hair extremely short and had affected wearing a long military cape, such as are worn by officers in the European war. He brought his hand up to grasp my right hand. "I'm so glad you decided to take Mae and Billy's advice," he said.

I returned his greeting. I saw no sign of Miss Marsh, but I had an impression that this suite of rooms continued well beyond the closed bedroom door.

"Mr. Surratt, I feel we've come to our understanding just at the nick of time," Griffith said, and gave a slight nod toward Bitzer. Bitzer swung his legs off the windowsill, covered the table of miniature ziggurats with what appeared to be a piece of stage drop cloth, and began to disassemble the wooden stand and map. Only then did Griffith release my hand, reaching inside his cape.

"Tomorrow we do not intend to offer a matinee of *Birth of a Nation*."

He briskly removed a sheaf of folded papers from inside his cape. "But with the theatre closed to the public tomorrow afternoon, I see it as our pluperfect opportunity to shoot and record you on the Gramophone." Griffith placed what I realized was a contract into my hands.

I stared at the papers. I realized that Griffith was deliberately manipulating me to suit his own cinematic prospects. I was but a pawn in his plans, albeit a valuable one. "I'm not at all certain that I can provide the sort of history you want," I told him. "I've never acted in front of a camera."

"Nonsense," Griffith said. "You merely have to do what all our theatrical troupe does, which is only to speak and act truthfully. You'll be in good hands, Mr. Surratt, with Billy behind the camera. And of course Miss Marsh and I also will be at the theatre tomorrow to make certain that all goes well." Griffith reached again inside his cape and withdrew a Waterford fountain pen. "I think you'll find our terms very generous and remunerative."

I unfolded the contract and briefly read its terms. I was to give up all rights to my "photographic likeness, commercial reproduction, or other graphical representation of identity" for a period of three years to the Majestic Motion Picture Company. In addition, I was to make myself available during this period for "the use of any and all personal reminiscences, private mementos, keepsakes, photographic souvenirs, and of any other private knowledge, written or otherwise, of the years 1861–1865." I was, in essence, to give up all rights to myself, and Griffith would use my words, my reflections, as he chose. I looked at the sum of money promised me on the last page, payable upon "acceptable delivery of Mr. Surratt's services as herein described." Griffith had been true to his word as to the payment. I was to be paid more than I had earned during all my decades as a shipping agent. It was even more money than had been offered for my capture after the murder of Lincoln.

I always had assumed that I would make a full confession to a priest at some time before the end of my life. It occurred to me now that this contract may be the only confession of which I am capable. But I still couldn't bring myself to sign the deed. "I must look it over carefully in my hotel room," I said, putting it off. "Why don't I drop it by tomorrow when I come for the shooting?"

"Capital," Griffith said, and shook my left hand. There was a distinct metallic click as he replaced the cap upon his fountain pen. "Well, will one o'clock tomorrow suit you for the shooting, Mr. Surratt?" Griffith seemed to be eager to end our meeting now that our business, for the moment, was concluded.

"I only hope I can give you what you want," I said as a fit of coughing overtook me.

Griffith shook his head good-naturedly and incredulously, as if dismissing my concerns. "Mr. Surratt, as Billy likes to say, Is the pope Catholic?" He straightened the folds of his military cape over his chest. "Or more appropriately, did Grant capture Richmond? I have no doubt whatsoever about your success tomorrow in front of our motion picture camera."

6.

Testimony by Louis Weichman at the trail of Mary Surratt, 1865, on the kidnapping events of March 17, Tuesday, 1865

I returned from my office one day at half-past 4 o'clock. On going down to dinner, I found Mrs. Surratt in the passage. She was weeping bitterly, and I endeavored to console her. She said, "John is gone away; go down to dinner, and make the best you can of your dinner." After dinner, I went to my room, sat down, commenced reading, and about half-past 6 o'clock Surratt came in very much excited—in fact, rushed into the room. He had a revolver in his hand—one of Sharpe's revolvers, a four-barrelled revolver, a small one, you could carry it in your vest pocket.

He appeared to be very much excited. I said, "John, what is the matter; why are you so much excited?" He replied, "I will shoot any one that comes into this room; my prospect is gone, my hopes are blighted; I want something to do; can you get me a clerkship?" In about ten minutes after, the prisoner, Paine, came into the room. He was also very much excited, and I noticed he had a pistol. About fifteen minutes afterward, Booth came into the room, and Booth was so excited that he walked around the room three or four times very frantically, and did not notice me. He had a whip in his hand. I spoke to him and, recognizing me, he said, 'I did not see you.' "

March 17, 1865

What folly, and what a fool to follow John Wilkes Booth! He is, after all, only an actor, if a famous one—he can accomplish nothing in the real world! I am aware of the bitterness with which I now pen these lines in my diary, unobserved for the moment from Weichman's prying eyes in our boarding house, but I cannot restrain my anger at Booth's rashness, or at his thoughtlessness. He momentarily exposed me to arrest by federal authorities, and may have endangered my future employment at Gardner's. What is perhaps most unforgivable to me, he has endangered my mother and sister; mother, sensitive to my inconcealable agitation this afternoon, broke out in tears. Booth has reduced my life to comical farce, and a low bumbling comedy.

I have written before of Booth's chimerical dreams—his insane dreams—to kidnap Abraham Lincoln, and to exchange Lincoln for the release of Confederate prisoners languishing in Union prisons. Not only had Booth proceeded with his plans, he has tried to drag me now into this incredible madness, as well. Booth had sent word to me this morning that now was the time to act, and that in the name of our friendship, I must come to him immediately. Booth had heard a rumor among his theatrical friends that the president was expected that afternoon at the Soldiers' Home, an asylum for maimed and invalided Union soldiers located a few miles north of Washington City, to attend a theatrical production of *Still Waters Run Deep.* Booth dispatched Davy Herold toward Surrattsville, to prepare his escape route over the Rappahannock and Potomac Rivers. He begged that I give an implausible excuse to Gardner and set off to meet with him. What he wanted of me I hadn't surmised. As it turned out, he had intended me to accompany him, along with the irrascible Samuel Arnold, and Lewis Powell to ride to a tavern a few miles below the Soldiers' Home, with the intention of intercepting the presidential carriage. I was horrified. It was one thing to help Booth save his life—it was very much another to be involved in the plot to abduct President Lincoln myself. But Arnold, brandishing a gun, made it clear that he would brook no backing out by now, and insisted that I take a revolver, too. My thoughts were in a turmoil. Fortunately, Lincoln and his party never appeared.

We waited for an hour or more. Booth finally rode his horse toward the Soldiers' Home, and inquired of an actor friend of his about the president's arrival. Booth later told us of the exchange.

"Hello, Ned. How is the house today? And is old man Lincoln expected here?"

"Why, no, Wilkes, Mr. Lincoln decided to stay back at the Executive Mansion, and present a flag to a distinguished Indiana regiment."

Booth had acted upon a false rumor, and had made false actors of us all. Furiously disappointed, he had us retreat ignominiously back toward Washington City, and my mother's boarding house. I was frankly relieved that the plan fell through the way it did—never in my wildest dreams had I imagined getting involved in something as dangerous, as treasonous, as this. I was certain that federal officers or the secret agents would come pounding on our boarding house door any moment. Even now, hours later, I remain furious at Booth. If he can so indiscriminately mix up the day of Lincoln's appearance, how can the others trust him to accurately take care of any of the myriad other details of his plan? I fear he is a loose cannon, and sure to get me killed—and over something about which I am utterly disagreed with him on. Why did I ever think Booth was my friend? How can I now disassociate myself from him?

7.

April 3–4, 1865

I carefully brushed wet shellac over the face of a smug Union colonel, his image chemically reproduced on the albumin photographic paper under my hands. All afternoon I have been printing positives on paper from the glass negatives which Mr. Gardner had exposed. Fifty or more positive paper prints now are hanging to dry from the ceiling joists of the studio attic above me.

To make each of these individual prints, I first had placed a sheet of photographic paper into a wooden frame with the glass negative atop it. Then I had briefly stepped out onto the roof of the building and exposed the negative and the paper underneath it to the fire of the sun. The light-sensitive element coating this paper is albumin, taken from broken eggshells, and more than once this afternoon, I have considered how many unhatched beings must give up their lives in order to produce these portraits around me. As a final touch, I have coated each positive print with shellac, as in the case of the Union colonel, to protect the fragile emulsion on paper. Tomorrow morning I will paste the backs of the prints to pieces of cardboard, or mount them in studio albums, and the photographic likenesses will be ready for sale.

The colonel, and my afternoon's work, were at last finished. I stood as upright as possible in the cramped darkroom attic and allowed myself to stretch my limbs. Mr. Gardner's business has shown no signs of slacking since the war has begun to, thank God, reach its end. Everyone knows that Lee cannot withstand Grant's advance on Richmond, nor can Lee possibly retreat and unite his forces with the other Confederate armies in the western theatre. In the Deep South, Sherman last year completed his terrible burning of Atlanta and his march to the sea, and even now is rapidly moving his federal armies through the Carolinas in order to join with Grant's forces at Virginia in crushing poor General Lee. It is just a matter of one more battle, perhaps two or three at the most. The indications are everywhere. Last month the *New York Times* printed its annual report, "The Dead of 1864," containing the names of all Union officers killed the previous year. The necrology report occupied less than two full newspaper pages, even fewer names than the accompanying printed columns of unclaimed letters at the city post office. The numbers of Union dead were decidedly on the decline.

I finished stretching my muscles with some satisfaction. It was almost five o'clock. When peace finally comes, Booth may be correct in predicting a prosperous future for me in the field of photography. As if in evidence of my skill, I looked at my fingertips, blackened daily by silver iodine from my work in the darkroom. The stains were much more indelible than the ink I use in writing my diary.

I repressed a slight shudder, recalling what I had written in my diary last month of Booth's farcical plans to kidnap President Lincoln. Thank God, the federal agents seem not to have gotten wind of our bumbling attempt. Gardner, despite a few days of sharp words and retorts directed at me, seemed to have accepted my excuse that an urgent personal affair had forced me to leave his studio early that day. I fervently hope that I have closed that chapter in my life, and in my journal.

I have in fact written little in my diary for the past three months. It is curious how much Booth's presence or absence determines the writing in my own diary. I am disturbed by this influence upon me. I consider how on some days I find myself dressing like him, affecting his neat manner of appearance and his way of using a formal black suit to distance himself from the world. Booth seems to have given up on his mad plans to kidnap the president and, as he had asked, I have collected names and possible routes for his escape to the south; but I am determined that with the return of peace I will back away from Booth, and turn once again to my own hopes, my own future.

Still, I cannot help but be troubled that Booth has not attempted to contact me, or even to thank me for my assistance. Perhaps with the imminence of peace, Booth has given up his plans to "go on his travels," as he expressed it. Perhaps Booth and Miss Ravenel, like myself and practically everyone else, have become bored by the war.

"Johnny! Johnny!" There was a high-pitched urgency to Gardner's voice as he clumped up the darkroom steps. Gardner thrust his head into the darkroom. There was a lurid, reddish glow reflecting off his face and ginger whiskers, but it was only the light from the darkroom's safety lamp. Gardner smiled with a broad expanse of exposed teeth.

"Why, the ball has begun, Johnny! The ball has begun!"

My own face must have shown incomprehension, for Gardner's features immediately twisted into an expression of vexation. "Well, don't just stare at me like a dumbstruck calf! Don't you understand, man? Grant has today just broken through the Petersburg lines! Our forces are at this moment advancing on Richmond!" Gardner advanced a step into the darkroom and took a deep, calming breath, but his eyes were full of a wild excitement. "The news was just received at the War Department by military telegraph," he said. "Now forget all this"—he waved his hands above us at my afternoon's work hanging from the ceiling—"and take what we'll need for the rolling darkroom. We can be at the front lines by morning."

The rolling darkroom was the horse-drawn wagon which Gardner had outfitted for developing and fixing his photographic plates outside the studio, and it was responsible for his reputation as the photographer "on the scene" at earlier battles. My employer already turned to run down the stairs. "I'll get the horses at the livery around the corner," Gardner shouted back to me. "We'll meet in the alley. And for God's sake, John Surratt, don't forget anything, as your life depends upon it."

I will admit that I felt my own heart beat considerably faster as I rapidly collected stacks of glass plates and vials of chemicals. It would be my first opportunity to work inside Gardner's rolling darkroom and perhaps to add to my own reputation as an epochal photographer of historic scenes.

Gardner had harnessed two horses and was standing beside his wagon when I rejoined him in the alley. The "rolling darkroom" deserved its cognomen. The sides of this wagon were far taller than wide, and it resembled a vertically slatted room detached from a house and precariously balanced upon four wheels. The structure included a roof, two open windows, heavy yellow curtains, and a set of back-door steps. A. GARDNER, PHOTOGRAPHER was painted on both sides.

Gardner was speaking in a low voice with two men standing in the alley beside the wagon. I recognized the ubiquitous E. J. Allen and his ruffian companion. Gardner motioned his companions to be silent and beckoned to me over their heads with his other hand. "Hurry, John, hurry, and help me put these things away."

Gardner had brought a jumble of his own photographic equipment and supplies, including a camera with a collapsible tripod, and I handed them up as he stood inside the wagon. A piece of canvas over the last item partially slipped away from my hand as I lifted it upward, and I found myself holding an item which seemed much more suitable for a curio cabinet than a photographic studio—an Enfield rifle, rendered useless by a bullet which had shattered the firing pin and traveled the length of the weapon. The bullet had cut a deep groove into the wooden stock of the piece, and it occurred to me that whoever had been holding this weapon at the moment of impact must have been very seriously injured.

Gardner gave me a significant look, and reconcealed the weapon under a roll of canvas on the wagon floor. It was time for us to be off. Gardner backed down the wagon steps, carefully locked the darkroom door, and turned to face us. Then, with great earnestness and an apparent sincerity, Gardner suddenly struck a Napoleonic pose in the alleyway, placing one hand inside his coat and extending the other to Allen and the pug-ugly. "Gentlemen, I am off to the front," he said. "God willing, we shall all meet one another on the great day of victory."

The three shook hands. They spoke a few inaudible words among themselves, before the two ruffians walked away down the alley. Gardner and I seated ourselves on a wooden bench behind the horses, and, with Mr. Gardner at the reins, we turned the rolling darkroom into the street.

Gardner kept up a low stream of muttered curses as we maneuvered amidst the late-afternoon traffic on Pennsylvania Avenue. We turned southward out of Washington City, in the opposite direction from the Navy Yard Bridge and my usual route into Maryland. Instead, Gardner steered the rolling darkroom toward the Long Bridge, the military's direct route of supplies over the Potomac River and into the Virginia war theatre. As we came into view of the bridge, Gardner's maledictions on the bench beside me now exploded into vociferous objections. Ahead of us on the final street was a confusion of mule-drawn ammunition wagons, two-horse ambulances, artillery caissons, and every other imaginable military vehicle. At this moment, a Union major rode up to the rolling darkroom, glanced at our military pass, and seemed to recognize Gardner. The major held up his hand to pause the other vehicles on the street and allow us to join into the line of traffic slowly moving across the river. The Potomac, forty feet or more below the bridge, looked roiled and muddy from spring freshets.

It took at least a quarter of an hour to cross the Long Bridge. The military vehicles ahead of us stretched in an unbroken succession across the wooden planks to the Virginia shore, and all traffic out of Washington City was restricted into one column to our right. I saw ahead two enormous signs nailed between the gatelike pylons at the center of the bridge: one, over the lane leading into Virginia, read NO PACE FASTER THAN A WALK. The other, hung so as to face the lane of soldiers and civilians returning from the battlefields, read NO SOUVENIRS. I thought of how rapidly the war was shrinking into an historical irrelevance. Already the relic-hunters, scavengers, and little boys were returning to its battlefields to collect the war, sell it, trivialize it. We Americans have no real need for history: we spit it out like a cherry pit. Would our descendants in the next century stand like tourists above the hills of the famous Civil War battles, ignoring the ghostly screams of the past from the valleys below?

Gardner had turned the rolling darkroom to the cleared side of the main road as soon as we had reached the wooded Virginia shore, and he was now intently studying a large, unfolded military map. I knew better than to test his patience by asking how he had obtained such a map, just as I had known better than to question how he had so quickly learned the news of the military telegram of the Union offensive.

Gardner flicked the reins, and, leaving behind the military caravan, we traveled for the next three hours down obscure country lanes and barely discernible military trails. We did not meet with another vehicle. The rolling, expensive farmlands of Virginia appeared surprisingly untroubled and peaceful despite the proximity of war. We stopped once at nine o'clock by my pocket watch to rest the horses and share a supper of cold oyster loaf and sparkling cider, which Gardner providentially had brought with him in a wicker basket. Gardner spoke to me few times during our meal, only one or two blunt interlocutions to confirm I had brought the necessary chemicals.

I was jolted awake once, after midnight, by a violent crashing above in the night heavens. I realized I had fallen asleep, and Gardner had driven the rolling darkroom onward for several hours. *Thunder,* I thought, and considered how frequently dramatic rainstorms had followed all the major battles of the war. Then, fully awakening, I realized the sound was artillery firing somewhere ahead of our wagon. For the first time, I considered the physical danger of traveling in a war theatre. I looked in the dim starlight toward Gardner, who only snapped the reins and, with his eyes fixed determinately ahead, urged the horses onward. Despite myself, after a few moments I fell back asleep.

I awoke at dawn to a wasteland, a blasted plain devoid of trees, littered with the debris of war. I was alone on the wagon. The horses had been unhitched and were hobbled a few paces away, trying unsuccessfully to crop at the trampled and muddy grass. A dirty, inconsequential stream meandered near the wagon, and was the only relief in this featureless landscape. I climbed down stiffly from the rolling darkroom.

I called out to Gardner, "Where are we?"

"Why, at the front, Johnny, at the front lines." Gardner's voice came from behind the wagon; he was urinating in the open field. He turned and smiled. "Where else would we be?"

I again looked at the field around me. What I had first assumed was a muddy stream I now realized had been a man-made trench for troops, either filled by the spring rains or deliberately flooded by the opposing army. Artillery shell fragments lay scattered in the grass. Scraps of boot leather or fabric were visible here and there, and, as the sun began to warm the air, there was an unmistakable stench of gunpowder, excretion, and death.

"My God, soldiers actually *lived* in these trenches?"

"Aye, Johnny, and for the last six months or so died here, too." Gardner walked toward me, unceremoniously buttoning the fly on his trousers. My employer's natural excitability seemed to have returned now that we were actually present on the battle-field. He handed me a pair of field glasses and pointed toward a far hill. I was able to make out clumps of blue-uniformed figures lying along the crest, and what seemed to be white dots scattered around them.

"We'll leave the horses here to rest. They may not care for what we'll find on that hill," Gardner said. "There's no sense in our car-rying any equipment until we can more closely see what's up there." Gardner had already started toward the hill, when he real-ized he had left me behind and turned and cried out irritably, "Well, are you coming along, John Surratt?"

My heart was racing as Gardner and I ad-vanced up the hill. I felt an excitement which I imagined was a pale shadow of what those distant Union soldiers must have felt when they charged up several days before. The grass was much thicker on the hill, and as the morning sun warmed the ground, grasshoppers jumped away at our bootfalls. What had appeared as white dots in the field glasses actually were dozens of sheets of paper, scattered some twenty feet or more below the top of the hill. I picked up several. Some were letters from home, some only sheets with individual names written on them. They apparently had been torn from the soldiers' uniform blouses by the violence of whatever had killed them.

"Oh, dear God." Most of the bodies lay at the very top of the hill, where the artillery barrage had caught them. There were roughly thirty or more mutilated forms in a company line. It was impossible to tell whether the artillery shells had fallen upon them from the front or from behind, but obviously the barrage had occurred just as the men had reached the exposed crest. The remains had been in the open at least two or three days. Few were recognizably human. I felt my legs begin to tremble under me, and I slowly sank to my knees. I spat weakly into the grass and tried hard not to vomit. "Oh, dear God," I repeated.

Gardner was walking along the line of bodies like a regimental sergeant on parade inspection. "Shaw! They are too far gone to be of use to us now." He spoke as if to himself. "Besides, they are fatalities of our side, and that never sells very well." Gardner looked down at one upturned soldier lying in the grass a few paces from the others. In the warm spring morning a cluster of yellow jackets had settled upon the face of this Union soldier, turning his features into a moving, golden mask.

For a brief, irrational moment, I wondered whether all the mutilated bodies on this hill beside me were not real. Were they, perhaps, only a malign artifice of my imagination? Gardner had removed his field glasses from his coat and was polishing the lens on his sleeve. I took another look at the bodies surrounding me. The dead were the dead, and this scene was altogether real.

Gardner was in an expansive mood. "Well, Johnny, so long as we've seized the high ground, in a military manner of speaking, we may as well take a survey around us." Gardner looked over the landscape before us, the field glasses glued to his eyes. Suddenly his body stiffened, and he uttered a blunt epithet. "Damn! Brady!" he exclaimed.

Gardner quickly turned and lifted me to my feet. He regarded me incredulously. "Damn it, man, this is no time to be praying!" He thrust the field glasses into my hands. About a quarter of a mile distant, I saw a photographic wagon similar to our own. Beside it was a short man in a full-length white duster looking nearsightedly at the battlefield in front of him.

"Quickly, Johnny, limber up the horses! We'll follow these damned entrenchments wherever they'll lead us." Gardner already was running down the hill, his coattails flying in the wind. "We must find *somebody,* and bring home the photographs." I ran blindly past the mute forms in the grass.

A quarter of an hour later, Gardner reined the horses to a stop beside an intimidating earthen berm. He had driven the rolling darkroom like a madman across the open landscape, but he had found what he wanted. Directly ahead of us and scattered behind this earthwork were a dozen or more dead Confederates, freshly killed, as if specifically to fill our request for photographic studies. "Excellent," Gardner said, and set the brake.

I was noticeably clumsy unloading the wagon, almost dropping the camera and tripod. Gardner cursed furiously. Seeing the bodies on the hilltop had impaired my coordination. Irritated, Gardner told me he would be responsible for preparing the wet plates and fixing the images. My job was to scout the area behind the berm and try to find other bodies to photograph.

"And please be more observant, Mr. Surratt, and do try to keep your head attached to your shoulders. There may still be a stray picket or sharpshooter about the neighborhood." As I left, Gardner was preparing to expose a half score of death studies.

The dead Confederates who had been the defenders of this earthwork had been overrun and killed to a man, and their bodies left where they had fallen. The figures in ragged gray uniforms were sprawled in shallow rifle pits, or concealed in a maze of deep, water-filled trenches behind the berm.

I cautiously slid down the muddy side of one entrenchment and advanced along the trench floor. Barely five feet wide, it had been dug so deeply that my head and shoulders were quite concealed from the surface of the ground. Mud and a layer of other filth at the bottom of the entrenchment made a sucking noise each time I withdrew my bootheels, a sound I knew would be audible to anyone ahead of me.

The trenchworks contained several offshoots and *culs-de-sac* hacked into the earthen sides. A plethora of paper sheets, regimental orders, and personal letters lay scattered across the bottom. It was clear to me that much of the past year Grant's and Lee's staff headquarters had been engaged in a lethal paper chase of enormous dimensions, as the war drew to its final moments.

Peering into one *cul-de-sac,* I started in fear upon encountering a dead soldier.

To my astonishment, the features appeared almost identical to those of the young Dutch-looking boy I had watched marching down Pennsylvania Avenue some four months earlier who had spilled orange pips down the front of his Union uniform. I glanced with trepidation at his sprawled body. He was dressed in a Confederate tunic and ragged, cotton trousers. How could this be? Had he been taken prisoner and temporarily gained his freedom by agreeing to fight for the opposing side? Or had some desperate Confederate soldier quickly stripped and exchanged uniforms with the corpse and so escaped with the victors? But on a more considered appraisal, I realized it was not the same youth—although they could have passed for brothers. A bullet hole in his head marred his otherwise peaceful features.

I heard a splash behind me in the mud; it was Gardner, walking up the entrenchment, carefully gathering and sorting the paper sheets around us. He elbowed past me to look inside the *cul-de-sac.* He, too, did not speak for several moments. When he did, his tone was congratulatory.

"Johnny, you have redeemed yourself," he said. He energetically patted my shoulder. "You have found absolutely the finest death study we could have wished for. Look at it, it's all there—the peaceful, almost angelic pose, the obviously mortal wound in the head, and the pathos of his youth. And there is the fact that he is the enemy." Gardner smiled at me. "I *want* this photograph."

He gave a worried look at the high banks of the entrenchment on either side of us.

"But, damn his luck, he *would* be shot in a place of perpetual shadow. Necessity is the mother of invention, John Surratt. I've a nice sunny spot near the wagon." Gardner began to roll up his shirt linen and coat sleeves, and he looked at me expectantly. "Well?"

I was shocked into speech. "Surely, Mr. Gardner, you are not proposing that we disturb this body?"

"And why not?" Gardner demanded, his sleeves fully rolled. "Brady and I frequently did the same, and much more, when we worked together. So do all war photographers when the light or some other condition is not usable." Gardner looked at me patiently, as if explaining facts to a child. "He'll still be *dead,* John, and I'll certainly arrange him in the same posture as I found him. That's the whole point." Gardner placed his hands underneath the dead man's armpits. "You can take him by his boots, and I'll take the business end, since you're so dainty."

I cannot fully describe the horrors I felt at lifting the dead boy out of the trench and moving his body across the battlefield. Knowing our reason for disturbing the body

313

made me feel a fraud. I felt my hands were contaminated. Gardner, despite our work, kept up a good humor and perhaps tried to increase mine. At one point, as we neared the rolling darkroom, he grinned, saying, "Well, Johnny, perhaps Monsieur Daoud is right. Photography *can* raise the dead."

It dawned on me how much of my life—of all our lives—is mere acting and deception; illusion and shadow.

We eased the body into a shallow, sunlit rifle pit. Gardner composed the boy's limbs and head so that he did, in fact, closely resemble his original pose. The wound in his head, although deep, was not particularly disfiguring. I remembered a classmate at school who had been struck in the head by a thrown baseball with no more apparent injury than this dead soldier.

Gardner retrieved a prepared plate and the shattered rifle from inside the rolling darkroom. He adjusted the weapon lengthwise across the boy's body. "For a greater dramatic effect," he told me.

Gardner unaccountably hurried throughout the exposure, and used only a single prepared plate. As soon as the exposed glass was safely inside its lightproof box, he handed it to me. "Johnny, I think it's time you got some field experience," he said. "Take this inside the rolling darkroom and develop it. I've other work to do."

Despite my apprehension at what we had done, I felt curiously honored by Gardner's request. I was being entrusted with the preparation of the most commercially valuable photograph we had taken that day. I carefully held the boxed glass as I climbed the wagon steps.

The interior of the rolling darkroom was arranged similarly to my upstairs working quarters, although much more cramped. Enough light diffused through the heavily curtained windows to enable me to see the glass vials of chemicals and the developing and fixing trays strapped to the interior walls. I heard incessant beating of winged insects against the outside fabric of one curtain. They were probably yellow jackets, attracted to the rolling darkroom by the sweetish smell of the chemicals.

As soon as I had placed Gardner's exposed plate into the developing bath, I saw that my employer had made a serious mistake. Whether from his haste or his overestimating the intensity of the sunlight, Gardner had grossly underexposed the plate. The glass negative in my tray was rapidly becoming translucent; the image was almost lost. The plate would print as only a paper rectangle of impenetrable darkness.

I snatched the glass out of the developing fluid, as if to save the image of the young soldier from the very fate he had suffered in life. My fingers were trembling as I held the four corners of the glass negative, and I knew that if the glass slipped from my hands, the photographic image of the young soldier would be irretrievably gone. But, at this same time, the chemical decomposition of the glass negative was proceeding apace, even as I held it. I forced my hands, and the glass plate, quickly into the cold water of the washing bath.

I considered what next to do. The water temporarily had slowed the action of the chemicals, and the ghostly negative image of the soldier was just visible on the glass. Perhaps it was salvageable. While I still held the plate under the washing bath, I tried to make out in the dim interior of the rolling darkroom the labels of the chemical vials on the tray in front of me. Nitrate of silver, pyrogallic acid, salt of soda, chloride of gold.

The names became a frantic litany in my mind as I tried desperately to recall all that Gardner had told me about chemically strengthening an image. I alternately poured chemicals over the negative and then washed it under water.

Gradually, and then with more acceleration, the pale image of the boy on glass began to darken and to acquire depth. I smiled in the dim light. When the image is reproduced, I knew, I will have saved most, if not all, of the boy's features.

I washed the glass plate a final time with a fixing solution and water and then stepped outside the rolling darkroom. I blinked at the direct sunlight, and I batted with my hands at the empty air above my head. "It's done," I said.

Gardner was making notes in a small, pocket memoranda book from the papers he had collected on the battlefield. He replaced the book inside his coat. We both glanced at the young boy's body in the rifle pit. Gardner then quickly assumed a brisk manner. "John, I believe we've done the Union cause, and ourselves, a good turn today. Now it's time that we steal a march on

Brady and get these exposures back to Washington City."

On our return trip to the city, Gardner was garrulous, while I remained lost in my thoughts. At one point, Gardner offered me the remains of the oyster loaf, but I had no interest in eating. Seeing so many soldiers dead had brought home to me how senseless the killing was, whatever one's side. Were the disagreements between North and South worth all that bloodshed? In an attempt at conversation, I remarked on the torn blouses of the soldiers and the number of papers I had seen scattered about the battlefield. Was it, I asked, the work of the relic-hunters?

"Oh, no, Johnny," Gardner replied. "If their uniforms are not torn open by the fragments of artillery, the soldiers do it themselves after they are shot. They know as well as you what your tumbling minié ball can do to human flesh. It's their final gesture, after they've been knocked off their feet by a bullet and before they're removed from the scene. It's a dying hope to locate the wound and discover that it is not mortal."

Gardner gave me a sly glance. "The relic-hunters and scavengers know what will happen to them if they're caught in the act. The Union army is protective of its dead. Personal effects and papers can be of great military significance." He gave a flick to the reins. "Had you been caught today pilfering the corpse of a Union man, you would have been summarily hanged, and there would be very little I could have done for you."

I started to retort that the Enfield rifle in Gardner's wagon was evidence of the same offense, but I was too exhausted to argue.

We reached the Virginia side of the Long Bridge by late afternoon. The Union sergeant at the bridge, noticing the name on the side of the wagon, asked, "Any souvenirs, Mr. Gardner?"

"Only photographic ones," Gardner replied, and handed him a business card, should he ever have the need to have his portrait taken.

The traffic into Washington City was mercifully light. I wanted only to assist unloading the wagon and to return home and forget this day's work in a long sleep. Gardner remained in high spirits.

"You've done very well today, Johnny," Gardner said, as we disposed our equipment about the second-story studio. "I had my reasons to doubt you beforehand—you seemed a bit squeamish to me—but you behaved as well as any man at his first battlefield." I longed to be told I was excused from further duties. Gardner looked across the studio at the doorway to the attic darkroom. "My only regret is that I cannot give you tomorrow off, as we must get these plates printed and made available to the public before our Irish competition on the battlefield does the same. I'm certain that the portrait of that boy you found today will be, commercially speaking, a big seller."

Gardner then smiled generously at me, pleased with my work. "But as you appear tired, I'll excuse you a few hours early this afternoon."

I thanked him and immediately began to take my leave, but Gardner had begun now rummaging into a wooden cabinet jammed against one wall. "And as a further reward, there's something I'd like for you to see before you leave." He turned, holding a large photographic print in his hand.

I had a fair idea of the subject of this print. Gardner had been selected to photograph Lincoln's second inaugural ceremony the

previous month. I had, of course, heard all about the details from him: how the Capitol dome actually had been completed just in time, and how the rainy and blustery March day had threatened to spoil the outdoor inaugural festivities, until Mr. Lincoln had arisen from his chair to speak on the steps outside the Capitol and a ray of sunlight had appeared from the heavens to shine directly upon him. Curiously, Gardner had refused all offers of assistance that day, insisting that I remain at the studio and take appointments for the few, strayed clients. Nor had he, until now, volunteered to show me any of the photographic results.

Gardner handed me the print. I tried to feign interest. "It's excellently composed," I said automatically. In my mind there no longer seemed any connection, logically or sentiently, between the photographs of the public figures of the war and the scenes of the war itself I had witnessed this morning. Then I realized the photograph was fatally marred.

"Yes, excellently composed," Gardner said ironically. He ruefully shook his head. "Notice how I included not only the dignitaries centered around Mr. Lincoln but also the large crowd below him in front of the wooden barricade. I uncapped my lens, and my exposure captured Mr. Lincoln just as he arranged his papers before speaking at the lectern." Gardner thrust a stubby finger directly at Lincoln's head. "And then *this.*"

Gardner shook his head. "In my excitement at having taken such an extraordinary portrait, I showed this negative to a high-ranking member of our war administration, and the damned fool touched Lincoln's image in admiration. The emulsion was still wet. Before I could stop him, my exposure was ruined. It's now commercially useless."

I carefully examined the imperial-sized print in my hands. The president's figure was well delineated, but the thoughtless finger touch had permanently erased Lincoln's features, reducing his head to an indistinguishable and light-colored nimbus. "It's a great tragedy," I said slowly, my eyes widening in astonishment at seeing a familiar visage. "Otherwise, this would be a valuable historical document."

"Aye," Gardner said, and returned the flawed photographic print to its locked cabinet.

I quickly took my leave, and made my

way down the darkened studio staircase, exiting into the street. I was relieved to be out of the studio and able again to catch my breath. What I had not told Gardner was that among the images in the crowd in the photograph of Lincoln's second inaugural, I had to my alarm recognized the figures of Booth, Powell, Atzerodt, and Herold. The insanity of Booth's plans and the seriousness of his intentions came crashing in on me in a wave.

8.

April 4, Tuesday, 1865

As I walked agitatedly through a pedestrian stream of late-afternoon Washington City shoppers, I could sense several people staring at my uncombed beard and soiled clothes. I glanced down at the tips of my fingers blackened by silver nitrate, and I wondered if the odor of death on my hands was noticeable to the passersby.

I felt my heart begin to race within my chest, and the anger within me begin to rise at the complacency of the passing crowds. I wanted to shout into their uncomprehending faces, "Don't you know what is going on outside the city? How can you live your lives so obliviously?" I wanted to knock the top hats off the gentlemen, push the ladies in their beautiful crinoline dresses into the muddy gutters, take a large club and smash all the shop windows along the street.

As I turned the corner at 7th Street toward our boardinghouse, all I could think of was a hot bath and sleep. At the sight of a strange carriage parked in front of the house, I felt another rush of anger. Doubtless it belonged to another boarder come to inquire about the rates, to take up more space, and to delay my chance for a rest and wash. I approached the front steps, and was surprised by the sight of George Atzerodt walking out of the side yard carrying a spade over his shoulder.

Atzerodt mumbled some words about my mother having hired him this morning to turn a spring garden in our side yard. He appeared embarrassed at being caught performing honest labor. Mother must have come to know him from my use of his services in sending messages from the studio. "The lady's waiting in the parlor," he said.

The confusion showed in my face. "What lady, Mr. Atzerodt?"

He shifted his spade and projected a brown stream of tobacco juice into the ground at his feet. "Mr. Booth's lady."

As I entered the parlor, Sarah Ravenel rose from her chair. "John," she exclaimed. Drawing up her skirts, she advanced toward me. She was wearing a fashionable, light gray riding habit and a hat covered by a laced "mask," a style of veil which is considered very current. "Mr. Atzerodt and I were beginning to become concerned for you."

She offered me her hand, which I took. It was covered in a white, kid-skinned glove. I was acutely aware of my muddy clothes and my need of a bath. "Sarah, this is a most unexpected pleasure," I told her. "But what brings you here? Is that your carriage outside?"

Sarah raised her figured veil. "They are all gone on a holiday," she said, smiling. Her blue eyes looked at me with a quizzical interest. "As we thought you yourself had done, John. But please sit down with me. You look very tired."

I took a place on the sofa beside her,

acutely conscious of my mother's bedroom hidden by the screens behind us.

"Mr. Booth insisted that I take advantage of this spring day and enjoy a carriage excursion with him in the city," Miss Ravenel explained. She looked directly at me. "I thought it best to wear my veil in public. We had just turned onto H Street when Mr. Booth recognized Mr. Atzerodt. As they were talking, your mother came out of the house and joined us, appearing very distraught. Apparently she had just received a letter from her tenant at Surrattsville, claiming he was unable to pay the year's rent. I suspect she was also becoming worried about your absence.

"Mr. Booth insisted at once on accompanying your mother to Maryland in his carriage, and to help her come to terms with the tenant. One of your boarders, a very shy man named Mr. Weichman, then arrived for lunch. He seemed so pleased to see Mr. Booth again and insisted upon riding in the carriage with him and your mother. Your mother's spirits did seem to lift. Mr. Booth told her that 'we may as well make a group excursion out of this necessary trip,' and that 'we all deserve a holiday.' "

Miss Ravenel's features betrayed a genuine pleasure at reporting Booth's words. She looked at me kindly.

"It's *you* that we were most worried about, John. Mr. Booth rented the second carriage to wait outside pending your return. We are both to follow them to Maryland upon your arrival. Mr. Booth assured your mother that you were probably sleeping late at the photographic studio after a long night's work. Unfortunately," she went on, with a frown, "you have arrived too late for us to use the carriage."

Sarah playfully tapped my knee. "Have you been out on a debauch, John Surratt?"

My body ached from want of sleep, and, frankly, I was irritated at Booth's casual dismissal of me. As a result, I replied more sharply than I intended.

"Quite to the contrary. I have just returned from combat at the front lines. Mr. Gardner and I have spent all morning photographing the war dead."

"Oh my!" A spot of color appeared on Miss Ravenel's cheeks, and her hands flew to her face. "You must think me a very foolish woman. I apologize, Mr. Surratt. I am a very childish woman, indeed."

Sarah Ravenel regarded me with a new seriousness. Perhaps for the first time we regarded one another as equals.

"John, there is something I must ask you," she said. "I don't doubt your physical courage in volunteering to accompany me to Richmond. And I know that you offered to do so both out of admiration for Mr. Booth and affection for me. But there is still likely to be cruel fighting between the armies when we make our attempt southward, and you now understand what that can mean. I also have seen the war personally."

Miss Ravenel looked at me with concern. "John, I must know, do you agree to this thing of your own free will?"

"Yes, of course! I am honored to do so. I only wait for you to tell me when." I should have then seized Sarah's hands in mine, but I was too shy. In an effort to make light of the dangers I had committed myself to—and that we both faced—I glanced at the stack of novels on the parlor table.

"Perhaps after this war is over and when we are perfectly safe, I shall write of our adventures together and dedicate the book to you." I tried to put a smiling expression into my eyes. "A romance of our daring escape southward."

Miss Ravenel looked at me with a renewed interest. "Do you often write of your experiences?"

"Yes," I admitted reluctantly. "I began maintaining a sort of literary record of my life last year." I wanted greatly to free Sarah, and myself, from the drab lighting of the parlor room and rekindle her spirits to their previous level of animation. "Would you like to see the room where I write?"

"I would like that very much, John."

I held her waist lightly as I guided her up the stairs to the attic bedroom. Once again, I felt my heartbeat accelerating. I saw no evidence of Anna or of anyone else in the boardinghouse. Perhaps in my mother's absence they all had arranged to take their suppers elsewhere.

I feared I had made a mistake when I opened the door to the attic bedroom. Ahead were the two narrow beds, much more noticeable than my small writing desk, crammed into the space I shared with Weichman. I was embarrassed to see that he had left his bed linens tossed and unmade this morning. And I was suddenly

330

afraid that, in the close confines of these quarters, the condition of my clothing and my body might prove disagreeable.

Sarah spun slowly about in the small attic, her eyes taking in the details of my meager existence. She then slowly removed her hat and veil. The declining sunlight at the high window shone off her auburn hair. Noticing my pinched, anxious expression, she said, "I see, John, that you, too, have much you'd like to escape in your past."

As she spoke, Sarah lowered her arms to her sides, with her hands opened slightly outward, the same pose she had struck when I first saw her seminude upon the stage.

At the thought, I experienced a powerful surge of arousal that I felt in both mind and body. I had been completely taken by surprise, or perhaps I wouldn't have acted as impulsively as I did. Despite my physical fatigue, and despite all the horrors which I had seen this morning, I felt an irresistible urge to take Sarah in my arms, to cup the ripeness of her breasts in my hands. I have never before felt so physically male. Nor was it something I could hide from Sarah—my physical state was plainly evident.

I closed the door and embraced her. Miss Ravenel at first demurred, and I thought she was physically refusing me. I then saw that she was turning away only to remove the jacket of her riding habit and the corset underneath. I watched as the small of her back was exposed as she unlaced the delicate bone stays.

Almost before I could have thought it possible, Sarah shocked me by stepping naked out of her skirt and half-shift. "Take off your clothes, John," she said. I did as she requested, throwing my clothes about me. Moments later I drew her into my bed.

Because of my Catholic upbringing, I had little experience in carnal love. Even as I lost myself in the perfume of Sarah's embrace, my senses were heightened. I heard Atzerodt outside the open window spading the earth, and was keenly aware of the danger of the imminent arrival of the other boarders, as well as the unsubtle squeaking of the narrow iron bed frame beneath us. Unlike any woman of my imagination, Sarah moved vigorously and without restraint. As I caressed Sarah's naked body, I couldn't help but remember her upon the stage. Then, in the frenzy of the moment, all thoughts were gone, and I felt, rather than saw, a spreading heat from between Sarah's breasts. I held her tightly as she clasped me to her for a long moment, crying out, "John, John." Moments later I reached my own climax. As we lay in each other's arms, our passions banked, I found myself falling asleep.

I awoke startled sometime later. The glass panes at the window were darkening, and Sarah had turned up the gaslight in the room. "John, we must dress quickly and go down to the parlor before they come back," she said. I hurried into my trousers, and, looking about me, considered whether I had time to change the bed sheets before my mother, and Weichman, arrived back at the boardinghouse.

Looking down at the bedclothes, I was startled by the realization that Sarah and I—whom I had known only as Miss Ravenel until recently—had made love. And although I had suspected it, as I looked at our bedclothes in disarray, it was evident to me from the unstained sheets that Sarah had given up her innocence in a sexual encounter prior to our own.

Miss Ravenel seemed to guess my

thoughts. Standing fully clothed with her hand at the bedroom door, she said, "There has been enough blood."

9.

After leaving Griffith's suite, I had remained on the trolley car past the stop at my hotel, and walked the remaining two city blocks to our old house at H Street. The neighborhood has been greatly altered by recent immigration; our former boarding-house now operates, as Miss Marsh had observed, as a Chinese restaurant.

Except for the garish lights in the front windows, the exterior of the house was unchanged. The drab, red-brick walls faced H Street blankly as if, after half a century, there were no secrets to be revealed. Perhaps there are not. The side yard where George Atzerodt once had spaded my mother's spring garden was now a paved alleyway for automobiles. The dormer window set into the house's third story, where Sarah Ravenel and I made love, was indistinguishable from all other dormer windows along this street. There were once small, boxed trees in front of the steps; they have been removed to make way for wider sidewalks and a paved street.

I became aware passersby were walking irritably around where I stood unmoving on the sidewalk. To them I was an impediment, a foolish old man who cannot decide where to go. Finally I walked up the front steps to the building.

The name of the restaurant was spelled in a string of incandescent lights across what was once our parlor window. I did not open the front door, which has become heavily coated with black and red enamel and is cut with a square window. I saw inside that some of the interior walls have been removed and that the parlor area has become lost in a maze of white-clothed tables and wooden booths, filled with shirtsleeved patrons eating dishes of chop suey and lo mein. Fantastic paper lanterns hung from the ceiling. It reminded me of Griffith's motion picture theatres. I decided I would not go inside.

"I am truly sorry," I said, almost at tears, apologizing to a ghostly woman who is no longer alive. "I am truly sorry." How things fell apart in my life so quickly, so irrevocably. That afternoon with Sarah had been perhaps my last happy moment in this house.

I did not want to miss the next trolley car. Although the nearest stop was but two blocks away, I felt barely well enough to cover this distance, and certainly not well enough to go on foot for the remaining eight blocks to the Willard Hotel. The trip back to H Street has taken me a long way. I walked carefully down the steps of our old boardinghouse to the street, my thoughts still dwelling on the past.

10.

April 10, Monday, 1865

I took the steps two at a time down to the street, my mood lightened despite my being late for work. In the past week, there has been much news: Richmond has fallen, and the previous day, Lee surrendered his army to Grant at Appomattox Court House. Except for a few minor *dénouements* in the remote theatres, the war is effectively at an end—and so are my obligations to Booth.

An impromptu celebration started throughout Washington City upon receipt of the news, beginning last night with a thunderous cannonading celebrating the Union victory by the federal forts surrounding the city. Mother went to church to light a candle for Isaac, which she vows to do daily until his safe return. I joined in the general festivities in the street, and, as a consequence, overslept this morning.

I refused to hurry through my morning toilet, knowing Gardner would be just as angry at my being ten minutes late as he would be at an hour's tardiness. I selected my attire with care, and even took a razor and scissors to reshape my beard. *As well to be hung for a wolf as a sheep,* I thought.

I have not seen or spoken with Booth since his return to our house from Maryland the previous week. I greeted Booth warily that evening, concerned that my friend would intimate what had transpired between Sarah and me and that he would consider my action a personal betrayal. Booth, however, seemed to notice no change, although he did glance oddly for a moment at Sarah. He took me aside only to give me his pair of theatre glasses and to tell me "they may be called for again." Sarah greeted Booth as warmly as usual and thanked my mother for her hospitality. Mother seemed glad to be home again and relieved when they took their good-byes. I supposed the trip had been tiring to her.

Later, I learned the details of the Maryland trip from Weichman. Booth had insisted that my mother and Weichman remain in the carriage while he went inside and talked with my mother's tenant in Surrattsville. He then returned with a large sum of cash, totaling both the previous year's rent and the current year's, and gave it with a theatrical flair to my mother, explaining that he had successfully come to terms with the tenant. I couldn't help but suspect, however, that Booth gave her the money out of his own pocket. My friend has always been impulsively, if somewhat ostentatiously, generous. Still, my mother needed the money, and I had no reason to doubt the spontaneity of Booth's act. Nonetheless, I am not at all sure that I like the idea of Booth giving money to my mother, nor am I clear why he went to such great lengths. On the trip back, Weichman said Booth had impressed him and Mother by pointing out wildflowers by the side of the road by both their common and their botanical names. Within a few years, he predicted, such flowers will cover the Civil War battlefields.

Gardner's studio was now less than a block away. My progress up 7th Street had been impeded by the almost frantic gaiety of the pedestrians I encountered. I've never heard before so many salutations of "Good morning!" and "What a glorious day!" and so many courteous raisings of the hat from perfect strangers. Everyone is in an expansive mood now that the war is over.

I stopped on the sidewalk to consider my situation and to allow myself a few moments of calm before facing my employer's certain anger. In spite of Mr. Gardner's irascibilities, I have become confident of my skills as a photographer; our war pictures have been selling well, especially the portrait of the pathetic boy soldier I found on the battlefield. The time is coming when I should set up a photographic studio of my own. Mother would then be relieved of earning the family's income, and, as my own man, I would be able to visit Sarah more frequently. Dare I trust Booth to loan me the capital to make a start?

"John." I turned toward the alley from where my name had been called. I was shocked to see the figure of Booth standing in the alleyway. Never have I seen him in such a state. For the first time, I believed his confession to me last winter that his age was accelerating. The Booth I saw in the alleyway now appeared at least a decade older than when I saw him last week. Usually so neat in appearance, his black suit was diskept and muddy; his face dissolute. I had the impression that he had not slept for several days. He motioned to me to step into the alley away from the pedestrians on the sidewalk. As I came closer, I saw that he was unshaven, and smelled of brandy.

"Dear God, Wilkes, what has happened?"

Booth steadied himself, as if favoring one leg. He spoke with such difficulty I feared he had been physically attacked. "What has happened, John, is that I no longer have a place which I consider home."

It took me a few moments to realize that Booth was referring to the fall of the Confederacy. "No, Wilkes, you've got it all wrong." I placed my hand on his shoulder, and with a thrill of pride realized that our roles had been reversed, and that *I* was encouraging *him.* "It means an end to the killing, and we both wanted that. You need not now risk your life or career to put an end to the bloodletting. What you intended to do was very noble, Wilkes. But now your plans are unnecessary."

Booth's gaze seemed to wander, and I tightened my grip upon his shoulder. I was worried that my friend felt that he had been denied his one great action of the conflict, and would now give himself over to dissipation. I spoke in a voice I hoped would calm him. "And you *have* found a home, Wilkes. You will always have a home with me and my family." Even as I said this, something within me shrank. But I felt the necessity of avowing nothing less.

With a familiar and undeniably gentle motion, Booth removed my hand from his shoulder. Another man might have brusquely struck my hand away, and I remembered how courteous my friend was, even more so when he was intoxicated.

"It goes deeper than that, John," Booth said. He looked down at his own hands as if they had become useless to him. "I have reason to believe that my talk about capturing Lincoln has been betrayed by an informant. I'm expecting arrest any day."

Booth squared his shoulders and looked beyond me to the open end of the alley. "But I still have the courage to call for my mail, and I'll make one more memorable appearance before I flee southward, and thence to Europe."

At that moment I felt regret at ever having known Booth, or even being seen with him in this alleyway. Booth's arrest would mean the end of my commercial ambitions, or of any hopes for Sarah. I shifted legs anxiously. I was now seriously late for Gardner's.

Booth, as usual, intuited my thought. "Oh, you needn't worry, John. *You're* safely out of it. I have destroyed all documents that in any way implicate your name or that of your family. They can't hang you simply for being John Wilkes Booth's friend. Even, if I may be so bold, his best friend."

Booth's eyes searched my face carefully. "Miss Ravenel is my greatest concern, John. After this Union victory, I expect a terrible retribution upon people like her and me. She is known to have been sponsored by me in the theatre, and she has already been under suspicion by the provost marshal's office."

Booth leaned closer. I involuntarily flinched at his brandy-soaked breath, but his dark eyes held mine steadily. "That is why I need you, John. Trust me, there will be talk of hanging, but not for Sarah Ravenel if you will play your part. I've arranged a carriage this morning at the Willard Hotel. It awaits only for you to claim it and to carry Miss Ravenel southward."

My thoughts froze in panic. Surely Booth couldn't be serious, now that the war was over. And I could not help but visualize my employer's increasing ire at my absence. "Wilkes, don't be melodramatic," I said. "All that you, Miss Ravenel, and I need do is to remain in Washington City and enjoy the peace. I can't imagine the government being concerned about a former actress or her friends. And you're too famous, too beloved, to risk arresting."

Booth took a step backward, as if my words had been a lead bullet fired into his chest. "A former actress? John, I asked you once to save a woman's life, an actress's. A beautiful young woman whose life had already endured enough pain. It did not seem to you then to be melodramatic."

My face reddened at his rebuke. Most of all, I wanted this conversation to be over, to gain some time to formulate my thoughts. Booth then committed something of a miscue of character, as the spirits he had so obviously consumed now claimed him. He stepped forward clumsily and embraced me at the shoulders.

"John, I will soon be gone, and so will Miss Ravenel, with or without you." His words seemed full of pathos. He drew his face close to mine. "If you can take Miss Ravenel to my friends southward, and if I can escape arrest, I promise to send a coded telegram to your house. You may, if you wish, join with her and me in leaving this damned country."

For the first time in our acquaintance, I experienced John Wilkes Booth as physically repellent. I noticed how his addiction to cigars had permanently stained his teeth brown, and, in the closeness of his embrace upon my shoulders, he stank of sour sweat and brandy.

Nonetheless, I couldn't put Sarah out of my thoughts. It was Sarah whose image propelled me forward. Perhaps, if I obliged her by escorting her to Richmond, I could convince her to come back with me as my betrothed, if after a few days she realized her flight was unnecessary, and that Booth's fears were groundless. If I were to leave on such short notice, I knew I would lose my employment with Mr. Gardner. But my association with him, in any case, was coming to a close. It was time to strike out on my own.

"Very well, Wilkes, I'll do it."

Booth embraced and thanked me effusively. He produced from inside his coat a surprising amount of cash, especially for someone who had been on a debauch, insisting that I take it for expenses. My commitment sealed, we said our farewells, and I turned to go.

"John." Booth called once more from the alley. He walked toward me very steadily, no longer favoring his good leg. "It occurs to me you'll need to protect Sarah along your trip. I'd feel much better if you'll take this."

He handed me an expensive-looking brass derringer. Booth appeared suddenly clearheaded and sober. I was astonished at his transformation. But I was given no time to reflect further. "It's capped and fully loaded. All you have to do is pull back the hammer and squeeze the trigger."

Perhaps he thought I hesitated to take it because of the cost of the weapon, or because it left him defenseless. "It's quite all right, John." Booth smiled. "I have another."

An empty carriage was waiting at the curb outside Gardner's studio, with two Union cavalrymen nearby. At the top of the stairs, I was surprised to find another Union soldier and also the obnoxious pug-ugly who enjoyed fisticuffs. I was apparently betraying some nervousness at my reception from my employer, and he grinned at my discomfort. The pug-ugly then nodded to the soldier, who stepped aside. With the weight of Booth's derringer swinging heavily inside my coat pocket, I opened the studio door and drew in my breath sharply. President Abraham Lincoln was standing at the center of the studio floor, rubbing the back of his neck. Apparently his photograph had been taken and the president had just been released from Gardner's headrest. My heart raced—the object of Booth's crazed plan to end the war stood impossibly before me.

Gardner approached me from behind the tripod, a look of black fury upon his face. He carried a lightproof box containing the exposed plate of the president in his hands.

"Ah, at last, my second honored guest of the morning." Gardner, smiling at me grimly as he approached, showed more teeth than courtesy. "Mr. President, may I present to you my sometimes assistant, Mr. John H. Surratt?"

The president and I shook hands. He was not quite as tall as the newspapers exaggerated him to be, but his arms and legs were unusually long, and the grip of his hand was extraordinarily strong. The fabric of his suit was stiff and uncreased, and apparently had been purchased just for this photographic portrait.

Mr. Lincoln's eyes revealed amusement. "I believe we have met before, Mr. Surratt," he smiled.

I bowed, flushing furiously. Although we had not, my involvement in Booth's plans almost made me feel as though I had. "I am certain that I have never before had this honor, Mr. President."

Mr. Lincoln continued to rub the back of his neck with a wryly painful expression. "Oh, I seldom forget a face, Mr. Surratt. It only seems fair, since my own features are so often charitably termed unforgettable. Are you quite certain we have not met before?"

I again assured the president that we had not previously met.

Mr. Lincoln seemed genuinely puzzled. He cocked his head to one side of his tall frame, as if mentally taking my measure. "Perhaps I knew your father," he mused.

I was finding this presidential attention uncomfortable. I looked to Gardner for assistance, and discovered him gripping the light-safe metal box so intently his knuckles had whitened. I hoped there would be no verbal explosion.

"Mr. President, Mr. Surratt is a very foolish young man with no sense of time," Gardner said, walking adroitly between the president and me and shaking his head, as if I were a particularly regrettable piece of work. "His late father was a Union postmaster, and if the president believes he has met the young man before, then that absolutely is the truth of the matter."

Gardner now made his way to the door at the darkroom stairs. He gestured to the light-safe box he held in his other hand, and said to me in a very pleasant and patient tone, "Now, Johnny, we must take no more of the president's valuable time. I'll need your assistance upstairs in developing this wet plate. I would also like to have a word of prayer with you about your promptness."

I took a deep breath. What I had to do was now infinitely more difficult, but my mind was made up. "Mr. Gardner, I have come by to request the rest of this day off."

I heard a long, low chuckle beside me. Mr. Lincoln folded his arms across his chest, grinning first at Mr. Gardner and then at me, though he chose not to speak.

Gardner appeared thunderstruck. He bent double, and raised his arms to his head. "Do I hear correctly?" he shouted. "Do I hear correctly? Dear God, with all the business cares of this day, do I hear correctly?" His question did not seem rhetorical.

I tried to explain. "Mr. Gardner, I have some urgent personal business to which I must attend, a consequence of this sudden coming of peace—"

349

"Peace be damned!" Gardner stamped his foot, and for a moment I thought he would tear out his hair. Gardner advanced at me holding the metal plate box in his hand like a weapon, before he gained enough self-possession to swallow his rage. His voice thick with a Scottish accent, he said, "John Surratt, now if you do not gae up these stairs with me—"

I heard a prolonged and dramatic clearing of a throat. We turned to see President Lincoln's gaze fixed upon us. He seemed to have become much taller, and a smile played at his bearded lips. He raised one hand with his palm outward in a gesture of peace.

"Oh, let the boy have his holiday, Gardner," the president said. Gardner grew quiet, and Mr. Lincoln slowly lowered his hand. He seemed deeply entertained by the scene before him. "We *all* need a good holiday," he said. He looked at me and winked. "I suspect there is a young lady involved, perhaps eager to join with the young man in watching the victory celebrations."

The president regarded Gardner, and although he maintained something of a straight face, he seemed to be even more privately amused. "I suspect that even you, Alexander, as a young man in Glasgow, occasionally let the badger out of the bag."

I turned toward Gardner. My employer stared at me in a silent rage, as if mentally picturing himself tearing me limb from limb. But there was no appealing such a presidential decision. I hurriedly wished the president well, and left to claim the carriage Booth had waiting for me and Sarah Ravenel. But I could not forget Mr. Lincoln's kindness, nor the innate generosity of his character. Could this be the man Booth had spoken of with so much venom? It made me wonder, if only for a moment, at the accuracy of Booth's other prognostications and perceptions.

11.

From the transcript of the trial of John H. Surratt, Jr., in the murder of Abraham Lincoln, Criminal Court of Washington, D.C., 1867

Q. Mr. Weichman, please tell the court what Mr. Surratt consequently admitted to you after his arrest of his travels with this woman, Sarah Slater.

A. Yes, sir. He said that they had started on their way to Richmond from Washington City, and after a great deal of trouble had managed to cross the Rappahannock; that after they got south of Fredericksburg, they saw some men coming toward them—five or six, if I recollect right. They ascertained that these men were Union prisoners, or Union soldiers escaped from southern prisons; they were, he said, nearly starved to death, and that this woman who was with him said, "Let's shoot the damned Yankee soldiers!" She had hardly said the word when the two of them in their carriage drew their revolvers and shot them, and went right along, laughing and paying no more attention to them.

Q. How many?

A. He said five or six dead.

Q. And he told you the name of his companion was Miss Sarah Slater?

A. Yes, sir, he did so.

I closed the book of my trial transcript on my writing desk at the Willard Hotel. *Lies, all lies,* I thought to myself. Louis Weichman, as a result of his testimony, had been appointed to a series of comfortable federal clerkships. He apparently saved his money; I read in the newspapers some years ago that he had moved West and had at last opened his business college. I rubbed my temples, a bitter survivor alone in a strange room. It has been an emotionally tumultuous day, and I was deeply fatigued. I opened my diary to the entry of my journey to Virginia with Sarah.

April 10–14, Monday–Good Friday, 1865
The single sentry guarding the approach to the bridge casually glanced at my credential from Gardner, and waved Sarah and me across the wooden planks of the Navy Yard Bridge over the Potomac. We were traveling as husband and wife. The military seems much less watchful over civilian traffic now that the war is effectively won. My credential to pass will soon no longer be needed—nor will I probably have employment at Gardner's studio when I return to Washington City. My relations with Sarah have altered everything.

Sarah, surprised at the white lie I had told the hapless young sentry, teased me gently.

"John, you are rushing our affair," she said, affectionately squeezing my arm. Sarah had assumed a rather desperate gaiety since I had called for her at the hotel. I attributed it to her anxiety at the dangers of our trip. She wore the same gray riding habit she had on when she called at the boardinghouse last week. I inwardly thrilled to her words—"our affair"—convinced anew that I had made the right decision in accompanying Sarah south.

"It's not an affair I would avoid," I said, returning her smile as I flicked the reins.

The road from the Maryland side of the bridge was a good one, partially walled with stone, and it ran directly down the countryside past Surrattsville before ending at the Virginia boundary. As my military pass was still valid, I saw no reason for us to travel surreptitiously; we would cross at the public ferries at the lower Potomac and the Rappahannock rivers, and thence to Richmond. We would be able entirely to avoid the war-wrecked city of Fredericksburg. As we passed by my childhood home at Surrattsville, I pointed it out to Sarah and noted the unusually large number of horses tethered outside the house and tavern. We did not stop on the road, and Sarah chose not to remove her veil.

We spent the first night of our journey sleeping outside the carriage, innocently in one another's arms. Sarah had seemed less inclined to talk the nearer we drew to Richmond, and had insisted that we avoid staying at any taverns or private houses. Booth providentially had packed for us some quilts and also a small wicker box containing teas, shaved ham, and other delicacies.

In the morning, our carriage was ferried without incident across the southern Potomac. There was but one more river to cross, the Rappahannock, and then onward to Richmond. This second crossing was the part of our trip I dreaded. The ferryman was a rough, slovenly fellow of an indeterminate age, and he stared greedily at the fineness of our clothing and carriage. The river water was darkened almost to blackness from the surrounding swamps. The heavy rope above our heads attached to the ferry was pulled by an emaciated-looking mule on the opposite shore, who drew us slowly over the river. The ferryman occasionally made pretension of helping the poor animal, launching a jet of tobacco juice into the dark waters as he shoved his pole perfunctorily into the river.

"We don't get much quality trade," he grinned, showing me a mouth full of yellowed teeth. "Deserters and spies, mostly, during the war." He glanced at Sarah. "Not at all like you and your lady there."

I said nothing, but was glad I carried Booth's derringer in my pocket. Sarah kept to the far end of the ferry, her back to us. On reaching the opposite shore, I paid him one of Booth's dollars.

We were now in Virginia, though not in the rolling, cultivated hills that state brings to mind. There were dark swamps and thickets on either sides of the Potomac and Rappahannock rivers, crosscut by innumerable creeks and hidden trails. Without detailed knowledge of the area, one could wander hopelessly lost for days. This wilderness, as if by mutual consent, had been largely avoided by both armies, although there always had been the danger of armed partisans. It was possible, if one knew the back ways and creek crossings, to arrive at Richmond undetected by the Union patrols on the main roads. I had hunted and fished here when my father was alive, and that was why Booth had asked me to map out his escape route along here when he fled the city.

I turned the carriage onto a sandy road that cut a straight line into the wilderness. "We are safe now, Sarah," I told her. "To-morrow we will be at Richmond, and your life begins anew."

Sarah, who had become visibly pale after our trip on the ferry, said, "I pray so, John. I pray so."

Over the next five or six miles I tried to improve Sarah's spirits, but she seemed even less inclined to talk. I remembered how easily Booth had entertained his guests on such trips, but the ability seemed beyond me, especially in the company of one whose affection I valued so much. It's an easier task accomplished, I realized, when one has little personally at stake.

All at once, our horse suddenly shied, and I had trouble holding onto the reins. Ahead I saw several blue-uniformed figures sprawled alongside the road. From my experience on the battlefield, I knew what to expect. "Don't look," I told Sarah. I got down from the carriage, tethered the horse, and then proceeded on foot the remaining twenty yards.

Before me lay the bodies of six Union soldiers, shot dead where they had been lying beside the road. Their uniforms were beyond tatters, and all had been at the point of starvation. They apparently had been resting after escape from a prisoner of war camp near Richmond, and had been surprised either by pursuing guards or by one of those savage, unpredictable attacks by Confederates in Mosby's guerrillas, with whom Booth had told me Lewis Powell once had ridden. I consoled myself that at least death had come quickly for these men.

I walked back to our carriage. The road and the green wilderness on either side were preternaturally quiet, and the only sound I heard was the scrubbing of my bootheels in the sand.

Sarah was standing outside the carriage waiting for me, trembling uncontrollably. She reached out to me with a wild look. "Will the death ever stop, John? The war was supposed to be over. Please make them understand that the death must stop." She began sobbing, and I realized I couldn't take her past the dead soldiers. I had noticed a path circling around the road, probably trodden by deer or wild pigs. "We'll go around," I quietly said.

The path led several hundred yards down a narrow incline to a concealed oak thicket with a surprisingly clear spring of water. Here I paused to water the horse, and Sarah removed her riding jacket. As I bathed her arms and temples with my handkerchief, she seemed to regain her composure.

"John, I should not have come with you in this state," she said quietly, as we were sitting beside the spring. She reached out and touched my arm apologetically. "You see, it is not just for myself that I am so frightened."

I embraced her affectionately, if only to demonstrate that she need not fear for my safety. Sarah responded with a physical desperation that surprised me. As she clutched me to her, I found myself becoming aroused. To our mutual surprise, we began the act of love.

Part of me knew that what we were doing was not due to desire, but rather to the need to counter the death around us, a need that somehow demanded that the two of us perform the *actions* of desire. In my haste, I tore at Sarah's clothing as I lay her on the ground, and she at my own. As I entered her, she cried out desperately. Despite our wooded seclusion, I couldn't shake off the sensation of being observed among the trees by eyes of both the living and the dead. Our physical intimacy was brief.

Sarah stood with her back to me as we dressed. "John," she said softly, "I think you misunderstood me when I told you I am frightened not just for myself." She turned to face me, tears running down her face. "John, I am with child."

It took me a long moment to understand her words. As I did, I realized Sarah could not be pregnant by me.

Time seemed to stop. I noticed some strands of Sarah's hair matted with dirt from our time on the ground. "John, my true name is Sarah Slater," she said. "I was once sponsored by Wilkes in the theatre." She took a deep breath. *"That* much is true, and much else." Sarah looked aside as if in shame. "Like you, with your intelligence reports, I have done certain favors for Wilkes after we first found one another again at that concert hall."

So now I knew, or I thought that I knew.

The edge of the woods around us seemed to close in on me, encroaching upon my field of vision. The image of Sarah in front of me blurred and her words seemed to come from far away.

"When I told Wilkes of my condition, he told me he would see that I and the child I am carrying would travel safely to Richmond. I would be taken abroad by his friends there."

I forced myself to concentrate upon Sarah's words. Even as the world I thought I knew—Sarah, Booth—dissolved before me, I wanted to hear all, to know how utterly blind in my perceptions I had been.

"Wilkes told me he would follow later," she said. She turned aside, as if ashamed to face me, and in a flat, emotionless tone of voice told me Booth's words.

"Wilkes told me that he was disentangling himself from a 'foolish affair of the heart,' which meant nothing to him now, with a much older woman."

Sarah seemed to force herself to continue. "Wilkes told me that this older woman had come to him out of loneliness of her widowhood, and that he had come to her out of the generosity and kindness of which he was sometimes capable."

"No!" I shut my eyes, but I saw the image of my mother and Booth together, and in a murderous rage *saw* in my mind's eye the two of them coupling at the Washington City house, in an obscene enactment of Sarah's and my lovemaking.

When I opened my eyes, my fury at Booth, at his utter deception and betrayal, made the remote setting in which Sarah and I now stood pale to insignificance. I felt cut off from my emotions, much as I had been on the battlefield. I found myself mechanically noting the details of the sumac bushes around us, the black gum trees, the scrub oaks, and Sarah herself.

"John, don't abandon me," she cried, and ran to me. "Remember, I didn't abandon you." She clutched at my clothing and began to weep. I felt my body become rigid.

"John, I swear to you I did not know the woman was your mother until Wilkes and I came by your house that afternoon in the carriage," Sarah said, her eyes imploring. "I admit that I played a part when we first met, but I am not playing a part now. I gave myself to you that day when I saw that you were in as desperate and uninformed a situation as I. I realized yesterday that I had made the right decision when you, rather than Wilkes, as he had promised, came to the hotel. I knew then that I could deceive you no longer."

Her face, stained with tears, pressed against mine. Although she was a better actress than I had given her credit for, I did not believe that she was playing a part now. "Please, John," Sarah said. "Please, dear God, don't abandon me."

Despite the anger I felt, and the overwhelming sense of emptiness her deception caused me, I embraced her. Could I forgive Sarah for deceiving me? Hadn't I deceived myself for the last year, I realized, and, without knowing it, had accepted a role in a play that was not my own? But it was time to play my own role. I looked at Sarah with an infinite sense of sadness. The thought of Sarah and Booth together was barely more palatable than the image of Booth and my mother. "Let's get you to Richmond."

I led the carriage out of the thicket and back onto the road, well past where the dead men lay, and handed the reins up to Sarah.

"There are more indirect routes to Richmond, but this road will get you there more quickly," I told her, a distinct coldness to my voice. "I must return to Washington City and try to comfort my mother." I handed her the purse of Booth's money. "Sarah, we are both through with concealment now. If you meet with either Union or Confederate soldiers along the way, I feel confident they will treat you kindly." There was some truth to my statement.

Sarah hesitated, but seemed to accept the inevitability of my decision. She took Booth's money. I was surprised to see that her features did not harden.

"John, you *should* be with your mother now," Sarah said softly. She withdrew a generous number of paper bills from the purse and handed them to me. "Use this to hire a horse on your way back, if you can."

Our eyes met in the sunlight. I wondered if Sarah guessed at my plans. "John, remember how I told you one night that you are as good, or a better man, than Wilkes Booth?" she said. "If you are able, will you find me in Richmond when this finally ends?"

I hesitated, but I knew now where my

heart lay. "Yes, I will." And in that, I, too, was not playing a part.

As I watched her figure recede down the yellow sandy road in front of me, I no longer perceived Sarah Slater as a romantic and exotic figure, different from myself. Instead, I saw her more clearly as she was, a frightened human being, her body carrying an unborn child, her clothing soiled and torn from our desperate attempts to know one another physically, headed toward an uncertain fate in a dangerous and altered landscape.

I now turned my attention to returning to Washington to kill John Wilkes Booth.

12.

April 14, Good Friday, 1865

I crossed the Navy Yard Bridge into Washington City in the late afternoon. My journey had been a hard one. I had returned near Surrattsville on foot, and, once near there, prevailed upon Dr. Mudd to let his horse out for hire, although he had at first been very unwilling.

Once again, I passed by my childhood

home, and once more I had not stopped. As a boy, how I had disliked the sound of my family's name and wished it were another's! It reminded me of the field rodents we would see, gray-colored and darting from the tobacco sheds at harvesttime. Now, with my mother's dishonor, there is even more reason to dislike my family name. I feel as if I want nothing more to do with my family.

I noticed on my return trip through Surrattsville that the tavern attached to our former home continued to enjoy a good trade. The tavernyard was again crowded with strange horses. This was a prosperity my father never saw. The last years of his life had been grim, as we slipped into near bankruptcy and he into unrelieved drunkenness after his failures as a farmer, tavernkeeper, and U.S. postmaster. In a sense, it was a relief when Father died—his misery was over, and with my mother assuming control of our family finances, we could begin to find our way out of our troubles.

I shuddered when I remembered my father's last, agonizing cry from his deathbed. "My God, I have failed! I have failed!" His shout had echoed throughout the rooms of our farmhouse, and my mother had wept at his bedside uncontrollably. And now, thanks to Booth's willingness to abuse our honor, my family had endured yet another stain on its honor. I touched the smooth metal of the derringer inside my coat pocket.

The weather over Washington City was cold, raw, and gusty, but there remained a carnival atmosphere in the streets at the celebration of peace. As I rode down Pennsylvania Avenue I saw that many of the government office buildings had closed early this Friday, and were covered with two- and three-story fabric signs: over the Capitol dome I saw a banner, AT HOME THERE IS UNION AND ORDER, and, above the U.S. Treasury Building, U.S. GREENBACKS AND U.S. GRANT. Among the crowds on the sidewalks was a surprisingly large number of former Confederate prisoners of war, released from the forts around the city, frightened and angry men in tattered, dirty clothing, wondering how to get home.

I went directly to our boardinghouse, but found no one home. I realized my mother and sister probably were at church praying for Isaac; the rest of the tenants were out as well. I wondered if our tenants would continue to stay with us and pay board, now that the war was over.

Mother had cleaned the attic bedroom and straightened the covers on my bed in my absence. Weichman had left the slovenly signs of his presence throughout his side of the room. Centered nearly on the counterpane of my bed was an opened envelope of a telegram addressed to me, which I assumed had been received and read by Weichman earlier in the day. "Get word to the others to come on. With or without them, Friday evening we sell—that night for sure. Don't fail. J. WILKES BOOTH."

I put Booth's telegram in my pocket and walked downstairs to the parlor. Very few times since we moved to the H Street house have I slipped between the dressing screens on the parlor floor and entered my mother's makeshift bedroom. I saw now that her bed was made, and an opened devotional along with a rosary lay on a mahogany bedstand beside her mattress. My mother's dressing table was pushed against the opposite wall; on top of it was her keepsake box. I opened it and found a few pieces of glass jewelry, which she no longer wore, and one or two of her favorite trinkets from her girlhood before her marriage. As an adult, the mystery of this part of my mother's life always had fascinated me, just as a child might be fascinated by the mysterious origin of the colored glass pieces of jewelry themselves.

I saw a medallion in her box as well, and picked it up. To my horror, I saw it was the St. Anthony medal which Booth had carried about his neck. One side was roughly engraved, scratched with a knife, "Te amo. JWB." She must have exchanged medallions with Booth, giving him the St. Christopher's medal, saintly protector of travelers, which I know my mother has worn since our move from Maryland. More confirmation yet of Booth's affair with my mother. But why her? I asked myself. I knew now that Booth had been associated with any number of older women. What need did he have of my mother's affections? I hesitated, and then returned the medallion. As a tacit rebuke, I left her keepsake box open, however.

I exited the front door of the house and went down the steps to the street. I touched again the derringer inside my coat pocket. It gave me a sense of secret power that lifted me above the unknowing pedestrians on the streets.

I had left Dr. Mudd's horse at a neighborhood livery to rest. I began my search for Booth on foot. Booth's comment that he still had the courage to call for his mail was, at least, correct. I found that at each of the city's theatres and at his hotel, he had been seen today, though he had left no word on when he would return.

At each place I left identical messages, sealed and marked urgent for Booth's attention, strongly warning him of the dangers of traveling the main road to Richmond down which I had sent Sarah. Instead, I left detailed, and deliberately inaccurate, descriptions of how he could best avoid detection to cross the lower Potomac and the Rappahannock. I was determined that if Booth should escape me and travel southward, he would wander aimlessly in the Maryland and Virginia swamps, allowing me plenty of time to catch up with him in Richmond.

It was early evening when I left the National Theatre. The gas lamps along Pennsylvania Avenue were already lit. The city thoroughfares were crowded with traffic. It occurred to me that Booth might be drinking at the Willard Hotel, and I made my way there.

Not even the prospect of peace had stopped the wartime clamor and confused din of the Willard's red-carpeted interior. Most of the noise seemed to originate from the far end of a corridor to my right. It led directly from the lobby to the barroom.

The wood-paneled, oval-shaped room was crowded with Union officers at the bar, each apparently trying to outshout the others. "Water! Water!" Half a dozen or more officers in front of me held up empty glasses to order more whiskey, and their cries for water provoked instantaneous outbursts of laughter from the others.

The officers seemed to be playing a game encouraging intoxication. I was one of the few civilians in the barroom. The newspapers had reported that at the final battle of Appomattox before Lee's surrender, the wounded and dying of both armies there had cried "Water! Water!" In the euphoria of peace, the drunken survivors of the war were now enacting a cruel parody of the dead in holding up their glasses and shouting for more whiskey.

In disgust, I started to turn away. Then suddenly I saw Booth's figure reflected in the mirror. Like me, he stood at the edge of the barroom. Booth's clothing and his body had regained his handsome and cared-for appearance, as if he planned an unannounced performance at the theatre later tonight.

I found myself jostled and cussed by a Union colonel unsteadily carrying two glasses of whiskey in each hand; some liquor spilled down my shirtfront, but I paid it no heed. I placed my hand inside my coat pocket.

As I shouldered closer to Booth, I was less than ten feet away. In the roar and laughter of the crowd, the pistol's firing might not even be noticed. Our eyes met, in the mirror. Although his expression did not change, I knew that Booth was aware I was in the room. And at that moment I realized he knew that I knew about his affair with my mother. Perhaps he had always known that I would discover it, and was deliberately waiting for me to kill him and perhaps end his isolation and misery.

"Water! Water!"

I caught Booth's attention with my eyes, and gestured for him to follow me. Outside, we stood out of the view of the traffic, partially concealed by an alcove of the Willard building.

Booth smiled. "John, I had prayed for your safe return." Without replying, I raised my derringer level to his face.

His features recoiled, to my satisfaction, and I kept the derringer leveled steadily on him. Yet, even in this moment, I saw that his fear was almost too theatrical, as if he were still playing a part. "You know of your mother and me," Booth said. Once again, he had intuited my thoughts.

"Yes, and I know *you,* Booth. Goddamn your soul." My hand was trembling with rage as I held the pistol at him.

Booth kept his dark eyes steadily upon me, and when he spoke, he betrayed no fear in his voice. "Then kill me, John. Do it here, now. Deliver me from all this obscenity."

I returned his gaze. "Obscenity? If you dare say one word against my mother, you die now, Wilkes."

Booth, incredibly, now regarded me with

a pitying expression. "You don't under-stand, John, and you never will, even after you pull that trigger. The obscenity is this life we are forced to live, among such men as in that barroom. My love for your mother was both an attempt to escape all this death, and my chosen way to let it destroy me." Booth smiled at me, and I began to tighten my finger around the derringer's trig-ger.

"I knew you were not really one of us, John," Booth said. "So deliver me from this degradation."

Booth slowly drew apart the lapels of his coat, exposing his chest underneath his shirt front, near his heart. "Do it, John. Join the obscenity of our time, and destroy life and what your mother loves. Destroy he who loves you."

Booth's pale face grew close to mine in the darkness. "Kill me, John," he whis-pered. "End my self-degradation. Kill me, kill me."

I lowered my derringer. It was now I who pitied Booth. "No," I said coldly. "I want you to live, Wilkes. I want you to live and understand that you're no different from those who cheapen life." I eased the hammer down upon the derringer Booth had given me, and then threw the disarmed weapon into the street. "That's where it belongs," I said. "In the gutter. That is where you belong, Wilkes." Without another word spoken between us, I scornfully left him standing in the street.

For the next several hours, I walked the streets aimlessly, unwilling to return to the H Street house, and uncertain whether I had acted correctly in sparing Booth. Could I return to my family and live with my mother in pretended ignorance of what we had learned of one another?

The distant tolling of the City Hall bell and the fetid stench of the Georgetown Canal alongside the street brought me back to my senses. It was nine o'clock. I was in southwestern Washington City, several blocks from the president's park and the Executive Mansion.

I turned onto Ohio Avenue. I had passed by three or four of the narrow, frame houses along the block before I noticed each had at its window a red-glassed lamp, or, in places, red window curtains only partially drawn on the scene within. Shadows moved on the stone steps of one house ahead of me, and as I walked nearer the streetlamp I made out a trio of women sitting outside on the steps in the night air.

"Do you want it, Johnny?"

"Two dollars and it's yours, Johnny."

"Take a sweet roll with me, Johnny, in my crib."

I had wandered into Hooker's Division. I stopped, shocked that these prostitutes had addressed me by name. The women on the stoops interpreted my hesitation as interest. One exposed her breasts under the gaslight. Another raised her skirt above her private parts; in the dim light I could see she wore nothing underneath. The youngest of the three was perhaps fourteen years of age. The two others appeared to be about the age of my mother.

I looked down at myself under the streetlamp. With my sun-darkened skin and dirty clothes after my four-day journey from Virginia, I must have appeared to these women as a "Johnny Reb," a recently released Confederate prisoner of war. I quickly resumed walking, to the sound of catcalls and insults of the women behind me.

Hooker's Division led me into a maze of

unlit streets among the poorest neighbor-hoods of the city, and I was soon thoroughly lost. Once, I heard a distant disturbance along a main avenue, with what sounded like a troop of cavalry rushing by. As the city bell struck eleven o'clock, I turned into an alleyway and saw to my relief that it opened to Pennsylvania Avenue.

Suddenly three cavalrymen appeared at the head of the alley. All three horsemen began to advance toward me at a deliberate pace. The two cavalrymen on either side of the alley unsheathed their carbines and held them at the ready across their saddles.

I regretted throwing away my derringer. I did not want to be robbed of my pocket watch by a trio of drunken Union soldiers. I looked behind me, preparing to run. At that moment, a hooded barouche carriage turned into the alleyway from the rear, blocking my escape.

The cavalryman at the center rode his horse to within a few feet of where I stood. The two on either side leveled their carbines at me. The horseman in front of me with-drew a small, dark card from within his uni-form blouse, and briefly studied it and, then, my face. His expression hardened.

"You also were with Booth," he said.

I was confused. I had expected a robbery and had involuntarily raised my hands. I tried not to back away or provoke the men with carbines. Booth had been at the Willard bar when I had last seen him. "I don't know or understand what you mean," I said.

The horseman replied to his companions, without taking his eyes away from me, "This man is one of them."

I began to stammer, asking what they intended with me.

The horseman at the center leaned toward me from his saddle. His voice was thick with anger, and he seemed ready to strike me. "Certainly you are one of them, you are a friend to John Wilkes Booth."

"I don't know this Booth you are talking about!" I said involuntarily, searching for the key to their sinister anger. I lowered my hands in emphasis and instantly regretted my mistake. At that moment, the barouche carriage rolled up behind me. I turned my head and saw the figures of two men getting out of the black-hooded vehicle. To my astonishment, I recognized one of the men as Mr. Gardner.

"I'm afraid you do, Johnny," Gardner

said. He let his palm fall heavily upon my right shoulder. With his other hand he withdrew from his coat a piece of cardboard identically sized to what the horseman carried. He held it close to my eyes.

In the darkness of the alleyway, I could make out a photographic print of my *carte de visite* pasted on the cardboard. Below my image was hastily written in ink, as if in a dream: WANTED FOR APPREHENSION IN THE MURDER OF PRESIDENT LINCOLN. My heart stopped in my throat. What had happened? What had Booth done?

Without releasing his grip upon my shoulder, Gardner turned in the direction of the second civilian, who was walking toward me.

"And I'm sure you know this gentleman, too, our mutual friend, Mr. E. J. Allen? Or, when he prefers to be known by his true name, Mr. Allan Pinkerton of the U.S. Secret Service."

13.

April 15–29, 1865

My mind was a confusion of scenes from that Good Friday night on. Pinkerton quickly thrust both my hands through a pair of iron manacles. I remember through my sense of shock the three of us jostled together in the interior darkness of the moving barouche. As I protested my innocence, Pinkerton cuffed my head with the flat of his hand. Gardner did not speak.

The trip took longer than I anticipated. I had a passing glimpse of shop windows. We were not traveling along Pennsylvania Avenue, but instead rode along some commercial thoroughfare. There was an indistinct roaring from a large crowd ahead of us.

The carriage slowed to a walk. The voices of the crowd were much nearer to us now, and I heard frenzied shouts of "Burn it! Burn it!" I had a moment of terror that a mob intended to set ablaze our carriage itself. Then the carriage jolted forward again, and with relief I heard the steady clop of the horse's hooves. Almost immediately, the carriage bumped over a curbstone, as it turned sharply to our right without braking, and then stopped.

Pinkerton treated me with little ceremony. He produced a black slouch hat from within his coat, pushed it down over my face, and dragged me by the manacles out of the carriage.

To my amazement, I stood at the L-shaped alley at F Street that led to the rear entrance of Ford's Theatre. There were half a dozen heavily built men in civilian clothes prowling about, shining bull's-eye lanterns into the alley's shadows.

Gardner steadied me upright, and with a quick, practiced motion rearranged my coat to conceal my manacles. Both men roughly grabbed me at my shoulders and quick-stepped me through the alley's rear door.

The back stage of Ford's Theatre was cavernous, but it hummed with activity and the evidence of fear. Every gaslight in the building seemed to be illuminated, and I blinked at the unaccustomed glare. Stage properties were piled against the walls, and blue-uniformed soldiers were poking through them. I recognized one painted backdrop as the dairy scene from *Our*

American Cousin. The floor was littered with pieces of costume and broken paste jewels, as if the actors had fled in a panic. A heavy drop curtain separated the three of us from a view of the front stage, but I heard the shouts of many more soldiers beyond it.

A warren of small dressing rooms had been jerry-built against the right rear wall, and Pinkerton and Gardner now led me toward them. Pinkerton opened the door to the largest of these and then pushed me inside. Gardner followed and shut the door behind him. I recognized that we were in the theatre's "greenroom," where the actors waited and rested before their entrances onstage. A few pots of greasepaint and facial creams rested atop a dressing table, and there was a cracked mirror on the wall.

Gardner began violently walking back and forth across the small room, like an enraged, caged animal. "Oh, this is an evil business of yours, John Surratt, an evil business." He gave me a baneful look. "And your evil business has ensnared me and my honest enterprise."

I still did not understand the unreal charges of the president's murder, or why these men had brought me here, of all places.

"Mr. Gardner, I swear to you—"

"Oh, don't you get sly with me, John Surratt!" Pinkerton rushed from his standing place against the wall, and he shook his fist a few inches from my face. I feared he would strike me.

"You know as well as I what your friends have done tonight," Pinkerton said thickly. "John Wilkes Booth has shot President Lincoln in front of hundreds of witnesses at this very theatre, and fled southward. The president lies mortally wounded at a boardinghouse across 10th Street. Your friend Lewis Powell has attacked and seriously wounded the secretary of state. And your friend George Atzerodt talked of killing the vice president, but he became too drunk to do so."

Pinkerton jabbed a stubby finger into my chest. "And you, John Surratt, have been arrested as a conspirator."

I scarcely listened beyond his naming of Booth and his act. How could Mr. Lincoln be dead when I had seen him only four days earlier? And how could Booth have committed murder when I myself had spared murdering him only hours ago? I looked down at the iron manacles on my hands as if they were only a dream, or at least *delirium,* and I was still walking the streets somewhere in Hooker's Division.

"You may well hang your head in shame, John Surratt." Gardner advanced toward my chair as he spoke, and then stood in front of me alongside Pinkerton. "You are not as clever as you think you are. Since last December, a very loyal clerk in the War Department has been informing Secretary of War Stanton's office of your suspicious activities."

Gardner shook his head bitterly. "I was your champion, John. Your deportment in the studio and on the battlefield betrayed no evidence of disloyalty. But your trips into Virginia have been observed, and we now know you aided Booth's escape."

I think it was only at this moment I truly realized that this scene at the theatre was real, and what the iron manacles on my hands meant.

"Sir, I was only trying to return a private citizen to her home, a Miss Sarah Ravenel."

Pinkerton sneered at me. "Sarah Slater, you mean. She's Booth's whore."

Gardner was determined to show I had not outwitted him. "You may well wonder, Johnny, whether it was just your bad luck that I happened to have prints of your *carte de visite* to circulate for your arrest." Gardner walked across this little room with his thumbs hooked inside his waistcoat as he spoke, and some of his anger seemed to leave him.

He patted his waistcoat pocket. "Not at all, not a matter of luck at all." He withdrew from his pocket a stack of *cartes de visite* and fanned them in front of my face like a deck of playing cards. "Mr. Pinkerton and his men found these prints very useful in identifying Southern spies during the war, and I always made it a point to encourage anyone with questionable sympathies to have their photograph taken. You were caught by your own vanity."

Gardner replaced the cards into his pocket and patted it again with satisfaction. "I have a regular rogues' gallery in my pocket here, John Surratt, and your face is among them." He gave a significant look at his companion. "Isn't that so, Mr. Pinkerton?"

"Exactly, Mr. Gardner." Pinkerton

seemed to have recognized a cue. He then placed the back of his hand, at first almost gently, under my chin. He forced my head backward and up as I sat in the chair, in a posture that was very painful.

"Now you listen to me, John Surratt," Pinkerton said slowly. "You shall be hanged for certain, as certain as dying men piss in their trousers, and I promise you that. There's an angry mob outside this theatre now, shouting for it to be burned down, and I'd like nothing better than to turn you over to them to be used dangling at the end of a lamppost."

Pinkerton withdrew his opened hand from under my chin.

"But my friend Mr. Gardner would be badly compromised in his business if his photographic assistant were publicly convicted as among the presidential assassins. Alexander has served our cause loyally for years, not only with his cartographic photographs for the military but also with his battlefield reports and photographic cards of traitors like you. I don't want his reputation compromised by the mistake of employing you. And my own intelligence services would be badly compromised by the revelations that we had concentrated upon watching you, rather than Booth, in the months before President Lincoln's murder.

"We dismissed him as merely an actor, and of no consequence," Pinkerton went on. "We thought Booth was your creature, and not that you were his." Pinkerton looked down on me with disgust.

"Secretary Stanton has been informed of your arrest, and out of compassion for any possible compromise to Mr. Gardner or me, he has agreed that you be kept out of the public eye and apart from any others arrested." Pinkerton looked around at the greenroom with satisfaction. "This theatre is now the most secure building in the city, and is sealed from the public. You'll stay here until Booth is captured, silenced, and executed, and you'll be forgotten as merely one of the hundreds of civilians my men are sweeping up in arrests tonight, for their possible conspiracy in the murder."

Pinkerton then brought his face very close to mine, and he spoke to me in a hoarse whisper. "And then you'll swing from a gallows, John Surratt, for aiding Booth in his escape route. I'll be pleased to do the job myself, in a cellar at Arsenal

Prison I keep especially for that purpose." I turned my face away from his rank breath.

He raised an accusatory finger at me. "I want you to remember this," he shouted, tears springing from his eyes. "While our dear president's life's blood is soaking out of him at a boardinghouse across the street, your life also is ebbing, Surratt. You're dead as soon as Booth is caught."

Pinkerton looked at Gardner. "Keep a sharp watch on him," Pinkerton said. "I'm going to arrange to have one of my men outside this door twenty-four hours a day." Pinkerton glowered down at me. "My man may not know who you are, Surratt, but he'll know that if you dare take one step out of this room, he's to break both of your legs."

There was a long silence after Pinkerton slammed shut the door. Gardner stood across the room from me with his arms folded across his chest. My body ached to stand upright, and I looked imploringly, first at my legs, and then at Gardner. He nodded. I found that my knees were trembling when I arose from the chair, and I had to lean against the wall for support.

Gardner looked at me sympathetically. "He means what he says, Johnny. Don't try to escape." Gardner looked at my imprisoned hands. "And those manacles will have to stay on."

Gardner began to shake his head ruefully at my standing figure. My condition apparently provoked his instinct to point me out as a bad example. "It is tragic, Johnny, it is indeed tragic. Do you know that Mr. Lincoln liked you? He told me so, after you so abruptly left my employ."

Gardner sighed, wiped his hands down his ginger whiskers, and looked at me as if focusing on a distant photographic subject. "But whether from the rashness of youth, the love of a woman, or the folly of choosing the wrong side, you must prepare your soul to be hanged.

"I am truly sorry," he said. "I am truly sorry."

I thought of Booth, and his betrayal, and of Sarah Slater. I even thought of my association with Gardner, and of the words he had just spoken to me.

They were far more than either of us had said to the dead soldiers on the battlefield.

To the best of my reckoning, I was kept imprisoned and out of sight at Ford's Theatre for two weeks following Lincoln's murder. Lincoln died across the street the first night of my imprisonment. I learned the news from Pinkerton's associate, the pug-ugly boxer. He had unlocked the greenroom door and thrown in some dirty quilts for me to make a pallet on the floor as best I could. Twice a day for the following days, he brought me what passed for food, and unlocked my manacles to allow me to wash and relieve myself. Frequently he would pretend to forget to call for a colored boy to remove and wash the chamber pot, and smile at me so that I knew he was pretending to forget.

I came to know every inch of this greenroom: its single dressing table, the two chairs, the solitary gaslight fixture always kept burning, the cracked mirror on the wall. I lost count of the number of times I heard the clumping of soldiers' boots outside the door and the shouting of men entering the theatre: each time my heart raced, my palms grew damp, and I saw the image of myself carried off to the gallows. I worried for my mother and sister, and how my unexplained absence would sicken them with anxiety.

On one occasion during my imprisonment, I stopped my pacing, and looked
amazed at my own reflection in the room's
mirror. I now resembled the broken and
stinking figure that had been Wilkes Booth
in the alleyway.

Pinkerton was a frequent visitor during
my imprisonment, and an additional torment. He questioned me closely about the
escape routes I had planned for Booth, and
although I tried to answer all his questions
honestly, he beat me and shouted that I was
lying. He strikes me if I do not sit quickly
enough in a chair when he enters the room.
He seemed to take an inner pleasure in
describing to me how I will be hanged after
Booth's capture, and in bragging of the
sweeps of retaliatory arrests throughout the
city. Lewis Powell has been arrested "at a
private residence in the city," he tells me.
Samuel Arnold, George Atzerodt, and many
others also have been taken into custody at
the Arsenal Prison. David Herold has been
identified as a conspirator to the assassination and has presumably fled southward
with Booth. From the incessant questioning,
I infer that neither Booth nor Herold has
been captured.

Once, after my afternoon's meal, I heard several pairs of footsteps and Gardner's loud voice outside the greenroom door, excitedly telling how he had so thoroughly photographed the interior of Ford's Theatre, "including even the late president's still-bloodstained state box." The guard unlocked the door, and Pinkerton and Gardner entered the room. I immediately seated myself in a chair. Pinkerton smiled, and silently held up for me to see my own red-bound diary.

"Well, Surratt, it appears you've told us all, despite yourself," he said, with an ugly smile.

My face burned with both shame and anger. To have this book found, and read, by such a man as Pinkerton was the greatest degradation so far of my imprisonment. I had made no entries in my diary since I had returned from the battlefields, but I was certain they had read of my intimacy with Sarah.

As if reading my thoughts, Pinkerton uttered a few rude comments about my family and my morals. I realized that the H Street house must have been brutally searched, and wondered how Mother and Anna had endured this affront.

My thoughts then turned to how I must help myself. I looked down at my wrists, now rubbed raw and bleeding from the chafing iron cuffs.

"Mr. Pinkerton, Mr. Gardner, might it be possible that I continue my diary? Could the manacles be removed, and a pen and ink be brought to me daily for a few hours?"

Gardner and Pinkerton seemed amused by my request. They exchanged puzzled smiles, then both indifferently shrugged. Gardner, on reflection, then seemed to adopt a Scottish piety in his voice.

"Of course, Johnny, why not? Your scribbling in your diary is like the condemned man's fervent prayers as he stands on the gallows' drop." He shook his head and stood over me in my chair. "It'll do no good for the hard facts of the situation, but it may benefit your soul."

Pinkerton took my request as an additional means to torment me. "And as soon as we're sure Booth is captured and dead, and can tell no tales out of school, your diary will disappear with all other traces of your existence, Surratt."

My diary remained with me when they left my cell. And for the next several days, an hour at a time, I wrote in its pages unfettered. As I considered that I was under a sentence of execution, with no certain audience to read my words after my death, I saw no reason to strike my earlier entries, and I wrote my thoughts uncensored, freely admitting my actions.

Several days later, Pinkerton and Gardner returned one afternoon to my *ad hoc* prison cell at Ford's Theatre. "Much news, Johnny, much news!" Gardner said, holding aloft a newspaper. I eagerly looked at the date when he offered me the folded pages. April 29. It was now fifteen days since Lincoln's murder and my arrest. Booth has been a fugitive perhaps two weeks. Pinkerton magnanimously pointed me to a chair, implying that he would strike me for being slow in seating.

It took me some time to find the article in the newspaper which Gardner, with evident amusement, was waiting for me to read. It was a copy of a letter the disgraced medium Monsieur Daoud had sent to Secretary of War Stanton. Daoud claimed that he had "clearly dreamed" that Booth was concealed at Ford's Theatre, and requested that the government act at once to examine the building. Daoud obviously also had sent a copy of this letter for publication to the *Washington Post.*

"I'm afraid that a prophetic miss is as good as a mile for our poor Monsieur Daoud," Gardner said, retrieving his newspaper and chuckling into his beard as if we shared a private joke. "By the way, the rebel army has surrendered in the western theatre. You may well be the last man in the war to die." Gardner looked pleasantly at his companion. "And we have other news, don't we, Mr. Pinkerton?"

For reasons which I could not fathom, I sensed the conversation between the two had been rehearsed. I tensed within the chair as Pinkerton folded his arms histrionically across his chest.

"John Wilkes Booth was shot dead by federal troops on April 26th, while resisting capture in Virginia," he said.

"All this while, Booth was close to home, so to speak. While we were scouring for him in major cities and Canada, the damnable man was lost in the woods and swamps less than fifty miles from Washington City.

Apparently his broken leg prevented him from traveling as far as he had planned. And apparently, *your* escape routes, John Surratt, came to naught in aiding our friend." Pinkerton looked at me ominously. "Before his death, he insisted that the pursuing troops peaceably accept the surrender of David Herold. Booth's body was wrapped in a saddle blanket and brought aboard the ironclad *Montauk,* where it has been positively identified and autopsied. His head was cut off from his body during the autopsy and temporarily lost—it is probably to be buried anonymously with the rest of his remains."

Pinkerton quickly pulled a photographic print from his waistcoat. "But here is irrefutable and damning proof that John Wilkes Booth was the man," he said.

I had expected to feel a sense of vindication, of triumph, at Booth's demise, given how carelessly he had manipulated the lives of my mother, myself, Sarah, and countless others to his will. But I found I did not feel it. What I saw in the photograph was a thing of horror. Booth's body lay clothed and intact, not yet autopsied, upon a wooden plank across two barrels. The photograph obviously had been taken in a cabin of the interior of the *Montauk,* and the black iron walls of the ship were garishly illuminated by kerosene lamps held behind the unseen cameraman. Several bearded men in surgeon's aprons posed with their autopsy instruments behind the table. Booth appeared emaciated, his clothing muddy and his face unshaven, as he had appeared to me two weeks ago in the alleyway. His left leg was twisted at a cruel angle.

I realized that a similar image would be taken of my own broken body after Pinkerton and his men hanged me from a basement gallows.

"Mr. Gardner, do you wish your trophy returned?" Pinkerton politely offered the print to Gardner, who carefully replaced it within his pocket.

"There is only one glass plate and only one print of that scene," Gardner told me. "I was the photographer."

Gardner then gave his companion a significant look. "And there is something else, is there not, Mr. Pinkerton?"

"Exactly so, Mr. Gardner." Pinkerton returned his eyes to me. "It seems your treacherous friend John Wilkes Booth shared with you the habit of keeping a diary, Surratt."

Pinkerton withdrew from his pocket a slender volume, handsomely bound in maroon leather. "This is Booth's diary," he said. "It's a damnable book, apparently composed during the twelve days Booth was a fugitive. It's part biography, part diary, and part excuse for his foul life."

Pinkerton flicked through the pages. "The presence of Booth's diary was noted by numerous witnesses at the scene of his death. Doubtless, it will be called for during the public investigation of Lincoln's murder. Secretary of War Stanton, Mr. Gardner, and myself all have read it."

Gardner drew his chair closer to me. "And there are problems, Johnny." Gardner stroked his beard in a worried gesture.

"Booth had made love with several ladies still most prominent in public life, as well as had amiable relations with some of Congress's most important legislators. He also seemed to have held certain strongly felt religious beliefs which present difficulties for the Church."

Gardner looked at me searchingly. "Not the sort of man whom we can present to the public as an unadulterated villain. And he could easily bring several innocent politicians down with him. So you see our problem here, Johnny."

Pinkerton approached and stood intimidatingly over my chair. "Surratt, we've come to offer terms. I don't give a fiddler's prick about saving your skin, but I value *my* skin and reputation, and that of Mr. Gardner. Your employer has spoken to Secretary Stanton of your skill in reproducing another's handwriting. We have been authorized to make a proposal to you.

"If you agree to reproduce Booth's diary, eliminating and rewriting entries at our direction, you may have your liberty."

Gardner withdrew a small book from within his coat and handed it to Pinkerton. It was a blank duplicate of the expensive book Booth had kept his diary entries in.

"Booth's original diary will be destroyed, and your version offered to the public as the authentic version," Pinkerton said. He looked at me cunningly. "Here's your chance to take revenge upon Booth, Surratt, as well as to save your skin. If you do as we say, and agree to live obscurely after we publish the diary, you may avoid arrest and trial."

Gardner tapped me upon the knee. "We also have been authorized to include the safe conduct of Sarah Slater out of the country." Gardner gave a significant glance at Pinkerton. "She is not yet within his powers, but she soon will be."

I considered Booth's treachery, and how little I owed him. I could have revenge, of a kind. And I thought for a moment of Sarah, of the smell of her lavender-scented hair the first time we embraced. Her life and the life of her unborn child depended on me. Perhaps, I thought with a start, even Booth would have preferred it this way. But as I reflected further, I knew in my heart that Booth would not have given a damn about the child, or Sarah. He was too full of himself, and of his own role in history. And damn him also, I thought.

I accepted the blank diary. I then took into my hands the secret diary of John Wilkes Booth.

14.

From the transcript of the trial of John J. Surratt, Jr., in the murder of Abraham Lincoln, Criminal Court of Washington, D.C., 1867

Q. What was your occupation in 1865, in the month of April?

A. [Everton J. Conger, witness for the prosecution] Lieutenant colonel, first District of Columbia cavalry.

Q. Will you state what articles you took from Booth's body?

A. He had two pistols. He had a large Bowie knife, or hunting knife, and sheath. He had some pine shavings, some daguerreotypes, some tobacco, a little Catholic medal. He had a diary.

Q. What kind of diary?

A. An ordinary pocket diary, six inches long, perhaps, and two or three inches wide.

Q. Did you make any memoranda at the time as to the condition of the diary when you received it?

A. No, sir.
Q. To whom did you give that diary?
A. To the secretary of war, Mr. Stanton.

Part Four

April 17, Monday, 1865

My name is John Wilkes Booth. From my earliest hour, I have been unlike the others.

I write this now with every man's hand turned against me, and as a stranger and friendless in this world. For two days, my companion and I have been wandering, wet, cold, and starving, in a wilderness called Zekiah Swamp. John Surratt's maps have proved useless, and we cannot even find the river to cross. The friends and safe houses of which John wrote to me, assuring me they would be waiting, either are not here, or they know us not, and turn us away. Last night, in the extremity of our cold and hunger in the swamp, I considered killing one of our horses with my knife and lying down between its legs for its animal warmth. I repented. Later, David and I took a handful of parched corn and ground it between the butts of our rifles, and thus staved off exhaustion and death for one more day.

The two of us have remained hidden like animals in the wet thickets. As we shared together this last rude meal, I recalled the prophecy of Daniel to one of the great fallen kings of the Old Testament: "Let his portion be with the beasts in the grass of the earth. Let his heart be changed from man's, and let a beast's heart be given unto him."

It was not always so.

I therefore intend to write, if only as a crippled fugitive jotting down his thoughts with a pencil, the true history of my life. As I begin this diary, with the imminence of my death before me, I shall write as honestly and frankly as possible. I myself may be the only reader of these pages, should I survive and successfully escape to a foreign land.

But whatever my fate, I have no reason to leave anything concealed, whether of my life as a presidential assassin and an outcast, or as a renowned actor and constant lover of women, or as a friend and benefactor to all mankind, which I believe fervently that I am.

Assassins on the stage are represented as morally degenerate and as the spawn of a wretched household. Yet I am able to quote by memory from the Good Book of one of the world's most wonderful religions.

Furthermore, my childhood years were blissfully happy.

My childhood home is Tudor Hall in rural northern Maryland, or as we simply called it as children, The Farm. It was to The Farm that Father, whenever he could, returned from his theatrical engagements. He was the nation's foremost tragedian. To his patrons in the theatre, it must have seemed but another of his eccentricities that he isolated himself with his family in the country for several months each season. But to my sister, Asia, and me, these one hundred and fifty rural acres, and Father's periodic returns to them, were a kind of Eden.

Father was a burly man with a remarkably handsome face, despite a nose broken in a drunken quarrel several years earlier. His embrace smelled of bourbon, and of love.

He affectionately delighted in teasing us children with his theatrical abilities. On the occasion of one of his returns, he actually changed into a stage costume on his own doorstep and gained admission into our house as a hunchbacked old Jew peddler. To our amazed eyes, this strange figure suddenly scattered bright pennies across the carpet for Asia and me to snatch up, before tearing off his mask and roaring with laughter at our expressions.

In my memory, of all my brothers and sisters, it is my older brother Edwin who stands silently at the edge of the scene, beautiful and remote like my mother. It was Edwin who traveled with Father to prevent our parent from drinking excessively before appearing onstage.

How strange that a man in my situation should find his thoughts turning so vividly to childhood memories! Even after spending two nights wandering in the swamps since leaving Dr. Mudd's, my broken left leg throbbing at each pulse, pursued by Union soldiers, these childhood joys are as real in my mind as the dangers now surrounding us. Perhaps these memories of childhood are like the insubstantial blue vapors of light that David and I saw burning and skipping from dark tree to dark tree on our first night in the swamp.

David Herold just returned to our campsite, advancing warily through the pine thicket, his carbine at half cock, fearing perhaps that I had been taken, or that he might be ambushed. Thank God he brings good news, and some food with a tin of boiled coffee. He has met with a Southern sympathizer, a Thomas Jones, along one of the swamp paths, who promises to come tomorrow and help us cross the Potomac. I hope that I can trust this man, and that Jones is his true name. I am not as credulous as David, and I know that generous rewards must have been posted for Herold and me since the night I shot Lincoln.

Mad, bad Junius Brutus Booth. The mad Booths of Maryland.

It has become too dark under the trees to write any further, and I dare not light a candle. My leg hurts excruciatingly at night. I tell Herold not to worry, that we will soon be across the Potomac. The boy sleeps beside me guilelessly. I must not alienate him—I need his help.

April 18, Tuesday, 1865
Since daybreak, rain has fallen in a gray, steady drizzle, and the green pine branches high above our heads slough and seemingly groan in the wind. David and I made our camp deep atop a pine-needled and forested hummock, the only rising and comparatively dry ground in the surrounding

swamps. Thomas Jones told Herold he would try to come this afternoon; and for now all there is for us is to keep covered in our saddle blankets below the trees and attempt to stay warm. I wonder whether Lincoln has had his funeral yet.

The mad Booths of Maryland. Everywhere I heard that calumny whispered about my father, and, in a later generation, about Edwin and me. My father's unfortunate alcoholic dipsomania was well known, and his free-thinking refusal to marry my mother with a clergyman present, until I was thirteen years of age, gave his children, to some eyes, the taint of illegitimacy. As if such a blessing should affect who or what we are.

But my father's madness was only madness to an envious world. Unlike our cruel and avaricious tobacco-farming neighbors, my father allowed no slavery on our farm, insisting that our black cultivators be paid and well treated for their labors. Father also forbade the slaughter of any livestock; he maintained that cows, sheep, geese, and all other animals had souls as precious as our own. Both on the stage and outside the theatre, Father publicly declared his friendship alike to Christian, Jew, and Muslim, and I can remember him majestically striding through the rooms of Tudor Hall in his dressing gown, declaiming in Hebrew. I honestly believe that Father's success and wealth from the theatre meant little to him, and he truly lived for his time on the farm with his family. We were his window into reality.

He had such high expectations for us. I was named for John Wilkes, the great defender of American freedom and a distant relation to my father. When I once asked him why he had given my sister, Asia, such a singular name, he told me, "Because that is the continent where man first talked with God."

As a boy, I sometimes stole apart from the others in my family. I would write my name in the dust, and repeat aloud the syllables, *John Wilkes Booth, John Wilkes Booth,* in a kind of incantatory rhythm, until I could sense the great man I would become. My actions were, no doubt, a consequence of having long and uninterrupted access to my father's library. Other than my dear sister, my constant companions during my childhood were Shakespeare and the Greek tragedians.

This isolation on The Farm was the cause of my only unhappiness. My sister Asia and I were permitted only infrequently to attend the local academies, or even see our father on stage. Father was away at least nine months each year, and always he took on his travels my older brother Edwin, both as apprentice and as his keeper. I fretted that I was losing my opportunity in the larger world to learn the theatrical crafts.

"It's not fair, Johnny," I can remember Asia consoling me when I confessed my unhappiness to her. She and I had been extraordinarily sympathetic to each other almost since birth, and our relation to one another was more like that of twins rather than younger brother to older sister.

Asia discovered a way to end my unhappiness. Concealing a copy of Foxe's *Book of Martyrs* from my father's library, she proposed that we secretly go into the woods and practice to become actors by re-creating the scenes illustrated in this book. These are my fondest memories from childhood. I can picture us at this moment, in a pine forest not very different from the thicket where I now lie injured, Asia raising her childish chin as I gathered sticks from the forest floor for her pretended immolation at the stake, or I, bound to the same tree as the martyred St. Sebastian, as she picked up imaginary arrows to pierce my body.

Later in the afternoon, a tall man appeared among the pine trees and began to shout loudly to unseen hogs in the woods. Herold excitedly started upright, his blanket falling from his shoulders. "Do you see, Mr. Booth? Do you see?" He pointed a finger at the man. "I was right, after all."

I would not rise, but I kept my revolver in my hand under my blanket, cocked and pointed in the man's direction as he approached. He called to his hogs in a peculiarly plangent tone of voice, as if he wished to be overheard beyond this pine forest. No hogs appeared. As he walked toward us, he swung his arms exaggeratedly at his sides, in what appeared to me as a crude pantomime of a farmer calling to his animals.

"Afternoon, gents." He touched his fingers to a gray and torn slouch hat. He seemed extraordinarily pleased at his charade. "You'll pardon the hog-calling, but if

413

I'd been spotted by any Yankees on my way here, I reckoned I'd have needed an excuse. He loosened a belt across his narrow chest and let fall a heavy canvas bag that appeared filled with dried corncobs. His clothing was very dirty.

"You must be Mr. Booth." He nodded with sly humor at me, and then at Herold. Without ceremony, he sat down on a fallen log facing us. "Your boy told me you-all were in a bad fix." He removed his hat and waved it downward at my broken leg. "I will say that both you gents are sucking hind tit, and that's for certain."

I kept my right hand clutched at my revolver concealed underneath my blanket. He was doubtless a plantation overseer, a professional brutalizer of blacks and the only type of Southerner whom I have ever actively disliked. The meanness of his class seemed a part of him, from the pinched features of his sallow face to the mocking courtesy with which he addressed his social betters.

"How do you know I am Booth?" I asked. "And are you indeed the man named Thomas Jones?" For a long moment there was no sound but the raindrops slowly falling from pine branches.

The man uttered a vulgar oath and leaned his sallow face closer to me, winking. "Oh, I reckon the whole world knows who you are, Mr. Booth. Your boy here, too. It's been in all the papers. You're the one who killed Lincoln."

He sat back on his log and hooked his thumbs in his ragged jacket, like an actor personifying pride. "And I am *indeed* the man named Thomas Jones."

David Herold, the poor, half-witted boy, was obviously delighted his name was published in the newspapers. I reminded myself that we needed Jones's help.

"Then can you help us cross the Potomac?" I allowed a slight note of imploring to come into my voice. "I had hoped to be in Richmond already, and on my way to Europe, but this broken leg impeded me. Our maps are wrong, we don't know where we are, and no one else will help us."

Jones allowed himself a slow, deliberate pause as he scratched his rib cage underneath his jacket. "Well, Mr. Booth, I could get you and the boy out of the swamp and across the river, all right. But not tonight, nor right away. Union boys are patrolling thick as ticks along the river, and the Washington newspapers say there's a million dollars reward for your capture."

My hand had never left the butt of my revolver underneath the blanket. "And why should you not claim the reward yourself?" I asked.

Jones surprised me. "Pride," he said. "Look at me, Mr. Booth, look at me." Jones stood up angrily from his pine log, and spread his ragged, soiled jacket in front of my eyes. "Niggers was all I knew, and I made a good living driving niggers before the war. When Mr. Lincoln abolished slavery, he made a ruined man of me. But, by God, Mr. Booth, you're the man who abolished Lincoln. I'm proud to help you."

Has it come to this? Will my great act be revered in the future only by the slave drivers, the failures, and outcasts of the South? Part of me burned to banish him from the scene, as unworthy of my great drama, and my hand involuntarily tightened on the revolver's butt. *As well as kill two as one,* I thought.

"But I still got me one nigger, and a boat for shad fishing," Jones said. Jones seemed momentarily to gather his wits about him, and his face resumed its habitually sly look as he glanced down at me.

"I heard the Yankee boys talking among themselves at Port Tobacco that if they didn't find any scat of you along the river by Friday, they'd turn north and search Fredericksburg." He smiled. "That's when we'll move. Three nights from now, in my shad boat. I'll come betweentimes and bring food, and newspapers, if you gents miss them."

I said nothing. Perhaps he sensed my moral distaste of him, or perhaps Jones sensed the revolver I concealed. "And, look here, Mr. Booth, look here." Jones grabbed up his canvas bag, and, in an elaborate show of good faith, began to toss out the corncobs. Concealed underneath them were fatback, molasses, and, thank God, some whiskey.

Jones's face took on an expression of mocking humility as he shook his head and looked down at his bag and the paucity of his gifts. "I know it's not what you gentlemen are accustomed to, but it's the best a poor man can offer," he said.

You need this man, an inner voice re-

417

minded me. I relaxed my grip upon the revolver, and, exaggerating my effort, raised
myself from my pallet on the ground. I
grinned at Jones and let my jaw drop stu-
pidly in an expression of what I hoped he
would think was kinship.

"Cooked or raw, it'll fill our craw," I replied. I deliberately slowed my speech to
mimic his dialect.

Jones slapped his thigh gleefully. "By
God, Mr. Booth, you're all right!" He replaced his torn hat on his head and smiled
at me knowingly. "I reckon you're one of us,
Mr. John Wilkes Booth."

I have insisted that David take most of the
food. I simply didn't have the stomach for it.
He eats greedily, like a child. The whiskey,
however, eases me.

David chats mindlessly of how we shall
escape to Europe to become famous, and
rich. He at last falls asleep, and I have an
hour or so to my thoughts. Jones may prove
trustworthy, and our prospects are at least
somewhat better for crossing the Potomac,
and thence across the Rappahannock and
to safety. Sarah by this time is among
friends at Richmond. John—who knows

where John is. Escaped to Virginia with his family? Under arrest? If I could have told him, without having him ruin the plan, he might be with me now. But it was not in his nature. He was not one of us, whatever my pretense. At any rate, where there is life, we are told, there is hope.

When I was ten years of age and my father was expected back at The Farm, I was delighted to see him one afternoon walking along the post road to our house and leading behind him a pony, a gift. I and this animal became inseparable. I named him Prince, and soon we were dashing together throughout the countryside, in reckless abandonment.

One day Prince took a bad fall. I was thrown free, but was nearly knocked unconscious; and my left leg twisted in such a way that I later reinjured it upon the stage. The accident happened near our tobacco fields, and the black hands went running to fetch Father. I remember the feeling of my body suddenly being lifted in Father's strong arms and pressed to his shirt bosom.

"Oh, is he dead, then? Is he dead, then?" Father's noble voice, so capable of enthralling entire crowds within a theatre, boomed across the dusty tobacco fields and over the heads of the black field hands I imagined silently standing in the background. He began to sob. "Is my beautiful, my darling Johnny, is he dead?"

Although I could have opened my eyes, I chose for a few moments more to remain limp in my father's arms. As I lay enclosed in a self-sealed darkness, I thought precociously to myself: *How moving this scene of father and dying son would appear upon the stage!*

I drink some more whiskey. I will sleep well tonight.

April 19, Wednesday, 1865

Jones returned as promised, bringing food, newspapers, and more whiskey. In his low, guiling way, Jones tried for an hour or so to engage me in conversation about my life, and my great act, but I do not trust this man's loyalties. At last, he left.

The weather continues rainy, and cold. According to the newspapers, George Atzerodt and Sam Arnold have been arrested, as I feared. I am universally vilified in the Northern press. Lincoln's funeral is to be held in the East Room of the White House, and the body sent home for burial. I have been a fugitive for six days.

Earlier this afternoon, a mounted Union patrol passed so near our thicket, we could see the flashes of the soldiers' blue uniforms between the vertical lines of the pine trees, and hear the curses of the enlisted men as they urged their mounts onward through the swamps. Our own horses whinnied at the scent of their own kind, and nearly gave us away. But the Union horsemen passed by and have not yet returned.

My father's death in 1852 changed everything. He died in my fourteenth year, away on his theatrical travels and while playing at an engagement in New Orleans. I can still visualize the newspapers' headlines, seemingly black-draped in massive letters: JUNIUS BRUTUS BOOTH, NATION'S FOREMOST SHAKESPEREAN TRAGEDIAN, DIES. Much later, from his friends in the theatre, I learned the details of his death.

Father was playing a lead in *The Iron Chest,* when he began to falter onstage and forget his lines. He had been traveling without my brother Edwin, who had begun his theatrical career. Having once escaped Edwin's watchful eyes, my father succumbed to his natural melancholy and alcoholic intemperance. The audience began to catcall and hiss as Father forgot line after line, until finally the great man advanced to the edge of the stage as if to face his tormentors. But, to the horror of the other actors onstage, Father seemed not even to recognize the audience's presence. Instead, holding his body like a wounded child, Father looked out over the rows of hostile strangers and began blankly to chant: "I can't read, I'm a charity boy, I can't read. Take me to the lunatic hospital."

Friends led him away from the theatre and aboard a Mississippi steamer bound for St. Louis. They sent word to Mother to travel West and receive him there. But by the second day of his journey, Father seemingly had recovered his sobriety and he insisted on drinking freely of the river, claiming the "father of all waters" would purify his body and spirit. He took a fever and died. His funeral was a time of national grieving, and his body lay in public at Baltimore for two days beside a large marble statue of Shakespeare.

After my father's death, Tudor Hall was sold. Mother was, perhaps, unwilling to continue the extravagant expenses of my father's agricultural experiments, and she also wished to live closer to Edwin in New York City. I was to remain in the South, as a boarding student at the St. Timothy's Hall of Baltimore. But even greater than the loss of my childhood home was my consequent separation from Asia. She had decided soon after Father's death that it was time for her to marry and start her own family.

Asia had been pursued for matrimony for some time by John Sleeper Clarke, a corpulent, clownish man who made his livelihood in the performance of low theatrical farces. Vainly did I try to dissuade Asia from marrying this man, who I felt was only trying to connect his name to the Booth family's greater theatrical fame. But they were joined in matrimony one afternoon in the last week that Tudor Hall was to remain in our family.

Asia came to me privately a few minutes after the completion of the ceremony, in her white bridal gown, wearing the floral tokens of her physical purity in a band cunningly woven about her forehead. At some distance from us in the yard, my new brother-in-law, Clarke, stood drinking at a table, and encouraging his hired fiddlers as they played the ribald tune "Sally in the Green Grass."

"It is you whom I love the most, Johnny," she whispered, kissing me. "It will always be you I love the most."

My dear God, why did my sister have to marry a *comedian*?

A few days later, I traveled alone to Baltimore and the St. Charles Academy. My school days were happy and uneventful. I excelled at games and at studies, having precociously read so much in my father's library. The priests at school were indulgent and kind to me, perhaps not expecting such humility and eagerness to please as they saw in me—a perception I deliberately cultivated. In return, I was filled with respect for the ritual and theatre of the Church.

On free days, I would slip away from the academy and wander the crowds of Baltimore, practicing my theatrical skills by pretending that I was a homeless orphan boy. In this solitary way, I came to love the city's stone quays, its harbor strangely forested with the masts of sailing vessels, and the marble porches at private homes of an almost cenotaphic whiteness. I reminded myself that Baltimore was the city of artists, of Francis Scott Key and of E. A. Poe, with whom Father told me he once had drunk a toast.

My brother Edwin's celebrated success on the stage, particularly in the New York City theatres, reminded me that I was lagging tardily in establishing my own career as an actor. Asia, furthermore, was writing letters to me candidly describing her unhappy marriage, and her possible physical abuse, at the hands of John Sleeper Clarke. I felt that my days of childhood and schoolboy innocence were at an end. I had a little money from Father's estate; although not yet sixteen, I was determined to leave St. Charles secretly at the end of the term and to strike out on my own as an actor.

I had prepared brief letters to Mother and Asia declaring my intention and promising to write.

In my early years in the theatre, I had my share of obscure roles, forgotten lines, and miscues, weeks and even months of hunger. Out of respect for my late father's reputation, I avoided billing myself as a Booth. Instead, I publicly billed myself in playbills as "John Wilkes," or, simply, "Mr. Wilkes." Gradually, the Southern theatres became kind to me, and I found my true calling.

As I traveled throughout the South during the 1850s, I could sense that our nation was on the verge of civil war. It made my heart sick. My own sympathies for the South, and its rich heritage and culture, far transcended my reservations over the institution of slavery. I saw the efforts of those in the North to impose their own beliefs on the Southern states as an effort to break the will and social structure of the South itself. Was not I of the South? The clumsy efforts of the abolitionists—and of many of the Northern legislators in Congress—drove me to despair, as I tried to imagine how the conflict would resolve itself. "The impending crisis" and "the irrepressible conflict" were on everyone's lips.

The beginnings of my own dissolution and fall from grace occurred as I was traveling by horseback along the old Charleston to Frankfort trail in the western Carolina mountains. I had an engagement to play *Politian,* and I was still more than a week's travel away. Throughout a long, dusky afternoon I had ridden alone along a path up a narrow valley of the Catawba River.

I was that day traveling through the southern territory of Lincoln's origins, although his history was not then generally known, and I would hear the facts only after his first inauguration. Here the president's mother as a young woman had entertained travelers by the wayside, and become pregnant with him out of wedlock before marrying the man now said to be Abraham Lincoln's father.

I stopped that night at a rudely built tavern where I entertained a small crowd of travelers and local people by reciting my lines from *Politian.* A fire was built outside in the tavernyard, and a great many toasts of cherry brandy were drunk in my honor. One remained after the others had left, a very young mountain girl with a charming, found-in-the-grass beauty. Later in the evening, I clapped out the measures of time in delight as she danced for me around the fire. I had insisted on buying a private bed, and with her arms wrapped around me we went there together. That was my first experience of carnal love. In the morning, I left her my gold watch, engraved JWB.

Months later, when the chancre appeared, it was like a bright and cruel jewel, a token of how I had both fallen and entered into the world.

The war was harvesttime for actors. Everyone wanted diversion. Theatre engagements and money practically rolled in upon me, and in the first years of my good fortune, I gave myself freely to the fleshpots of the wartime theatres. Wooing hearts on the stage and wooing hearts in the *boudoirs* became one and the same art to me. Later, I began a succession of more serious affairs of the heart, of which Laura Keene was the first.

April 20, Thursday, 1865

This morning the skies are somewhat clearer. David and I dry our clothes and discuss our plans for escape after crossing the river. Jones has promised to return again this afternoon.

I first met John Surratt's mother in October 1864, when I went to visit John at his house. I had become famous on the stage and frequently was recognized on the streets. The newspapers called me "the most handsome man in America," a title which always embarrassed me. My theatrical fame by the time of this visit had eclipsed even my brother Edwin's. I memorized the words of one reviewer:

"Mr. Booth has created an altogether new style of acting, so different from his late father's or anyone else's. His artistry upon our national thespian boards is not unlike the new poetry being written by Mr. Whitman, or the republican principles now being espoused by Mr. Lincoln."

I nodded pleasantly to those who recognized me from the theatre as I walked that day along Pennsylvania Avenue, but as I turned down H Street, I had quite another errand in my mind other than pleasing my admirers. John Surratt had told me of his family, and I was determined to learn more of this young man's life.

Mary opened the door hoping to find a potential tenant. She startled at the sight of my expensive clothes; it was clear I was not a poor government clerk come seeking room and board. Her expression then turned to confusion, and a kind of pleasing surprise; I was sure she recognized my features from my public *cartes de visite.*

"Wilkes Booth," I said, and slightly bowed. "I am a friend of your son John."

Mary recovered magnificently. "I have indeed been told much about you, and the warmth of your friendship, by my son," she said. Mary drew herself up in the open doorway as she spoke, so that I could not quite see beyond her to what I knew was the drabness of the house's interior hallway. "Unfortunately, John is away for the afternoon seeking work," she said. "He will regret the occasion of missing you." Mary tactfully did not mention my theatrical fame.

Perhaps it was at that moment on her doorstep that I succumbed to the temptation of what later would happen between us that afternoon. When we discover that our acquaintances lack sufficient mystery, then *that* is the temptation. "May I wait inside in case John comes home early?" I asked. "I'd be vexed to have missed him."

She hesitated, but I intimated a loneliness, and perhaps more than that. Mary brought her right hand up to the side of her hair and blushed slightly. "Very well, Mr. Booth, you may wait. I admit that company has become a rare pleasure for me." She led the way into the parlor. There were, as I had expected, the usual furnishings: the marble-topped table with books, the camel-backed sofa, now somewhat threadbare, and the hammocked cushions. She sat across from me on the sofa. We talked of novels and of the stage. "As a young girl, Mr. Booth, I was once a very ardent reader of novels and romances," Mary said.

She gave a little laugh, with a slight undertone of bitterness which I think that I was intended to hear. She then brushed at the front of her black frock as if removing imaginary household dust, although I understood the intent of her gesture was to emphasize to me the current drabness of her clothing.

"But that was when I was a young girl," Mary said. "I subsequently was married for many years to a man who, whatever his other virtues, considered novel-reading and theatre-going to be idle pastimes, and not suitable for a woman with responsibilities in the kitchen or the nursery." She again laughed, but this time I thought the disappointment in her voice was intended, whether I heard it or not.

I felt the need to put her at her ease, and I told some amusing theatrical anecdotes about my father.

"I have a confession to make, Mr. Booth," Mary said, giving me a coquettish look from her chair across the parlor. "When I was a young girl in Maryland—when *you,* sir, were yourself in Maryland at your family's nursing room—I kept hidden in my bedroom a steel engraving I had torn from the pages of a popular publication, an engraving of your father, Junius Booth, in *Julius Ceasar.*"

She smiled, and I found it exciting to be able to renew this memory of youth. "I suspect that *many* young girls secretly kept such an engraving," I said, and we laughed together.

There was a short silence after our laughter died. I heard the clock ticking on the parlor mantel. I wondered at what hour John intended to return here to H Street after his search for work, and considered how within four hours I was due onstage at Grover's National to perform *Pescara.* The silence seemed to remind Mary of her present circumstances.

"I sometimes dreamed in my girlhood of going to Baltimore and becoming an actress," Mary said after a few moments. "But that was before I became a wife to a tavernkeeper, a sorter of penny postage in rural Maryland, a mother, and a widow." She straightened the folds of her frock. "I now feel that on some days I *have* become an actress, although in a role and in a play I would not have chosen, Mr. Booth."

I was intrigued. "I understand your situation," I told her.

My words seemed to have a dramatic effect upon Mary. She suddenly arose in a fit of passion and advanced toward me, twisting her hands in front of her in a gesture of both hopelessness and anger that would have appeared beautiful upon the stage.

"Do you truly understand, Mr. Booth? You say you do, but I fear that you do not, my beautiful young man. Do you understand what it is like to be a woman suddenly cut off in the prime of her life by a husband's cruel death, condemned to an existence, whatever her good works and hopes, of eternal widowhood and constant financial anxiety and concern for her children? To wear dresses only of plain bombazine and to spend her days totaling the insufficient accounts of a boardinghouse, while she sees her children's lives slipping away from her, and her own life passing her by like an unfulfilled dream outside the window? You say that you do, sir, but I fear that you do not."

She looked at me from eyes that were distraught and accusatory. But of course I did understand. I am John Wilkes Booth.

In response, I crossed the room and undid her hair, allowing it to fall to her shoulders. She gasped, both at my boldness and at the possibilities of our situation.

"Mary, come with me someplace else," I said, and I led her by the shoulders to her own small *boudoir* behind the parlor screens. Mary followed me almost willingly, although she looked around the familiar furnishings of this room as if they belonged to another.

"Mr. Booth, you mistake my intentions, sir," she said. I saw that she could scarcely believe that her words of complaint, spoken only a few moments ago to a young man half her age in her parlor, could have a resolution even more dramatic here in her bedroom. In my answer, I placed her upon the bed. I undid her bodice and gently removed the St. Christopher's medallion that hung around her neck.

"It's all right, Mary," I said. "It's quite all right. What we do is a gift to us from God."

I removed the St. Anthony chain from my own neck. Mary watched me remove the medallion as she sat passively upon the bed, half-undressed, but she did not speak, and I knew that she was inwardly considering herself and not my actions. She kept her hands folded in her lap, and I was certain that she was judging that having compromised herself to this point, she had no further choice but to play her part as best as she was able. I gave her this necessary time for privacy.

After a few short moments, she said, "Wilkes," and with some hesitation began awkwardly but tenderly to fumble at my clothing.

I knew she was trying to call back to her memory the actions that had once pleased her drunken and loutish husband in their marriage bed, or that she now imagined would please a much younger man. In response, I placed my left hand over her eyes and began to direct her hands.

Together we loosened our clothing. Mary's body now has more of a maternal than an erotic beauty, but she still retained the outlines of her figure as a young woman I had seen in the daguerreotype on the mantel; and I knew that she, like other women, found my body to be beautiful. I continued to guide her hands in ways that were to her as a widow both familiar and new. I was reminded of my first physical intimacy with Laura Keene. Much of the pleasure to me of this act is in my ability to play a role, anticipating what the woman might expect or hope from an ideal lover. Thus I entered into her, and we continued our act of love.

Afterward, I insisted that we go to church together, in an act of penance, and light a candle for Isaac.

Jones returned to our thicket, calling to hogs. I put away my diary and painfully straightened the blanket covering my shattered leg. I was determined not to show physical weakness in front of him.

Jones casually tossed us a canvas bag with our day's food. Although I knew it would contain a jar of harsh whiskey, I refrained from reaching to it, despite the pain in my leg. Jones looked at me in a high humor.

"The Yankees've moved out toward Fredericksburg, and I reckon you boys can move out, too, tomorrow night. I made sure my nigger knows what's good for him. He'll leave my shad boat tied up at Pope's Creek."

David Herold laughed aloud and clapped his hands. Jones spit aside a stream of brown tobacco juice and looked at me with a patronizing manner.

"That's about five miles from here. Think you can hop and ride that far, Mr. Booth?"

I looked at him steadily. "I am sure I can, Mr. Jones. And once this boy and I have crossed the Potomac, my friends will help me there."

Jones's eyes shifted to a point in the pine trees about twenty yards distant, where our horses, half-starved, were hobbled and concealed. He disregarded my rebuke.

"You'll not be needing them horses, Mr. Booth. Not after you two push off tomorrow night in my boat." Jones kept his face in profile to mine, refusing to turn his head in my direction. I watched as his throat visibly constricted. "I'm a poor man ruined by the war," Jones said. "After you leave me, you'll not be needing them two horses."

I forced myself to rise upon one elbow and made my voice sound kind and gentle. "I understand, Mr. Jones. You are most welcome to our horses after we're gone."

Jones slapped his palms together in delight, and Herold started upright in wonder. "Deal!" Jones's shout carried throughout the empty pine thicket, and for a moment I thought of unseen Union patrols. Jones remained unconcerned, and advanced toward me as if to shake my hand at a horse swap. But, instead, he reached inside his pocket. His face became a rictus grin as he talked.

"Six days, Mr. Booth! For six days the goddamned whole world has been wondering where you are, and all that time I'm the only one that knowed! Six days, and I could have practically spit and hit the trees you boys been hiding behind! And now I'll have your horse to prove it."

To my astonishment, Jones then produced one of my theatrical *cartes de visite* from within his pocket. "You reckon you could sign this, Mr. Booth?" Jones held my photographic image down to me. His voice was imploring. "Sign it with both our names? It's proof. It's proof that I was the only one that knowed, Mr. Booth."

Wearily, I took the card and the pencil Jones handed to me. I wrote and dated both our names, in order that this man will have no reason to stay with me any longer. Also, I can keep his pencil with which I will continue to write these pages, my having worn to a nub the one I happened to have in my pocket the night of the murder. (Pencilless! And I will doubtless have to pay Jones something to buy his silence. I have but a few dollars, and my money is at Richmond. I should have been in Europe now.)

I will be glad to be quit of this man tomorrow night. Jones says he helps us for pride, but I think there is something more. For now, I have solitude, and I will write of more pleasant matters.

I subsequently revisited the H Street house later in October 1864, after sending John Surratt a note asking that he and his family receive me. John opened the house door to me. On entering inside to the parlor, I immediately bowed and introduced myself to Mary as if this were our first meeting. I acted before she or John had time to speak, and I was greatly aided by Anna, who was gushing about excitedly at my presence. Mary hesitated, then acquiesced to my false greeting. I honestly believe this little charade was the first falsehood of her life, and I was touched in my heart that for the sake of love she would seal her lips.

While I was on my theatrical travels the following weeks, the love which Mary could not speak in public she poured out to me in her letters. Her correspondence was a source of affection and amusement to me, as I lacked that kind of close contact with my family. I had felt myself estranged by the war from Mother and Asia.

"Dear Pet," Mary wrote to me later that fall, "Have you returned safely from New York City? How is the theatre there, and how do the ladies dress? . . . I feel, my dear Wilkes, that you have filled me with a greater happiness than I could have thought a woman of my position, and of my age, would again experience."

As these letters accumulated, I saw an opportunity. I needed help in my Southern plans—perhaps Mary's son John could act both as the brother I missed and as a confidant and aide in my plans. I knew John's knowledge of the swamps of Virginia would prove invaluable in my escape after my great deed, and I knew John would be flattered by my attentions. My own family had slipped far away from me. Asia's husband refused to admit me to his house, despite my sister's pleadings, supposedly because of his distaste at my political sympathies. Edwin, attending to my mother at New York City, too, was a strong Union man, although I sensed something more. Mother and Edwin, although always kind to me, had never been close, perhaps because I had not shared their tacit disapproval of Father. It was I who had grieved most when he had died. I perceived an opportunity to re-create something of a second family for myself with the Surratts, a family that would cater to my needs and wishes. And doesn't everyone desire that?

I was disappointed when, in November 1864, I returned to the city to consider playing in *The Apostle* at Ford's, Mary was unable to slip away for a lover's tryst at the Willard.

Nonetheless, I was undeterred in my efforts to enlist John Surratt's aid, first to carry medical goods and intelligence reports southward, and without his knowledge, to gain his assistance in the one act that would write my name forever in the history books, and, I prayed, make the South whole again. All my previous work upon the stage may have been but preparation for this one great, dramatic event.

For the past three years, I had been quietly sympathetic to the cause of the South: it was the side of *gentlemen*—those who refrain from using foul language in the presence of ladies, or who consider their rural estates as Edenic retreats from the evils of large cities, as did my father. And as the war degenerated in its totality and its brutality toward all civilians, it became evident to me that the leaders of the North desired nothing less than the subjugation and *deliberate physical humiliation* of a people who had given me a home and whom I saw had unwillingly inherited the burden of slavery. This was as true of the people of the South just as surely as I had inherited the burdens of my own father's theatrical tradition and name. I despaired that this cruel war would continue to play itself out upon our national stage until both sides had exhausted themselves to their limits—until, as Mr. Lincoln stated in my presence at his second inaugural speech in March, "every drop of blood drawn with the lash shall be paid by another drawn with the sword." But by the fourth year of the war, I found that there were other gentlemen in Richmond who considered my ability to move freely in Northern cities very useful to their ultimate victory.

In late December 1864, I received a curious letter from Mary Surratt. It arrived at my hotel a few days before our planned trip to Ford's Theatre with her family. "My dear Mr. Booth," she began, "We have sinned greatly, both against the laws of God and the laws of nature." Mary intimated a change in her "spiritual and bodily existence" and said that she thought it best that we did not meet again privately. "You shall continue as you are, my dear Wilkes, as a wonderful and kind gentleman, and I shall continue as what I have become."

A wonderful, kind gentleman. Perhaps, but one not without sin. I had by this time renewed my acquaintance with Sarah Slater. I had been a good friend to her at Richmond, and I continued to look after her interests at Washington City. And there was also Lucy Hale, the daughter of Republican

Senator Hale from New Hampshire. She had met me at one of the dancing "hops" given for young people at the National Hotel, and, for a time, we convinced ourselves that we loved each other. It was, of course, through the influence of Lucy's father that I was able to secure a ticket to Lincoln's second inaugural. I had planned originally to secure my place in history that day. I had placed a derringer inside my coat pocket. I had gotten tickets for my conspirators, as well, and had gathered them about me among the inaugural crowd. While I had initially toyed with the notion of capturing Lincoln, I soon gave that up in favor of another, bolder act. I was certain, of course, that attempting to kill Lincoln would likely lead to my death. But it honestly was of no concern to me, despite the assurances by my Southern friends and several key politicians in Congress that I would be delivered, and taken safely out of the country. All of my life, I have had the conviction that I shall die violently at some desperate end, although I have shared these thoughts with no one. I remember thinking that morning that as a result of my personal suffering, at least, perhaps *others* shall be delivered. Few men, I knew, could claim to be as altruistic.

I was introduced to Lincoln as one of the distinguished guests inside the Capitol Building before Lincoln went outside to deliver his address. Despite the crude humor celebrating the president's rustic appearance and manners, I found him to be a gentleman, and very captivating in his person, and yet his actions in this war have been nothing short of barbarous.

As we shook hands, I noticed underneath his white shirt cuff the remarkable, olive-colored tone of Mr. Lincoln's skin, which to my knowledge no one has yet commented upon, and the abrupt, almost primitive way in which he combed his shock of gray-black hair.

"I believe we have met before, Mr. Booth, or at least at a distance," he told me. "Two years ago, my wife and I both had the pleasure of watching your performance in *The Marble Heart* at Ford's Theatre."

I was somewhat taken aback by this personal memory. "You are very kind, Mr. President," I said, and bowed. "It was not my best performance."

In his response, I discovered that Mr. Lincoln could be a great physical toucher. He brought his other hand down upon my left shoulder and looked at me humorously with his remarkable gray-blue eyes. Usually, I abhor being touched by other people against my will, but I found this gesture of the president's to be strongly affecting.

"I know that, Mr. Booth," Mr. Lincoln said. "But so long as *they* don't know that"—he indicated with a smiling turn of his head the large crowd waiting for both of us outside the Capitol Building—"I reckon we can both get along fine with our audiences."

Mr. Lincoln abruptly left me to deliver his speech outside. I followed in the wake of the crowd, and briefly stood outside on the Capitol steps. I saw Herold, Atzerodt, and Powell among the spectators below us, as I had asked. That old busybody Gardner was setting up a camera on a tripod. But I was puzzled and angry by my seeming inability to act decisively when I stood but a few feet from Lincoln. I had been *upstaged,* and my scene stolen, by an actor much less talented and much older than myself. I left the inaugural scene frustrated.

Then the events crowded down. Sarah informed me that she was pregnant by me. She had done me good service, making me intimate to so many military secrets she had overheard at the dance hall, and I was determined to act honorably toward her. How could I do otherwise when she was carrying my son. In early April, the Southern Confederacy collapsed, and my friends advised me either to act decisively or flee. My old physical malady also briefly returned, although in time I passed into good health.

It was in these last weeks of March 1865 that I discovered my remarkable ability to read the signs hidden in the still or moving pictures of nature. I believe this gift was due to my impending fatherhood, when it is possible that a new passage opens up in the mind of a man. I was taking a solitary walk in the suburbs of the city at night, considering the consequences of my proposed action, when I both saw and *heard* in the windward motion of tree branches a prophecy of my act.

"Booth will not hang, Booth will not hang," was the song in the wind. The tree branches themselves were silent, but I *heard* this message through the moving wind in the voice of a beautiful woman, even

more beautiful in my imagination than my sister, Asia. *Booth will not hang.*

Several days later, I finally understood. I was to be both father and son. I was no longer a mere actor. I understood that I would have my time publicly reviled and wandering in the wilderness, even as I am just now writing these lines hidden in a pine thicket. But I was to be both a national and a personal savior. I am a type of Christ. I was to murder Abraham Lincoln.

April 22, Saturday, 1865

Failure. I write this still on the Maryland shore. The Potomac, two miles wide at this point, separates me from freedom and escape. For eight days now I have been a fugitive, and I have managed to travel no farther than what a man with two good legs could have ridden in a day.

Jones did not betray us, or at least not in the manner I had feared. He did indeed put us into a small boat on Friday night and push us out into the Potomac. For the next six hours, Herold and I drifted, our small craft caught first by one dark current and then another. Herold had assured me he could read a compass and navigate the river, but he was helpless as a child. At day-break, we maneuvered our little boat into a freshwater inlet concealed by willow trees. I had hoped we were at last in Virginia. As the light increased under the trees, Herold stood up in the boat and gazed at the scenery around us.

"I believe I know this place, Mr. Booth," he said. "It's Nanjemoy Creek. I recollect that I used to fish here with my father. It's on the Maryland side."

I could have screamed, both at his stupidity and at the desperate nature of our situation. Instead of crossing the river, we simply had drifted upstream on a tidal current. Now there is nothing for us to do but remain hidden, and wait until darkness to try again to cross. My broken leg is fully suppurating, and the flesh below my calf is as black as any Negro's. I can bear its pain only by lying lengthwise along the boat.

As we wait and sleep fitfully through the long spring day, I notice for the first time in the swamp the rhythmical humming of the cicadas. It is a soothing chorus—yet is it not a kind of *accustomed* horror, surrounded by insects that care not for us, and whose song is not for us?

On reading these pages, I notice a strange convergence of time. *In medias res* is how I began my story, as do all good playwrights. But now there are only two past episodes to recount before my diary once more becomes totally of the present. I fear my own life is forfeit, that I will never see Sarah or John again, and that the present can only drift me to certain death. But at the same time I feel I am writing a secret and unrevealed drama of *other* lives, to which I do not yet see the conclusion.

I last spoke with Mary Surratt in the first week of April 1865, preceding Lincoln's death. Sarah and I chanced by her boardinghouse in a carriage. I had been talking to Sarah of her condition, and my plans to send her safely southward. Sarah had secretly intimated, I believe, of my plans against Lincoln, and she urged me to make arrangements for her travel as soon as possible. When Mary came up to our carriage, I seized upon this opportunity to help Mary in her financial crisis. In part, this was only the courtesy I felt was due to an old lover; but I confess that I was also curious as to why Mary had so abruptly ended our affair. I immediately arranged the trip to Surrattsville and instructed Sarah to wait behind us for John's arrival. As usual, she understood my motives perfectly, for it was also a perfect opportunity to throw Sarah and John Surratt together again in the hopes they might solidify the bonds between them, and ensure John's help in taking Sarah to Richmond. The presence of Weichman in the carriage kept this trip from being too awkward for Mary. Later that afternoon, after I had made my own arrangements at the Surratt farm and tavern, I had the opportunity to speak with her privately.

"We made love but once, Mary," I said. We stood in a windswept field of flowers near the tavernyard, the sunlight on her face. Her features still retain much of the beauty of her youth, but in the direct sunlight I could not help but notice the small patterns of tired flesh now present at the corners of her eyes. I was certain Mary knew that at that moment I was thinking both of her beauty and of her age. She seemed embarrassed at reading my thoughts, and turned her face away.

"Mr. Booth, I have become old," she said. She kept her gaze downward upon the field of ragged robins in bloom around us, as if contemplating the irregular and individually torn blue petals of these flowers. "In ways too personal for me to explain to any man, I have changed," Mary said. "I have practically become an old woman before your eyes."

"Nonsense, Mary," I said. "People become old, and then they become young again. And surely you realized when I visited your house in December that I was speaking of you when I praised Anna's beauty?"

Mary suddenly brought her hands to both sides of her severely styled hair and stood shaking her head from side to side, near tears.

"Oh, Wilkes, stop it, stop it." I was impressed by the elegance of her gesture and said nothing. "Did you not see that, other than trying to give my poor daughter a few precious hours of her youth, I was doing penance that night for my own presumption of thinking and acting like a young woman? You are kind, Wilkes, but you are too kind. I fear that Our Lord requires a more demanding judgment of us. It is my hope, when I am again able to make my confession, that I receive divine forgiveness for what I have done. I hope to be brave enough to make that confession before my death."

"There is no death," I told her, shocked by the honesty I heard in my voice, "unless one wishes it."

Later that day, I insisted that we exchange medallions. I carved an inscription on St. Anthony for her with my knife. But I realized that my time with Mary, and indeed with all my Washington friends and intimates, was drawing to a close.

It will be dark in an hour, and we will try again to cross. I have some time now to write of Lincoln's death. How many times will that scene be reenacted on the stage, or on painted dioramas, or prepared photographs? Yet will I always be the villain, and remembered and revered only by the Thomas Joneses of this world? My last meeting with Jones makes me fear so. Jones had led us to his hidden boat and charged us eighteen dollars for it, as well as keeping our two horses. As we had pushed off, he stood on the shore clutching his right shirt pocket, where I knew my signed photographic trophy was kept. He gave me a sly look.

"I'm more than just a nigger-driver, Mr. Booth," he told me. "I can read and write as fair as the next man, I reckon. There's a book to be made of you, Mr. Booth."

With the right toe of his boot, Jones nudged our boat out into the Potomac while I lay lengthwise across its bottom, speechless with pain. In front of me, Herold floundered with the oarlocks. "Whether you boys live or die, it's your own lookout," Jones told us, and grinned at me. "But there's a fortune to be made just by writing a book that I knowed you, Mr. Booth. I can tell your story. And I got your horse and your photograph to prove it."

As we drifted away, he was but a small, mocking figure on the shore. This is not how I wish to be remembered. My plan had more drama, more consequence, than that.

In the week preceding Good Friday, I had determined upon my action. I had safely removed John Surratt, unaware of my plans, from the Washington scene, so that Sarah could escape arrest. All that remained was for me to seek the president out, and to kill him. The only untoward incident that occurred was on the Tuesday prior to the assassination, when I happened to meet on

Pennsylvania Avenue with the insufferable Louis Weichman. Mary had sent him to hire a carriage for a trip that day to Surrattsville, and he approached me for the use of mine. He was too lazy, I suspect, to want to attend to the livery business himself. I had by now had my fill of the Surratt family, and their interminable needs. Impatiently taking out my wallet, I told him, "Here is ten dollars; take it," plainly meaning that Weichman could hire a carriage at my expense if he would only quit my presence. But, on reflection, I saw an opportunity. Speaking more kindly to Weichman, I told him of the theatre glasses I had left at the boardinghouse, and asked him to please carry them down to the Surrattsville tavern for me. They could be useful on my flight after the assassination. And, seeking to confirm my private arrangements with the Surrattsville tenant, I made up a nonsensical story for Weichman about how I planned for a hunting excursion soon into southern Maryland. I asked him to tell the Surrattsville tenant to be certain that our "shooting irons" would be in readiness. I had Weichman repeat the message to me until I was certain he remembered it.

On the morning of Good Friday, I arose

late, had a fine breakfast, and innocently flirted with a young lady seated next to me in the dining room of the National Hotel. I then went to the barbershop, and thereafter learned that Lincoln himself was expected that evening to attend the performance of *Our American Cousin* at Ford's Theatre. The performance was to be a "benefit night" for Laura Keene. I was amazed at my good fortune. I would not even have to present my card at the Executive Mansion in order to gain admission to Lincoln's house to kill him. *For the good hand of his God was upon him,* I happily repeated to myself, excitedly walking down Pennsylvania Avenue and recalling this line of Holy Scripture from my childhood. I promptly arranged for my conspirators to strike that night throughout Washington City, but I reserved the main drama at the theatre for myself.

By nine-thirty that evening, I was dressed and had arrived at the theatre. Gaining entrance to Ford's was childishly simple.

I ascended to the dress circle. No one in the audience turned their backs as I walked around the circle of chairs toward the president's box at the stage right. I had arranged for the slow-witted boy I have been befriending, Johnny Peanut, to leave the state box unlocked and to hold a horse for me in the alley behind the theatre. The door was unguarded.

The most difficult part for me was waiting to hear my cue while standing in the dingy passageway leading to the interior box. I silently mouthed the lines of the other actors, unseen and below me onstage, until Act III, Scene 2—"you sockdologizing old *mantrap!*"

At that I rushed the box and fired my derringer at the back of Mr. Lincoln's head. At first, in the noise of the laughter below us, I did not hear the report of the pistol. There was only a small cloud of blue smoke between me and the president, and I believed that the cap in my derringer had misfired. *I've failed,* I thought.

In the gaslight, I then saw Lincoln's head jerk to his shoulder in a sudden spasm, and I realized I had succeeded. It was the first violent death in which I have participated. "How like a birth," I calmly thought to myself, as if hearing another's voice. There was a dreadful screaming of a woman in our box, which I wished would stop. I recognized the woman as Mrs. Lincoln.

There were another gentleman and lady seated in our box. The gentleman rose and advanced toward me. He wore the uniform of a Union major. I dropped my emptied pistol, and with a gesture long practiced on the stage, I drew my Bowie knife and brought it in a slow, graceful curve to meet his throat, and I would surely have spilled out his life's blood there, but he was wearing a civilian white collar underneath his uniform blouse, one of those stiff stand-up affairs John so favors, and to our mutual surprise the edge of the knife glided harmlessly over the thick layer of cardboard around the major's throat. I laughed aloud.

I then grasped this man's right arm, turned it upward, and plunged my knife into the soft flesh at his elbow and up to his collarbone. He gave a hoarse cry, and I felt his body shudder in my grasp.

As he fell away from me, there was blood on my clothes. Mrs. Lincoln's mouth opened in horror. To effect my escape, I leapt to the stage.

I felt my left leg break as I landed upon the stage. It was the same weakened limb I had injured in a childhood fall from the pony my father had given me. I wanted to turn toward the audience and scream out my pain, but the words that came were *"Sic semper tyrannis!"*

The audience had not yet realized the president had been shot, or the significance of my fall to the stage. Harry Hawk, the dear fool, had thought someone was shooting at *him,* and had fled center stage in his *American Cousin* costume. I did not feel the pain as I ran past the drop curtains and toward the rear door of the theatre. Of all those standing backstage, only Laura Keene, who had been waiting for her next entrance, seemed to have realized what I had accomplished.

"Oh, Johnny, what have you done? What have you done?" she cried out, looking ridiculous in her layers of facial paint and her stage clothing.

I reached the alleyway and forced myself up into the saddle of my horse. "Mr. Booth! Mr. Booth! My fifty cents!" Johnny Peanut was holding tightly onto my bridle. I saw then that all my plans for escape could come to naught because of this poor idiot boy. I had forgotten to give Peanut his fifty-cent piece. In my haste, I kicked with my good leg into his face, and I was free.

Concealing my blood-splattered clothing and my dagger underneath my cape, I rode in very good time to the Navy Yard Bridge, and crossed without a challenge into Maryland. The military sentinel who waved me onward was very inattentive, and so I did not have to kill that young boy.

I was barely eight miles along the road to Surrattsville, near the place called Soper's Hill, when I heard the clatter of a horse and rider close behind me. *A Union cavalryman,* I thought, and instantly regretted my plan to leave fresh horses and weapons at the Surratt tavern, still several miles ahead. But I then recognized a familiar, immature voice.

"Mr. Booth! Mr. Booth! Wait for me, please!"

It was David Herold. I had told this boy simply to make himself useful to others in the killings, but he had followed me on his own volition. We reined in our horses at the top of the hill, and as our gasping animals got back their wind, I questioned him in the darkness.

"Did Lewis kill the secretary of state?"

"Yes, sir. I saw him running from the house with blood on his hands."

"And did George assassinate Vice President Johnson?"

"I think so. He was doing an awful lot of drinking, Mr. Booth."

We rode together to the Surrattsville tavern. There, by my private arrangement with Mary's tenant, we received fresh horses, Spencer repeating rifles, and, thank God, some whiskey. My broken bone had torn at my flesh since riding from Washington, and, in remounting my horse, I nearly fainted from the pain. I realized that I needed David Herold if I were to continue my escape, and I asked him to ride with me to Dr. Mudd's farm, where my leg could be splinted.

He could not refuse me. Dr. Mudd had me carried upstairs to his bedroom. (At this same time, I later read in the newspapers, Lincoln's unconscious body was being carried across 10th Street to a bed at a boardinghouse opposite Ford's Theatre.) Mudd broke up an old wooden hatbox and began to splint my leg.

The sly doctor had been in the thick of us from the beginning, even before I had recruited John Surratt and the others. Yet, I wanted to give my old friend an opportunity plausibly to deny that he recognized me, and, in a moment alone in the bedroom, I slipped on a false beard I had earlier that day placed in my coat. Of course, with the lack of spirit gum, the beard kept slipping off my face at the *most* inopportune moments, so that Mudd and I had to pretend that we did not recognize one another, or that Mudd did not notice my frantic fumbling to replace the whiskers back onto my face. These were the first, few horrible hours after the assassination: our tragedy was in danger of becoming a farce.

In the morning, Mudd sent breakfast to Herold and me and then ordered us both out of his house. Did my clever friend remember to destroy the boot marked with my initials which he so angrily slit from my left leg? I distinctly remember Mudd tossing it underneath the bed on which I lay. Acting on John Surratt's latest information and maps, David and I then rode our horses into Zekiah Swamp.

It is very dark. Tonight we will once more try the river with the intent to cross, though I have a greater desire and almost a mind to return to Washington City and in a measure clear my name.

April 23, Sunday, 1865

Success. Whether from divine intervention or by blind chance, we drifted in the night undetected across the Potomac and find ourselves in the morning on the Virginia shore. I believe we are in King George County. I remain concealed in the boat, which we leave drawn up underneath a pine bluff by the river, and Herold searched for nearby townships and help. He returned with a horse and saddle, bought with most of my Union money. I am very weak, scarcely able to write in my diary, but for the boy's sake I forced myself in the saddle, and we rode the eight miles to Port Conway and the Rappahannock ferry.

The road toward the ferry is crowded with Confederate ex-soldiers returning home. I am one of the few on a horse. I see no Union patrols accompanying them, as the government apparently is still searching in force for me about Fredericksburg or Richmond. Curiously, Herold and I excite no attention as we join into the columns of anonymous, gray-tattered men making their way down to the Rappahannock. Many also are lame and halt, and they scarcely raise their heads at the sight of two more refugees in civilian black suits, one crippled, moving among them. I am pleased for our safety, but I must admit that I am somewhat worried that I am not recognized: have I changed so much from my injury or from my confinement in the wilderness that I am no longer recognizable? Do they know how much I sacrificed for them, as well as for their brothers in blue uniforms in the opposite army?

We crossed at the Rappahannock ferry. Herold chatted among the soldiers grouped on the ferry, but I remained on my horse, as I cannot endure to stand. The ferryman was a rough-looking man, and he stared suspiciously at our civilian clothes. I consider the large rewards which the newspapers say are posted for my arrest, and the certainty that someone along my travels must betray me. For all I know, Jones has now sold his story of my life, and is leading Union avengers after me. The rope dragging the ferry to the opposite shore sang in the pulley above my head.

I looked down from my saddle to the reflection of my own face in the black water of the Rappahannock River. My features were distorted across the flat surface, as when John had seen me in the darkened mirror at the Willard Hotel. But although John knows of his mother's affair, he also knows that I entrusted him with the safe journey of my unborn child and the deliverance of the woman whom I love. Will John forgive me? After all, are he and I not like brothers?

On the opposite shore, I paid the ferryman the last of my Union dollars.

I rode, and Herold walked, a few miles down the main road to Richmond. I tried not to complain of the increasing agony in my leg. We passed by the disturbed gravesites of six Union soldiers. Feral hogs from the surrounding swamps in search of food have rooted up and desecrated these poor men's remains. As we silently passed by, I saw the largest hog gnawing on a skull in a cruel reenactment of death and resurrection in this first springtime of peace.

I will write no more this day.

April 24, Monday, 1865
We have escaped the nightmare of the swamps. Herold and I proceeded several miles toward the township of Bowling Green, and thence toward Richmond. But the agony in my leg became so great that I begged Herold to walk up to a farmhouse

we saw from the road and ask if we might rest there a few days. I remained on the road, out of sight of the house. I instructed Herold to describe me as a "Mr. Boyd," and to tell whoever was there that I was "a gentleman from farther South, lately injured in the war, who only wants to return home."

Our hosts are the Garrett family, a kindly old man with his wife and five children. They invited us up to the piazza of their house, and for the first time in more than a week I began to feel comfortable. Their two-story frame house is well sited, on a sunny hill with rosebushes away from the main road, and distant from the outlying marshes and rivers. Their five children vary in ages from two grown sons to boys and girls perhaps eleven or twelve years old. The younger children gathered around my chair on the piazza and stared at the stranger their father had invited into their family. I was reminded of my own happy childhood at Tudor Hall.

The old man Garrett has heard news of the assassination of Lincoln, but I am sure he has no idea of my true identity. I have told him that I also was an actor in Maryland before the war.

"I've heard of Junius Booth, but not this Wilkes," the old man told me. "Have you ever met the Booth who shot Lincoln?"

"I saw him once onstage in Richmond," I said. "About the time of John Brown's raid."

"Is he an old man or young man, Mr. Boyd?" This question was asked me by Joanna, their youngest daughter of perhaps twelve years of age. Her eyes were wide with wonder at me.

"Sometimes very young, and sometimes very old," I replied.

Later, the old man and his wife brought us a dinner on the piazza, and I was able to eat a little. Mr. Garrett invited us to stay with his family for several days until my leg healed, but I insisted that Herold and I sleep in an outlying tobacco barn I noticed on their property.

"I would not dream of imposing further upon your hospitality by taking your beds," I reply. I shift my lame leg in my chair with what I know is a graceful stoicism. "You have already been too kind to me." I see the old man and his wife exchange a furtive smile; the family is pleased to have such a

467

gentleman among them. But I fear that if Union patrols come, these good people will suffer if I am found under their roof.

After dinner, Herold napped, and Mr. Garrett fashioned a rude wooden crutch for me. I was able to move about the farmyard a little. It is now ten days since Lincoln's death. It was a beautiful April afternoon, and I reminded myself that it is no sin for man to limp.

Little Joanna and her younger brother Richard, who is about ten years of age, followed me about the farmyard like a pair of curious puppies. The children bashfully confessed to me that they did not know what I meant when I told their father I was an actor. Despite the excruciating pain in my leg, I decided to lead the children in a game, explaining theatre by reclining with them under the falling white petals of an apple tree in full bloom in the farmyard. Together we pretended that it is winter and that the petals are falling snowflakes. The children were delighted. Later, I amazed them by magically causing the needle inside my box compass to move, merely by passing over it the iron blade of my Bowie knife.

(It is still flecked from the dried blood of that major at Ford's Theatre.)

For a moment, I am very happy.

April 25, Tuesday, 1865

This morning Herold walked to the nearby town of Bowling Green, to see if he could barter for some new shoes. After breakfast, I entertained the little Garrett children with my stagecraft. I plaited some spring rosebuds into Joanna's hair. My leg was paining me somewhat less than usual, and I had almost forgotten that I was a fugitive, until little Joanna pointed out to me below the hill the blue flash of uniforms, as a mounted Union patrol rushed past the farmhouse on the road to Bowling Green. I reached for my revolver underneath my coat, and ordered the children to run to their parents in a voice that frightened them.

No soldiers came to the farmhouse. Herold returned, shoeless but uncaptured, within a few hours. The boy apparently does not realize that he is too trifling in appearance to draw the attention of our pursuers. He reported that the Union patrol had searched the town and then moved on uneventfully toward Richmond. But I will admit that I am badly frightened. I am determined that in the morning we will move on, and to whatever fate awaits us at Richmond.

Booth will not hang, I silently repeat to myself in a kind of personal catechism, *Booth will not hang.*

Perhaps I will not successfully escape and never again be united with Sarah, or my mother and sister, again. If so, I am determined to die violently resisting, rather than be returned for hanging. I will insist that David Herold be peaceably surrendered, as this boy did nothing and followed me only from, perhaps, a misplaced sense of hero worship. I do not fear death, and fret only that my body will be mutilated by my angry captors after my death, and my gravesite deliberately kept unmarked.

The public never knew my best drama. It was necessary for Mr. Lincoln to suffer and die, both for his presumption as an actor and in order for the people to *see,* to understand, that only by losing everything can we begin anew. Similarly, I have suffered, and will probably die, both for my presumption in attempting to be a greater actor than my father and for my great visions. By rising above and destroying whatever my beloved father hoped for me, I briefly had the power to create myself anew.

My act should not be considered political, nor the demented violence of an outcast. The newspapers say that I am a madman. To be mad, we gather, is to live in a world that is totally symbolic; nothing is random, like the cicadas' song, and one is never alone, like the so-called sane.

Little Joanna runs laughing toward me as I lie reclined in the sweet grass and sunshine writing this. And so we all move on, from the eternal love of a parent to expulsion by death, and behind us a door closes, so like the door to the greenroom when I first entered onto the public stage.

I bid farewell to my mother and sister, to all my mothers and sisters. I always tried to do good. I bless the entire world.

J. Wilkes Booth

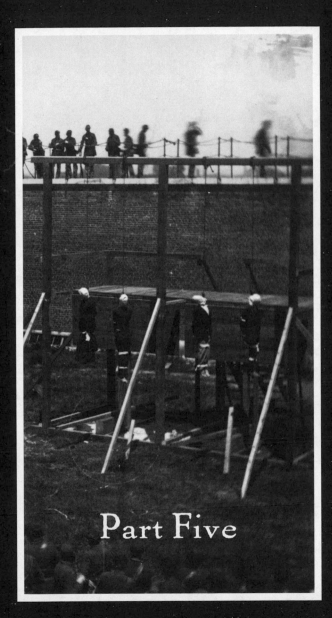

Part Five

From the transcript of the trial of John H. Surratt, Jr., in the murder of Abraham Lincoln, Criminal Court of Washington, D.C., 1867

A. My name is Everton J. Conger. My occupation in 1865, in the month of April, was as lieutenant colonel of the 1st District of Columbia Cavalry.

Q. Colonel Conger, will you give to this jury an account of the capture and death of Booth?

A. My command of twenty-six cavalrymen arrived at Garrett's house about twelve or one o'clock on the morning of the 26th of April. We were acting on reliable information received at Washington City and elsewhere, and we were under orders received directly from President Johnson to attempt to capture Booth alive, if at all possible, and determine the exact nature of the conspiracy.

Q. And what occurred when you arrived at the Garrett farm?

A. We awakened the occupants of the household, and I will admit that my men treated the members of the Garrett family rather roughly. They at first denied that there was anyone else there except for a "Mr. Boyd" and his friend. But when I threatened to burn the house and to hang old man Garrett, and when I produced a photograph of John Wilkes Booth, the children of the household began to cry. They told us the men we sought were asleep inside a tobacco barn on the property.

Q. And what did you then do?

A. I ordered my men to dismount, and deployed them about the barn at intervals of about five feet apart. It was very dark. I lit a candle, advanced to the front door of the barn, and called out for the men inside to surrender.

Q. Tell us what was said, by both you and Booth. We want to get before the jury the precise occurrences in their order, exactly as they occurred.

A. Booth's voice responded from within, "Who are you? It may well be that I am taken by our friends." I recognized Booth at once. I had heard him several times upon the stage, and his voice carried very well from within the interior of the barn.

"We are no friends of yours, and we know who you are," I replied. "You are surrounded. If you don't come out, we will set the barn on fire and burn you out."

"Colonel, that is very hard," Booth replied. "There is a young man here who very much wants to surrender." Herold then thrust his bare hands through the barn door, was seized, and I ordered him tied to a black locust tree in the barnyard.

Booth then called out to me again from the interior of the barn. "Colonel, I do not want to shed blood. I have had half a dozen chances to shoot you, but I do not wish to do it."

I will admit that I became very alarmed at this statement. I immediately put down the candle I was holding, drew my revolver, and stepped back into the darkness surrounding the barn. I then gave my men orders, loud enough for Booth to overhear, to place brush into the open slats of the barn, and to prepare to light it. Sergeant Boston Corbett was directed by me to see to this detail.

"Your time is up," I shouted out to Booth. "I am going to fire the barn." There was no reply from within.

Q. And then what occurred?

A. This tobacco barn was an old wooden structure, and, on my order, it burned very quickly. In an instant, it was illuminated from inside. I advanced cautiously to the barn door and could see Booth distinctly. The sudden light must have blinded him. He stood very erect, though he dropped a crutch to his side as I watched him. He was standing underneath the arch of fire that had become the barn's roof. Booth as an actor was said to have "the form of an Apollo," and it occurred to me at that moment I was watching an Apollo in flames. Booth dropped the carbine he was holding in his other hand, and drew a revolver as if to place it at his head. In an instant there was the crack of a pistol. I saw that Sergeant Corbett had shot Booth from an opening in the slats of the barn wall. Booth fell forward upon his face.

Q. And you are certain this Sergeant Corbett is the one who shot Booth, and that the assassin did not kill himself?

A. Yes, sir. In the morning, I saw Corbett in the yard, and with considerable profanity I rebuked him and asked why he had shot Booth. Corbett drew himself to attention, and, pointing upward, he said, "For the greater glory of God." I had the sergeant placed under arrest, as we had been under strict orders to take Booth alive if possible, but it is my understanding this Corbett later received his liberty at the express request of Secretary Stanton.

Q. And what did you do when you saw Booth was shot, and you saw him fall?

A. I was upon Booth in a moment to take away his weapon, and, with the assistance of my enlisted men, I dragged him into the yard and out of the intense heat of the barn. Booth was still alive, though barely conscious, and he died a few hours later, about the time of daybreak.

Q. And at any time during the hours Booth remained alive after his capture, did he speak to you or anyone else of John Surratt, Mary Surratt, or any other members of the Surratt household?

A. No, sir. He said very little. I had my men place Booth with his face upward on the piazza of the Garrett house, and one of the women of the family brought a sponge soaked in brandy and water and moistened Booth's lips with it. This seemed momentarily to revive him.

"Kill me, kill me," he whispered.

"But we don't want you to die," I told him. "We want you to live."

Booth then asked me to look at his mouth and see if there was any blood in it.

He apparently thought he had been shot through his chest and was bleeding internally. In fact, the bullet had struck him at the back of his neck, a few inches below his collar band, and he had lost the use of his limbs from his head downward. He said no more until about daybreak, when he began to utter a rasping noise and with great difficulty he asked me to please raise his hand marked JWB to his eyes.

I did so. Booth then stared at it for a moment.

"Useless, useless," he said, and expired. I ordered my men to sew his body into a bag made of my saddle blanket, and with Booth's remains my company and I proceeded back to Washington City.

Q. Thank you, Colonel Conger.

From the diary of John H. Surratt, April 19, Wednesday, 1916

It was almost time for me to meet with D. W. Griffith. The very thought of it made me feel even more fatigued. My fever had grown worse overnight, and I had begun breathing with difficulty—my lungs felt as if a great heaviness were pressing upon them. I shook my head resolutely. This was no time to let the frailties of the body overtake me. I looked at the court documents and photographs spread across my desk at the Willard Hotel. Among them was the photograph of Boston Corbett, the soldier strange beyond any literary invention, who shot Wilkes Booth. Attached to Corbett's print was a copy of his medical record from the War Department:

> *Subject is a slight man of below average height, keeps his hair noticeably long, and is a devout Methodist. Having chatted with some prostitutes on the street and then perused the eighteenth and nineteenth chapters of Matthew, he returned home and took a pair of scissors and made an opening one inch long in the lower part of his scrotum. He drew down his testes and cut them off. He then went to a prayer meeting, walked about some, and ate a hearty dinner. He later called on Dr. R. N. Hodges, who on discovering the wound, laid it open, removed the clotted blood, and sutured it. . . . The injury was treated on July 18, 1858. Subject was later*

accepted into the United States Cavalry, where he distinguished himself by the ferocity of his fighting, his earlier self-mutilation apparently being no handicap to the performance of his soldierly duties.

And so Booth was right, in his own way, in foreseeing the scene of his death. He had not hanged. I took a final look at all these stacks of documents, as if to fix them in my mind, before leaving for the National Theatre.

July 7, Friday, 1865

I wrote and dated this entry after the fact, but I shall remember the events of this afternoon for the rest of my life.

I estimated that I had been held as a prisoner for more than two months now since the assassination of Lincoln. I finished writing the "official" diary of John Wilkes Booth, a forgery reproduced by me in Booth's handwriting of the events Pinkerton and Gardner required, which I copied down on the blank pages of the book identical in appearance to Booth's true diary. I created in this spurious diary an historical Booth who is a misanthrope, and racially baleful, rather than the subtle manipulator and egotist he was. The country prefers its villains to be utterly evil, rather than stained with shades of gray. More to the point, the references Booth made to the participation of others in government have been excised. It was made clear to me that there can be no official implication of a broader plot by those in power. The government, and the Union, Pinkerton pointed out, are shaky enough without further scandal and intrigue. And a mention of that sort in a diary would necessarily have to be thoroughly investigated. Pinkerton and Gardner have taken both my forgery and Booth's authentic diary, and I have heard no more of them.

I assumed that Booth's real diary will be destroyed, and my forgery introduced publicly in its place. But I have no idea whether or not Secretary Stanton will keep his promise to spare me, or Sarah.

How many of these men—Stanton, Pinkerton, Gardner—must have read of Booth's intimacy with my mother before the diary was turned over to me! No one spoke to me of these passages, and I, of course, deleted them from the document I forged.

Perhaps it was all of God's plan that Booth's diary be destroyed, and that in that act, any public knowledge of my mother's part also die. Booth was part of my being now, and I, through the diary, am part of him. But there was also a part of him that will be forever lost to a world that would try to understand him.

The afternoon in question, I heard footsteps outside the greenroom door. Gardner and Pinkerton entered, the latter unlocked my manacles and placed a full-length white duster coat over my shoulders. Gardner looked at me with an exceptionally grim expression. For a moment, neither man spoke. Finally, Gardner placed his right hand on my shoulder and directed me toward the open door.

"It's time, Johnny," he said. I assumed he meant Stanton had betrayed his word, and I was being taken off to Arsenal Prison to be hanged. Curious, I felt an absence of either courage or fear.

Outside in the theatre alley, I was surprised to see not a hooded barouche carriage, but Gardner's rolling darkroom wagon. Gardner and Pinkerton seated themselves beside me on the wagon without an explanation. Gardner took the reins, and the wagon turned onto F Street.

From the trial of Mary E. Surratt, in the murder of Abraham Lincoln, United States Military Commission, District of Columbia, 1865

[R. C. Morgan, witness for the prosecution] On the night of 17th of April, I was in the service of the War Department. About twenty minutes past eleven o'clock, on the evening of the 17th of April, Colonel Olcott gave me instructions to go to the house of Mrs. Surratt, 541 H Street, and superintend the seizing of papers, and the arrest of the inmates of the house. When informed that the carriage was ready to take her to the provost marshal's office, Mrs. Surratt requested a minute or so to kneel down and pray; whether she prayed or not, I cannot tell.

I had sent for a carriage to take the women arrested in the house to headquarters when I heard a knock and a ring at the door, and the prisoner, Paine, came in. Said he, "I guess I am mistakened." Said I, "Whom do you want to see?" "Mrs. Surratt," said he. "You are right.

Walk right in." I then told him he would have to go to the provost marshal's office and explain. He moved at that, but he did not answer.

The next morning I went down to the house, and Lieutenant Dempsey, the officer in charge, showed me a photograph of J. Wilkes Booth, that he had found behind a picture, which he turned over to the provost marshal.

The rolling darkroom was moving slowly through heavy Pennsylvania Avenue traffic. I realized from our direction and the crowds around us that I was being carried toward the Arsenal Prison. The mob residents before me were turning out to witness the public execution of the Booth conspirators. Pinkerton told me several weeks ago that Atzerodt, Herold, and Powell were being tried at the Arsenal grounds, and that their hanging was a foregone conclusion. I concluded that I was to be now the fourth to be hanged. Pinkerton, seated at my right, kept a hard grip upon my shoulder. Gardner, behind the reins, was uncharacteristically silent and withdrawn.

From the trial of Mary E. Surratt, in the murder of Abraham Lincoln, United States Military Commission, District of Columbia, 1865

A. [Weichman, a witness for the prosecution] Yes, sir, George Atzerodt came very frequently to the Surratt house. I questioned Mrs. Surratt once on the wisdom of admitting a man of such character to our household, but she replied that she felt sorry for the old man, and that she was in the habit of employing him for small tasks about the house.

Q. And also Lewis Powell?

A. Indeed, sir. I was present in my room the day your soldiers searched the house, and Powell arrived there seeking Mrs. Surratt's help. He exclaimed that it was the only friendly address he remembered in the city. Mrs. Surratt appeared confused, claiming she did not know the man by that name, but it was I who positively identified him to your officers as Lewis Powell, or, as he claimed to be, Lewis Paine, the attempted assassin of our secretary of state.

Q. And did John Wilkes Booth visit frequently at the Surratt house?

A. Oh, yes, sir, Booth was a very frequent visitor to Mrs. Surratt's residence. I overheard her once refer to him affectionately as "Pet" in my presence. He came and went very freely. I can see John Wilkes Booth now, as clearly in my memory as in any photograph, arriving at the H Street house in his expensive rented carriage, and standing in the parlor with his gloves in one hand and his riding whip in the other.

Finally, the rolling darkroom arrived at the prison. A large crowd had gathered outside the high brick walls. It was a very hot day, and I was indistinguishable from most of the other civilian males in the crowd, many of whom were also dressed in white dusters. Gardner showed a pass to a guard at the gate, and he and Pinkerton led me into the interior courtyard of the prison.

Several companies of soldiers in blue uniforms were assembled in loose formations on the prison courtyard. The sparse grass had been beaten down by the exercising prisoners who were kept here, and the few blades of grass remaining were dried brown from the heat. In front of the rear brick wall at the prison's courtyard, four gallows had been constructed. Four empty graves were dug and waiting beside the gallows.

Without speaking, Pinkerton and Gardner took me by the shoulders and quick-marched me across the courtyard. To my surprise, they did not lead me to the three-story prison building overlooking the yard, but in the direction of what appeared to be an administrative, smaller building forty feet or so in front of the gallows.

From the trial of Mary E. Surratt, in the murder of Abraham Lincoln, United States Military Commission, District of Columbia, 1865

[Anna Surratt, witness for the defense] I plead with you gentlemen to spare my mother as a godly, innocent woman. She has never, to my knowledge, breathed a word that was disloyal to the government, nor have I ever heard her make any remark showing her to have knowledge of any plan or conspiracy to capture or assassinate the president or any member of the government. When we lived in Maryland, I have known her frequently to give meals, tea, and such refreshments as we had in the house, to Union troops when they were passing. Sometimes she received pay for it; many times she did not.

From the trial of Mary E. Surratt, in the murder of Abraham Lincoln, United States Military Commission, District of Columbia, 1865

After mature consideration of the evidence adduced in this case, the Commission finds the below accused

George A. Atzerodt . . . . GUILTY
David E. Herold . . . . GUILTY
Lewis Powell . . . . GUILTY
Mrs. Mary E. Surratt . . . . GUILTY

. . . and the Commission does, therefore, sentence her, the said Mary E. Surratt, to be hanged by the neck until she is dead, at such time and place as the President of the United States shall direct. . . .

From "The Fate of the Lincoln Conspirators. The Account of The Hanging, Given by Lieutenant Colonel Christian Rath, The Executioner." McClure's Magazine, October 1911

"I often wished that Annie Surratt would give her mother something to put her into everlasting sleep, but she seemed to share my hopes that her mother would be reprieved. Annie was a daily visitor to the prison, and often ate her meals with her mother, staying nearly all day. . . .

"The night before the execution Paine sent for me and said: 'Captain, if I had two lives to give, I'd give one gladly to save Mrs. Surratt. I know she is innocent, and would never die in this way if I hadn't been found in her house.' We hurriedly sent word to the War Department and in an hour had orders to take Paine's statement. Then I was filled with a great hope, and thought the woman might be saved after all.

"That night I took the rope to my room and there made the nooses. I preserved the piece of rope intended for Mrs. Surratt for the last. By the time I got at this I was tired, and I will admit that I rather slighted *the job. Instead of putting seven turns to the knot—as a regulation hangman's knot has seven turns—I put only five into this one. I really did not think Mrs. Surratt would be swung from the end of it."*

I was taken upstairs into a whitewashed second-story room of the building overlooking the courtyard and the gallows. This room was empty, except for two cameras mounted on tripods and a stack of prepared plates at the center of the room. Gardner moved one of the cameras to the open window on the left facing the courtyard, and commanded me to put the second camera at the open window on the right.

Below us on the courtyard a hundred or so civilians had been admitted inside the walls. Along the walkway at the top of the brick wall behind the gallows, soldiers with rifles were leaning down and looking on from a railing. It was very hot. To my surprise, four prisoners were now led into the courtyard. From the civilians and the soldiers atop the brick wall, I heard a murmured chant of "Shame! Shame! Remember Booth the murder!" The first three prisoners were Atzerodt, Herold, and Powell. In shock, I recognized the fourth, preceded by Father Wiget reading from his prayer book, as my mother.

"No!" I shouted from the camera, recoiling in horror. It was as if a light illuminated my eyes: my mother, because of her affair with Booth and my own friendship with him, had been arrested and sentenced to death. I have been brought here to photograph her execution, in lieu of my own execution.

"I cannot," I said, stumbling backward away from the window into the whitewashed room.

"Johnny." Gardner approached me and laid a heavy hand upon my left shoulder. "Do it. Do it so that you and the woman carrying an unborn child shall live."

Gardner's face had a pained expression. "If it were my decision, I'd let you go with no further hindrance. You've suffered enough. I've read your diary, and that of your demon friend, John Wilkes Booth." Gardner turned his head toward Pinkerton, who was leaning against a wall. "You always gave me honest labor for my money, Johnny, and I think that you truly meant no great harm to our country. But you may have noticed that my friend

494

here, Mr. Pinkerton, is not of such a forgiving nature. So do it, Johnny, and live."

Through the open windows, I could hear the sentence of execution being read aloud. Gardner pushed me firmly toward the window. The four condemned were standing on the gallows. A man behind my mother held an umbrella to shield her from the heat.

"You must," Gardner said, looking at my shocked face. I looked at him blankly. "Some may call what you do here today an act of matricide, and no man would willingly speak of that. Such is what our friend Pinkerton is counting upon—your silence." Gardner's features took on a pained expression, as if recalling his own undescribed youth in Glasgow. "All the old ones can give us, Johnny," he said, "is a chance to live. It is what your mother would most want for you herself, as you well know. And this is all that we can ask of them. Their death, and their forgiveness. There is nothing more you can do for her anyway."

Gardner turned my head toward the wooden box of the camera in front of me. I looked through the open window almost involuntarily. On the gallows trap, the four figures were being prepared for hanging. Their arms were being tied behind them with strips of white cloth, and their legs bound together. Beside me, Gardner already was at his camera, exposing plates.

On the gallows, Herold said nothing, looking down at his shoes. Over the hot, unmoving air of the courtyard, I could hear Atzerodt shouting. "Gentle-*mun,* gentle-*mun,* I hardly knew Mr. Booth! I hardly knew him!" He was struggling against the binds around his arms.

Powell, even with his death imminent and his open grave before him, seemed in ruddy good health. He looked toward his executioner with the same distant and benevolently good faith he had shown in Booth. "You know best, Cap'ain," I heard him say.

The crowd below me became quiet as the executioner approached my mother. Her arms and legs bound, she was wearing a black alpaca bonnet and a black bombazine dress. "Oh, please, don't let me fall," she was crying. "Please don't let me fall." Time seemed to stand still. Then the noose was placed around her neck. Father Wiget read aloud from the text of extreme unction.

Canvas hoods were put over the heads of all four, and they were left standing alone on the gallows. Two soldiers underneath the gallows prepared to knock away the trap's wooden supports. With trembling fingers, I placed a wet plate inside the camera.

The trap fell sooner than I expected. Several in the crowd startled back, as I wanted to. I forced my mind to see the hanging images as only fixtures upon glass, frantically struggling against gravity.

Eventually, the four bodies ceased moving. My eyes remained glued to the camera, my feet frozen in place to the floor. It was as if I, too, had died, and for a time, I lost all thought of what was going on around me.

Ten or fifteen minutes later, the crowd, apparently satisfied with the spectacle, began to leave the prison courtyard. From the window I could hear their continued murmur, "Remember Booth the murderer."

Four enlisted soldiers entered the room; I noticed Pinkerton had disappeared. I walked toward the soldiers to give myself up to their custory, but they passed by me, and, at Gardner's direction, began to remove the cameras. Gardner collected the exposed plates, including the one from my camera. He took me by the shoulders and led me out of the building. I did not look at the four mute forms on the gallows.

I found myself alone with Gardner outside the prison, at the steps of the rolling dark-room at the curb. He had the exposed plates in light-safe boxes underneath his arm and appeared eager to develop, print, and sell them.

"Well, Johnny, you're free to go now. After what we've done here today, Mr. Pinkerton and Mr. Stanton are certain you'll never talk, or be believed."

Gardner handed down to me two books which I recognized as my diary and Booth's diary. There was also a large bank draft payable to me. "I'll offer you some further assurances," he said. "I have reason to believe that we may very rapidly have a new political leader other than Mr. Johnson. If there is a change in presidential administrations, it is just possible that at some time in the future you may be found out and arrested. If so, just keep your mouth shut, and remember our little agreement about Booth. Remember that you have powerful friends on your side. So you're free to go, Johnny."

"Free to go where?" I asked, looking at the high, brick walls of the Arsenal Prison.

My question seemed to infuriate Gardner. "Anywhere you please, damn you! Go to the South and find that actress you sacrificed so much for. Or go to Europe, or go to the West. That's where the future is, Johnny, the West. The point is, you're free to live your life."

But I was not free, and never would be again.

Gardner fidgeted a moment on the wagon's rear steps. "Do as I say, Johnny." He glanced down at the plates he was holding. "What I have here is the end of the story, and I plan to offer to the public in album form a complete and official photographic history of the war. I'm certain it will make my fortune. Then I'm off to the West myself to explore the possibilities of the photographic market there."

Gardner seemed to realize that the wet plates he was holding must be developed immediately. He took a final, long look at me, smoothing his ginger whiskers with his free hand, and as he did so, his sardonic nature returned. "So go where you please, John Surratt. Or go to the devil!" The door

499

to the rolling darkroom slammed shut behind him.

I was alone on the street, alone with the
ghosts of my past. With my diary and
Booth's diary in the pocket of my white
duster, I hailed a cab and proceeded toward
the Washington City train station.

Mr. Woodbridge (Republican, Vermont)
from the Committee on the Judiciary sub-
mitted a report relative to the arrest of
John H. Surratt; and moved that it be laid
on the table, and ordered to be printed;
that on November 24, 1865, an order
was issued from the War Department re-
voking the reward offered for the arrest of
Surratt; (and)
that in their opinion due diligence in the
arrest of Surratt was not exercised by the
executive department of the Government.
—39th Congress,
House of Representatives
2nd Session, 1867

April 19, Wednesday, 1916
Having gained entrance to the National
Theatre, I looked across rows of vacant
chairs receding into the shadows of the the-

atre. In the extreme back row, I barely discerned the figures of Miss Marsh and, seated next to her, Griffith. Offstage, at my left, I saw a cylinder-recording Gramophone machine with a large morning-glory-shaped metal receiver. Standing near the empty stage, I was startled as lights suddenly illuminated above me. I was momentarily blinded, setting off a small fit of coughing. I was reminded briefly of the colonel's description of Booth trapped inside a burning tobacco barn, underneath a flaming proscenium.

"Mr. Surratt," I heard D. W. Griffith call to me. "You're here! Did you bring the contract with you? Are you ready to begin committing your memories to film?"

I hesitated, realizing the momentousness of the decision I'd made this morning. Unable to talk of the assassination while the principals were alive, I now found that I was about to turn down perhaps my last, best chance to record my recollections. But the more I'd thought about having my words, my diary entries, and my photographs edited for the screen to suit the purposes of an evening's entertainment, the more I realized how impossible it was for me to go through with it. How could I allow what had happened to my mother, to Booth and the others, to be cut and tailored for little more than a vaudeville amusement? I thought back to my revulsion over Gardner moving the body of the young Confederate soldier to better capture the light for commercial purposes. Could I entrust Griffith with the memories of those who meant so much more to me?

"Mr. Griffith, I must apologize to you, for I have reached an unfortunate decision regarding my participation in your film. As grateful as I am for your hospitality and the generosity of your offer, I'm afraid I've decided not to sign the contract, or permit the use of my diaries or recollections. As impressed as I am with your movie, I've come to feel that it is not the proper forum in which to remember my mother, and the calamitous events in my life that took place so long ago."

Griffith rose from his seat and strode angrily toward the stage. "So you want more money, Mr. Surratt, is that it? My offer isn't generous enough? I've been utterly straight with you, Mr. Surratt, and I'll not offer a penny more, not a penny, sir."

"Mr. Griffith, I understand your anger. But

I assure you that I am not merely angling for more money. I've made any number of mistakes in my life, particularly during the last days of the Civil War, but I will not make another now. I cannot be in your film. I will, of course, reimburse you for the expenses you've outlaid on my behalf, and I apologize once again for using up your patience and your time. But I cannot go forth with this. And that is final.''

I claimed my parcels of books and photographs at the Willard Hotel desk and was preparing to leave for Union Station when I saw Billy Bitzer standing in the hotel lobby. He was dressed very neatly in a suit and vest.

"I really feel lousy," Bitzer said. "I mean, I feel lousy for you, Mr. Surratt, besides for myself. I know how much you wanted to set the record straight. And you thumbed your nose at a hell of a lot of money.

"D.W. doesn't know I came here," he went on. "But I know you're the one who had to have taken those photographs. I respect what you did, Mr. Surratt. I was hoping the movies would be the way for you to tell your story. But maybe there's no way for us in the movies to tell a story like that in the right way." Bitzer looked away at the lobby's revolving door, embarrassed by his honesty.

"I wanted atonement," I whispered, more to myself than to him. "I wanted some sense of absolution for my sins. But there can be no atonement. Lincoln is dead. Booth is dead. My mother is dead. And soon I will be."

Bitzer shrugged uneasily. To my surprise, he insisted on paying for a taxicab and riding with me to the train station. During the ride he seemed agitated, and eager to talk. "D.W. will still make his movie about Lincoln, Mr. Surratt. But Jesus, it may not be until 1929 or '30. Louie Mayer has asked him to do a war movie, too. Woodrow Wilson put a goddamn bug in D.W.'s ear about going overseas to make a war film, and put in real fighting, see? So now D.W. wants Mae and me to go with him to France."

Bitzer nervously lit a cigar inside the cab. "Jesus Christ. The western front and all that crap. Can you see me there, Mr. Surratt? Now I'm going to be in France making a movie for D.W. and some kraut cousin of mine is going to shoot my keister off."

I expressed my sympathy. Despite his blunt manner and foul language, Bitzer could not quite conceal that he was an artist behind the camera. I felt sorry for him, as only the very old can feel sorry for those who are still young.

The train to Baltimore was making its final boarding as Bitzer and I walked down the steps of Union Station. I checked again to make certain I had not misplaced my valise or parcels. Bitzer stood for a moment on the platform, rocking slightly back and forth on his heels. He lit another cigar.

"In a way, it's a goddamn shame, Mr. Surratt. You could have told us a lot about the Civil War years. It would've been a different picture story, that's for sure."

The train beside us sounded a last bell for passengers. "Well," I said, "what is real is never caught on film."

"What?" Bitzer cupped a hand to his ear. He apparently had not heard me. I smiled and shook his hand.

On the short ride from Washington to Baltimore, as I huddled in my seat from fever and fatigue, I reflected on the aftermath of the assassination and my mother's execution. After leaving Gardner, I had made my way overseas to Europe, where I lived in disguise as U.S. agents the world over hunted for me. I had made inquiries after Sarah to friends of Booth's in Richmond, but she seemed to disappear without a trace. Perhaps, given events, she no longer wished to be associated with someone so intimate with Booth, and the assassination. Or perhaps her feelings for me had changed.

My forged diary of Booth was accepted as authentic. And Gardner, Pinkerton, and others kept their word to aid me when, two years after my mother's execution, I was arrested and tried on charges of Lincoln's murder.

Gardner succeeded in issuing his photographic album in 1866, *Sketches of the War,* fully expecting it to make his fortune. He included among the mounted photographs in the album numerous pictures of my mother's execution. But rather than making him money, the photographic album was a commercial failure for Gardner. No one wanted to look at those terrible photographs again. There was instead a kind of national desire to bury those images with the bodies. By the end of the century, many of Gardner's original glass negatives had been bought up at odd lots; I bought some of Gardner's negatives and prints myself at bankruptcy auctions shortly before his death.

After my trial and acquittal in 1867, I no longer tried to locate Sarah—my own life had been so branded that it did not seem fair to me to attempt to draw her back into a life she clearly would rather forget. Whatever became of Booth's child I never knew. My sister, consumed with grief over the part my actions had played in our mother's death, never spoke or wrote to me again.

A decade later, having pursued an obscure life as a shipping clerk, I married a good-hearted if somewhat plain-looking woman from Baltimore, with whom I had several children. But my dreams and ambitions had died with Lincoln, and my mother. The artistic soul Booth refered to in me shriveled and disappeared, if ever it existed.

Eventually, my sister persuaded the government to release my mother's body from the Arsenal Prison, and to have it reinterred at a public cemetery in Baltimore. Booth's body also was moved, his remains collected by his family and eventually reinterred in an unmarked grave within the Booths' Balti-more plot. I long ago stopped paying atten-tion to the persistent rumors I had heard or read that Booth did not actually die at the barn in Virginia. Every few years there are requests to exhume the body to determine whether those pathetic shreds of tattooed skin and fragments of bone really were the man who once pretended to be my spiritual brother.

As I arrived in Baltimore, dusk had darkened the skyline. My chest felt encumbered by a great weight. Perhaps, if I was feeling strong enough, tomorrow I would visit my mother's, and Booth's, graves. After all, there is little more I can do for them, or for myself. For fifty years my diaries had rested on a shelf, undisturbed if unforgotten. Hav-ing now relived those memories that I had kept so fiercely at bay for so long, I found them slipping through my fingers like ashes. Tonight, I decided, despite my fever and the warmth of the evening, I would light a fire in the kitchen stove. And I would place the torn fragments of the diaries in my possession in the hot grate, and watch the pages curl and twist in the flames. Ashes to ashes, dust to dust.

After the light, there is only darkness.

Sources and Acknowledgments

Readers of the historical novels about the Civil War, like the generals who fought it, prefer to "defeat in detail," vigilantly looking for any misstatements of fact or the commitment of literary anachronisms on which they can bring an overwhelming verbal firepower. In regard to nineteenth-century social customs and the science of photography described in this novel, I have made what I hope is a good-faith effort not to disturb the reader's sense of credibility. Diaries and newspapers from the period of 1861–65 were consulted frequently, not only for the great events of the day, but also for such details as laundry, diseases, marriage, and entertainment. Margaret Leech's social history of our nation's capital during the Civil War, *Reveille in Washington,* and Robert Reed's *Old Washington, D.C. in Early Photographs* were invaluable sources. The accurate depiction of American genteel clothing is patterned from the 235 plate illustrations in Alison Gernsheim's *Victorian and Edwardian Fashion: A Photographic Survey.*

Such seeming verbal anachronisms as "traffic," "suburbs," and "theatre of war" were, in fact, in usage by the mid-1860s.

I altered willingly a significant biographical fact in this novel: John H. Surratt never worked as Alexander Gardner's photographic assistant. I made this novelistic change in order to introduce photographs into the text, and I acted out of respect both to history and those individuals whose lives were destroyed by it. Photography always is an exchange between the quick and the dead, and on viewing photographs of the Civil War dead, I have for years felt that it is *they* who quicken to life. We are forced to see their individuality and their undeniable historical authenticity, often more powerfully than we see our own. I therefore made this change in Surratt's biography, so that the figures in this historical novel do not appear in the reader's mind only as costumed actors, as if in a literary version of a D. W. Griffith film. Out of respect for history and their tragic lives, they appear in photographs in this book as they actually existed and suffered—often seen through Alexander Gardner's photographic lenses.

Gardner, and not Mathew Brady, is now recognized historically as the preeminent photographer of the Civil War. The twentieth-century art and military historians William A. Frassanito and D. Mark Katz have done much to restore Gardner to his rightful place. Gardner was the photographer officially designated by the U.S. government to record Mary Surratt's hanging in 1865, and the historical photographs reproduced in this novel, unless otherwise noted, were taken by him or his assistants. Gardner as an historical figure did perform military intelligence work for the Union, and was an acquaintance of Allan Pinkerton, of the famous detective agency. At the time of the Lincoln assassination, however, Pinkerton had been dismissed by the U.S. military. His fictional character is an amalgam both of Pinkerton and of Col. Lafayette C. Baker of the U.S. Secret Service, also a shady and dangerous personage of the time.

The details of nineteenth-century photography as practiced at Gardner's Washington City studio are taken from descriptions in *Harper's Illustrated Weekly* and the *Atlantic*

Monthly for the 1850s and 1860s and from early photographic manuals. At one point in this novel, the fictional John Surratt writes, on viewing the historical photograph of Lewis Powell, *He is dead, and he is going to die.* This observation was, in fact, written by Roland Barthes, in the late twentieth century in *Camera Lucida: Reflections on Photography.* The sentence is included verbatim in this novel for the reason that no one has ever better expressed the haunting beauty of this particular photograph; and full credit is here given to Barthes for having written it first, and so well.

Many people testified under oath that the historical John Surratt fled his mother's Washington City boarding house after the Lincoln assassination. Others testified, however, to having seen Surratt in upstate New York the day of Lincoln's assassination. That discrepancy would prove crucial at his trial. He was recognized in Italy and returned to this country for trial in 1867, two years after the death of his friend John Wilkes Booth and the execution of his mother, Mary Surratt. John Surratt was acquitted, and lived fairly obscurely as a shipping agent. Sarah Ravenel, or Sarah Slater, who is known to scholars of Confederate espionage as "the lady in the veil," was an actual personage who, according to testimony, was seen several times in the company of John Surratt. Her postwar fate is uncertain. The historical John Surratt married Mary Victorine Hunter, and fathered seven children. The excerpts from the criminal trials of John and Mary Surratt printed in this novel usually are reproduced verbatim, although frequently similar testimonies have been combined into one dramatic speaker. The full court summations and stenographic records are found in Benn Pittman's *The Assassination of President Lincoln* and, U.S. Government Printing Office, *Trial of John H. Surratt.*

The fictional characters of John Surratt, Mary Surratt, and John Wilkes Booth enter this novel with certain theatrical and chronological liberties. The historical John Surratt was briefly liable for the Union draft, but he was exempted for undisclosed reasons shortly before conspiring with Booth to kidnap Lincoln. The question of an affair between Mary Surratt and Booth is conjecture, although historically persistent. Mrs. Surratt's lifelong piety is unquestioned. Surratt and Booth were reported attending a theatrical performance together in early 1865, but I have predated the first revival of *Our American Cousin* at Ford's Theatre to late December 1864, and recast some roles and lines.

D. W. Griffith's rising cinema career and the 1915 production of *The Birth of a Nation* occurred during the last two decades of the historical Surratt's life. Griffith's remarks throughout this novel usually are his actual words, reproduced either from his effusively autobiographical reminiscences of the 1910s and '20s, or from the promotional copy for his movies. The historical Surratt did once appear on a lecture tour, although he declined to speak of his mother and Booth. The historical Griffith, subsequent to *The Birth of a Nation,* did direct the movie, *Lincoln.* There is no record of the two men having met.

Thomas Jones, the slave overseer who aided Booth's escape, eventually self-published his book on the presidential assassin, and was nearly lynched by angry veterans. The details of the capture and death of Booth in this novel are factually accurate, taken from the testimonies and published reminiscences of those soldiers and civilians present at the scene. Lt. Col. Conger, one of the commanding officers of the capture party, is presented as the dramatic speaker, but some details corroborated by his subordinates have been folded into his account for dramatic reasons. Booth's family is well-documented in Stanley Kimmel's *The Mad Booths of Maryland* and Gene Smith's *American Gothic.* The historical Booth's diary is now on permanent display at the Ford's Theatre museum. The question of its completeness, the reason for its missing pages, and its whereabouts after being taken from Booth's body have long been issues of dispute. William Hanchett is perhaps the best academic authority on this diary's provenance. Booth's historical diary became known to the public when it was introduced into evidence at John Surratt's trial in 1867.

Many of the episodes which the character Booth describes in the "secret" diary of John Wilkes Booth are factually verifiable, and all are emotionally congruent with what is known historically about his character. The question of whether Booth was part of a larger government conspiracy against Lincoln is examined in *Come Retribution,* by the scholars William Tidwell, James O. Hall, and David Gaddy. A subjective but important source is Asia Booth Clarke, *The Unlocked Book: A Memoir of John Wilkes Booth by His Sister.*

John Wilkes Booth as a magnetic, attractive, manipulative, and violent character continues to command the American imagination in a way not fully explained by the facts of his life or of his notoriety. In searching for any explanation to an image of our collective experience, we inescapably read facts subjectively, just as we are fated to "read" photographs and even documentary cinema from our own field of personal experiences. I have provided the lengthy sources above for, as Nathaniel Hawthorne wrote in the preface to *The Scarlet Letter,* "whomsoever, induced by the great interest of the narrative, may desire a sight of them." As with Hawthorne, I have not confined myself to a recounting of documents, but rather have attempted what Hawthorne described as "the authenticity of the outline."

I wish to thank my honest literary agent, John Ware; my good editor at Doubleday, Roger Scholl; and also numerous other friends and organizations who encouraged me during the writing of this novel, including but not limited to: Stan Ashley, Jan Craft, Frank Day, Michelle Farmer, Ruthie Hinson, Paul Hogroian of the Library of Congress, Kurt Neiburg, Ron Rash, Robert Scarborough, the Surratt House and Museum in Clinton, Maryland, Karen Swann, Mark Winchell, and the staff and management at the various restaurants where I have worked while completing this manuscript.